# THE CUTTHROAT KING

*For Olga*
*There wouldn't be a Silk without you.*
*Thanks for being my sister.*

# CONTENT NOTICE

*For the Dictionary and Pronunciation Guide, see the end of the book*

CONTAINS SPOILERS

The Cutthroat King is a dark gaslamp fantasy romance written for adults and contains themes and situations that may not be suitable for every reader.

The following subjects are included in the novel. Be aware, this may not cover all triggering subjects.

- Physical Violence
- Gun Violence
- Assault
- Death
- Kidnapping (not on page)
- Torture
- Adult Language
- Nudity
- Graphic Sexual Encounters
- Fire/Electrical injury

## CONTENT NOTICE

- Drugging/Poison
- Animal Death
- Parent Death (not on page)
- (Implied) Violence Against Children

# THE CUTTHROAT KING

## A GWEN ST. JAMES AFFAIR NOVEL

## NICOLE MCKEON

TOWER ROOM

# CHAPTER 1

They say the Cutthroat King is a monster. They say he can kill a dozen men, rob a dozen homes, and disappear into the shadows. They say he knows everything that happens in New London and owns half of Scotland Yard. That is why he's never been caught, why he is the undisputed ruler of the criminal underworld.

I hope they are right because my life has fallen apart, and I <u>need</u> a monster. So, into the night I will go and hope I find him. If you read this, please commend me to whatever gods you pray to.

—From the diary of Willow Beauregard
November 22, 1902

NEW LONDON, OCTOBER 4TH, 1902

THE DIAMOND-TIPPED AWL DIGS A CLEAN, STRAIGHT LINE INTO THE brass to connect the last two runes in the sentence. Energy floods the metal, and with a crunch of turning gears, the toy soldier stands and marches across my worktable. I blow an escaped strand of white-blonde hair out of my eyes and smile.

There's something endearing about this tiny clockwork toy. Generations of affectionate children have worn down his paint until bare metal shows through at the corners of his red hat and jacket. Somewhere along the way, his rifle has been lost, but he still strides determinedly back and forth, guarding the neat row of tools behind him.

"You are a dashing little fellow," I say as he spins on his heel and sets off in the opposite direction. "Quite the pride of your regiment, I'm sure."

He ignores me and continues his patrol. When I pluck him off the table and press the button on his back, it pops up and disengages the sentence. The clockwork soldier freezes as the runes stop channeling energy into the gears, making him safe to store.

"And now, back to the box with you. Don't worry. You'll fight for king and country again soon."

He doesn't answer—no toy ever does—but I fancy he's glad to be fit for duty again. It's as clean a repair as I could've hoped for. A bit of oil in his joints for good measure, and I'll return the toy early for a nice tip. With my apprenticeship only weeks away, I need every spare coin I can hoard.

Behind the counter, Ethel claps her hands. "Oh, well done! I thought that one was beyond fixing for certain. Or that you'd have to cut it up and replace the brass. Poor little thing was so scratched and worn down I could barely read the engravings. It must be what, fifty years old?"

"Closer to a century, at least." The pad of my thumb slides across the runic sentence to ensure my engraving leaves no ragged bits of metal that might scratch the pudgy little fingers of its owner. "Artifice like this wasn't meant to last so long. It's terribly inefficient. Modern artificers would never power a children's toy with static electricity. I bet half the dents and scratches are from toddlers throwing it after being shocked."

2

Ethel shrugs, dismissing my observations in favor of filling out the time card for the repair. She bends over the paper, brow furrowed, lips curved in a contented smile. Her pen scribbles away.

She doesn't care much for the science of repairing gadgets. She's good at tracking the receipts, keeping accounts, and reassuring customers—sometimes even convincing Papa to finish a repair when he'd rather be working on his invention. In fact, she's the best shop manager we could hope for.

If I could convince her to manage the finances, I'd kiss her feet. But those kinds of numbers aren't her strong suit, and Papa wouldn't hear of it.

I waggle the toy to catch her attention. "How much is this one?"

"One and four, for the rush," she says.

That means I can put a few shillings into my apprentice fund, two toward this month's mortgage, half a pound into next week's supply order, and fifty pence for Ethel's salary. If nothing goes wrong in the next week—and if Papa finishes his backlog of orders —all the bills will be paid, with enough left over for my replacement.

I place the little soldier on the front desk so Ethel can tie the receipt to his leg with a piece of white string. "Papa hasn't mentioned interviews, has he?"

"No," Ethel sighs. "He'll probably wait till the last possible moment. He doesn't like thinking about you leaving."

He's had time to get used to the idea. It was his plan, after all. He just doesn't want to pay someone else twice my wages. Shame burns my cheeks. How can I think such ungrateful thoughts? Papa took me in when others would've sent me to an orphanage. He gave me a home.

I grab a rag and scrub the oil and grease from the table as if the force of my arm can also scrub ungratefulness from my mind. Then I clean and replace my tools, letting the familiar task settle my heart. He wants this apprenticeship as much as I do, though for different reasons. He's only busy and absent-minded, like all inventors.

The workshop door slams open, and Papa strides in with an armful of rolled papers. His lean, inquisitive face is lined with worry, the tips of his pointed ears red with frustration.

"Have a look at this, will you?" He pushes my tools aside to spread the schematics atop the table.

I wince but resist the urge to put everything back in its place. He doesn't mean to disrupt my things. Brilliant inventors are known for being careless when inspired—or frustrated.

The tip of my finger runs across the blue pencil markings, and disappointment settles in my gut. "This isn't the Lord Rutledge's water heater."

"No, it isn't."

"But Lord Rutledge's job is the most important repair we've taken and he needs—" I start, but he talks over me.

"Remember the slippage I've been getting when I increase the power output? I've had an idea about how to control it. We assumed it was best to dump the excess energy, but what if we funneled it here, instead?" He taps the new addition on the sketch.

If he's been working on his blasted invention rather than fixing Lord Rutledge's water heater, we could end up days behind on the biggest repair we've ever taken. Having the business of a peer of the realm could change everything for us, raise the reputation of our mechanica, perhaps high enough to compete for business with true artificeries.

But he's clearly not in the mood to hear that. He's eager to drag me into hours of brainstorming about power ratios and slippage. And while I love puzzles, there are more pressing matters to address.

"You said you were going to interview apprentices."

He waves that off. "There's plenty of time for—"

"Papa." My fingers rest on his arm in the hope my touch will focus him. "I leave in two weeks."

"I know."

"If I don't have time to train my replacement before I go—"

"I know." His tone says he's done with the subject. Normally, I swallow my misgivings to keep the peace, but the deadline looms like a guillotine.

"You'll have no one to keep up with the smaller orders if you don't bring someone on for me to train. I don't want to leave you without help."

"We can talk about this later."

"There isn't time to—"

"Can't you let me enjoy the time we have left without worrying about how I'll get by when you're gone?"

All of my arguments die in my throat. Papa is many things, but sentimental isn't one of them. His voice, his face are too unguarded.

"Papa, I—"

The bell above the door jingles and two men in black bowler hats and frock coats stand silhouetted in the doorway, framed by sunlight. They're of a height, with unremarkable builds and forgettable faces—like two copies made from the same mold.

They stride down the aisle in silence. Ethel gives me a tight smile as I join her behind the counter.

"Welcome to Beauregard's Mechanica," she says in her best customer service voice. "What can I help you with today?"

They stop short of the counter, standing shoulder to shoulder. Their hats and coats are identical, fine dark wool, expensively tailored. A barely noticeable insignia on their lapels catches the lamplight. I squint to make out the shape without staring. It looks like a slanted S with a line through it from tip to tip with a few flourishes on either side. The embroidery is very fine. Whoever these men are, they belong in the Artificer's District, not on Penny Lane.

"Good afternoon," says the man on the right. "We'd like to speak to Archibald Beauregard."

Ethel glances at Papa, who doesn't normally engage with customers because his service etiquette leaves much to be desired, but their expensive clothing must have caught his attention.

"What can I do for you, gentlemen?" Papa asks.

The men exchange a glance. The one on the left gives a polite bow. "We have a business proposition for you."

Anger flares in Papa's cheeks. "I've already told him I'm not selling. My blood and sweat built this shop, and I'd die before—"

Left Hat holds up a hand, cutting Papa off mid-sentence. "We have no interest in your shop, Mr. Beauregard." He pulls a folded sheet of paper from his pocket. "We're interested in this."

Papa takes the paper, glances at it, and the color drains from his face. Shock? Fear? I ease the wooden panel under the counter aside and let my fingers rest on the shotgun Papa insists we keep there. The idea of using it makes my palms sweat, but he's drilled into me the importance of knowing how to use it.

"Where did you get this?" Papa asks in a small, stunned voice.

"From the records of the Royal Institute for Practical Sciences," says Right Hat. "They keep copies of schematics for all inventions nominated for the Silver Moon Award."

"They were most accommodating," Left Hat adds with a smile.

Their flat voices send a chill up my spine. Oh, they're polite enough, but their eyes are hungry. Ethel steps closer to me.

"Yes, well." Papa folds the paper stiffly and hands it back. "I was disqualified."

The men exchange another glance and Right Hat makes a dismissive gesture. "Our organization is not burdened by the same... shortsightedness as the Institute Council. We see great promise in your invention."

"And we have a proposal for you," Left Hat adds. "Might we speak somewhere more discreet?"

Papa's expression is a marvel: confused around his eyebrows, hopeful in his eyes, and suspicious around his mouth. "Of course, of course. Let us speak in my office. Willow," he lowers his voice as the Hats head toward the back of the shop, "make sure we have privacy, please."

6

His eyes dart toward the front, giving me a pointed look before he closes the office door behind them.

Ethel leans close as worry clouds her face. "Who are they?"

"I don't know," I whisper. "But keep your voice down."

The shotgun rests on the countertop as I flip the sign to *closed* and lock the door.

"We aren't supposed to close for another two hours!"

Ethel is wonderful at her job, and a devoted friend, but she's also grown up in a safe part of New London. She's never been exposed to the more unsavory things people do when times are tough and business is bad. And her parents have certainly never been strong-armed by street toughs.

Luckily, Papa handles those interactions. Violence makes me nauseous, but fear for him means I'm never far away, often watching through window cracks or listening through holes.

"This is only a precaution," I tell the smaller girl in a confident voice meant to soothe her nerves, even if I don't quite believe it myself. "In case they're expecting company."

Ethel catches her breath. "You mean—you don't think they work for... for *him*, do you?" She glances around. "Like the Ratcatchers?"

"Him?" I ask, frowning. "Him, who?"

Ethel grabs the neckline of my leather apron and pulls me down to whisper, "The Cutthroat King!"

After disentangling myself from her clutches, I pat her hands. "Of course not. What would he want with us? Like I said, this is a precaution. That's why Papa asked for privacy. No need to worry."

After a wary glance at the front door, Ethel returns to organizing and record-keeping, but her gaze strays toward Papa's office. Only shadowed shapes can be seen through the frosted glass of the small window, which doesn't ease the mind of a worried daughter.

Since there's nothing to do but wait, I clean up the tools scattered by Papa's carelessness, then study the schematics he spread on my workbench. As much as I resent the invention for the time and money it drains from the shop, it's a work of genius. Using artificery to convert natural energy, like sunlight or wind, into electricity that powers rechargeable batteries could change the course of the future.

If he succeeds, every home in New London will have an Aetheric Charging station, and safe electricity will compete with artificers to power people's lives. Several families may even share one station to power batteries for light, heat, and other gadgets that make life easier.

Unfortunately, no matter how brilliant the idea is, Papa will never find an artificer willing to test it. Dwarven street lamps provide the wealthier half of the city with twenty-four-hour sunlight, dwarven heaters keep houses warm, and dwarven engines power autos, ships, and dirigibles.

No artificer would undermine the guild by helping Papa build the Aetheric Charger. And while the two of us know more about artificery than anyone without a guild sanction, neither of us has the depth of knowledge needed for such delicate work.

One wrong rune or misplaced line on a power source of that size might destroy several buildings. Without the knowledge that only guild apprentices have, the invention will remain nothing but a dream that sucks money from our pockets like a hole in a dam.

Which is why Papa pushed me to apply for the coveted apprenticeship. And by some miracle, I've been accepted. I'll be the first elf—the first non-dwarf, in fact—ever to apprentice with the Artificer's Guild.

They'll never admit me to the guild when my apprenticeship is over, of course, but that doesn't matter. When it's done, the Mechanica will have two guild-sanctioned repairists, and Papa's invention will finally have the delicate hand it needs to restart his once promising career.

I sigh and shove the papers away. In two weeks, the invention, the shop, and the constant worry of finances won't be my burden to bear anymore. Not for a while, at least. It isn't the Artisan's Guild like I dreamed of, not a place to study light and color and balance, but it's something. Something of my own. Something that can't be taken away.

The door to Papa's office swings open, and Right and Left Hat walk out with smiles on their pale, waxy faces.

"A carriage will be round to convey you to the site at eight o'clock, sharp," Right Hat says.

Left Hat snaps his watch closed and drops it into his pocket. "Don't be late, Mr. Beauregard. We have a schedule to keep."

Papa bows, smiles, and wrings his hands, looking so servile it shocks me into silence when I would have asked *what site, what schedule?*

They unlock the door without being asked and let themselves out to the jingling of the doorbell. Ethel and I stand frozen, but Papa is vibrating with energy.

He stares after them for a long count of ten, then grips my fingers in shaking hands. "Willow, my girl, this is it! The break we've been waiting for! Our problems are solved!"

I want to say, *we wouldn't have any problems if you'd finish your commissions on time instead of fiddling with that cursed invention,* but what comes out is, "Papa, what do you mean?"

"Those gentlemen were members of a scientific institute called the Covenant of Silver..." His brows furrow as he tries to remember the name, then waves it off. "Oh, Silver something-or-other. Anyway, they're researching alternative energy sources, and they've heard of my invention! I told those stiff-necked old pedants at the Royal that my ideas wouldn't stay buried, no matter how hard they tried to scrub my name from the records. And I was right! A threat to public safety, indeed." He scoffs.

"How does that solve our problems?"

He blinks as if my question doesn't make sense. "Don't you see? They want to fund the research! They've already recruited several artificers but they're on a deadline, so they want me to test my prototype immediately."

The sense of foreboding planted in my stomach the moment those waxy-faced men entered the shop blossoms into sick apprehension. That means he doesn't need me to finish the invention. Is my future about to crumble before my eyes?

All I can think to say is, "What about the Robertsons' water heater?"

"Water heater?" Papa demands, incredulous. "You're worried about the water heater? Willow, this is bigger than a thousand water heaters! It may change the world. And for this first test alone, they'll pay me fifteen thousand pounds."

The smack of Ethel's hand against her mouth is loud in the silence that follows. Fifteen thousand pounds? That wouldn't only discharge our mundane debts, it would pay off the rest of the mortgage, too. Papa could spend as much time as he liked inventing whatever he wanted.

I would have time to finish the art pieces I've been working on. I could expand my little indoor garden. Perhaps finally begin thinking about romance. It would be nice to have a partner someday.

But if Papa doesn't need me at the mechanica anymore, what reason would he have to keep me around? "Wait, my apprenticeship is only weeks away."

He waves my worries aside with an impatient flap of his hand. "Oh, I'll be done before then. The deadline is days earlier. I'll be back well before you need to leave."

I pull my hand from his, severing the last point of contact between us. "How can you be sure? Papa, have you verified their claims? And what if something happens to extend the test? Two weeks isn't enough time for the rigor you'd need to test something so dangerous and complex." My thoughts spin in a hundred different directions as all the potential hurdles spring up in my mind. "You'd need months, if not years, and a dedicated crew, and I still need to prepare and train someone new to cover the simple repairs and handle the finances. We don't have time to—"

"Willow." Papa stops my anxious pacing by taking my shoulders in his hands. I'm tall for a woman, nine or ten inches above five feet, and our eyes are level. Looking at him now is so different from my childhood, when his hands on my shoulders would gently wake me from nightmares, saying, *Willow. It was only a dream.*

It feels like he's saying it again now, only this time he means something entirely different.

"You're an adult, now, not the skinny, bedraggled little sapling I found standing outside my door. You can handle this."

"It's just—"

"I didn't think twice, you know. Of course, I didn't expect the difficulties of raising a child on my own, or realize how many dreams I would have to give up to ensure you were safe and cared for. And I've never regretted it. You are a joy to me. But"—he releases me and clenches his hands as if grasping something only he can see—"everything I've worked for is finally within reach. Is it too much to ask that you help me now?"

My objections, my worries, my plans, and even my fears for the future shrivel and die at that request. How could I say no to the only person who's ever loved me, who's given up so much of his life for me; the only person who stayed?

If this is his chance to revive the promising career stolen from him by short-sighted academics, how can I stand in the way? After all, there will always be time for me to pursue my dreams. Won't there?

I swallow the lump in my throat and firm my jaw against a chin that's determined to tremble. "Of course not, Papa. I'll take care of the shop. Besides"—I square my shoulders and force cheerfulness into my voice—"you'll be back before my apprenticeship starts, like you said."

The smile he gives me is full of such affection and excitement that I wonder whether I've ever seen him truly happy before. He capers around the room, catches Ethel about the waist, and turns her into a graceful spin.

She giggles as her round cheeks flush with embarrassed pleasure, and the two of them dance down the length of the shop and back.

"Of course, I will! Oh, ladies, this will change everything! No more fixing worthless trinkets for pennies and scraping by to survive."

I smile as they twirl to a stop before me, grinning like children. Ethel puts one hand on her chest to calm her racing heart, and Papa kisses both of my hands with a loud smack.

"You will remember this as the day our lives changed!" he says as he hurries off to pack.

It doesn't take him long. He carries an unevenly bulging suitcase to the door, balanced atop the trunk housing the Aetheric Charger. His hat is askew, and his tie is crooked from rushing, but his eyes are fixed on the street.

A glossy black carriage pulled by sleek mares waits at the curb. Such a fine vehicle is painfully out of place on Penny Lane. The strange insignia painted on the door looks like the symbol embroidered on the Hat's lapels.

It might be a rune, which wouldn't surprise me. Master Artificers are often hired to make carriages more comfortable or safer. Some artifice dampens sound inside the passenger compartment or reduces strain on the horses by transferring the energy from the shocks into forward momentum in the wheels.

As they approach and the lines solidify, though, it's clear that it isn't a rune at all. At least, no rune I've ever seen, and repairing second-hand artifice means I've seen a lot.

The symbol resembles a slanted S with a line through it at an angle, from tip to tip, with strange flourishes and dots on either side.

"Have you ever seen insignia like this?" I ask.

Papa gives the door a cursory glance before handing his bag up to the footman. "It's the symbol of the organization. Covenant of the something-or-other."

This is it. He is leaving. A pit opens in my stomach.

Instead of saying, *Papa I'm nervous about this,* or *please don't go, there is so much for you to do here,* I straighten his tie. "This is the chance you deserve. Don't worry about the shop. I'll take care of everything until you get back."

He smiles and rolls his eyes heavenward. "The Muses have truly blessed me. No man could have asked for a more dutiful daughter." He tucks the flyaway strands of hair behind my ear, as he did when I was young and too focused on a project to notice my hair slipped out of my braid. "I'll be back before you know it."

With that, he swings himself into the carriage and pounds on the roof. Leather reins smack the horses' rumps, and the driver pulls the carriage into traffic. A shiver makes me wrap my arms around myself. Early October shouldn't be quite so cold. I run my palms briskly up and down my arms.

There is plenty of time. He'll come back. He always comes back.

The carriage grows smaller as it carries Papa into the evening bustle of New London, and leaves me alone in the growing dark.

# CHAPTER 2

*A note appeared on the stoop this morning. The writing is in Papa's hand, but the envelope and paper are so mangled Ethel and I can scarcely make out half a dozen words. There was a silver coin inside. My heart stopped when I saw the cutthroat man stamped on its face. Ethel nearly fainted, but all I can think of is that I may still have a chance to find Papa.*

*—From the diary of Willow Beauregard*
*November 20, 1902*

THE EDGE OF THE SILVER COIN BITES INTO MY PALM. I SHOULD loosen my grip but the pain forces me to stay rooted in the moment–in the winter air stinging my cheeks, and the faint clop of hooves echoing off cobblestones–instead of repeating all of the very *good* reasons this is a very *bad* idea.

If I don't distract myself from the fear bubbling in my chest like an over-full teapot, it will spill out, and I will lose my nerve... as well as whatever chance I have of finding my father.

So I bite the inside of my cheek for good measure and avoid the muted glow of the flickering electric street lamps as I ghost into the one place in the city even I have the good sense to avoid: the Thieves' Market.

In truth, it isn't a market at all; merely a decaying neighborhood guarded by the bones of an abandoned church. They call it a market because the fools who walk through the square in front of the church–fools like me–are the merchandise. If I was not so scared, there would be something compelling, if not beautiful, in the ruins that still stand in spite of neglect and decay.

*But I am scared.*

Gooseflesh cover my arms despite my coat, and I have nothing but a coin for protection as I display myself to any criminal who happens to be watching. I truly am a ninny.

A gust of wind howls through the square, tearing the last leaves from the nearby trees. They skitter along the cobblestones to disappear in banks of shifting fog that obscure and reveal the city in waves. The sound echoes back like rasping laughter.

Lovely. Even the wind thinks I am a fool.

Strands of my hair escape to join the fun, sliding from beneath my hood to blow across my face like a white flag. The momentary blindness makes my heart leap into my throat. Without being able to see what is in front of me, my imagination conjures up a hundred possibilities for who, or what, may lurk in the darkness.

A cutpurse with yellow teeth and hard eyes? A murderer with a sneer and a raised knife?

I press my back to the cold brick of the closest building and fight the windblown hair away from my eyes. "Are you trying–to get–me killed?" I demand in a ragged whisper as I stuff the unruly locks back in place to clear my vision.

My muscles are tensed to run, but the square is still empty. A slow, relieved breath calms my racing heart. I may need the

Cutthroat King's help, but I would rather not get robbed–or worse–to secure it. Not that I have much to steal. I already sold everything of value.

Slinking past the next alley and squinting into the fog-softened darkness takes all my concentration as I strain to hear the slightest noise. What do I expect? Sneaky rustling, or perhaps an evil chuckle? I have no idea what criminals sound like. Even the scent of the still air, heavy with coal smoke but blessedly free of the summer stink of fish, manure, and exhaust, is so bland it tells me nothing.

After several long minutes of shivering in silence, barely daring to breathe, bitter disappointment replaces my fear.

No shadows move through the shifting mist. No rough laughter echoes off the old stone houses. And no lingering odor of liquor or onions or even sweat lingers on the air. My only company is the mocking wind and the rattle of dead leaves. And probably more than one rat.

Of course the streets are empty. Anyone with common sense is already safely inside, letting the night see to its own business. That's exactly where I should be: warm in my bed.

Suddenly all of my hopes—and fears—seem ridiculous, and my trek across the dark streets of New London feels like a fool's errand. Did I truly think I could simply walk up to a criminal, present them with the coin, and my problems would be solved?

"Of course, ma'am, I'll help you find your missing father," they'd say with a helpful smile. Right. I should know better but the silver coin was a piece of hope I could not let go of. Especially now that my father has been gone more than a month.

"Mistress Willow, please don't do this," Ethel said mere hours before. "You're the best repairist in the city, you can work for another mechanica to save the money. Just wait a while and hire a private detective instead."

As if I could afford that. I thought I'd done so well managing the books, portioning the money every month like a miser with a single fistful of coppers to fill a dozen hands. But I didn't know about the other loans: the ones papa kept in a ledger in the lower desk drawer of his office.

I found it while ransacking the shop for anything that might fetch a price. The number of red zeroes in the liabilities column still makes me dizzy. Even if I work for the best shop in the city, I can't make enough money to pay the loans before they come due.

I could abandon the shop and the loans and let the bank repossess the building. It would still take me months to save enough money to hire even a shabby detective. And my father may not have that kind of time.

If he's still alive.

The thought makes me brave. Jaw clenched, I leave the shadows and strut across the square, passing through the light of the dwarven lamp that is engraved to store sunlight during the day and release it at night. Unfortunately, the light imparts no warmth, and I fight back a shiver.

My heels clack on the damp stone like the ringing of a dinner bell; and still nothing. How does one attract a criminal? And if a criminal appears, how can I convince them not to rob or murder me long enough to show them the coin? An embarrassed flush warms my cheeks.

If the Muses are watching me, they're laughing.

This is foolish. The entire affair was nothing more than a throw of the dice, anyway. Stuffing the coin into my pocket, I spin on my heel and set off toward home with chagrin making my heart heavy. I will tell the inspector I simply could not do it.

I'll have to find another way to rescue my father.

A hand shoots out of a recessed doorway and clamps over my mouth. The motion is so fast I think, at first, it is only a pigeon sailing past. Before I can make sense of what is happening, my shoulder blades slam into a wooden door.

A man presses his body to mine from breastbone to knees, flattening me against the wood so I cannot move. He grips my upper arm with the hand that isn't practically suffocating me and pins my free arm away from my body.

Away from my pocket and the all-important coin inside.

I should be panicking, but all I can think is that I passed this doorway and didn't see anyone, didn't smell or hear anyone. And my senses are far sharper than that of any human.

"Why is a delicate bird like you strutting around the Thieves' Market?" His voice is low and rough, but warm. Criminals aren't supposed to have voices like that, are they? Voices that sound like sun-warmed honey? Then again, how the hell would I know? He is probably a cold-blooded killer. Perhaps that's how he lures unsuspecting victims to their deaths. The thought gives me back my voice.

"I have a coin," I mumble into his palm, but the words sound like gibberish against his calloused skin. His grip tightens, his fingers digging into my jaw muscles not quite enough to hurt, but enough to let me know he can make it hurt if he wants to. A bolt of terror hits me, and welds my muscles to my bones so tightly that I cannot fight back even if I was brave enough to do it.

He whispers against my ear, "No, no. Don't speak. Don't even move. You shouldn't be here, dove. The Market is not for the likes of you."

Yes, I figured that part out.

But he isn't hurting me. I may still have a chance to carry out my plan, to find my father and perhaps even save our shop if I can just get my hand into my pocket...

He continues in the same low tone, "I'm going to release you, and you're going to turn around and walk yourself out of this neighborhood. You will not stop walking until you're safe behind a locked door. You will not speak, and you will not look back. Nod if you understand me."

With no other option, I nod.

He eases his hand from my mouth so slowly that our fog-dampened skin clings for a moment before peeling apart, like lifting my arms from a leather couch on a hot day.

When I don't speak, he nods. "Good girl. Now, leave and never come back."

I search his face for a trace of kindness, a hint that he won't hurt me if I disobey him, but even my sharp eyes can only make out vaguely angular features, no more than pale smudges beneath his hood. It is as if the cloak he wears is made of darkness, blurring the edges of his body to blend with the shifting shadows. No wonder I never saw him in a cloak like that.

Whether he is kind or not, I won't get another chance like this. And I cannot leave knowing my father is out there somewhere, and that he needs me.

"I have–" I whisper, but he lunges at me and clamps his hand over my mouth once more. This time, his grip isn't so gentle, and his voice isn't soft.

"Do you have any idea," he growls, reaching down to hike the hem of my skirt, "what happens to pretty girls who wander into the market unprotected?"

Gooseflesh breaks out on my legs as the wind tickles between my knees and slides up the inside of my thighs through the thin cotton of my chemise. Terror rips through my body. It wasn't as if I walked here ignorant of the danger. I'm not stupid. But I did foolishly believe I would be a bit more stoic about it, if things went badly. Now that things are going badly, I am so far from being stoic that I start shaking. A whimper escapes the fist of fear constricting my throat.

He nods. "Yes, Dove, and worse than that. Whatever you're looking for, you won't find it here. This is no place for you."

His words trigger a memory that drags me out of my body and into the past.

*Fat raindrops splattered my head and shoulders, plastering my hair to my skin and soaking the rags I managed to scrounge as clothing. I stood before door after door, hoping they would open. And when one miraculously did, I stared longingly at the light and warmth just beyond the threshold, only to hear the words, "There is no place for you," before the door closed and left me in the dark and cold.*

Alone.

I was always entirely and absolutely alone. Until the night the door stayed open. Until a kind hand pulled me across the threshold into warmth and light. Until my father changed everything.

I cannot let fear stop me from trying. No matter what he does, I must try. My father needs me.

"I have a coin!" I shout against his hand, but the words sound like *uh habba con.*

That muffled sentence acts on him like electricity on the toy soldier. He stiffens, releasing my hem. His hand falls away enough to free my lips. Energy thrums through every cell of him, animating his body to such a degree that the vibrations of it electrify the air between us. I have repaired artifice that behaves that way when the runic sentences are too damaged to retain energy.

If not handled carefully, they usually explode.

I tense to run, but he's still too close. He would only grab me again if I tried. And I have a promise to keep. So I repeat, slowly and clearly, "I have a coin."

"Don't say that." He leans into me, close enough for his warm breath to brush over the shell of my ear and send shivers down my neck. "You don't want to say that. You want to be in your bed, warm and safe. Take it back. I'll pretend I didn't hear you, and you can return to your life like this never happened."

This is my last chance. If I don't do it now, I won't be able to maintain my courage. My hand dives into my pocket with Elven speed, faster than any human can move, because I'm terrified he'll try to stop me. He doesn't.

Breath caught in my throat, I hold the silver coin up on one palm. His grip tightens for a heart-stopping second, then loosens.

"I have a coin," I repeat, panting. "I have. A coin."

He sighs and frees me, retreating a step, shaking his head as he backs out of the doorway. "Moon and stars be damned, woman. You have no idea what you've done."

Except I do. I have just taken the first step toward finding my father, and, possibly, damning my future. Not that my future was very promising, in any case. But he doesn't need to know that.

So, I bite my lips together and wait. I can sense him glaring at me even if I cannot see his eyes. Frustration and disapproval make the air around us colder and more brittle.

He sighs and says, at last, "It is your life I suppose. Or, it was. Let's go."

He takes me by the upper arm the way I have seen wealthy ladies and gentlemen walk together, but there is nothing refined about the way he drags me through the market. I may as well be a disobedient child being taken home for a reprimand.

It isn't until we enter the wide mouth of the abandoned church and the grim atmosphere swallows us that the reality of what I have done smothers me.

The future my father and I planned, my failed apprenticeship with the Artificer's Guild, even quiet days in the shop filled with the scratching of my awl, fade like the shifting fog outside.

Will I ever watch a repaired toy soldier march across my work-table again? Or stand in the sunlit corner of my room as the window breeze ruffles the feathery leaves of my ferns?

Is darkness my future now? Whatever bravery I managed to cobble together fades. My lungs seize and the air is too heavy to breathe. My captor hauls me along but my feet drag on the uneven floor because I cannot muster the strength to pick them up.

When I stumble, he catches me by both arms and holds me against his chest so my wobbling knees don't drag me to the floor. "Weakness won't help you now, so there is no use in going pale. You've made your bed. Best muster up the strength to lie in it. If you don't, I'll be forced to carry you." His fingers tighten and he pulls me close enough that the tip of his nose almost brushes mine, close enough to smell his breath–is that cinnamon?–and says in a husky voice, "Unless you want that? Do you, Dove? Want me to carry you?"

No. No, I don't want him any closer than necessity demands. I can still feel the brush of the wind between my legs, and the memory makes me jerk backward. I right myself, though my knees are still weak. He lets me go. Which must mean he had no intention of carrying me, only of scaring me enough that he wouldn't have to.

I imagine I hear a smile in his voice when my captor says, "Good girl. Let's go. And no fainting spells, eh?"

The faint light of the street lamps leaks through the broken windows to reveal a flagstone floor littered with splinters of the pews that must have been here once. Refuse is scattered here and there, detritus left behind by people who used the mostly intact roof for shelter in bad weather.

I might have hidden here, once upon a time. When the weather is particularly bad and the shelters are full, a place like this, cold as it is, keeps people alive. But the years have not been kind to the old building, and neither have the residents of Thieves' Market. Whatever could be torn apart and sold or burned, including the carved wood wainscoting, has been.

A bit of fellow feeling rises in my chest. I, too, have sold everything of value: every gadget, every bit of art, furniture, even my clothing to hang on to the shop long enough for my father to come back. But he never did. And I doubt worshippers will ever return to this place, either.

The church and I are both cold and empty.

My captor negotiates the broken floor with the grace of a cat, seeing better than any human has a right to see in the dark, and guides me around the worst of the mess without looking. When we reach the back of the transepts, he knocks on a bit of flagstone flooring in a staccato rhythm that must have been a signal.

The floor moves.

I flinch but he holds me fast as the flagstone lifts and slides away with a dry scrape that, for a moment, fills the hollow space with noise. At our feet, a hole opens wide enough for a person, revealing a set of steps that disappear into the center of the earth.

"Mind your head," my captor says as he uses his grip on my upper arm to urge me toward the hole.

My leg muscles lock up. If this man truly is taking me to the Cutthroat King, I must force myself down the stairs. But what if he's not? What if he has something else in mind? Something worse. I try to tell him that my legs won't move, but the only sound I can force past my lips is a terrified whimper. Likely he will only manhandle me down the hole, as he did earlier. This is my bed. But I cannot seem to force myself to lay in it.

"Don't make this worse than–" he starts to say, and stops. When he reaches for my face, I want to pull away, but only my eyelids flinch. If I could feel shame for being such a ruddy coward I would.

He runs the pad of his thumb across my cheekbone in a caress that is more threatening than comforting. "Poor little dove. I cannot release you, now. It is too late for either of us to turn back. And you are walking into the fox's den. Don't let them see you cower."

*"You are the best repairist I've ever trained," my father said proudly. We stood outside the Guild Hall with a dozen dwarves, waiting for the doors of the examination hall to open. Anxiety curled through the crowd like a hunting animal, growling and hissing until every one of us trembled.*

*The other candidates chatted uneasily, using company to take the edge off their nerves. But no one spoke to me. They were dwarves, and they belonged here. I was the only elf, the only outsider.*

*It did not matter that I was a test case, a way for the League for Equal Representation to prove to the humans that elves and dwarves presented a united front. That we would fight together to ensure hereditary titles and power belonged to everyone, not only humans.*

*To the other apprentices, though, I was more than a political puppet. I was a threat. The elves have the Artisan's Guild, their accusing eyes said. I had no right to poke my nose into hundreds of years of dwarven secrets. Why couldn't I stick to my own?*

*My father turned me away from their accusing eyes and said, "They cannot give you a test you will not pass. You will be the first elf ever to apprentice as an artificer, and that makes some dwarves nervous. Their guild is the source of their political power, as the Artisan's Guild is for us. That means some of them will not want you here. They will try to intimidate you into leaving. Don't let them do it. Don't let them see you cower."*

That was my father's dream. I would finish my apprenticeship and while they would never grant me membership to the guild, we would be the only licensed repairists in the city employing a true artificer. I could take over the shop, and he would be free to focus his attention on his inventions at last, to restart his stalled career and recapture the stardom that faded too fast.

The memory makes my shoulders straighten. My father gave me a future worth having, one an orphaned girl with no hope of even a hot meal could never have dreamed of. Taking this chance for him is the least I can do. His secretive employers have done something with or *to* him, I know it. Which means saving him, and the Mechanica, is up to me.

I gather up my secret hopes, my fears, and everything that doesn't align with doing my duty to my father, and stuff them down deep inside myself. I know what it is to be abandoned. I will not abandon him.

Jaw clenched so hard it hurts, I step down into the dark.

# CHAPTER 3

*Papa still hasn't returned. We've had no communications from him, and as much as I tell myself he is merely so distracted by work he's forgotten to write, I cannot make myself believe it. Without him here, our license to operate under the guild is at risk, so I cannot take on any more repairs. We've started selling whatever will fetch a price.*

*—From the diary of Willow Beauregard*
*October 25, 1902*

NEW LONDONERS HAVE BEEN TRYING TO ERADICATE DARKNESS FOR hundreds of years. Street lamps, dwarven lanterns, electric lights, candles, and torches soften the night and brighten the shadows. Interior paint is chosen for how well it reflects light, and decorations are designed to capture and return every stray bit of it.

My workspace is surrounded by lamps, and even my small room has two huge windows that let in sunlight during the day. At night, the stored sunlight of dwarven street lamps lights the wealthy parts of the city, and an electric street light on Penny Lane joins the moonlight that leaks through my windows.

As the underground passage engulfs me, I realize that despite my jaunt through the nighttime city, I have never known true darkness.

We leave the last faint light of the stairway behind us, and I learn that the dark is a living thing. It covers and surrounds me, worms into my ears and eyes, and even my lungs until I breathe only in short gasps.

But the damp air pressing against my skin invades my nostrils anyway, carrying the smothering stink of mildew and fetid water. My breath catches in my throat. If I knew the way out, I would turn and run.

My captor, however, doesn't seem to notice the oppressive dark. He drags me forward as if it is noon on a clear day. It must be familiarity that lets him navigate this pit. Because even my eyes, far more sensitive than any human's or dwarf's, are utterly defeated by the blackness. Only his confidence stops me from curling into a ball and screaming until my throat is sore.

I try to count my steps at first, thinking I can distract myself from the terror riding the back of my neck like an angry cat with its claws dug in. But that doesn't work. There are too many.

Then I think I can memorize the turns and find my way out if I need to escape. But I lose count, just as I lose my sense of direction and time. All I know is that we are walking down. Down and down and down, into the bowels of the city... maybe the bowels of hell.

Tons of earth and rock are above, separating me from the sky, pressing in from every side, waiting for a weakness to exploit, to come crashing down and bury us so deep no one would ever even think to search for our bodies.

"How far is it?" I force the words past the tightness in my throat, desperate for any distraction, but they are strangled by the darkness.

I needn't have made the effort. My captor doesn't answer.

Minutes pass. Hours. Days and years and whole ages of the earth slide by in the nothingness until, *finally*, a dim orange light appears. It is far enough away that it's only a less black spot in the dark, but I cling to it with every scrap of my attention. If I stop looking, it might disappear.

As the light grows brighter, the faint smudges of old stones are visible, forming an arched tunnel over us, narrow enough that I can touch both sides at once, and so low that I would have to duck if I was any taller. They were laid so long ago that hopeful plant roots have dug through the mortar in places. Uneven flagstones line the ground, cracked and worn smooth in the center from the passage of countless feet.

The faraway echo of laughter and rough voices raised in song reaches my ears, loud enough to hear between footsteps. Finally, the smell reaches me: the sour tang of ale, of body odor, and... meat pasties? Hope flutters against my ribs like a caged bird, growing stronger as we near the light.

I lean toward it, every cell in my body yearning to escape the clinging dark, but my captor clicks his tongue and pulls me tight against his side. "I would not be so eager if I were you."

A shiver skitters down my spine, due in part to the rumble in his voice, and in part to the warning. But I would throw myself on the mercy of the King without a coin or a bargain to offer if it means escaping the dark.

Several corridors join and branch off of one another like crooked city streets or tunnels in an anthill, and I can't keep track of them as he hurries me through first one room and then another, turning left and left, then right. One room made of blackened brick, one carved directly out of the bones of the earth, and the other might have been the catacombs I've read about beneath monasteries or great churches.

Light and sound increase as we approach what can only be a large gathering of some kind. Blood pounds in my veins and throbs in my fingertips. This must be it, where the Cutthroat King holds court.

My fists clench as we near a wide, arched doorway that leaks light and laughter into the dreary shadows we pass through. Part of me aches to run toward it even as I dig in my heels and drag us to a stop short of the door.

It yawns like a portal out of some faerie story: on this side of it is everything my life had once been, and whatever hopes I cherished for the future. And on the other?

My captor pulls me across the threshold and into what I can only describe as an underground dining hall. Pillars of dubious sturdiness, some reinforced with iron bracers, hold up a high, barrel-vaulted ceiling.

Ramshackle tables covered in mismatched tankards, vessels, and flatware of all kinds line the right and left walls. Humans, elves, and dwarves of every shape, size, and skin tone sit on benches and chairs or stand in groups eating, drinking–always drinking–gambling or chatting.

And all of them are a little dirty. A little drunk. And a *lot* intimidating.

I try to take everything in, noting flashes of knives, brass knuckles, and even a few barely concealed pistols. The rumors are true. The Unseen Court is real, and I am standing in it. I sidle closer to my captor, which is foolish because he isn't any more likely to protect me than any other criminal in this place, but at least he is familiar.

He leans down to whisper in my ear, "Welcome to the Undercroft, Dove. Good luck. Don't let them see you sweat."

Before I can think to stop him, he disappears into the milling bodies. My stomach drops and I clutch the silver coin to my chest.

"Will you save me from this crowd if something goes wrong?" I whisper. Not likely.

Maybe if I hover at the edges they won't notice me. I take a few careful steps backward and bump against something hard.

"Watch it, sweetheart," a deep voice rumbles.

A ruddy-skinned mountain of a man grabs my shoulders with hands the size of dinner plates and moves me aside as if I am no more than a broom or an umbrella that happens to be in his way.

"I'm sorry," I croak, watching the other attendees melt out of his path as he cuts across the room.

"No need to apologize to 'im," an old dwarven woman cackles.

She sits in a shapeless lump with her back against a pillar, wearing a series of scarves and blankets like a tree wears leaves. The bright yellow scarf around her neck makes her brown skin glow despite the wrinkles of age fanning out around her eyes, which are dark and penetrating.

"A man that big knows 'e's in everyone's way. 'E should be the one apologizin'." She narrows her eyes and flicks the edge of one scarf at me. "I never seen you at court. First time?"

"Ah...I–" I fiddle with the coin as my cheeks start to burn.

"Don't fret, duck. Proceedin's will start a'fore long. Tithin' first, then complaints, then supplicants. You can stand 'ere, by me. No one will bother you, if they know what's good for 'em."

I try to show her my appreciation but cannot tell if I give her a grateful smile or only a grimace. I'm not properly connected to my body anymore. But, thankfully, it isn't long before her prediction comes true. At some unseen signal, the crowd separates up the middle, pushing to either side of the room and dragging chairs and benches with them.

Soon a clear aisle opens from the door to the front, where a wooden throne sits on a wide stone dais.

Even from this distance, I can see the spoons carved into the wood. Various vining flowers and—to my surprise—willow leaves and buds, twine in and around the spoons.

I whisper to my new friend, "What do the spoons mean? The ones carved on the throne?"

She responds with a buzzing snore, snuggled so deeply into her scarves and blankets that she looks like a caterpillar poking its head out of a cocoon. The sound is particularly loud in the sudden silence but no one looks at the sleeping woman. Their eyes are trained on the front of the room.

A man prowls out of the shadowed double arches wearing a bent crown of silver spoons. The tight-fitting britches and loose black shirt belong on a poet... or a pirate. The clothing contrasts sharply with his fair skin and makes him look like he stepped out of the past. But he wears them with such casual aplomb they might as well be the height of fashion.

He isn't particularly tall or broad, not the physically imposing figure I have created in my mind. And there are no guards to protect him. But he moves with a languid, confident grace more intimidating than mere size. As if the most dangerous men and women in the city were of no more concern to him than the pigeons that crowd the streets above.

He sinks into his throne, throws one leg over the armrest, and leans back on his opposite elbow. His dented crown catches the light of the oil lamps scattered about the room. It should look childish, but he wears it with the same disregard with which he sits in the chair, and that makes it fitting, somehow.

I draw a slow breath to calm my nerves. Despite everything I have heard, he's only a man; handsome in a sharp way, lean and charismatic, maybe, but still just a man and not the monster we've all been led to believe.

Maybe the stories have always been merely that, stories meant to instill fear, to keep people who don't belong out of the Undercroft. Maybe I can do this, after all. The old woman said the proceedings would include tithes, complaints, and then supplicants. I must be the latter.

Leaning against the pillar next to the sleeping dwarf, I have an uninterrupted view of the dais where I can settle in for the wait.

Two men carry a trunk to the front of the room and place it on the flagstones before the King. They open the lid, then stand on either side. A queue forms that snakes from the front of the room into the entryway. People take turns depositing all kinds of things: necklaces, coins, leather pouches, handfuls of gems, pocket watches, an ivory hairbrush, folded bills, a bolt of blue watered silk more beautiful than anything I have ever worn, and even a very fine bit of artifice.

I lean forward, trying to get a glimpse of the beautiful little teapot but it disappears into the chest before I can see enough to appreciate it.

The tithing continues for another ten minutes, and by the time it is done, the chest has overflowed, and several offerings are left on the floor. How often does the King receive these donations? Once a month? A week? Surely not every day.

Staring at such wealth makes my heart skip a beat. A mere fraction of that chest would pay off all our debts and secure the future of the shop. He must be one of the richest men not only in the city, but on the island.

Yet the King appears bored as he picks his teeth, only glancing once and while at the offerings. The last tithe, a beautiful little French doll with a glass face, is placed carefully at the foot of the chest, and the crowd heaves a collective sigh of relief. The guards turn to pack the chest, but the King sits up so abruptly the people standing closest to the dais flinch away.

"Someone hasn't paid their dues," he says, in a familiar, sun-warmed honey voice.

I gasp loud enough that the people near me should be staring but everyone else appears as shocked as I am. They glance at one another, trying to ascertain who is referring to. But I cannot drag my eyes from the man at the front of the room because I still have gooseflesh from the sound of that voice.

*Gracious Calliope*, had I shown my coin to the Cutthroat King *himself*? My stomach flips as though trying to find somewhere to hide. No. No, that is a ridiculous thought. The King wouldn't be abroad on the streets, he wouldn't escort lowly supplicants to the Undercroft.

Would he?

I had never seen the face of my captor, and I'd been so preoc-cupied I hadn't thought to examine his clothing. I can only stare in mute discomfort as he picks at his cuticles and says, "There is still time, Mr. Coulter."

The rest of the room is abuzz with tension as they exchange excited or nervous glances, but Mr. Coulter never appears.

The King sighs and waves a dismissive hand. "Very well. Send out the Ratcatchers. Shall we call it the normal bounty for whoever finds him first?"

Sinister laughter and sharp smiles punctuate the faces in the crowd. A few people even slip silently out, walking with a purpose. The chest slams shut, the lock snicks into place, and the guards carry all that wealth back into the shadows.

Everyone should relax after such a tense moment, but the anticipatory energy only grows.

"Very well, you wretched lot," the King says, and a strange light enters his eyes. He swings his leg down and braces his elbows on his knees. "Bring forth your complaints."

A hush falls over the crowd as an elderly woman with iron grey hair and a severe expression stomps to the front of the room. Despite the anger evident in every line of her face and form, she keeps her eyes downcast.

"Welcome to court, grandmother," the King says. "Who has wronged you?"

The old woman's voice is brittle, but it vibrates with anger. Her hands curl into fists in her apron. "I always paid me dues, majesty. I never been late, not once. But the Ratcatchers said I owed twice my regular fee though business ain't changed. When I told 'em I needed time, they tore up my shop. In all the years since Grover left me the business, goddess rest his soul, I never shorted my dues! They smashed my product and took all my ready cash. I can't even pay my shop boy."

The King tilts his head to the side in a motion that reminds me of the way a cat stares at a mouse hole. "Did you recognize them?"

"The Ratcatchers? No, majesty. They was new, and rough. Not like Tom and Kumar."

The King's voice sounds lazy but there is an edge to it. "They put their hands on you, grandmother?"

She nods. "And I've the bruises still, to prove it." A bit of pride enters her voice as she reaches into her pocket. "Did manage to snag this in all the kerfuffle, though. I ain't lost *all* my skills."

"Bring it to me."

The old woman hesitates, her smile fading, but after a deep breath, she drops the object onto the King's palm before scurrying back to her place. His cheek twitches below his right eye and the edges of his mouth curl into a grimace. But the expression disappears as quickly as the light reflecting off the silver coin on his palm.

A perfect match to the coin currently clutched in my hand.

"Gwil," the King says, and a burly man with a chest like a keg steps out of the crowd. His tanned skin is sunburnt, and he wears common work clothes–trousers, suspenders, and a vest in sensible shades of brown and grey–but my eyes drift to the black mourning band on his left arm. He must be one of the Ratcatchers.

The King waves a hand and says, "Take care of it. And when you find Tom and Kumar, bring them to me."

Gwil nods and strides out of the room to the murmuring from the crowd. I wonder if I am the only one who noticed the slight emphasis the King put on the word *when*.

"Take what you need from the coffers at the Divvy tomorrow, grandmother," the King says as he settles back into his throne. "The imposters will be found and punished. You shall watch it happen."

With a bob of her head, the old woman slips back into the crowd, and I cannot help but think that judgment was... just. Is the lazy grace and dangerous expression only a disguise? He may not have been *kind* to the old woman, precisely, but his decision smacks of consideration. Perhaps even concern.

The chance that he may accept my offer–or at the very least not dismiss me out of hand–makes the claws of fear loosen their grip on my neck ever-so-slightly. I may have a chance. A real chance to find my father.

Someone else steps out of the crowd, and this time my height does me no favors. I edge around the people in front of me until I can see the dark-skinned dwarven man striding forward, his long, elaborately beaded mustaches swinging like pendulums as he approaches the throne.

"What brings the head of the Black Cats to court?" the King asks.

The dwarven man's jaw works for a moment before he rolls his shoulders and raises his chin. "Ambrose, majesty." His voice is deep and rumbly, like a rockslide, but it is drowned by the surprised murmurs of the crowd. "He squealed about the warehouse job. Constables were waiting for us. We lost a grease man and killed a guard to get out."

"That's a lie, Cecil, and you know it!" A slender man with fair skin pushes through the crowd, his nose and cheeks red with fury.

"Yeah? Tell that to Jamie. Oh, right, you can't. He's dead, isn't he? Now constables are crawling all over the docks. We won't get a shipment through for weeks, at least, because you couldn't keep your mouth shut!"

"How do I know it wasn't you who–"

"Endangered the entire Undercroft–"

"Say anything to absolve yourself from–"

The crowd watches the men scream at one another, rapt, but no one else appears to notice the King. He uncoils from his relaxed position like a snake rearing up, his eyes hard and dark as onyx. By the time he speaks, he's within arm's reach of the arguing men.

"Ambrose," the King's voice stops the fight with the same efficiency as scratching out the final rune on a bit of artifice. Silence strangles every sound in the room but the King's question. "Have you been visiting the Silk Purse?"

Fear washes the angry red from Ambrose's cheeks, leaving him almost as white as my hair. "N-no, Majesty. Of course not. You forbade it."

"And you always follow my directives"–the King circles him, one finger pressed to his chin–"do you not?"

"Of course, Majesty."

"Because you are loyal."

"I am."

"And you are careful to follow the code."

"Always."

The King stops inches from Ambrose, their noses nearly touching. "Then you will not mind... looking into my eyes?"

If Ambrose were a mouse frozen before a cat, he could not look more hunted. His lashes flutter as if he wants to raise his eyes but cannot force himself to do it.

"Ambrose..." The King's voice sounds like it rises from the depths of the earth, cold, hollow, and compelling. My own eyelids tremble with the desire to follow his directions but I am already staring at him so hard I am locked in place.

Ambrose must feel the same compulsion because he silently shakes. A bead of sweat slips down the side of his face.

Then he turns to run.

The King's hand shoots out, clamping around Ambrose's throat before he can complete the turn. Ambrose's eyes flare, then narrow, and a knife blade reflects the lamplight like a fish leaping out of the water. The impact makes everyone flinch, though we remain silent, stunned into disbelief.

Ambrose has buried a knife to the hilt in the King's side, below his ribs. The terror of New London's underground, the bogeyman mothers use to frighten wayward children, has been stabbed. But he does not release his hold on the struggling man. Instead, he raises his arm, lifting Ambrose off the ground as if he weighs as much as a small child.

Face turning dark red, Ambrose releases the knife and grabs the King's wrist with both hands. His feet drum uselessly against the King's shins in a desperate rhythm.

The King smiles tenderly. "As always, a coward refuses to choose his own fate. And, thus, it is chosen for him."

Ambrose's face is purple, his eyes bulge, and his mouth is open as he desperately sucks at the air, back arched.

"Goodbye, Ambrose," the King murmurs as the struggling weakens. Slows. Stops. "It appears"–he drops the body with a dull thump–"the Black Cats have an unexpected opening in the ranks."

I cannot pull my eyes from Ambrose's limp body. His limbs are twisted the wrong way, head turned toward me, mouth open as if to scream, or shout a warning. And since his bloodshot eyes are locked on me, I hear the imagined word, *Run*, whispered as if in my ear.

There had been no trial. No request for evidence or proof. Merely an allegation and summary execution.

The King casually pulls the knife from his side and lays it on Ambrose's chest as if the dead man is some fallen warrior king. "Are you satisfied, Cecil?"

The dwarven man looks sick, but his jaw is set. "Aye, majesty. Though his foolishness will cost us a month's income."

"Perhaps, you should take that as a lesson and learn to keep a closer eye on your second in command. Especially if you know his weakness."

"Isn't love every man's weakness, Majesty?" He says absently, but his eyes are still fixed on his dead partner.

"Only if the man is weak," the King replies.

He turns and strides toward the throne as if more than three inches of steel hadn't been jammed into his side mere moments before. I cannot see the blood staining his black shirt, only catch the wet shine of the soaked fabric when he passes through a pool of lamplight.

He retakes his throne, swallows a mouthful of wine from a goblet I had not even noticed, and says, "Any further complaints?"

No one speaks. No one even moves.

"Very well," the King claps his hands and smiles. "Shall we invite the supplicants to come forward?"

The sleep-tinged voice of the scarf-woman says, "That would be you, duck."

# CHAPTER 4

*Scotland Yard turned me away. They said I have no proof he's been kidnapped, and unless I produce evidence, I must be content with the fact that, "Sometimes men leave." But Papa would never abandon the shop. I've tried everything else I can think of and there isn't much left to sell.*

*—From the diary of Willow Beauregard, November 15, 1902*

MY HEART CLIMBS SO FAR INTO MY THROAT IT CHOKES ME. I CANNOT walk out there now, with Ambrose's broken body on the ground. It is too easy to imagine hanging by that man's hand, my feet kicking at his shins as I fight for air.

No. My captor was right. I most definitely should not be here. I slide backward a few careful steps, using the taller men to screen myself from the throne as I angle toward the door. I may not remember the way out, but the tunnels cannot go on forever, can they?

Of course they can. And my common sense knew it when I came here, I didn't listen. Because, despite everything I clearly don't know, I am certain of one thing: I am the only person looking for my father. And nothing I have tried so far has worked. It was easy to convince myself this was a viable option when I was still safe in the shop.

Before I saw a man get strangled to death.

"Now's your chance, duck. And the last one you'll get, likely."

I squeak in surprise and spin to find the dwarven woman staring up at me from her nest of scarves. The sound is loud enough in the silence that, for the first time, dozens of pairs of eyes turn in my direction. Most are curious, some are measuring, and a few are outright hostile.

The King's voice fills the room, reaching out to touch me even as I hide. "Ah. There you are."

My skin goes cold. Blessed, merciful hammer, it was him. I had forced the Cutthroat King himself to drag me into the Unseen Court.

"Well? Do not leave us in suspense. Approach." He gestures grandly at the stairs before the dais and grins like a shark. "I insist."

The temptation to run seizes my muscles, but the onlookers have no intention of missing a show. They crowd in, herding me toward the front of the room like terrified sheep sacrificing a member of the herd to the wolf. Someone gives me a solid shove in the back, and I stumble into the aisle clutching the front of my coat in one hand and the coin in the other.

Ambrose's body is only a few feet behind me.

I don't want to look at the King, but I cannot help myself. He lounges on the throne, secure in his power, a cold, hungry light in his eyes. My mouth goes so dry that my cheeks stick to my teeth. Swallowing convulsively doesn't help.

One corner of his mouth curls in amusement, and he raises an eyebrow as if to say, *Afraid?*

His voice and my father's blend in my memory, becoming a joint exhortation. *Do not let them see you cower.*

When staring at the wolf, it is easy to forget this room is full of predators. Showing weakness before the Cutthroat King is dangerous enough, but there are also dozens of criminals at my back. Who knows how many of them would happily end my life?

I straighten my spine, drop my shoulders, and throw my hood back. If I am going to do this, I should at least appear confident. This isn't the first time I've tried to fix something so delicate that one misstep would cause it to blow up in my face.

And my father needs me.

But the speech I rehearsed is hidden behind a wall of terror I cannot push through, one so heavy my lungs can't move beneath the weight of it.

*Say something. Say anything, damn you.* "I need your help."

The crowd murmurs in amusement.

One dark, sardonic brow raises. "Help? You are no subject of mine to make such a request."

"But–" I scramble for a response but the only thing I can think to say is, "I have a coin!"

"And you will explain how you came by that coin before it is taken from you."

Prickles of dread, like tiny pointed feet, race down my spine.

"Now, if you please."

How much do I tell him? If I lie, will he know? He certainly seemed to know Ambrose was lying. And the possibility of repeating that terrifying scene electrifies me.

Almost without my permission, the words start pouring out. "I work with my father in a repair shop. Over a month ago, two men offered him a temporary job with their organization. He should have been home by now, but"–my shoulders shrug in a nervous twitch–"he hasn't returned. He hasn't contacted me. Someone delivered an envelope to my doorstep yesterday. This was inside, along with a smudged note." I open my fist to display the silver coin embossed with a cutthroat man.

His expression makes me feel like a child trying to convince my father that I did, in fact, see a monster in my closet, thank you very much. So I dig out the crumpled letter as well. It has been folded and unfolded so many times the paper is wearing thin at the creases.

My father's hurried scrawl is immediately recognizable, but the ink had not dried before the letter was stuffed inside the envelope. Most of the words are smudged beyond recognition. And whoever delivered it hadn't exactly been meticulous about its condition. The dirt and mud stains further damaged the letter, leaving it only partially legible.

The paragraph isn't a long one, and the only words I can make out are *danger, I'm sorry, protection,* and *seek to find me.* "I don't know where he came by the coin. But he must have found a way to send it to me so I could use it to help him."

"How...fascinating," the King says, not sounding fascinated in the least. "But you are no subject of mine, and neither is your father. Therefore I owe you nothing."

If I was a subject, would he owe me something? Something like protection? How did one become a subject of the Cutthroat King? Swear fealty, surely, but what else? What responsibilities did that entail? I don't know enough about how this world works to risk making such a commitment.

The only option I have is the one I walked in with, and now that one of his subject's bodies lays on the carpet behind me, even that sounds like a far worse trade than it did a few hours ago.

But my father is out there, somewhere. And if he has to sneak correspondence to me, something is very wrong. I owe it to him to do whatever I can. Like he did for me. So I force my voice to be calm and confident when I say, "I understand that, Your Majesty. So I have come to propose a trade."

His small, amused smile is far from comforting. "Have you, indeed? What sort of a trade?"

Take a deep breath. I can do this. "I offer you my service as a skilled repairist in return for finding and returning my father."

"I have repairists of my own," he says, waving a hand at the crowd.

"I also have some skill at artificery. Enough to be accepted as the first non-dwarven apprentice to the Artificer's Guild."

Surprised mutterings rise from the crowd, but the King doesn't seem impressed. He uncoils from the chair and slinks down the steps, holding his elbow in one hand while tapping his lips thoughtfully with the forefinger of his other.

His eyes fix on me. Running away is a capital idea, but I remain locked in place by the chains of his gaze.

"I don't need your professional services," he says, circling me like a man deciding whether to buy a horse. "What else can you offer?"

My mouth goes dry. There is that voice, again: the sun-warmed-honey voice he used on me before, only this time it isn't comforting. "I... I have nothing else."

He stops just behind my right shoulder and picks up a lock of my hair, letting the strands slide through his fingers. "Oh, that isn't true at all."

Lascivious chuckles punctuate the silence.

"What–" I swallow to work a bit of moisture back into my mouth. Which isn't easy as he runs the tip of one finger from just below my ear, down my neck to my shoulder. Disgust ripples down my arm. This is not what I planned. Nowhere near it. "What do you want in exchange?"

The King starts walking again, tapping his lips while his gaze roams over every part of me, crown to toes. "Let's see. You want me to find your father. That will require detective work. This is a big city, after all. My people must be fed, housed, clothed, and paid, as they cannot do their jobs while they search. That will bite into my coffers quite substantially."

"I-I can offer–I mean, I am skilled–"

"In return for such lavish generosity, I shall require something rather substantial."

"I have already sold everything that would fetch a price." Everything but my plants, which still sit in their tranquil little indoor garden in the sunny corner of my room. I want the peace of quietly tending them more than I have ever wanted anything. Anything but a home. A place to belong.

"I don't want your possessions," he says, waving a dismissive hand. "I want *you*."

"Me?" I squeak.

What could he possibly want with me? In this room alone I have seen women more beautiful, with wicked smiles and ripe curves, some of them who make a living giving pleasure. I am too tall, too thin, and certainly not skilled enough to pay for this trade with my body.

My knees wobble so hard that it takes every bit of concentration to remain standing. If I cannot control myself, I will collapse in front of the most dangerous person in the city.

My head shakes without my permission.

"Yes." He holds my chin between his thumb and the knuckle of his forefinger. "You. In whatever capacity I choose. Whenever I choose it. If I require my boots shined, you will shine them. If I require my goblet filled, my back washed, or my... needs to be serviced, you shall see to them. For as long as it takes me to return your father, you will belong to me."

A trade was one thing, but agreeing to be at the complete mercy of a murderer for an unspecified amount of time was something else. No. No slagging chance. Not even my father would ask for such a sacrifice.

Except that he did. The letter in my hand was proof. I could not deny him that after everything he'd done for me.

"For three months or until you find him, whichever comes first," I blurt.

Holy gods, what have I done? In heaven's name, why have I done it?

"A year," he counters.

"Six months, but you may never lay a hand on me in anger. Or require me to hurt anyone. Or... or force me to perform any service for anyone else."

"I am not accustomed to sharing." The low growl in his voice makes a little tingle of terrified anticipation race up my spine.

"How do I know you will keep your end of the bargain?"

One dark brow quirks up. "If I recall correctly, you are the one asking a service of me."

"But I have everything to lose, and you have nothing to gain."

"Oh, I wouldn't say that," he chuckles. "I assume you have heard rumors about me? Stories told to frighten children?"

I nod. Too many to count. I never believed them, not really. Not until the envelope and coin appeared on my doorstep.

He eases closer, bringing us less than a foot apart. The rust scent of his blood makes me swallow convulsively. "Do any of the stories claim that I lie?"

A thoughtful frown pinches my brows together as I sort through as many tales as I can remember. Cheating, stealing, blackmail, bribery, smuggling, the list goes on and on, but lying isn't on it. Still, a man doesn't rule the Unseen Court because of his honesty.

"No," I admit. "But they are stories for a reason."

The muscle in his jaw ticks as he thinks, his eyes cold and dark as charcoal. Finally, he nods and draws a small dark knife. I flinch away, but he takes my hand and places the hilt on my palm, wrapping my fingers around it.

Then he holds my wrist and sets the tip of the blade against the hollow in his throat. "I will help you find your father in return for your complete service for six months, or until your father is returned safely. I will not lay a hand on you in anger, require you to serve anyone else, or require you to hurt anyone. If I do not keep my word," he intones, "may this knife pierce my flesh. Does that satisfy you?"

I accept with a jerky nod and pull the metal away from his skin as soon as he releases my wrist.

A smile colors his voice when he leans in close, his cheek brushing mine, and says into my ear, "We have an accord, Dove. And I intend to enjoy it."

The air comes to life, crackling with pins and needles against my skin, as if his promise established an invisible runic sentence between us. But the sensation fades as quickly as it arrived.

He releases me and steps back, leaving me to wobble as I catch my balance. I did it. I really did it. People are chuckling and pointing, but I barely register them over the pounding blood rushing through my ears. Black closes in at the edge of my vision.

I am going to faint. I really am a ninny.

"Welcome to the Unseen Court," he announces. "I am certain you will be a valuable *member* of our society."

I simply stand there, dumb and mute, with ringing in my ears.

"Come along," a friendly voice says, and a solid arm wraps around mine. It is the dwarven woman with the scarves. She's pulling me out of the crowd and into the dark, behind the throne. "Breathe, fergodsake."

What just happened? What have I done? Tied myself to a murder–no, the *king* of murderers–for six months, that's what I've done. Six. Months.

That's not entirely true. He may find my father before then.

The thought doesn't help much. It took the King less than two minutes to kill a man.

"Almost there, ducky, then you can relax a bit."

Relax? I am never going to relax again. I just made the worst decision of my life.

The dwarven woman releases my arm and opens a carved wooden door. For an instant, my past and present collide, and the darkness of the corridor becomes the darkness of a rainy street. The door opening in front of me, spilling warm firelight into the hall, becomes my father's door and the glow of a small forge.

I stand before both of them, frozen by the possibilities of my future. How many times will my life be changed by walking through a door?

"Don't dawdle." The dwarven woman tugs at my sleeve. "The King staked his claim on you and welcomed you to the court, but that don't make you safe. Not entirely. Let's get you behind closed doors, quick-like."

Blinking, I allow her to pull me into a room with stone pillars and a vaulted ceiling high enough that the firelight doesn't quite reach it. It smells good. Like sandalwood, leather, and rose, beeswax from a candelabra by the four-poster bed, and bread and sausages from an earthenware tray by the fireplace. And something else I've never smelled before, something musky and salty but sweet and tinged with sweat. A strange smell, but it isn't unpleasant.

The floor is covered in rugs of various shapes and sizes, layered so deep my booted feet sink into the fibers.

"Where are we?" I ask, coming back to myself fully for the first time since hearing the King say *I want you.*

"Why, the King's chambers, of course. Where did you think I would take you?"

The King's chambers? "Is this where I am to wait until I have a room?"

She puts her fists on her hips, or what I assume to be her hips under the shapeless bulk of scarves and blankets, and blows a bit of iron-grey hair out of her eyes. "He claimed you in front of me and everyone. Where did you think you'd go?" Her eyes widen and her hands fall to her sides. "Cor blimey, girl. You really did pawn yourself in the Unseen Court without knowing what you were about, didn't you?"

I did not need to be reminded of that lapse in judgment, so I said, "My name is Willow. What is yours?"

"My name?" She clucked her tongue and headed for the door. "We don't give our names down here, ducky. That's an Upstairs thing, that is, and you'd do well to remember it. But you can call me Tildie."

"Why don't we give our names?"

"Most folks down here, well. Maybe they don't want ties to their old lives. Maybe they want to become someone else. Maybe they got family to look out for. There's as many reasons as people, I expect."

"How do I know who I am speaking to?"

She laughs. It's a worn, friendly sound, and balm for my nerves. "You don't unless they tell you. And it's probably best that way. The King called you Dove, so if you don't want every criminal in the court who 'eard your story to 'ave one more piece of information about how to find you, I'd let the name stand." Tildie reaches the door, then turns back and holds a hand out, palm down, as if I am a dog in need of training. "Stay 'ere. 'E'll come for ya when he's good and ready. And don't open that door. Not for anyone. 'Ear me?"

I nod and clasp my hands together in front of me. "Yes. Can you tell me—that is, will he—the King I mean—will he..." The words shrivel up and die as I look down at my body. I cannot make myself say it.

She pats my hand. "Don't fret. The King follows the code, same as any of us. Most of the time. That"—she gestures at my skirt with the end of her scarf—"is something as can only be given freely or fairly paid for. Though I s'pose that agreement of yours might be seen as payment, mightn't it?"

My chest constricts into a cage too small for my lungs. "I suppose it might. Will I see you again?"

"Maybe so, duck. Maybe so."

Before she can close the door I say, "Tildie? Thank you. Thank you for your kindness."

A wink and then she's gone. And I am alone in the private chambers of the Cutthroat King, monarch of the Unseen Court. By all accounts an assassin, thief, cheat, swindler, smuggler, just about every other crime one can think of, and—via firsthand knowledge—a murderer.

If he's so dangerous, why does he have such soft carpets?

That is the least common sense thought I have ever had.

My knees give out at last and I sink to the carpet in a limp heap with tears making my vision fuzzy. Every desperate measure I tried over the last two weeks had failed. It is uncomfortably ironic that this is the only option that might work and it is the most desperate measure of all.

And even now, with so much at stake, I have no guarantee. I've made a pact with a criminal. He swore on a knife, but is that enough? What moral convictions will make him keep his word? None. So my father is missing, my apprenticeship is gone, the shop is on the brink of collapse, and I do not have even the solace of my plants to hold back the gut-wrenching uncertainty of the future.

With an irritable swipe of the back of my wrist, I wipe the tears away and take a deep breath. He was right about one thing. Crying won't change my situation. And I chose it. I'll make the best of it as I always have.

In fact, I will approach this problem like I approach fixing a bit of broken artifice. I take a deep breath in to gather all the distracting thoughts and exhale to release them, letting my heart-beat slow.

The first thing to do is acquaint myself with the situation. When a customer brings in a broken gadget or a bit of damaged artifice, they'll explain what they think is wrong. But it isn't until I examine the piece myself that I get a true picture of the problem.

So, I push myself to my feet. Perhaps the decor will give me some insight into the man. It is certainly better than thinking about what he might do when he finally arrives.

Velvet drapes enclose the four-poster bed, plush and green as moss. Soft beneath my fingers, and newer than the rumpled blankets and pillows. Apparently, the King cannot be bothered to make his bed.

A liquor cabinet with mother-of-pearl inlay stands against one wall, well stocked and outfitted with crystal glasses. Comfortable chairs sit by the fire. More pillows than any self-respecting man could need are scattered across the room, suggesting he lazes about quite often. A bowl of incense burns on the side table.

Every texture begs to be touched, and I don't bother resisting as I meander around the room and study each piece, letting my fingers drag across their surfaces. There is something hedonistic about this room, a stimulus for every sense. But it isn't pretty or pleasing. There are too many disparate pieces, no symmetry, or even the proper complementary colors, patterns, and shapes to make such a hodgepodge of decoration look purposeful.

It is as if he courts every sense but vision: incense and perfume to smell, velvets and silks to touch, food to taste, even the crackling fire and–was that a phonograph in the corner?–to hear. Does he have something against beauty? I turn in place, because there must be at least one angle that shows the room to better effect, when I notice a door partially hidden behind a tapestry in the corner.

Could it be an escape? It may be nothing more than a broom closet, but I'm halfway across the room before I stop and sigh. I cannot run away now. I've made a bargain. Besides, I have no idea which way to go.

Still... it cannot hurt to look, can it? Just in case.

The tapestry is heavy, hung on an iron rod bolted into the grey stone, and very old. Someone draped it in folds, so the design is difficult to make out, but if I pull the corner–

"Trying to escape already, Dove?"

# CHAPTER 5

*My name is Willow Violet Bowbriar, and this is my first entry. It is my 21st birthday yesterday. Mr. Boragard says that makes me 7 years old for humans, and 14 for dwarves, and all girls old as me should have their very own diaries to write my most private thoughts.*

*He says I can call him Papa if I like. I don't really want to, but it makes him smile and I do want him to be happy. And he gave me a pastry for my birthday, too, which is more than my real Papa did.*

*—From the diary of Willow Bowbriar*
*January 17, 1848*

WHEN I WAS A SMALL CHILD, PERHAPS 18 YEARS OLD, AND STILL living on the street, I had an unfortunate run-in with one of the orphan gangs near the docks. I hadn't eaten much that week because pickpocketing was my most successful skill, and people have a habit of keeping their hands tucked safely in their pockets in the winter. Scavenging became the only way to keep myself from starving.

Shopkeepers and delivery men tend to watch their wares rather carefully, but dock hands and fishermen are messy, driven by the necessity of speed. Edible bits of discarded fish were often overlooked when they unloaded the day's catch. But cold weather made the scraps freeze quickly. That day was colder than most, and I was forced to search farther and farther downriver for something edible and fresh enough that it would not make me sick.

I was too desperate to be careful. The One Tear gang, the city's oldest and largest gang of orphans, found me in their territory. I was older than every one of them in human years, but elves age at approximately one-third the rate of humans and half that of dwarves. So I was about as helpless as any other six-year-old, and I couldn't stop them from making a spectacle of tossing me into the Thames for violating their borders.

The film of ice along the river's edge cracked when my body struck. I remember thinking it was my bones snapping. Frigid water closed over me, and the cold locked my muscles so tightly that I barely managed to fight my way back to the surface. A burly fisherman who saw the affair dragged me out before I could drown.

Hearing the King's voice now, unexpectedly, makes my lungs and muscles seize as if I've been dropped again into icy water. Only no one will rescue me from the most dangerous man in New London. And he thinks I am trying to escape.

*Move*, I tell myself, but it takes several seconds to force myself to turn. He stands on the other side of the room, half cloaked in darkness, leaning one shoulder against the bedpost. His arms are folded, and his ankles crossed as if he's been relaxing there for several minutes. As if he did not kill someone and suffer a stab wound less than an hour ago.

Light from the candles slants across his sharp features, casting downward shadows that make his face look skeletal. Death hangs about his shoulders like a cloak... and my fate is in his hands. He could cancel our agreement or simply kill me if he chose. There would be no one to hold him accountable either way.

"No," I choke and gesture clumsily at the tapestry. "No, I wasn't trying to escape." Even though the thought had crossed my mind. "I wanted to see the embroidery."

"A great admirer of textiles, are you?" The edge in his voice tells me this is a rhetorical question, but I answer anyway.

"I am, yes. Admiring art brings glory to the Muses."

He raises a sardonic brow. "Piousness? A quality one does not often see from a second-class repair shop employee. Surprising."

My spine stiffens. Sharp words push against my lips, but I swallow them back. Angering the man isn't a wise way to begin our arrangement, especially if I want to stay alive. "A thing being surprising doesn't make it any less true."

"A philosopher as well? How lucky for me. Well, admire it to your heart's content. But first–" He crosses to the armchair by the fireplace, sits, and extends his legs in a languorous stretch that pulls his trousers tight against his thighs. "Be so good as to take off my boots."

His command smothers the little ember of resistance kindled in my chest. When I hatched this plan, I didn't consider that he might demand something of me other than what I intended to offer. Skill with my hands is the only value I possess, after all. And while taking off a pair of boots is infinitely less complicated than repairing a piece of artifice, it is not less dangerous. Not when the person wearing them is The Cutthroat King.

"If a simple task is too trying, perhaps our bargain was not well struck. Perhaps"–he shifts his hips, sinking further into the cushion with a blatantly sensual movement–"we should redefine the terms of our arrangement."

"No," I blurt, forcing myself to hurry across the room. "No, that isn't necessary. I agreed to the terms of our arrangement, and I intend to honor them."

"Do you, indeed?"

"Yes. I have to find my father. I owe him that much."

"I doubt that."

My mouth pops open in surprise. "Why would you doubt it?"

"Because no man alive is worth the price you've agreed to pay."

"I would not have agreed to the bargain if he wasn't," I say, my spine stiff.

He snorts. "Oh yes, you would have. Women do more foolish things for less worthy men."

"My father," I say, forcing my voice to remain calm, "saved me from the streets. He gave me a home and a skill to make my way in the world. This is the least I can do to repay his kindness."

"Kindness?" His scoffing tone makes me grind my teeth. "You sold yourself to repay mere kindness? Little Dove, you must raise your standards."

That comment stings enough that it makes me angry, and though I am used to swallowing my emotions, the words escape with less tact than usual. "*I* know the value of kindness.

"And I do not?"

I lock my jaw to stop any more foolish words from slipping past my lips. He smiles as if he won the argument. That smile is a sharp, dangerous thing that flays my unsteady nerves.

"Soon enough, you will learn that no one knows the price of kindness better than one who has never received it. And now that payment is within my reach, I intend to collect every cent."

My blood runs cold. "Our agreement stipulates that you cannot lay a hand on me in anger."

"I am glad to see you remember the terms. Repeat them to me."

His smug expression makes me want to growl, but I manage to keep my voice calm. "That you will find my father and, in return, for six months..." The words lodge in my throat.

"Say it."

"In return, I..." deep breath, "I belong to you."

"In whatever capacity I choose," he reminds me.

"So long as you never lay a hand on me in anger," I repeat, raising my chin as if the words are a dare or a shield, or both.

"And you intend to keep your end of the bargain to the letter?"

What can I say to that except, "I do. So long as you keep yours."

"I am glad to hear it." He offers me his right foot and smirks. "Get to work."

I swallow the desire to tell him to remove his own boot and decide that I will do what he requires, but I do *not* have to enjoy it. I'll smile to his face, focus on my task, and pretend he doesn't exist otherwise.

The supple black leather glows orange in the firelight, encasing his leg to mid-calf. Removing the boot will require a fair bit of leverage and wiggling. That's likely why no one wears boots like these any longer. It is the twentieth century, after all. Wearing such things in 1902 should make him ridiculous. Unfortunately, the man sprawled comfortably in the armchair before me is anything but ridiculous.

Darkness clings to him despite the firelight playing across the lean lines of his body. He isn't a big man, though he is a few inches taller than me, making him somewhere between five-foot-ten and six feet. It isn't his height or build that intimidates: it is something in his expression and the confident way he holds himself. Which, come to think of it, he certainly should not be doing after being stabbed less than an hour ago.

So much for ignoring him. "Shall I fetch something to clean and bandage your wound before I remove your boots?"

A queer look passes over his features like a cloud across the sun and disappears as quickly. "No, you shall not." He wiggles his foot at me.

"Pulling on your leg will hurt your wound," I warn, unable to stop myself. I don't want him kicking me for my trouble if a bolt of pain shoots up his side when I tug on the boot.

He only stares, boring a hole through me with his eyes, and folds his hands like a long-suffering instructor. Very well. If he wants to die from a blood infection, who am I to complain? So long as he does not die before finding my father. A twinge of guilt niggles at my stomach for thinking something so unkind, but I ignore it.

Wiping my sweating palms on my skirt, I take hold of the heel and pull. Nothing happens. I climb up off my knees and readjust. When I tug this time, the leather slides easily down his calf, and I topple backward, flinging the boot and landing on my behind with a surprised *oof.*

I catch myself on my forearms but wince at the sound of tearing fabric. Lovely. My only dress was already old and thin enough. Now, my bare elbow pokes through my right sleeve, and the tips of my ears burn at my clumsiness.

But the King does not laugh at me. He stares down the length of his body at my position on the floor the way a cat stares at a mouse. It isn't until that moment I realize that falling backward has rucked my skirt up above my knees. My stockings and garters are on shocking display.

But worse, my bare thigh is visible where the skirt and chemise have slid up to settle near the bend in my hip. And his eyes are locked on the exposed flesh. A thrill of fear runs down my spine, and I shove the fabric over my legs as heat blooms in my cheeks.

Tildie said, *That is something as can only be given freely or fairly paid for. Though I s'pose that agreement of yours might be seen as payment, mightn't it?*

He would not consider my clumsiness an invitation, would he? I hurriedly climb to my feet and pull off his other boot, ignoring the heat of his eyes on my skin.

"Where should I–" I hold up the boots and glance around the room. "Do you store your boots somewhere?"

He rocks up and to his feet. Though our height difference isn't significant, he towers over me when he closes the distance between us.

"Such a willing servant," he mocks, leaning close.

I bite my lips closed and lean away, but I cannot pull my eyes from his as he bends down, bringing our faces only inches apart, and plucks the boots from my hand. He walks back toward the bed, leaving me by the fire, flushed, embarrassed, and somehow ashamed.

Such a willing servant? Am I to uphold my end of this agreement and do his bidding only to be mocked for it? As much as I would like to throw my frustration at him like daggers, making him hate me can only jeopardize my chance to find my father. And I will not risk that, not after the trouble I took to get here.

It is only six months. I can endure anything for six months. Besides, I have a lifetime of experience in being biddable. So I take a deep breath to gather all my worries and exhale to release them, letting the embarrassment subside. At least, until the King slides his black britches down his legs.

Gasping, I turn my back to him, my heart thundering and heat rushing into my cheeks once more. Most women are married at my age, even Elven women, but my entire adult life has been focused on keeping the shop afloat. That hasn't left me much time for romance. Not while wrestling our finances back from the edge every time my father has a new idea for an invention, or convincing the bank to give us a few more days to make our mortgage payment.

Luckily, the King's shirt is long enough to cover... well... the important bits. But the look of his muscled thighs in the firelight won't fade from my memory any time soon.

"No need to be so prudish, Dove. I have no intention of changing my habits simply because you are now part of them. You may as well get used to it."

I don't turn until I hear the rustling of blankets and the creak of the mattress. "Where am I to sleep?"

"Is there something wrong with my bed?"

The mocking challenge in his voice makes my hands curl into fists. "Yes. *You* are in it." I say before I can think better of it. This must be the day I am fated to make all of the worst decisions of my life.

He relaxes against the wall of pillows, arms spread wide, revealing a deep triangle between the muscles of his chest. "What keen observational skills you have. A great benefit as a repairist, no doubt."

"Do you intend to mock every word I say?"

"Now that you mention it..."

I have years of practice managing my father's temper, keeping my cool while I cajole him into a more reasonable frame of mind. But something about this damned man has me so on edge that controlling my tongue is almost impossible, despite the danger he presents. "Is that how this arrangement is to be? I do what you ask of me only to suffer the sharp side of your tongue for my trouble?"

"If I decide to use my tongue on you, Dove, you will not suffer. That I can promise you."

My lungs seize at the innuendo. "That's not–that isn't what I meant!"

"Isn't it?" he asks, arching a dark brow. "Then you will have to be clearer."

"If I were as clear as glass, you would still choose to misunderstand me."

"Is that so?"

I don't notice the dangerous tone in his voice because I am truly angry. "Of course it is! But I suppose I should not expect anything else from someone who delights in the pain and discomfort of others."

He throws the blankets aside and stands, his gazed locked on mind as he stalks toward me. If I had not seen the sleekly muscled power of his legs before, they are on full display now. But I cannot drag my eyes away from the flat coldness of his expression.

Blessed Muses, he is going to kill me.

I back up, but he continues to advance, and my heart pounds against my breastbone like a bird trying to fly through a closed window. How could I have been so stupid, so careless? I've never had such trouble holding my tongue, no matter how much my father or an angry customer vented their anger at me.

Is it some sick punishment of fate that the one person I finally snap at is the man who holds my life and future in his hands?

Hands that strangled someone to death not an hour ago? How could I have forgotten?

"I-I'm sorry," I stutter.

"Oh, don't apologize now," he says, pursuing me as I retreat.

My back hits the wall on the opposite side of the room, and I gasp. There is nowhere else to go. My palms flatten on the rough stone behind me. His hand shoots toward my throat.

The King has me pinned against a wall for the second time tonight, and I cannot believe how bloody stupid I am. I cringe, expecting the crushing pressure of strangling hands, but his fingers glide across my skin almost like a caress. Which is all the more terrifying because I know exactly what those hands are capable of.

"Why apologize when you know you are right?" he asks, leaning in close, his eyes roaming over my face. "I do enjoy the discomfort of others. I thrive on it. Would you like to know why?"

I shake my head, biting my lips together.

"Because people will lie to you when they're comfortable. They will play at being virtuous and deceive themselves as much as they deceive others. But discomfort? Pain? Those things tear the lies away and strip them of their masks. I would much rather see people for who they are than who they pretend to be. So..." His fingers tighten enough to make me stiffen, and my hands fly forward to press against his chest in reaction. "Who are *you*, Little Dove?"

The question seems significant somehow. Maybe more important than anything he has said to me so far. But what answer does he want? My mind flies over possible responses, trying to find one that will make him loosen his grip.

"Your servant," I blurt, panting and dropping my eyes. "I am your servant. For the next six months."

He releases me and steps back, a frown pulling the corners of his mouth down. I must have answered wrong.

"So you are. Unless you break our agreement now and leave."

Is he trying to chase me away? Because I would love to run

back to the surface and lock the doors of the Mechanica behind me. But he swore not to hurt me. And he hasn't. This is the best chance I've got of finding my father. So I shake my head.

"A pity. "

Without another word, he returns to the bed, leaving me cold and trembling in the shadows. "Sleep wherever you want, so long as you do not leave this room. Tomorrow, you will tell me of your father. And then, we must convince the Unseen Court that you belong to me. If you want to stay alive long enough to see him again, that is."

# CHAPTER 6

*I may die of embarrassment. Papa found me in the alley with Tadgh O'Connor.*

*He said I have "too much promise to waste time on stupid human boys" and that if I work hard, I might get an apprenticeship with the Artificer's Guild. Little does he know I am never leaving my room again.*

*How can I show my face on Penny Lane knowing Tadgh may deliver mail at any moment? I never even got a kiss.*

*—From the Diary of Willow Bowbriar*
*May 3, 1883*

I GASP AND JERK UPRIGHT, BLINKING AT THE DYING FIRE AS MY HEART pounds. It takes a moment to remember that I am not at home but sitting in the chair next to the hearth in the room of the Cutthroat King. Which, to be quite honest, is rather concerning.

But he's still sound asleep, and my muscles are so stiff and achy that I cannot feel much aside from resentment. Sleep had been impossible. Every breath, every rustle of shifting blankets, or creaking of the ropes beneath the King's mattress made me flinch awake. After the most exhausting day and night of my life, I'd managed no more than a light doze.

And it was my fault.

Blaming it on the King would have felt much better, but I was the one who sought this arrangement, even if I hadn't been aware he would require... whatever he wanted of me. At least he didn't force me to share his bed.

I climb out of the chair and stretch. The long muscles up the center of my back are knotted from sleeping in a strange position, and a groan escapes as I dig my fists into my lower back, bending and arching, at least as far as my corset will allow.

After working out the worst knots, I glance down my body. The view does not look promising. Several long mirrors are propped against the grey stone in various parts of the room, and while the fire is low, there are enough lamps to let me see that my simple grey day dress is a rumpled mess.

But, as it is my only dress, I must make due, at least for now. Perhaps I can retrieve my belongings later. I comb my fingers through my hair, untangling knots until the mass is wavy but manageable.

"You could have sold your hair for a few months' wages, you know."

His voice makes me start so violently I pull a handful of hair from my scalp and wince at the prickling pain before glaring in his direction. The King stands in a loose black shirt and black britches. His hair is tousled from sleep, falling across his forehead and into his eyes. That should make him less intimidating, make it easier to see him as nothing more than a man, but it doesn't.

The lock of hair I still hold, a sort of pale silver blonde, is silky against my calloused palm. Though my coloring has brought me only surprised glances and grimaces, and now and then, someone making a sign to warn off evil, it is hard to imagine cutting it off.

"I will admit, that possibility never occurred to me."

He shrugs. "Plenty of wealthy old women in need of wigs. They pay top dollar, too. Remember that for next time."

Next time? The purpose of selling myself to this ruthless man is to ensure there is no next time. I turn away before I can say something unkind, my fingers flying through the familiar movements of plaiting until a braid hangs in a neat tail down my back.

A woman enters a moment later, carrying a tray. The smell of food hits me so hard my stomach sits up and howls. Her lip quivers as she tries not to smile at my gurgling belly, but she sets the tray on the circular table close to the hearth and departs without saying a word.

Before she can close the door behind herself, the King says, "Wait. Is the dress finished?"

"Aye, majesty."

"Good. Have Silk bring it in an hour."

She bobs a quick curtsey and disappears.

"A dress?" I ask, but my eyes stray back to the food.

He crosses the room, amusement tugging at one corner of his mouth but never reaching his eyes. "I do not intend to starve you, Dove. You are of no use to me if you are weak."

Did I imagine the emphasis on the word *use*? The reminder that he could demand physical service from me sends a shiver of dread up my spine, but it can't compete with my ravenous stomach. The pastry I grab is buttery and flakey and makes my mouth water so much that I have to swallow.

"You'll give yourself an upset stomach, standing to eat," he says as he plucks a sausage from the tray. "Sit."

And put myself within arm's reach of him? "No, thank you."

His amusement fades, leaving his expression sharp as a blade and his voice just as dangerous. "Sit. Down."

I sink into the chair and the smell of sausage and mushrooms, eggs, bread, butter, and honey wafts toward me.

"Eat."

I can't. Nerves have stolen my appetite entirely. If I try to put anything else in my mouth, I'll sick it up. Muses, what have I gotten myself into?

"You said you needed to learn more about my father," I say, picking at the flakey pastry to give the appearance of obeying him.

"I need to know enough to find him, yes." Between bites of sausage, he asks me about the shop, my father's height, weight, and eye color, the men who brought the offer of employment, and the symbol they wore. And even more about our shop and my father's work.

His questions are cool and clever, like a mathematician figuring sums in his head, but his voice and body language are as casual. He may as well be asking me about the weather. Our conversation is almost normal for a moment. As I answer questions, I forget I'm sitting across the breakfast table from a killer.

"I searched every registry available," I say, rubbing my fingertips across my forehead. "The Covenant of the Silver Dawn simply doesn't exist, not as far as the guilds or the city are concerned. Not every business is required to register, but considering how much they offered to pay my father, there must be some trace of them. Who spends such money without recording it anywhere?"

He leans back in the chair and folds his arms across his chest. "Someone with powerful connections who isn't interested in being watched. But they do not hide their name unless they gave a false one."

I swallow, remembering standing alone and watching the only person who ever loved me disappear into the city.

He runs the side of his forefinger across his lower lip, back and forth, as he thinks. With his hair falling over his forehead and his shirt undone, he looks less like a shark and more like a man. A regular person discussing an interesting topic over a meal. Strange how his appearance can change so drastically, even when he is wearing the same clothes.

"There are many powerful people in New London with the funds, the connections, and the motivation to create something that would disrupt both the guilds and the electric companies. If that is their goal, secrecy is the safest option. But my fingers are in enough pies that I should be able to find out. The electric companies are a good place to start. They have hired my assassins more than once."

I stop breathing. Is my father in danger of assassination? Having a guild sanction makes our shop a target, which is no secret. Other shops do not like the competition, and sanctioned mechanicas have been sabotaged in the past.

The Artificer's Guild is strict, and the dwarves do not hand out sanctions easily, particularly to elf-run shops. Our political power lies with the Artisan's Guild, and both they and humans see our foray into repairing artifice as a threat. Unless, of course, we pay them a quarterly fee for the privilege of our sanction.

The politics of who can earn money in which profession has never escaped me. But in the grand scheme of power and money in the city, my father is no more than a weed in a badly-tended garden: easily overlooked and not worth the effort to pull.

The idea that anyone would want to hurt him is so absurd that I blurt, "Assassins? That's ridiculous."

That crocodile smile is back on his lips. "Industrial espionage comes in all forms, Dove. It is, in fact, one of my favorite games. No man has more to lose than the man who has sacrificed everything to slake his greed and desire for power."

"I always thought those who loved had the most to lose," I hear myself say. If I cannot keep my stupid mouth shut, I really should bite out my tongue.

"Love?" He scoffs. His attention slips back to me, sharp and penetrating, making me feel like a strange bug pinned to a board for inspection. "Do you know how many powerful men sacrificed everything on the altar of power, including love? Their wives and husbands, their children, their inheritance, all of it. All for a bit more power."

"What good is power without love? Without people to share your life with?"

His smile is mocking, and more than mocking. It cuts between pity and scorn. "Are you truly so naive?"

I want to raise my eyes to meet his, to challenge such cynical views, but the last thing I need is more discord between us. If I make myself disagreeable, he could make my life harder just so I will break our contract and he can be rid of me.

"Perhaps I am," I concede, though I would rather have said, *You must be very lonely.*

One dark brow raises in what I can only interpret as a combination of disbelief and disappointment. Before I can stop myself, I ask, "If you don't believe in love, what do you believe in?"

He runs the tip of his tongue along the sharp edges of his teeth, stands, and brushes a few crumbs from his trousers. When he unbuttons the top button to tuck in the black shirt, I jerk my gaze away.

"I believe in power," he says. "I believe in the primal forces that motivate mortal nature: hunger, greed, ambition..." He holds one hand out to me, and the hardness in his eyes tells me not to refuse. My fingers glide across his palm, and he pulls me to my feet. "And lust."

I swallow against the sudden dryness in my throat and take a hesitant step backward. That razor-blade smile curves his mouth again, but his eyes are sharper. "Don't be such a coward. I have no intention of taking you to my bed. I prefer enthusiastic lovers. Somehow"—his eyes rake me from simple braid to practical, worn leather shoes—"I suspect you aren't enthusiastic about anything."

That stings, but if he notices me flinch, he does not care. "We have a business arrangement, you and I. Nothing more." He turns as the door opens and takes a bundle of shimmering cloth from a dark-haired woman, who gives a quick bob of her head before retreating. "You'll wear this today."

He tosses the fabric over the bedspread and bends to slide his stocking feet into a pair of black leather boots.

"Where shall I change?"

He sighs. "I told you I have no intention of taking you to my bed. Your half-naked body isn't tempting enough to alter that. Change here."

The idea of removing my clothes in front of this shark of a man makes my fingers freeze and hover over the buttons of my dress. He rolls to his feet, and since I cannot bring myself to look up, I watch his hips shift, and the muscles of his thighs flex as he approaches me.

Seeing his long fingers—fingers that strangled a man to death last night—brush mine aside and reach for my collar sends a bolt of fear through my body. I flinch away, hastily replacing his fingers with mine. They tremble as I shove the buttons through.

He chuckles. "Wary little dove. You flew willingly into the fox's den. I wonder whether you'll fly out again."

The door creaks and I pull the edges of my dress closed in a rush, my cheeks burning.

"Make certain she is dressed," the King says to the dark-haired woman who enters. "I'll return for her shortly."

Relief hits me in a wave so staggering I nearly collapse onto the bed. But the woman is less gentle than the King. She hauls me upright and pulls my dress off without so much as a hello.

"I can dress myself," I say, taking half a step back and folding my arms across my chest.

She looks me up and down, raising one dark brow. "Get to it, then."

Scowling, I grab the fabric. It is heavy for being so light, softer than I knew any fabric could be, and it slides through my fingers like water.

"Quicksilver," I breathe, watching the metallic shimmer play over the surface. "What is it?"

She snorts. "Hell, if I know. It's pretty and expensive, though. The King must like you if he's letting you wear it."

I start to say that he barely tolerates me and mocks me every chance he gets, but he mentioned last night that my safety may depend upon convincing the court that I belong to him. The thought makes me shudder, so I search for the collar and hold the garment up to disguise my unease. "What is it?"

"It's a dress," she says slowly, watching me like she's unsure whether I comprehend English.

Lifting the heavy fabric by the shoulder straps proves, beyond a doubt, that the garment is *not* a dress in the traditional sense. "It looks like a really, *really* expensive chemise."

"Does it matter what style it is? He wants you to wear it. So unless you plan to tell him no"—her tone says I really shouldn't do that—"take off your corset."

"What? Why?"

The woman rolls her eyes and takes the shimmering fabric, holding it up for me to examine. "Does it look like this will sit right over a corset?"

I grit my teeth, remind myself this is the price I am paying for my father, and try to hold myself steady as she pulls at my laces. "Blimey. D'you always lace your corsets so tight?"

"No," I grunt. "I rarely wear them."

"Why?"

"I'm a repairist. I spend most of my days in overalls and an apron."

She spins me and tosses my corset cover and corset unceremoniously on the bed. "Then this is sure to be quite a change for you, isn't it? Arms up, princess."

My teeth lock together, and I shimmy through the opening as she tries to work the fabric over my head. "Are you... well acquainted with the King?" I ask as the cold material slides over my shoulders.

She chuckles. "Don't know that I like what you're implying by that question."

"No, I meant no"—I twist, trying to narrow my shoulders

enough to slip through the tighter waist— "offense. It's only that I don't know what to expect and…"

The skirt slides over my hips, and the weight of yards of fabric pulls the bodice into place in a rush, leaving me staring at the woman's face. What had the King called her? Silk? She's pretty in an aggressive way, with a riot of dark curls, fine, dark eyes canted up at the corners, slashing brows, and a mouth that looks more fitted to smile than frown, which is what she's doing right now.

I don't trust her, but I have to be honest and say aloud, "And I'm scared."

Her brows rise at that. "At least you aren't stupid. Anyone who isn't afraid of the King is a fool. But he's civil enough to those who keep the Night Code. Turn around."

"What is the Night Code?" I ask as she unravels my braid.

It has been a long time since anyone but me touched my hair, and I cannot pretend the sensation ins't nice. By the time my father adopted me, I was too old to make friends with girls my age. They spent their time with governesses or in schools of one kind or another while I was already at work in the shop. So, aside from Ethel, there are not many women in my life. Is this what it would have been like to have a friend?

"There aren't many rules in the Unseen Court. We probably wouldn't follow them if there were. But the ones we have are simple enough." She recites the list like a schoolgirl at her lessons. "Keep quiet. Us before them. Pay your dues. And: freely given or fairly paid for."

"Keep quiet makes sense, I suppose," I say.

The Unseen Court exists because people don't talk about it. Rumors spread, but never enough to make anyone believe the place is real, and certainly not enough to help anyone find it. If they did, the Chief Inspector at Scotland Yard wouldn't have offered me a deal. In fact, I found the place only because of the coin carried by the Unseen Court or those invited by the King.

And paying dues is simple enough, as well. If you want the

King's protection, you pay the King's tax. Tildie already explained *freely given, fairly paid for.* "What does *us before them* mean?"

Silk turns me by the shoulders and looks me over with a critical eye, sometimes pulling at seams or adjusting how the fabric lays. "Some who join the court have no ties to the upper world. This is the closest they'll get to a family. But others have families or something to protect. Their loyalty would be split if it weren't for the code. They might sacrifice us for the sake of them."

"Shouldn't someone be loyal to their family more than anything else?"

She rolls her eyes at me. "Sure. But if their families aren't also court members, it creates a... conflict of interest, you might say. And that ain't safe for anyone." After a few more tweaks, she brushes my hair off my shoulder and shrugs. "You're as ready as you'll ever be. Chew your lip some. And pinch your cheeks. You need a bit of color. Come on."

I feel naked, exposed, and catching my reflection in a mirror near the door certainly doesn't help. Enough fabric swims around my hips and ankles to get lost in, but it skims the skin across my breasts and torso. If I had worn a corset, every line of it would have shown through the fabric, cover or not.

The sleeves are not quite sleeves, but draping fabric split up the center so that bare skin shows from my fingertips to my shoulder when I move my arms. And while the neckline is low, it isn't my décolletage that is embarrassing; it's the fabric itself.

It hugs and drapes, showing the curves and hollows of my body in tantalizing glimpses when I move. Common fashion in New London may be snug across the torso, but it hides the shape of the body beneath structured garments. This dress hides nothing and highlights everything.

And because of my pale skin and paler hair, the silver makes me look like a specter. It certainly doesn't help that the fabric slides against my skin in a sensual caress as I walk.

Heat crawls from my chest to my neck and burns in my cheeks. "I cannot wear this."

Silk sighs, returns from the door, and grabs my shoulder. Her grip is not unkind, but it is forceful. She leans close and hisses, "Did you think the King would parade his woman in front of the court wearing a high-necked walking dress? This isn't the Upstairs, Dove. And if you want to survive here, you'd better get that through your head."

"I'm not his woman," I sputter.

"Oh really? Why did he take your bargain, then?"

I open my mouth to respond, but the truth is that I don't know. He must have some plan for me not relating to a physical relationship if he has no intent of taking me to his bed. And truthfully, I'm more than a little grateful I have not had time to wonder what it might be.

"It don't matter," Silk says, holding up one hand before I can speak. "What matters is that the thieves, cutthroats, and murderers in the Undercroft believe you are. Because if the King hasn't claimed you, you are living here without protection..."

She lets the insinuation sit, and a chill that has nothing to do with the naturally cool nature of the underground runs down my arms. "I thought the code said freely given or fairly paid for?"

Silk takes me by the wrist and hauls me toward the door, saying over her shoulder, "The Code only matters if someone catches you breaking it. Now keep your chin high, and for god's sake, don't embarrass me out there."

# CHAPTER 7

*The faerytale book Papa bought me says banshees are*
*supposed to wail before people die. But I was the only one*
*who cried when my parents died.*

—*From the diary of Willow Bowbriar*
*March 30, 1848*

THE DOOR SWINGS OPEN WITH A GUST OF COOL AIR TO REVEAL THE
Cutthroat King standing in a pool of slanting candlelight that cuts
across his features, making them harsher and more aggressive.
The hints of humanity I glimpsed over breakfast are gone.
Narrowed eyes, flared nostrils, and a clenched jaw make him look
like a predator.

What did he call me earlier? A dove in a fox's den? That is
exactly how I feel with his eyes on me.

"Think she'll do, my lord?" Silk asks cheekily.

The King flexes his hands and rolls his shoulders, shifting
from looking like he is about to attack me into a more relaxed

stance. It's like watching someone put on a mask; instead of a fox about to leap, he's a bored cat, loose-jointed and confident.

He circles me once, his expression unimpressed when he says, "This might have been a mistake."

My cheeks burn with a mixture of embarrassment and anger. This damned dress hadn't been my idea. He chose it without consulting me, so it is his fault if I am not suited to it. At that thought, guilt makes my chin drop. He provided me with a dress more expensive than anything I own, judging by the quality of the fabric. Perhaps he thought he was doing something kind, and I am simply ungrateful.

After a deep breath I force my body to relax and determine to keep my unfair thoughts to myself. Luckily, the King doesn't notice. He waves his fingers at Silk in dismissal.

She gives a respectful nod, then whispers as she passes. "Don't embarrass me."

She walks through pools of light with an easy stride until she disappears in the dark, leaving me alone, again, with the King.

A line forms between his brows as he considers me. "Come here."

Chin raised; I close the distance between us, stopping a long arm's reach away.

He points at the ground a foot in front of him. "Here."

The desire to tell him no makes my jaw clench, but I cannot spend the next six months in constant conflict with this man, sick with fear at every word, every glance. He made an oath in front of his court. Unless he breaks it, he is still my best hope of finding my father.

And if he does break his word, I have a backup plan.

So, holding my breath, I close the distance until no more than a scant few inches lay between us. The well-oiled leather of his boots, the warm, earthy hints of tobacco smoke clinging to his clothing, and the resinous touch of cedar wash over me. Those scents are echoes of his habits, of things he has touched or eaten.

It is the scent of shadows, of secrets whispered behind closed doors.

"When did you smoke tobacco? Or is that cologne?" I ask, dazed.

"Why? Do you like the scent of me, Dove?"

I swallow. "It isn't displeasing."

He clicks his tongue against his teeth, sounding disappointed again. "Such a mild answer. Always a mild answer. No. I do not wear the stuff. The last thing I need is a recognizable scent. You could benefit from something pleasant, though. Did I smell lavender in your hair last night? Or was that rosemary?"

"Rosemary," I say, surprised.

He gives me a thoughtful look, one that suggests he is planning something I probably will not like. Despite the discomfort of his proximity, I cannot help but admire the man. If I were an artist and not a repairist, I would count myself skilled indeed if I could sculpt a face like his. A vision of how handsome he would be if he smiled assaults my mind, but I force it away and remind myself to stay alert.

This is no time for my imagination to interfere.

"I'll have rosemary brought in for your bathwater," he says as if making an important decision. A little glow of gratitude springs to life in my chest, only to be doused when he continues, "You need them both."

Our gazes lock, his probing to see if I will respond unkindly, and mine only able to maintain contact for a moment before I look away. Pitting my will against his won't get us anywhere, no matter how much I want to try.

He slides one finger beneath the shoulder of my gown, and I fight not to flinch away as his skin brushes across my collarbone. "Yes," he sighs, "this was most certainly a mistake. But I shall endeavor to make the best of it. And so shall you."

With that, he wraps an arm around my ribcage and pulls me tight against his side. It isn't an embrace. He probably thinks keeping me close is the best way to ensure I do not turn and run.

He pivots on one heel, pulling me down the corridor and into the dark.

Lamps light the corridor at regular distances, so I try to pay attention to the twists and turns between the King's room and... wherever he's taking me. But the warmth of his hand and the pressure of his fingers on my ribs, resting just below my left breast, makes noticing anything else impossible. Without a corset, the contact is terribly intimate. But I cannot afford to be distracted, not now that I have a chance to see what I was too shocked to notice last night.

I have to remember as much of the layout of the Undercroft as possible, or my backup plan will be worthless. Details. That's what I need. Details. Something to focus on outside the heat of his hand and the scent of tobacco and cedar. The walls! Surely, there are details in the walls that will help me navigate these tunnels if I need to escape.

Unlike the roughly quarried grey stone I recall from my trip beneath the church, these walls have high-quality masonry that peeks through layers of cracked plaster and faded paint. But the brick in the barrel-vaulted ceiling has been patched and repaired so often that there is no consistent color or pattern.

It almost appears to have been created separately from the walls, which are close enough that the King and I would have been forced to touch shoulders if he hadn't already held me against his side. A fact I am not supposed to be thinking about.

I focus on the floor, which was cobbled not unlike the streets in older parts of New London. So many feet have walked these paths that the rounded tops are smoothed flat. Now and then, other corridors turn left or right, winding away either into complete darkness or lit at intervals by lamps, either dwarven lamps that require charging in the sun, or oil lamps that must be filled and trimmed.

The corridor looks so much like a twisting back alley, what my father calls a *snicket*, that I keep expecting to look up and see the sky. But every time my gaze rises to the ceiling, I remember that tons of rock and earth press down on these flimsy stone corridors, and my heart leaps into my throat.

What I would not give to stand beneath the sky.

"Do you hear that?" the King asks in a low voice.

For a moment, I think he's asking because he can hear my heart pounding. But the distant echo of voices, so different underground than it is in the open-skied world above, makes me ask, "What is it? The Unseen Court?"

"No. The Court has already seen me claim you."

*Claim you.* Those words do something uncomfortable to my stomach, something I do not have the time to examine because, as we near the intersection, the light, heat, and noise become overpowering. The King leans down to bring his lips within an inch of my ear, and his voice—that damned voice—slides across my skin like a warm velvet caress. "Don't faint on me, now."

We turn left into a cavernous room as long as a city block and taller than a three-story building. I blink against the light and catch my breath, my fingers tightening in the silky fabric of my skirt. After the dim privacy of the King's room and the near emptiness of the corridors, this place is a slap in the face.

It's much like Covent Garden Market. People with carts, stalls, and stands sell food, produce, and goods of every variety. The air is heavy with body heat and rich with cooked potatoes, meat pies, sweat, and the dung of a few feed animals. And all of them selling and buying beneath the light of a dozen huge dwarven lamps hanging from the wood beams bolted into the stone ceiling by chains as thick around as my arms.

I never imagined anything like this place could exist in the dark tunnels beneath New London. My voice is heavy with wonder when I exclaim, "It's a market!"

"Keen observational skills," the King repeats. "Hopefully, you are clever, too." Mocking, as usual, but his grip tightens on my side in a distinctly possessive manner he hasn't displayed before.

In fact, almost everything about him changes. He seems to grow taller, more commanding, and levels a proprietary gaze at the crowd. These people, this room, and every shadow belong to him. They are *his*. And the way his palm slides across my ribs to settle on the flat of my stomach just above my hip bone says that I, too, am his.

I bite back a little squeak of surprise as he leans down to run his nose along the column of my neck.

"Shall we go shopping, my dove?" he asks, his voice that of a doting lover. "Didn't I promise you some rosemary oil for your bath?"

I swallow and fight not to pull away or—Muses forbid—lean into the intimate touch. "Mhmm" is the best I can manage.

He laughs. Actually, really laughs, and the sound draws the eye of everyone around us. Their gazes flash to me with a mixture of shock, awe, and appreciation. A few stare in fear, though I cannot tell why.

The King doesn't seem to notice any of it. He glances at the staring crowd. "A man must keep his pet happy, mustn't he?"

A few of them chuckle uncomfortably, some leer, and others try not to notice either of us, turning back to their business with a single-minded determination I admire. I wish I had something, anything else to keep my mind occupied. But the King walks down the center aisle with me tucked against his side as shoppers hurry to open a path for us.

His fingers make distracted little circles on my side, my stomach, sometimes sliding up to the underside of my breast. I keep my eyes locked forward and try to ignore the crowd, but it is impossible not to see their heads turn, to feel their gazes as we pass.

Most of my life has been spent in the workshop behind a table. When customers see me, they see a repairist with her hair tied back and grease smeared on her cheeks. I look like someone else now, someone very different than the person I see in the mirror every morning. Someone decidedly not me.

Knowing people are looking at me and not seeing me is disorienting. Which probably does not help sell the fiction that I belong to the King. I must relax. Perhaps I can ignore their gazes by focusing on the goods for sale.

Crockery, soap, clothing, ribbons, makeup, shoes, hats, and more are displayed on tables, in booths, and carts. That is all normal and familiar. But there are also more weapons than I have seen in my entire life: pistols and rifles, knives and daggers, brass knuckles, and other dangerous things I don't have names for.

"Roasted peanuts!" shouts one man surrounded by stacks of brown paper bags.

"Fine silk and linen!" shouts another.

"Wrapped candies! Caramels and hand-dipped chocolates!"

The King stops me with the pressure of his hand, making the fabric of my dress slide against my skin, and asks, "Would you like a chocolate?" as if my stomach was in any condition for sweets.

The elf woman behind the stall watches us with a combination of admiration, hope, and terror, the tray in her hands full of things that would have made my mouth water at any other time. It isn't her fault I am queasy, so I give her as kind a smile as I can manage and start to decline, but the King leans in close enough for his low voice to reach only my ears.

"You need the sugar. You didn't eat this morning, and you're trembling."

I try to smile, to keep up the appearance that I am happy to be here with him and not strung so tightly I might break. "I can't eat," I whisper.

Without looking at the vendor, he extends his right hand and says, "Chocolate."

She complies with a quick bob of the head and a "M'lord."

The fingertips of his left hand rest lightly on my neck, his thumb along the line of my jaw as he lifts the chocolate to my lips and says, "Open."

What else can I do without embarrassing myself or breaking the illusion he claims will keep me safe? I open my mouth. A trace of a smile is in his eyes, almost as if he is daring me to defy him as he slips the chocolate between my lips. For a heartbeat, I'm tempted to spit it back out at him, but he slides the pad of his thumb across my lower lip, pressing my mouth closed, and the chocolate hits my tongue.

An involuntary sound of pleasure curls up and out of me as the rich, smokey flavor and sweetness unfurl in my mouth.

"Another?" he asks.

I cannot help but nod, increasing the pressure of his thumb on my mouth. Muses, I am hungry, and my body doesn't seem to care about how upset my stomach has been. With the tip of his thumb, he presses my mouth open, and slowly, so slowly I'm tempted to bite his fingers, he places the second chocolate on my tongue.

The fine tremors of fear that have been constant since first stepping into the Undercroft begin to subside. Within a few seconds, I am more awake, more aware. Dammit, he's right. I do need the sugar. The mocking light in his eyes says he knows I know it. He releases me, then slides his thumb into his mouth without breaking eye contact. I can't blame him for licking the left-over chocolate from his thumb, only... he isn't.

He is licking the taste of my mouth from his skin.

He makes a purring sound, one that sends heat cascading from my breastbone to my thighs. The tip of his thumb rests on his bottom lip for a heartbeat before he says in a voice richer and darker than the chocolate, "Mmm. Sweet."

A shiver of awareness that has nothing to do with fear runs down my spine, and I cannot drag my gaze away from his face, his finely carved lips, those dark eyes, and lashes so long it looks like he's wearing kohl.

"Would the lady like a box?" the vendor asks.

Her voice shatters the fragile moment, and the sounds and smells of the market come rushing back to pound against me. The smirk on his face tells me the King knew exactly what he was doing, and the thread of desire I felt moments ago snaps like an overtightened piano string.

"Yes," he tells the vendor, pulling a coin from his pocket. What-ever the coin was, it must have been more than enough because the look of shock and gratitude on the vendor's face is almost ecstatic.

He pulls me back against him, pretending we are no more than a pair of lovers out for a stroll, and drags me down aisle after aisle to peruse the goods; potatoes, pretty gowns, knives, cabbages, apples, needle and thread, and a scrap vendor who has enough copper, brass, and aluminum for me to start a whole shop of my own.

I wish I could pay proper attention, but all of my focus is on maintaining the illusion and trying to forget that every person here, every vendor, is a criminal of one stripe or another. Ones who believe I belong to the king of criminals. My chocolates may have been made by a thief or a swindler. And the man holding me as if he wants nothing more than the pleasure of my company is the worst of them all.

I need to remember that the next time he tries to make me forget it.

"Ah," he says when we reach a table covered in potted plants and dried herbs. "We'll find your rosemary here."

I forget everything as soon as I see the stall. My gaze flies over the variety of plants displayed on the table and lands on broad, waxy leaves that are dark green and frame small, delicate white flowers.

"Is this Carinachea?" I ask, bending to touch the leaf.

"Indeed it is, my lady," the elven man behind them says, surprised. "How do you know it?"

I trace the scalloped edge of the leaf with one finger. "I'm fond of plants. Too fond, maybe."

"Are you, now? What makes you love them so?"

I cannot stop a blush. "There is just such peace and richness of life about them. They don't require you to be any sort of person. They never ask anything of you. They simply exist and let you enjoy"—I gesture at the abundance on the table—"all of this."

He laughs. It's a jolly sound that makes me smile. Both stout thumbs are tucked into a belt that can't contain his round belly, and his cheeks and forehead have the perpetual tan I've seen on all serious gardeners. "That's fair enough, to be sure."

"I've been searching for a Carinachea for ages, how did you come across it?"

"It fell off the back of a delivery wagon," he says with a roguish wink, and the moment of joy is gone.

In my excitement, I'd forgotten where I was, and with whom.

"Not much call for them down here, but a few folks have homes Upstairs and I've got better prices than anything they have up there."

I straighten and back away. "I see. Thank you."

The King asks for rosemary water, and the vendor sets several sprigs in a boiling pot. "Quarter of an hour or so," he says.

Normally, I would stay to watch, but the magic of the place has faded, and despite the heat of so many bodies, I shudder. It is not the reminder of where I am that makes me uncomfortable as much as it is proof that the world I knew isn't as it seems and probably never was.

If I had met that fellow Upstairs, as he called it, I would never have guessed what he did for a living or wondered how many people lost money at his hands when important shipments went missing.

I run my father's business. I know what happens when shipments go awry, and there are bills to pay. My parents died in debtors' prison for exactly that reason. And here I am, willingly living in that world and keeping dangerous secrets. I turn and stumble down the aisle to the next vendor, not caring whether the King follows me or not.

"Why so sad, Willow?"

Hearing my name makes me freeze. A frail woman with skin as pale as a fish belly sits behind a simple table, her short white curls a halo around her head. Unlike the other tables, she has no wares or sign in her clothing or stall that she's been paid much.

She stares up at me through rheumy eyes, a line of concern between barely-there brows.

I slide out of the flow of foot traffic and rest my hands on the table. "What did you call me?"

"Willow. It is your name, isn't it?"

"That is a rude question," I say, taking my cue from Tildie. So far as I know, no one knows my name in the Undercroft. Perhaps it would be smart to keep it that way.

She gives me a knowing smile that sends a fan of wrinkles out from each eye and folds her hands on the table, her bony fingers and skinny wrists sliding out of threadbare sleeves. "As you will. I only ask why you are so sad."

"How long has it been since you've eaten, mother?"

She blinks at me and shrugs. "Hours. Days. It doesn't signify much."

The little box of chocolates makes a plunking sound on the table as I set it in front of her. "Do me a favor and eat these, will you? They're too rich for my taste."

Long fingers close gently around the paper box and tap it once, twice, three times before she says, "May I give you a favor in return?"

"If you wish."

She holds out her hand, palm up, expectant. Curious, I rest my palm on hers. Her skin is cool and papery, but her fingers move confidently as she turns my hand over and drags her fingertips across my palm and along my fingers as if drawing invisible lines. When her fingertips reach my wrist, she stops, and her already pale skin loses all trace of color.

She grips my wrist tightly in both hands and pulls me close. "You are in danger," she says in a ragged whisper. "More danger than you know. Betrayal. Fire, blood, and death. They are all in your future." Her voice rises from a rough whisper to a shout. "Beware! Beware the white lady!" She drags her thumbnail hard across my wrist, tearing my skin in a thin line, and smears the blood with the pad of her thumb.

I jerk out of her grip, but not before she licks my blood from her fingertip. There are red streaks on her teeth when she says, "To protect what you love, you must sacrifice what you are. Remember my words. *Remember!*"

Suddenly, the King is there, and he's dragged the old woman from behind her stall by the front of her shirt, holding her several feet off the ground. Just as he did with Ambrose. Power and cold fury radiate from him, but his voice sounds casual. "Weren't you warned about practicing witchcraft here?"

"You said do no harm!" she screeches. "I've done none."

The King grabs me by the forearm with his free hand, holding my wrist aloft. "Does this count as no harm, old woman? Does it?"

"Less harm than you will do to her!" She spits, her sleeves falling back as she grabs at his forearms. I gasp, and my stomach flips. Strange boils cover her exposed skin, discolored and textured like calluses made of tree bark. Beneath them, fat purple veins trace up her arms and disappear beneath her sleeves. The stories say channeling magic damages mortal bodies, but I never thought to see proof of it with my own eyes.

He releases my arm and slides a dagger from his belt. Fear closes my throat.

"It isn't that bad," I say, grabbing his arm. "It's barely a scratch! Please don't do this."

He ignores me and sets the tip against her throat, where a bead of dark red blood wells and slips down the blade.

"Please!" I beg.

My fingers tighten in his shirt, but I hold still for fear I might cause the knife tip to sink further into her flesh.

He holds the dagger level, balancing the blood on the blade, before dropping the old woman. She lands on the stone floor with a gasp, crumpling to a heap of tattered clothes and frizzy, white hair. Before I can help her, the King pulls me against him in a grip like iron.

"Look at me, witch." The command in his voice is absolute, and my gaze follows hers as if invisible hands have plunged into my head and forced my eyes toward him. Her eyes are locked on his face, full of fear and anger. He tilts the dagger, letting the lamp-light slide along the blood pooled there.

"You know what this means," he says, his voice low and hard. "Give up your coin. Leave the Undercroft and never return."

Wincing, the old woman braces herself to stand. Rather than giving the King the silver coin, she drops it on paving stones and spits at his feet. Traces of my blood color her spittle.

The market has gone silent, and shoppers and vendors alike skitter out of the old woman's path as she hobbles toward the door. Before she reaches the wide entryway where two guards wearing the black bands of Ratcatchers wait, she turns and says over her shoulder, "Remember my words, girl. And thank you for the chocolates."

Then she is gone, and after a moment of silence, the market buzz returns as if an old woman hadn't just been exiled from their midst. The King plucks the discarded coin from the ground and rests it on his palm. With a deft twist of his wrist, he lets the drop of blood slide down the tip of the knife to land on the silver coin. He cleans the blade on his thigh, drops the bloody coin into his pocket, and takes my hand.

Nothing is romantic about his embrace this time, nothing mocking or playful as he herds me out of the market and back down the cool, dim corridors. I want to say something to break the tension, but so much energy radiates from his body, from his palm into mine, that I don't dare speak until we are safely behind the door to his room.

"Must she truly be exiled?" I ask after the door slams shut. "Witches are outlawed in the city; how is she to find work or care for herself?"

"She knew the rules about witchcraft in the market." His gaze hardens. "And she drew your blood."

"Truly, it is no more than a scratch." I turn my wrist over and expose the thin red line. "See?"

His Adam's apple bobs, and his jaw clenches and unclenches several times.

"I have had worse injuries while engraving. Look, my hands are covered in scars. This will only be one more."

He lunges for my wrist, and holds it up as if I haven't seen it, growling each word one at a time. "She damaged my property. Or have you forgotten that you belong to me?"

My mouth goes dry, and my traitorous lip trembles. An old woman, witch or not, now lives on the street for my sake. I don't wish that life on anyone.

Guilt joins my exhaustion. I am so tired, I am hungry, and I simply do not have enough energy left to control my emotions in the face of his anger. As much as I want to be strong, to yell or scream at him, I cannot. My chin wobbles, and I look down before he can see tears gather in my eyes.

He drops my arm in a huff, says, "This was a mistake," and jerks the door open. "Do not leave this room for any reason, or you will regret it."

# CHAPTER 8

*I cut my hand today. Papa says blood is the price of being a repairist, and my first scar is something to be proud of. But it slagging hurts. Papa said I shouldn't use dwarvish curses, but they are the ones who came up with artifice anyway, and I don't think the Smith will mind.*

*—From the diary of Willow Bowbriar*
*August 8, 1857*

Sharp rapping on wood shocks me awake, and I sit bolt upright, my heart pounding as I blink in confusion. What's wrong? Where am I? It takes several seconds of blinking at the unfamiliar room for my sleep-addled mind to remember that I am not at home in my small room. I am not even above ground.

I am, in fact, lying in the bed of the most notorious criminal in Britain. Understandably, that realization does not calm my wildly beating heart, nor does it stop me from flailing to free myself from the clinging blankets.

"One moment!" I shout as the knocking increases in intensity.

My bare feet sink into layers of carpet as I roll out of the bed and hit the floor. A wave of dizziness forces me to grab the footboard to steady myself before I stumble forward. After the King left, I'd yanked the door open to find two Ratcatchers standing guard on either side. They'd given me warning glances that said chasing after the King was a bad idea.

So, alone for the first time since entering the Undercroft and as safe as I was ever likely to be, I'd bolted the door from the inside—the King could knock just like everyone else for all I cared—and climbed onto his bed. After a good cry, I promptly fell asleep. Which, judging from my decided lack of coordination, had been a bad idea.

I rub the sleep out of my eyes as I reach for the door and freeze. It could be *him*. What would he do to me for locking him out of his room? After his display of anger, my bit of exhausted rebellion feels like a childish temper tantrum. One that might get me punished. If it is him, stalling won't help.

"Yes?" I croak.

"I've got your supper, duckie." The thin, rasping voice is comfortingly familiar despite only having met her once. Tildie. Relief makes my knees weak as I slide the bolt aside. Her calm, knowing expression is as comforting as a warm cup of tea. She enters the room with a wood tray balanced negligently on one hand.

"Tildie. I'm so glad to see you."

"I don't doubt it," she chuckles. "Where d'you want this?"

"Ah..." I search the room. There is no dinner table or anything so formal. "The table by the hearth, I suppose?"

She snorts. "Don't ask me. Eat it wherever you like. So long as you do eat it. You're far too thin, and the Undercroft is a cold place. You need a bit of padding to keep you warm."

"Is that why you've bundled yourself in so many layers?" I ask, eyeing the blankets and scarves that obscure her short frame.

"What, this?" she asks, plucking the tasseled end of a scarf after setting the tray on the table. "Nah. I can hide all sorts of things in this mess. Pockets everywhere. Besides, makes it hard for someone with violence on their mind to find my innards. Know how tricky it is to slip a knife through this much fabric?"

That makes a chill run down my arms. "I suppose I hadn't thought of that." I glance down at my body, noting how exposed this dress leaves me, without so much as the boning in my corset for protection.

She catches the direction of my thoughts. "Don't think nothing of that, duck. The King don't wear armor, either."

"Yes," I say, rubbing the gooseflesh on my arms. "I noticed that when he was stabbed."

She nods. "That makes him scary. Walkin' about half naked like that, well. That's a real show of power, innit? Proves he ain't scared of nothing bad happenin', not to him and not to you. It's proof he can protect you."

No wonder he'd gotten so angry when the witch drew my blood. It wasn't only that she'd manhandled someone who belonged to the King, but she'd thrown doubt on his ability to protect me.

"Is everything he does calculated to protect his power?"

She snorts as she hobbles toward the door, her blankets and scarves swaying with her bowlegged gait. "You try to rule a kingdom of thieves and murderers, and tell me what *you'd* be concerned with."

After Tildie leaves, I eat so fast I barely have time to taste the food. My stomach goes from painfully hollow to stretched and heavy. Somewhere along the way, numb detachment slides over me. I should be angry that he locked me in this room, but I am only vaguely relieved to know nothing else is expected of me.

So long as the King looks for my father, I'll stay wherever he tells me to. For now, at least. I wrap myself in a throw blanket and wander around the King's room, looking more closely than I had during my previous inspection. Nothing I see contradicts my first impression: the King is a man who likes physical comfort.

As I run my fingertips across various surfaces, the tapestry in the corner catches my eye. Gold threads catch the fitfully burning fire and reflect it in shimmers, drawing me forward almost like the cloth is weaving a spell. Before I realize I've started walking, I am pulling the edge of the tapestry until the fabric lays straight.

"You... you are a work of art," I breathe.

Silk threads in hundreds of colors and millions of stitches blend to create a vision of the forest I can fall into: the scent of damp leaves, fresh wind, soft earth beneath my feet, and the lonely call of an owl floating on a breeze that raises gooseflesh on my arms.

"I have never been in a forest," I tell the fabric as I trace the raised lines with the tip of my finger. "I've never even left New London. You may be the closest I ever get."

White birch trees weave pale green leaves into a bower over the heads of two figures: a man with stag's horns and a woman with a crown of flowers. They are beautiful in a way that only exists in faerietales, standing beneath a full moon with their palms pressed reverently together. Silver threads become the moonlight on her dark skin and flowing gown and shimmer in the chains and jewels hanging from his antlers.

My fingertips run gingerly across the threads where their hands meet. The composition centers on this single point; lines, color, and contrast all lead the eye here. Whoever embroidered this had the heart of a painter, I think, as I examine the expressions of the lovers. Were they meeting in secret? Perhaps marrying with no blessing but that of the moon, since a thrice-turned rope binds their wrists together?

Tears prick my eyes. Something in the composition, in the muted colors of the forest and the suggestion of eyes in the shadows, promises that this quiet moment will not last. That even this perfect, faerietale love is doomed.

"Obyrron and Titania."

I squeak and spin to see the King leaning one shoulder against the bed frame, his left hand pressed hard to his ribs beneath a cloak so dark he nearly disappears into the shadows behind the bed. If the hood hadn't been down, I may have glanced past without seeing him. Still, how had he gotten in without my hearing him? Had I truly been so enamored with the tapestry?

When I release the edge of the fabric, it falls back into folds that obscure the scene. "A Midsummer Night's Dream?"

He chuckles, but it is a pained sound and more rueful than amused. "Not quite the same tale Shakespeare told."

"Any news of my father?"

"Nothing yet. Have patience. Here."

The vial on his palm catches the light of a nearby lamp. I cross the room in a few quick strides, but my eyes are on his chest, not the glass. He is curled slightly over his left side as if protecting his ribs, and lines of strain bracket his eyes. "Are you hurt?"

"You are an art lover, aren't you?" he says, ignoring me and holding out the vial with the hand not pressed to his ribs. "Take this and call for a bath."

I fold my arms to make it plain that I will not take the vial until he tells me the truth. "You are hurt."

"The moment my business becomes your concern," he says with a grunt as he pushes away from the bed and grasps my wrist, "I will tell you. In the meantime"—he wraps my fingers around the vial—"do as you're told."

The temptation to argue with him is almost overwhelming. Pain is clear in his voice and his bearing, in the way he guards his injured side, and in how he wants me not to notice. Was he injured looking for information about my father? The guilt of that possibility makes me sigh and hurry for the door.

"If you are injured," I say after the bath has been ordered, "I can help you. Injuries are common in a repair shop, and I'm not a bad healer."

The King leans back to sit on the foot of the bed, letting his legs stretch out as he sighs and shifts uncomfortably. "Some wounds"—he eyes me, a warning in his voice—"can't be healed."

A train of people carrying steaming buckets troops into the

room without notice. They arrived far faster than I would have expected, so I watch them rather than responding to his warning. One by one, gallons of hot water are emptied into the copper tub in the far corner. Steam rises into the air like a beacon, curling in a luscious promise of warmth as they exit.

None of them are servants, per se. They don't wear uniforms or livery. Perhaps they are merely whoever was near at hand when the order went out, which seems rather dangerous for a man in a precarious position of power. Then again, he does wander about without a guard, armor, or visible protection of any kind. Maybe that, in itself, is a statement, as Tildie claimed.

"The bath," he orders after the door closes.

With my thumbs, I press the cork out of the vial with a little popping sound, and the musky bite of rosemary makes me close my eyes in pure pleasure. The familiar scent is a comfort I did not know I needed, and makes unasked-for appreciation warm my insides.

After everything that happened, he'd gone back to the market. No. He'd likely sent someone. But he hadn't needed to. The masquerade had begun, and no one would doubt him after that performance. So... why?

I retreat to the fireplace, mind spinning, and turn the chair so it faces away from the bath at the back of the room. "I won't look," I promise.

"It will be rather hard to bathe if you don't look."

Heat burns in my chest and neck. He had mentioned that I might be required to scrub his back, but I would rather pretend he didn't. "I'm certain you've bathed without an audience before."

"Get in the water, Dove."

My spine stiffens. "I'm not... but the bath is for you!"

"The bath is for you. You need it. You stink of stale fear."

Blood heats my cheeks, and not from embarrassment. "If I stink of fear, it is your fault!" I shoot to my feet and square my shoulders at him. "If you don't like the scent of it, maybe you should stop going out of your way to scare the hell out of me!"

One dark brow rises, and he comes to his feet as well. Hunger burns in his eyes, not arousal, but something else I cannot place. It makes my outburst seem like a red cloak waved in front of a bull. "Perhaps I would not be forced to scare you if you would do as you are told."

"Fine. I will. If you bathe first and let me see to your wound."

He stops, surprise replacing the hunger. "I am not wounded."

"Liar," I blurt, and immediately want to slap my hands over my mouth for being seven colors of fool. Provoking a man this dangerous is stupid in the extreme, so why can't I hold my slagging tongue?

But he only says, "I do not lie."

"Prove it," I demand, folding my arms over my chest. I've pushed this far, and my blood is still too hot for my common sense to get the best of my frustration.

A slow smile curls one corner of his mouth into a crooked grin that is exactly as attractive as I feared it would be. "Another bargain, eh? As my lady wishes." He performs a mocking half-bow, then pulls his shirt off in a single, graceful move.

My heart stops. I do not know what I expected to see, but the muscles of his torso and a fine dusting of black hair across his chest and abdomen were certainly not it. Bruising should have colored his ribs at the very least, but he looks as if an unkind hand has never touched his skin.

My mouth pops open, which is terribly embarrassing, but I cannot pull my eyes away. He is as lean and dangerous as a coursing hound, and without so much as a scab or a scar from the knife wound I saw him take two days ago. Where is the wound?

He smirks, and his long fingers fall to the lacing on his britches. "Keep staring like that, and I'll find excuses to undress more often."

I spin and slap my hands over my eyes as if the pressure of my palms can force the memory of his body out of my head. Damn and damn and damn this man again! Turning as he passes behind me, I keep my eyes averted until the sound of splashing tells me he's sunk into the water.

It is bad enough knowing he is naked a mere fifteen feet away, but worse still, knowing I will be forced to do the same once he is done. I wish, most fervently, that I had made any other arrangement but this one. The sound of soap sliding over his skin sends shivers down my arms.

"Why do you enjoy torturing me?" I moan into my hands.

His chuckle is dark. "Have you never seen how lovely you are when you blush? When your eyes are wide, pupils dilated, and your lips part ever-so-slightly?"

Lovely? That is a word no one has ever applied to me. Which means it is yet another barb designed to irritate. Well, I will not give him the pleasure. Instead of covering my eyes, the heels of my hands press tightly over my ears, but that doesn't stop me from hearing him laugh as I retreat to the other side of the bed.

His bath seems to take hours, though the mantle clock says less than ten minutes have passed.

"Your turn," he says, voice amused as I try to keep my back to him while navigating the room. I doubt he has the common decency to dress before speaking to me, and his naked body is the last thing I want to see.

After draping a blanket over the backs of two chairs for a makeshift screen (which makes the King roll his eyes in exasperation), I crouch behind it to undress and bathe faster than I have ever bathed in my life. Every sound from his side of the room tightens the skin along the back of my neck as I imagine him walking around my hastily devised wall.

Scrubbing my skin with the rough cloth till it is raw takes no more than a few minutes, though I will admit the soap smells heavenly. It is my hair that will be the problem. It reaches my lower back and usually takes me a quarter of an hour to wash and untangle.

I refuse to be naked near that man nearby any longer than absolutely necessary, so I pull the dress back on while my skin is still damp, and lean over the tub to wash my hair. My skin is still hot and tingly from the force of scrubbing, and my hands are tangled in my hair when the King says, "Come here."

I rush through the last of my braid, leaving it hanging damp down my back, and join him at the closet door I'd mistaken for an exit. Standing close to him makes me edgy, especially when his dark eyes glint in far too suggestive a way.

Perhaps I should not be so modest and embarrassed, especially since I agreed to this arrangement knowing what he may demand of me, but the King makes me nervous on a fundamental level. It is not merely the nerves of being a virgin but of being *prey* and having no power.

He watches me approach, fingers resting lightly on the door handle next to the tapestry. "When I open the door, don't scream," he says, "and don't run."

No one ever says things like that unless they're talking about deadly animals. Of course, that would also be good advice for dealing with the King. I lift the hem of my skirt, just in case I need to leap out of the way. "You're not keeping animals in there, are you?"

"In a manner of speaking."

With that, he lifts and jerks open the door. The wood must have settled badly over time, making the door fit tight in the frame, because it pops as it releases, making me flinch.

Lamplight doesn't reach the back of the closet, but the massive shape inside is still visible. I take half a step back in spite of myself. A low humming and whirring, so low humans would probably never hear it, echoes from the dark, followed by metallic clinks I immediately recognize as the sound of brass.

A construct dog prowls out of the shadows. Lamplight glows on the dull brass skin, picking out the delicately engraved runes and rivets so cleverly set that they are almost flush with the skin.

Its enormous head reaches the middle of my thigh, and it stares at me with unfathomable eyes made of black glass. I hold my breath as it stops between the King and me, head swiveling soundlessly between us. It doesn't need to breathe, but its massive shoulders still move as if it did.

"It's modeled after a mastiff, isn't it? Muses, it's beautiful," I breathe, clasping my hands to stop myself from touching it.

Excitement stretches a grin across my face. I've only repaired one construct, a small bird that hopped back and forth on a branch and sang for its owner, but it was one of my favorite repairs. Constructs are notoriously expensive. It is far cheaper to buy a real pet or hire someone to complete whatever task one needs done than it is to commission a master artificer to make one.

And this is the largest construct I've ever heard of.

"The craftsmanship is exquisite," I say, crouching to get a better look but keeping my distance. "This is the creation of a master. See the runes engraved along the seams? They should make the brass lighter and strong enough to withstand significant damage. And can you hear the gears and belts? There must be noise-dampening runes engraved inside as well! I bet there are pistons in your joints," I tell the dog. "What fluid was used for your hydraulics?"

"Ripper does not speak," the King says. The strange note in his voice makes me glance up at him, only to see that his expression is just as baffling, a mixture of humor and bemusement.

"Of course, he doesn't." I stand, feeling rather stupid. Part of me wants to explain my habit of talking to inanimate objects so I do not appear stupid, and the other half knows it would be a pointless conversation. "He is extraordinary, but I'm sure you already know that. Who built him for you?"

He clears his throat and looks down at the dog. "Ripper, you will protect this woman from harm."

Ripper turns to face me and sits his metal rump on the ground.

"He can take orders?" My eyes widen, and my breath comes short. "But, constructs don't think. They behave according to set patterns inscribed by the artificer."

"Tell yourself that every time he follows my directions if it makes you feel better."

"But—" I circle the dog, peering at the runic sentences to decipher every one I recognize. "Constructs are good at simple tasks, like hopping back and forth on a branch and singing, or following a set path, or digging. But they do not have minds. You cannot inscribe additional orders or alter them once the construct has been completed. They merely follow the same set patterns, over and over." This limitation can become quite problematic if they are damaged and continue to swing a sledgehammer or wield a shovel despite being in the wrong place. Yet another reason constructs are so rare.

But Ripper turns his big black eyes toward my face, and his tail wags twice as if he understands. A substantial dent warps his side, but luckily doesn't affect the runes that keep him running.

I slide my finger along the dent. "What happened here?"

"Any time you leave this room," the King says, ignoring me but sounding deadly serious, "keep the smiling man coin in your pocket and take Ripper with you. You are never to leave it or him behind."

"As if I would want to. Look at him! I could learn so much just by observing him. But what happened to his—"

"Don't concern yourself with it. He still functions."

"But I could repair—"

"No."

One word shouldn't crush me so thoroughly, but the thought of getting my hands into Ripper's gears and returning him to perfection has wormed into my mind and given me an unexpected sense of purpose. "Please? I cannot stay in this room for the next six months with nothing to do, and I truly—"

"No."

"I can fix him!"

The lump in my throat is so big I can barely take another breath around it. I hate begging him, but I have nothing to bargain with, and the need to do something meaningful is too compelling to ignore despite my fear of his reaction. The dog has excited every part of me, both the artist and the artificer.

The King searches my face as if he's never seen me before, his expression one I cannot read. But both of his hands are curled into fists.

"Some things," he says softly, "cannot be fixed."

My chin wobbles, but I clench my jaw. I don't know why fixing the construct is so important, but the need to repair it digs its claws into my chest and won't let go. "I refuse to believe that. Something so beautiful should not be left damaged. Won't you let me try?"

He searches my eyes. Meeting his gaze is like falling down and down into the darkest parts of the earth where light cannot reach. But the depths of the earth are hot, I've been told, and there is warmth in his eyes, though it is far beneath the surface.

His eyelids flinch ever so slightly, and he releases me from his gaze to walk away. "Fine. Do what you can, if it pleases you."

An ember of excitement takes fire in my chest. "I can go home and retrieve my tools—"

He raises one hand to cut me off, no softness in his expression or his voice now. "No. I'll send Gwil with you to the market tomorrow for supplies. But be warned: the construct is too damaged to repair. It will never be what it once was."

With that, he leaves. And he doesn't come back.

# CHAPTER 9

*I dreamed about that day again when they came for Mamma and Papa. It didn't matter how much I screamed or pleaded; the constables couldn't hear me. When I woke, my pillow was wet. Now, I cannot get back to sleep, and the only person who can keep me company is the little asparagus fern by my window.*

*—From the diary of Willow Beauregard*
*June 12, 1882*

RIPPER AND I APPROACH THE BUSTLING MARKET, AND FOR THE FIRST time since entering the Undercroft, a sense of independence fills me with the confidence of agency. Which is only slightly marred by being forced to rely on Gwil—the big man I ran into my first night in the Undercroft—to lead me through the maze of tunnels. When we reach the market, the Ratcatchers near the door nod at him and allow us inside.

He takes position behind me and to my right, leaving Ripper on my left.

"I don't mind if you give me a *bit* more space," I begin, but Gwil cuts me off with a shake of the head.

"I'm not losing a finger because I was too far away to stop someone from doing something stupid."

I stop. "Would he really cut off your finger?"

Gwil merely stares at me as if he is unsurprised I've asked such a stupid question.

"Surely your presence alone is enough to dissuade anyone with ill intentions."

His blue eyes lock on my wrist, and he raises a brow at me. The scratch has already healed, but his point is taken. Even the King hadn't been able to curtail the activity of his people entirely.

I'd like to argue with him, but he doesn't seem the type to argue back.

"There's no chance I can convince you to give me a little more space? Now that Ripper is here?" I ask one last time.

Gwil shakes his head and folds his arms. "No chance, lady."

I sigh and turn down another aisle. It looks like I've simply got to get used to having two shadows breathing down my neck. At least I'm no longer stuck in that room.

There is so much to take in now that I am free from expectations and can wander the market at will: gadgets, food, tools, and plants. But I focus on the tools, rattling off the names of things I will need to repair Ripper while Gwil digs coins out of his pocket and hands them to vendors.

"For someone who don't belong to the King, you spend his money freely enough."

I turn and smile at Silk, who stands with her hands on her hips and a jaunty grin. Her dark hair hangs over her shoulder in a complex braid, and her split skirt looks far more comfortable than my dress.

And it isn't just Silk whose clothing defies the standards I am used to conforming to. Undercrofters have a distinct sense of style that functions like an act of defiance, a sartorial middle-finger to the refined expectations of the world above. There are people here with more than enough money to fit themselves up in the finest fashions, but they choose not to. What would it be like to join in that act of defiance?

But for now, I have other things to keep me busy. I gesture at Ripper with my chin. "I've got something to fix."

"That so? Well, bully for you, then. I see you've got another shadow, as well. All right, Gwil?"

"Go away, Silk," Gwil says, sounding like an older brother trying to get rid of his younger sister.

"Nah, I don't think I will. It's been ages since I've shopped. I think I'll stick around a bit. What's on the list today, Dove?"

Before I know it, we are wandering the market together.

"Let me get this straight," Silk says after popping a roasted peanut into her mouth. "You didn't want to commit any crimes to earn enough brass to find your father, so you thought working for the most dangerous criminal in Europe was a safer idea?"

"I don't think I have the makings of a criminal, and I wouldn't have been much use to my father in prison." As much as I wish I was hard and clever, like Silk, I don't have the temperament. My time in the Undercroft proves that.

"Suppose not. Too late to change things now, in any case. You'll have to learn on your feet."

"Learn what?" I ask, turning into a new row of vendors, carts, and stalls and letting my eyes roam over the offerings. A tinker's stall halfway down the row looks like he may have the tools I need.

"How to protect your pockets, for one thing," Silk says. "Gotcha!"

I spin in time to see Silk grab the wrist of a young boy I hadn't noticed. His eyes are round, his teeth clenched as he plants his feet and tries to jerk his arm out of her grasp. His clothes are too small, revealing knobby wrists and ankles visible through threadbare socks.

"Let me go," he snarls, but Silk is stronger than she looks.

"Knowing whose pockets to dip your fingers into is half the job, you little gutter snipe," she tells the boy. And though she pries his fist open and retrieves a coin from his grubby fingers, her voice isn't unkind. "Gwil?"

The burly Ratcatcher hauls the boy up by the back of his jacket until his feet dangle a few inches from the stone floor, and shouts for one of the Ratcatchers near the door. Other shoppers have turned to watch, their expressions amused or disapproving.

"No!" the boy shouts, flailing uselessly.

The Ratcatcher ignores his struggles and carts him off down the row. A few people jeer or clap as the pair nears the end of the aisle. An elven man with dark skin slides out of the way and bumps into a pale fellow with his back turned. He spins to give the elf a dirty look but locks gazes with me instead. And for a moment, my blood runs cold.

The colorless, waxy skin that looks stretched too tight over his skeleton sends butterflies of recognition fluttering in my chest. He ducks back into the milling crowd. The entire exchange lasts only a heartbeat, fast enough to make me wonder whether I saw what I think I saw, or if, in the confusion of the jeering crowd, I am imagining things.

"Did you see that man?" I ask, scanning the crowd and finding nothing.

"Which one? The market is full of 'em."

"He was a pale human. Waxy faced. Wearing dark clothing."

"You've just described half the blokes in here." She flips the coin that was nearly stolen, snatches it out of the air, and drops it back into her pocket.

"Why put it back if it's so easy to pick?" I ask, eyeing the fabric as it gapes open several inches, begging for a quick pair of fingers to slip inside.

"Because an easy target is irresistible to a bad dip. Makes 'em predictable. Means I only have one spot to protect instead of many." She pats her pocket affectionately.

It was a good thing I'd never chosen a target like Silk when I was young. Then again, I hadn't picked pockets long before I found my father. "I didn't think there would be thieves in the market. I mean, aside from... well, everyone, I guess. Why steal from one another down here?"

"To keep in practice. Because we can. But it happens here less than it does Upstairs because we still have to tithe, so it's less profitable."

I glance down the aisle, remembering the boy's stricken face. "What will happen to him?"

She shrugs. "He'll get beaten."

We stop walking, and I stare at her in dismay, "Beaten?"

"Of course. He can practice down here and maybe get a good hiding if he botches it up. But if he makes stupid mistakes like that Upstairs, they'll toss him in a school or reformatory, and that's if he's lucky."

I know the stories about reformatories. Politicians claim they rehabilitate and reform delinquent children, but no one is foolish enough to believe them. Even as a child fighting not to starve, I preferred life on the street, as tenuous as it was, to places like that.

Had my father not taken me in, I likely would have ended up in one. But beating the boy didn't seem like much of an improvement, and I told her so.

"Would you rather him make mistakes down here, where a bit of pain is the worst he can expect? Or up top, where they'll exploit, abuse, and starve him?"

"Is beating him necessary? Aren't there other ways to teach him, kinder ways?"

She turned on me, her eyes hard as agates. "Kinder ways to teach him to *steal*? Where do you think you are, Dove? You think we pledge loyalty and pay homage to the King of fucking murderers because we've got safe, gentle homes to return to? There are no schools here. That boy is growing up to be a thief, with only thieves and criminals to teach him. Kindness is for people who can afford it. In this life, kindness isn't a gift. It will only get him killed."

I swallow hard. If my father had not opened his door, I might have lived this life and learned these lessons at the end of a fist or a leather strap. Will the boy be lucky enough to find someone kind, someone willing to open a door and invite him inside?

"You were kind to me," I say, daring her to respond. "Are *you* trying to get me killed?"

She smirks and takes my arm in hers as if we are the best of friends. "You? No. Oh, don't mistake me. I am using you for my own benefit. And right now"—she stands on her toes and peers down the aisle at a food vendor, a speculative light in her eyes— "I'd benefit from a meat pasty."

"Come into the Garden, Maude," plays softly on the gramophone. The gentle music, crackling fire, and glowing dwarven lamps make the room cozy. The bundle of flowers I bought—several bundles to be fair, now displayed in random containers—make my cage feel almost like a space I can call my own.

Sheets of brass, tools, screws, and other equipment litter the back of the King's room between the tub—which now, unaccountably, is blocked from the rest of the room by a folding dressing screen—and the tapestry. Ripper stares up at me, patient as only a creature who is not alive can be. I should be glad to start repairing him while I wait for the King to find my father.

But all I can see is the face of that boy when he realized he was about to be dragged away and beaten.

He couldn't have been more than thirteen. I've had my pockets picked by children half that age and twice as stealthy. I was one, in fact. Which means he is probably new to the trade, likely shoved into life on the street by some tragedy.

After they dragged my parents to debtors' prison, I stole to collect enough to pay their debts. I brought my booty to the guard every day, and he took my coins, rings, and other baubles with a solemn nod. Until he saw me approaching one evening and shook his head, his eyes sad. After that, I stole to survive.

And here I am, again, somehow having come full circle: another parent relying on me to save them from a situation I do not fully understand while I am unprepared and ill-equipped to do anything useful. Ripper makes a huffing noise, and I blink at him, drawn out of my reverie.

"Something to say, boy?"

His tail wags.

Crouching, I force myself to focus on the damage, not the past or my current impotence.

"Whoever created you was an artist," I say, running my fingers along the articulated joints of his paw and squinting at the careful lines of runes etched and sealed in lines along its seams. "You should not have been abandoned. I wanted to be an artist, you know. But making money in the arts is hard when you need to support yourself. Ripper?"

His ears swivel toward me, just like a real dog's might, though no expression alters his metal face. "Are you going to bite me if I take you apart?"

His tail wags.

"That is not a promising response."

But I cannot fix him if I don't. So, I mark the center of the first rivet with my awl, then position the drill on my mark. "This may hurt a little," I mutter, though Ripper has no nerve endings. "Please don't bite me."

I begin drilling. The bit chews through the metal at a steady pace, then slides through the head with a hollow sound just before the rest of the metal falls into his chest cavity with a muted *ping*. "There! Easy enough, right?"

Ripper tilts his head at me.

After that, rivets come apart one after the next, and I find myself falling into the rhythm of the work. Once the rivets holding his damaged ribcage are removed, I can slide the panels off one at a time. They are fitted like the joints in a suit of armor, giving the dog a full range of motion.

"There is more to you than meets the eye, isn't there, my friend?" I murmur as I turn the panels over. More engravings decorate the inside of his brass skin, but they don't look like any runes I have ever seen. These symbols swirl, almost like fine penmanship, and hint at a language entirely different from the runic artifice I am familiar with.

"What is this?"

The hydraulic pump that cycles fluid through his limbs and joints is the size of my joined fists, and not all of the markings engraved on it are runes. Not runes I recognize, at least. "And these?"

In truth, it doesn't matter. Not yet, anyway. First, I have to use these panels as templates to cut and shape the replacement pieces. "I wish I could simply hammer your original panels back into shape, but that would damage the artifice. And damaged artifice is far more dangerous than a dented side, I'm afraid."

I sink into the task of measuring, cutting, hammering, and polishing pieces of brass until they match the damaged panels perfectly. Without the sun, it is easy to ignore the clock on the mantle and work until my vision blurs.

It must be at least a day since the dwarven lamps in this room were charged, and the stored sunlight has waned until details are impossible to make out in the firelight alone. Working with sharp tools and hammers now would be begging for an injury, so I shuffle back to the chair, drag the blanket over myself, and fall asleep in front of the dying coals, too tired to worry about where the King has been, or when he may return.

# CHAPTER 10

*Excuse the quality of my penmanship, for I am so upset I can hardly stop my hands from shaking as I write. Papa's invention blew the back wall off his office this morning. He stormed out covered in dust and wood splinters with a cut across his fore-head, ready to spend all of our savings on repairing the wall and buying new equipment. It took me two hours to calm him enough that he did not ruin us. It worked, but he is not speaking to me.*

*—From the diary of Willow Beauregard*
*April 30, 1899*

THE FIRE HAS BURNED TO COALS, SO THE ONLY LIGHT IN THE ROOM comes from the open door, where the faint outline of a woman is visible against the hall lamps. She lights a candle and slinks into the room, all liquid grace with a curving profile and yards of dark hair falling around her shoulders.

The King follows her into the room, elegantly lean in the dim candlelight. He allows her to drag him toward the bed as one of the Ratcatchers leans in to pull the door closed. He takes the chamberstick from her, sets it on the table near the bed, and pulls her flush against his body.

A shocked blush makes my skin hot. He said he did not intend to curtail his normal activities simply because I now shared his room, so I should have expected this would happen at some point. Still, I shouldn't be watching her hands run up his stomach to his chest; I shouldn't hear the low sound of pleasure she makes as he pulls her against him. But where am I supposed to go?

Anywhere but here.

I won't make it through the door without being noticed, but the closet isn't that far away. Spending the night inside doesn't sound particularly pleasant, and my elven ears are far too sensitive to block out all sound. Still, anything would be better than hearing the woman gasp and giggle as he does... something I shouldn't be wondering about.

Quietly, I lever myself out of the chair with the blanket wrapped about my shoulders, trying hard not to hear the unmistakable noise of kissing. He said he had no intention of taking me to his bed, and I'm grateful she is in it and not me. But that doesn't mean I want to hear it.

I ease past the tools laid neatly on the floor and grip the door handle. Slowly, slowly, it turns, and the latch inches out of the strike plate, only to catch. I forgot that the door sticks. I'll have to lift it without making the wood pop. Muscles burning, I raise the weight of the door an agonizing millimeter at a time.

Almost there. I can close myself in the closet and plug my ears with the corners of the blanket. A little further... the King groans, a guttural sound of pleasure that makes a shiver run up my arms and heat run down my legs. Panicked, I pull the handle too hard.

The wood comes free with a *pop*.

The giggling and rustling stops.

I freeze, then leap into the closet and slam the door behind me, my eyes squeezed shut.

"Bloody, fucking, everlasting hell," he growls, slurring his words. He's been drinking.

*Oh, Calliope's harp,* how I want to disappear.

"Is that your lady, majesty? She can join us if you like. No extra charge."

I am going to expire of shame right here on the spot.

The mattress squeaks in protest, accompanied by a little sound of feminine disappointment and a heavy masculine sigh. "Not tonight, I'm afraid, Mona."

"We can continue, I don't mind."

"Take your share and extra from the Divvy tomorrow for your lost wages. Go."

"But, majesty—"

"Go."

The bed squeaks and the door opens and closes. I refuse to move. If I try hard enough, I might just slip into the shadows and never return.

"You may as well come out," he says, his voice acid.

I exhale in a silent rush. "I'd rather not."

"Think I'm going to force you to take her place?"

My stomach drops, and I blurt, "I refuse."

"You don't have that right, Dove. Remember? Consider it an order. You've deprived me of the comfort of a warm body. Why should you get the comfort of shadows?"

"I didn't mean to interrupt. I'm sorry."

"Are you? I doubt that."

Shame and embarrassment, I've learned, are dry tinder for the flames of anger, and mine blazes up faster than I have ever experienced. Shoving the door open, I stumble into the light of the dying fire. The King is standing near the hearth, having dropped a log onto the coals, his arms folded over his bare chest.

The sight of his exposed torso and burning eyes smothers my

anger as fast as throwing a wet blanket over a banked fire. I cannot lose my temper now, not when everything I have done is riding on his help. My throat is tight but I draw on years of practice to school my tone. "You cannot think I wanted to overhear your... *activities*." I glance at the bed and drag my eyes away. "I was trying to give you privacy."

"By slamming closet doors loud enough to wake half the Undercroft?"

"There was nowhere else to go. I wanted a room of my own, but you made me stay here. If you're angry, you have only yourself to blame."

My calm tone does not have the desired effect.

"Oh," he says, stalking toward me, fury making his eyes hot. "I am. I berate myself for being a fool every damned time I look at you."

That stings and only makes my blood run hotter. I should be trying to make an ally of him, make myself someone he likes and trusts, but the fear and discomfort I've bottled up since descending into the dark are so close to boiling out that my eyes hurt. "*You* are the one who proposed the nature of our arrangement. If you want your privacy, I am happy to find myself a new room."

"Where will you run to, little dove? Where will you be safe when half of the members of the Unseen Court know you are helpless, friendless, and have a failing business ripe for the picking?"

A chill slips down my spine.

"Oh yes," he says mercilessly, "you told all of them exactly how to take advantage of you when you stood in my court begging for help."

"I didn't beg," I insist, trying to regain my sense of outrage but failing in the face of what I've done. Weakness steals through my muscles. Muses, how could I have been so stupid?

"You may as well have." He raises my chin, forcing me to meet his gaze. His lips are swollen from kissing, but his jaw muscle flexes, and his heavy brows are drawn low over his eyes. "I gave you a way out, did I not? I told you not to force my hand. You did it anyway. You left me no choice but to claim you in front of the court or feed you to the wolves. And now you are angry I did not let them chew on your bones? Is your precious father worth such a sacrifice?"

"Yes!" I shout, my anger finally exploding as I shove him out of my space with both hands. I may not be built for strength, but repair work requires muscle, and as an elf I am stronger than the average human. "He's worth a hundred of you!"

The King should have stumbled backward, but he retreats only a step, one brow arched in amusement. "I knew it. I knew you had a temper hidden somewhere behind that gentle mask. I knew, deep down, that you were a liar."

"I am not a liar," I try to snarl, but the sudden change in his manner robs me of balance.

In fact, the truth of his statement makes me feel more naked than I had when bathing behind the draped fabric. Every altered word, every softened tone, every time I've concealed my tears or said exactly the opposite of what I meant to keep the peace or make someone happy, comes hurtling back at me like a thrown handful of stones.

"Why hide from the truth?" he asks, holding my neck between his hands, his thumbs running from my collarbones up to the tip of my chin. "There is power in admitting what you are, what you want."

He could snap my neck if he wants to. And yet, that possibility is not as frightening as the truth in his words. No, not truth. He is cruel and only wants to hurt me, to pay me back for ruining his night.

My fingers curl into fists. "I'm not hiding from anything. I only want my father back."

"Liar."

"I have no reason to lie."

"You," he whispers, stepping closer and flattening my hand on his chest, "want to be free. But you're afraid to admit it. And"—his voice lowers until the sound of it is like a caress—"you want me to touch you. Tell me I'm lying."

"You're lying."

"Now"—he leans down until our lips are a breath apart— "Make me believe it."

Everything in my body, the storm of anger, confusion, and fear, yearns to close the distance, to be swallowed by the darkness of his presence so I do not have to be alone in my head, in the tempest swirling in my chest.

But I do not move. I cannot. Not to answer the wild beating of his heart beneath my palm or to silence the traitorous desire in my gut.

He's baiting me, just as he always does: hot to cold, from touching me to ignoring me, insulting one moment, complimentary the next. This is simply another way to amuse himself by torturing me. Maybe he is beautiful, and maybe he is compelling in a terrible way. But so is a snake.

"You are a bad person," I breathe against his mouth.

He inhales as if sucking my words into his lungs, then nods, making our lips brush. "Yes. I am that." One hand on the small of my back presses me against his chest, and my hands slide up to his shoulders to push him away.

"I am a bad person." The fingers of his other hand thread through the hair at the base of my neck. His breath smells of whisky and cinnamon. "And you would do well to remember it. And *you* are a liar. I won't forget it. Now—" He releases me and crosses to the bed.

I wobble forward, dizzy from anger and his proximity, barely able to pay attention as he continues, "You robbed me of a bed companion, and I am tired from a long day of searching for *someone's* father. So, you'll have to take her place."

I can only stand there, slack-jawed and unsteady.

He flings back the covers with a dramatic flick of the wrist. "Get in."

My mouth goes so dry I can barely force out the words. "You said I could sleep where I—"

"Enough with sleeping in the damned chair. There are dark rings beneath your eyes, and I'm tired of looking at them. You need rest, and I need a bit of peace. You will be sleeping here for the foreseeable future. So get in. Now."

When I simply stand there, staring at the bed, he aims one more carefully pointed arrow in my direction. "If you want to end our arrangement, all you must do is speak the words."

I've always been careful not to burden anyone else with my emotions, keeping them tightly controlled so they don't spill over and damage my relationships. Letting them free in a moment of weakness has left me more drained than I could have imagined. I don't even have the will to fight back.

The idea of escaping the Undercroft to tell Chief Inspector MacSweeney everything I've learned is so damned tempting. But I've been through too much to stop now. Besides, the last month of my life has been characterized by stupid decisions. What's one more?

Bottom lip firmly between my teeth, eyes averted, I strip off my dress. Never have I unbuttoned a garment so fast. It slides over my hips and puddles on the floor. At least my corset cover and corset create a protective layer between him and me.

When my dress is folded neatly and draped over the chair, I turn toward the bed. He still stands on the other side, watching me with firelight reflecting in his dark eyes.

I slide beneath the covers, and cannot help groaning. The pleasure of lying flat without having to curl my legs is almost unspeakable. Sleeping in the chair had been horribly uncomfortable. I can admit that, at least.

The bed dips as the King climbs in. I turn on my side, my back toward him, and scoot as close to the edge of the mattress as possible. That leaves a few feet of empty space between us.

Space another woman occupied mere minutes ago.

Had I not interrupted them, she would have shared his bed.

That makes feeling the mattress shift as he moves and listening to the blankets slide across his skin particularly disconcerting. When he turns toward me, I stiffen and stop breathing, clutching the blanket to my chest like a shield.

He punches his pillow and flops onto it. "Waiting for me to touch you, Dove? It's not going to happen."

"Good."

"Go to sleep."

As if I could sleep with his half-naked body mere feet away. I don't know if I'll ever sleep again. But I do know one thing: I'm tired of not knowing what is happening in the search for my father. If I must continue suffering the King's barbs and ill-humors, his absences and unannounced rendezvous, it isn't too much to ask to know what my discomfort is paying for.

A kernel of determination wriggles into my tired heart like a seed being planted. I defied the King to his face tonight. And I am still alive. He hasn't sent me away or broken our contract. Tomorrow, I must do it again. And again, until I get my way.

# CHAPTER 11

*Papa legally gave me his last name. My past is sealed behind a closed door, and I've become someone new. I am Willow Beauregard now, and Willow Bowbriar has ceased to exist. Strange how a name can hold so much power. It reminds me of the stories in the faerietale book Papa bought me so long ago. If you learn a faerie's true name, you have power over it. Was this always my true name, or has taking it changed what I am?*

*—From the diary of Willow Beauregard*
*February 15, 1881*

AFTER A NIGHT OF THE BEST, AND WORST SLEEP I'VE HAD IN DAYS, the King and I stride down the corridor I've come to think of as the main passage. Ripper remains in the room, as he cannot function properly without so much of his artifice removed, but I find myself wishing for the comforting sound of his metal paws behind me.

"The Divvy?" I ask, rubbing my palms against the gooseflesh on my upper arms. It was easy to forget how cold the Undercroft is while ensconced in his room where a fire constantly burns.

"If a member of the court falls upon hard times, they withdraw money from my coffers until they can provide for themselves."

Flummoxed, I stare at his back. That was not what I expected from the King of thieves and criminals. "That is... rather generous."

"Generous?" He glances over his shoulder at me, one brow raised. "Is that what you think it is?"

"You said you are giving them money to care for themselves," I counter. "What else would you call it?"

"If a man does not care for his horse, the horse dies. He is then left afoot. Caring for the horse is a good investment. Caring for the people is also a good investment."

"You make it sound like mere pragmatism, and yet—"

Stopping, he turns to face me, one finger pointing at my nose. "You are making the willful mistake of seeing altruism where none exists. It is a foolish mistake that will only hurt you. When someone shows you who they are, Dove, believe them."

Biting my lips together shows my willingness to drop the matter, and he gives me a single nod before he turns and takes another passageway, leaving me to follow in his wake.

With the exception of his uncomfortable exchange, he has largely avoided speaking to me since we woke in the dark. We'd shifted in our sleep until we were close enough to breathe one another's exhales. His breath tastes like cinnamon. I could have happily spent the rest of my life not knowing that.

His proximity caused enough discomfort that I was more than happy to accept a bit of distance. But every effort I've made to start a conversation where I might ask questions about my father has been ignored. In fact, the only words he said to me this morning were, "Wear the white gown today."

As I hurry after him, hoping the movement brings a bit of warmth back to my limbs, the only comfort I have is knowing that he slept as badly as I did. In a perverse way, the shadows beneath his eyes please me, which is terribly unkind.

With a sigh of resignation, I admit to myself that this place—this man—is truly having a negative effect on my character.

LESS THAN A QUARTER of an hour later, we arrive in the great hall. The King whispers something to Gwil, who hurries away, before he directs me where to stand: behind the throne, of course, a little to the left. No one stands on the right.

Someone hands me a carafe of wine as members of the Unseen Court enter the room, arranging themselves in double lines before the dais. Two Ratcatchers sit behind tables with strong boxes in front of them and a list of names in their hands.

"Mary Thornbridge," says a small elven woman when she limps to the front. Her clothes hang off her frame like moss on tree branches in the winter, and her cheeks are hollow.

The Ratcatcher checks his list, makes a mark beside her name, and passes her a handful of coins.

A narrow-chested human with slumped shoulders is next in line. "Harcastle."

"Smith."

"Nine-tooth."

"Jonny-b."

The King sips from a silver goblet and lounges on his throne, watching people receive the fruit of his generosity with a beneficent expression. After an hour, we've barely made a dent in the line of recipients that stretches through the hall and into the corridor beyond.

The iron chandelier above the throne throws cutting light across their features, making their eyes look hollow. Now and then, someone receives their Divvy, and either nods at the King in thanks or approaches to kiss his knuckles.

Gwil appears a moment later with an apologetic smile and tosses a finely woven wool shawl over my shoulders without a word. It is blessedly warm. The gooseflesh disappears as I stare at the back of the King's dark head, his hair curling over the collar of his shirt. I cannot decide whether to thank him or knock this heavy carafe against his frustrating skull.

He claims this generosity is just good business, and yet I have seen nothing that makes me believe he is as heartless as he claims to be. He can be cruel, yes; autocratic and pragmatic. But heartless? I am not so sure. The man is too contradictory to be easily defined.

Then again, perhaps I am doing exactly what he warned me against and assuming good intentions where only selfishness exists. But, despite my dislike, I cannot shake the notion that he is not bad, not entirely. The thought only adds to my determination to have answers. And to take a few more matters into my own hands.

The court fears him, yet a sort of reverent affection is mixed with their wariness. He may be a big, scary dog, but he is their big, scary dog, and perhaps that makes all the difference. They know what he is and what to expect from him.

They do not, however, quite know what to make of me. Sometimes, they stare or open their mouths as if to speak before thinking better of the idea. More than one person gives me a respectful bow or curtsey. I have done nothing to earn their respect, so I can only assume it is a result of my proximity to the King.

At least, I assume so until I notice the stares and sidelong glances and catch the words "white lady," whispered behind hands. The King holds up his empty glass, flicking a glance in my direction in a subtle command.

"I didn't expect the court to be such a superstitious lot," I mutter as I lean down to refill the cup.

"No one prays harder to the goddesses of fortune than those

who live their lives outside the protection of society. They will believe anything that gives them hope."

"I suspected criminals to be clear-eyed realists, given how often they faced the world's callousness."

"What makes you think everyone in my court is a criminal?"

That makes me pause. I have never broken a law—at least, not since coming to live with Papa—yet here I am. Might it be so very different for them? "But they look at me as if I may burn them where they stand."

"Can you blame them? You are rather an otherworldly crea-ture. Particularly in that dress with your hair down. You may as well have walked out of a faerietale."

I hesitate mid-pour as realization strikes. "Is that your game?"

"What?" he asks, but the corner of his mouth curls ever-so-slightly.

The pieces fall into place at last, and I feel seven colors of stupid for thinking, even for a moment, that everything the King does is not calculated for his benefit. "You are using me to make the people think you've got a white lady under your control."

"Not so loud," he says, but his tone is amused. He swirls the wine, watches the lamplight reflect on the deep red liquid, and swallows a mouthful. The muscles of his throat work and the tip of his tongue darts out to catch a stray drop as he makes a pleased sound. I do not watch its passage across his full lower lip.

"Is that why you wanted me beneath your thumb?" I demand.

"Could you blame me if I did? Control of a white lady would be quite a coup."

I retreat to my position behind his chair so I don't say some-thing stupid. All this time, I wondered what could make my service a worthy trade for the effort it would take to find my father. And now I know. If the people believe he controls a spirit or a faerie who may grant blessings–or curses, depending on her mood–it would only make the King appear more powerful.

If asked about faeries and spirits, they would likely laugh and mock the question. Faeries and spirits? Those only exist in stories.

Even so, they wouldn't go wandering about in haunted manors or faerie circles, either. Which means some of them see me as unnerving at best, and potentially dangerous, at worst.

Unfortunately, I cannot curse anyone, bless them, heal them, perform miracles, or disappear into the shadows. My pale skin and paler hair have been anything but a blessing. The sun is particularly cruel to me, and other mortals aren't much better. I was often turned away as a child by superstitious people, certain my coloring and pale eyes were a sign that I was cursed.

A white lady, indeed. Would that I had such power! I would not be here, enduring the mocking smiles and cruel barbs of the Cutthroat King if I had. Then again, as far as they know, he dotes on me. Which, I realize with a sudden start, gives me some small measure of power. If I ask a favor or make a statement in front of the people, and he denies me, that would create a crack in the picture he's using me to paint.

Something he would not be doing if he didn't require the illusion of power he didn't possess. So, something is happening in the Unseen Court that makes my ability to bolster his power important.

I ruminate on what might make the King nervous enough to turn a pale elf woman into a white lady while watching humans, dwarves, and elves walk through the line to accept their Divvy. It is almost like seeing a baroque painting come to life. Dramatic light on dramatic figures, the tension of want and hunger, every shadow full of mystery, and every expression a reflection of an inner world the viewer will never have access to.

A man with an injured leg limps to the table, accepts his handful of coins with a nod, and turns to hobble back down the center aisle. Before he completes his turn, his heel shifts on an uneven flagstone, and his ankle rolls hard to one side.

I watch him fall as slowly as if time has taken a deep breath. His eyes widen, and his arms swing to the side to correct his balance, but his knee has already given out from the strain. Coins fly from his fingers and bounce off the stones with a dozen metallic cries.

He is too far away for me to break his fall, but I find myself moving anyway. He lands on his hip with a grunt, his lips white with pain. Someone steps out of the line to lever him up by one arm, so I gather the spilled coins. People pull their feet away from me as if a touch of my fingers means death.

"No," the man says, waving his free hand at me, the panic in his eyes almost matching his pain. "Please don't trouble yourself, lady."

"It's no trouble," I assure him and wait till he's regained his balance before pouring the coins into his cupped hands, ensuring my fingers do not touch his.

He bobs his head in gratitude, but sweat beads his upper lip, and his gaze strays toward the King as if my assistance will earn him some sort of punishment. I want to ease his fears, but I doubt anything I say will help now. But his eyes widen; he's no longer looking at the King.

When I turn, it isn't the King I see either, but the chandelier above him—and the bolt sliding out of the mortar. It tilts, and wax splats on the ground near his feet and splatters one of his black boots. The cast-iron circle must weigh at least sixty pounds, if not more. And it is going to crush the King. My stomach flip-flops, and a chill runs from my shoulders down my spine.

"Look out!" I scream and lunge toward him, but the chandelier is already falling.

Gasps and screams rise from the court as the King leaps from his chair with shocking speed. One heartbeat, he lounges with a negligently held glass of wine, and the next, he flies toward me in a long, low leap.

He wraps his arms around me as the chandelier hits his wooden throne with a deafening crash. I land hard on my back with the King's arms beneath me, all the air whooshing from my lungs. Bits of cast iron snap and explode, buzzing past my ear and smashing into the stone with sharp cracks. Splinters of rock flake off from the impact, making people cry out as they try to protect themselves from the sharp pieces arrowing through the room.

The King flinches. He spasms, jerking against me as a hiss of pain slides between his teeth, hot against my neck. When he pulls me to my feet, his eyes search my face and torso.

I am fine, but the dais is in ruins. Cast iron has become a popular metal for large production pieces, poured into molds by the dozen. It is durable but brittle, and the heavy circle has snapped in several places, biting into the wood of the throne and sending shards flying for twenty feet in every direction.

A few pieces are embedded in the mortar of the closest pillar.

"Is everyone alright?" I ask, spinning toward the stunned crowd.

A few bystanders have minor cuts, but nothing to be concerned about. Luckily, they'd been far enough away from the impact not to suffer any real damage. Had they been any closer... The thought makes me cold.

"Were you hit?" I ask the King, remembering his sharp exhalation.

He ignores my question and wraps an arm around my waist. "Our lady is shaking." The crowd chuckles uneasily. "She's had enough excitement for one day, I think. Gwil, escort her back to my chamber and guard the door."

"But—"

"I'll join you when the Divvy is finished," he says, which sounds more like a threat than a promise.

Gwil hurries me up the stairs, but I have to slow to pick my way through the broken bits of metal. The pieces of chandelier that remain intact bit deeply into the wood just where the King was sitting, and they've been tampered with.

Breath held, I stare up into the darkness where the chandelier used to hang. Humans and dwarves would never be able to see details in the high ceiling from this distance, but I can. And what I see makes my blood run cold.

# CHAPTER 12

My first piece of art sold today! Papa says the untouched metal sheets must be saved for repairs, so I have been hoarding scraps. Mr. Grindstone arrived this afternoon to retrieve his teapot (his cat had knocked it off the stove, damaging the runes for heat storage), and he saw my little rose lamp.

He was so impressed with the way the petals lit up that he bought it before even picking up his teapot! He said no dwarven artificer could have made a prettier lamp, which was quite a compliment, as he was a master artificer before he retired. His hands are too arthritic to repair his own pieces, which is a shame.

Anyway, he gave me hope that I may have the talent to apply for an apprenticeship with the Artisan's Guild, just like Mama and Papa. Perhaps Blessed Calliope and the other muses have made me an artist after all.

*—From the diary of Willow Bowbriar*
*August 8, 1866*

~

WHILE WE WERE GONE, SOMEONE PLACED A MAKESHIFT WORK TABLE against the back wall and left my tools haphazardly atop it. The first order of business is, of course, to organize them. The familiar act helps settle my mind, at least a little, so I can focus on Ripper's repairs instead of what I saw in the Great Hall.

I hammer runes into brass for hours. By the time the King enters our room, a line of people is carrying hot water buckets behind him. He ignores me as they fill the tub, sitting on the edge of the bed to remove his boots as if no one else is here. They don't look at either of us and leave as soon as their buckets are empty.

When the door closes, he says, "Lock it."

My leather gloves hit the table with an irritated slap before I turn to tell him what I saw, but the words dry up and wither in my throat. His torso is bare and smeared with blood. "Calliope's voice, you were hurt!"

"The door, Dove."

I'm across the room in seconds, but my fingers hesitate over the bolt. "Shouldn't I call for a doctor?"

He peels the trousers off his long legs. "There is a medical kit under the bed." Though his expression is calm, pain colors the edge of his voice.

"Why didn't you say something?" I ask as I crouch to retrieve the heavy leather sack.

"I did not realize our pact required me to report to you."

"Fine," I snap, standing with the bag, "But you could have come back with me. I would have—" But he's already walking toward the tub.

A sheet of blood makes his back look like a gory illustration from a dime store penny dreadful. He must have been in terrible pain this whole time. My stomach twists. The combination of anxiety and nausea destroys my ability to control my temper.

"Muses, what were you thinking leaving this untreated so long?"

"I must be at the Divvy." He lowers himself into the tub with a grunt. "Just as I must rule over the Unseen Court when it meets."

"Of course. Can't have anyone thinking you're a mere human who can be injured."

He laughs, and the sound is completely incongruous, given the wound and bloody water. "Can't have them thinking that."

My gorge rises. I've handled many injuries in the mechanica, both my father's and my own. But I've never seen anything as stomach-turning as the flap of skin hanging open on his back. "You"—I swallow back bile and try to control my voice for his sake as I place the medical kit on the table nearest the tub—"you are begging for an infection, leaving this open so long. It was foolish."

"Are you scolding me, Dove?"

He's looking at me over his shoulder, a gleam in his eye as if I am a mother and he an impudent boy.

"Yes! Were you trying to bleed out? This needs stitches!"

"No stitches. But if you clean and dress it, I would... I would be grateful."

I pause, my mouth open for more scolding, but no words come out. Did he just ask me nicely rather than order me? All the angry steam I built up evaporates, leaving me unbalanced yet again. Will I never be on solid footing around this man? "Alright."

Cleaning the wound without causing him more pain is impossible, and every time he flinches, I jerk my hands away. "I'm sorry."

"Why?"

"I didn't mean to hurt you."

"You didn't. The wound did."

I carefully dab the last of the blood with the wet cloth, ensuring the flap is closed. "This is as clean as I can make it. I won't be able to wrap it until you're out of the tub, though."

He stands, leaving me at eye level with his well-muscled backside. His complete disregard for nudity is getting out of hand. I'm determined not to stare as he towels off until I realize that if he bends to reach his legs and back, the wound will hurt awfully and likely make him bleed more.

"Here." I snatch the towel before he can stop me, try to ignore the fact that I am standing right next to his naked body, and begin gently wiping the rivulets of water from his skin.

He sounds bemused when he says, "This isn't part of our arrangement. I am quite capable of drying myself."

"Not without significant pain, you aren't," I retort, sliding the towel up his thigh. Water droplets cling to the fine black hairs and trace rivulets down the unblemished skin stretched tight over his muscles. The King is pale, but not nearly so pale as I am, and is sun-kissed enough to suggest he spends at least some time out of doors. When does he have time to spend in the sun? The darkness of the Undercroft is complete. And I would be lying if I said that fact did not wear on me more than a little.

I cannot spend much time in the sun without burning and blistering, but I still miss the daylight. It is no wonder there was such a large chandelier in the great hall. People must have enough light not to go mad.

Which reminds me... "Someone tried to kill you."

The towel—and my hands on the other side of it—slide across the round muscles of his arse, and I fight to keep my attention on the conversation.

The amusement that has characterized his voice and posture the last few minutes evaporates faster than my anger had. "What makes you say that?"

I try hard to focus on what I need to tell him as I gingerly dry the area around the wound. An injury he received protecting me.

I swallow. "When Gwil escorted me out, I saw the bolt on the ceiling. There were fresh chisel marks in the stone. And someone notched the iron of the chandelier so it would shatter when it fell."

He turns to face me. Water droplets cling to the edges of his dark lashes as he searches my eyes. His eyes aren't any color I've ever seen: grey so dark that their splintered depth can only be appreciated up close. "You are sure of this?"

"My night vision is significantly better than yours. I am as sure as I can be without examining the ceiling up close."

He regards me for a moment as if I am a puzzle piece that does not fit, then his expression clears, and he nods once as if everything finally makes sense. "I suppose you will not get your father back if I die. You warned me, and I protected you. We are even, are we not?"

I hadn't been thinking of my father at all when I realized he was in danger. But if I tell him that, and he interprets my actions to mean I care about whether he is hurt, it will give him yet more tools to manipulate me.

He pulls a roll of clean linen from the medical bag and offers it to me. "Will you dress my wound?"

The roll looks too fine, too insubstantial to stand against such an injury. "You need a doctor. You must have one in the court. I'll tell Gwil to—"

"There are doctors, but none have a personal stake in keeping me alive."

Does he truly think the only reason I would treat his wound is to further my own goals? I cannot decide whether that is an indictment of him or of me. He presses the linen into my outstretched hand.

"Fine," I say, taking the fabric. "Will you tell me more about the search for my father?"

"Another negotiation? Very well. But not tonight."

As I wind the fabric around his torso, trying hard not to notice the way he winces when I near the injury, I search for something, anything to distract him and myself. And, almost as if my brain dragged the memory from some dark corner, the witch's warning comes to mind. *Betrayal. Fire, blood, and death. They are all in your future.* I am not close enough to anyone in the Undercroft for them to betray me, but the King is. The witch never said the betrayal would be against me.

"Is someone plotting against you?"

He stops breathing for a heartbeat. "What do you mean?"

"Well, aside from the chandelier," I say slowly, speaking as I think, "you've been stabbed, and I would have sworn you've come back wounded before. You encourage the people to think I am a white lady, and you posture as if you do not need guards or medical attention when you clearly do."

Tying the knot over the wound makes him suck a pained breath through his teeth, but there is no help for it. The dressing must be tight.

He turns and chucks me beneath the chin. "Someone is always trying to kill me."

My fists clench. This is nothing to dismiss. The more I think of it, the more certain I am that this is a matter he must take seriously, and he is brushing me off. "Why do you do that?"

"Do what?"

"Evade. Push aside my questions without giving me real answers."

He carefully slides a clean shirt on. "I wasn't aware our agreement involved me being questioned like a suspect at Scotland Yard."

I point at him and grind out through clenched teeth, "There! You're doing it again."

"And there you are, getting angry again. You know, I like your temper, Dove."

"Well I don't like—" It strikes me, all of a sudden, that I do not know his name. I have been thinking of him only as the King. And that, no doubt, grants him a sort of power. Power I would rather he didn't have. "What can I call you?"

He may as well be made of stone, he goes so still, and his voice sounds like it echoes out of the bottom of a cave. "Why do you ask?"

"Because I want to swear at you," I admit, flinging my arms out in exasperation. "I'm tired of you calling me Dove while I have nothing to call you."

"Your Majesty has a nice ring to it."

"Oh, go to hell," I growl and flop into the chair.

"Loot at that. You swore at me just fine without a name."

"Keep talking," I mutter as I fold my arms, "and I'll do it again."

"Swear at me all you like, Dove. I rather like it. It's more honest than anything else you've said." He eases onto the bed, grunting as he tries to position himself comfortably on his uninjured side. "But I am done answering questions tonight. Ask me again tomorrow."

I want to force him to answer my questions and take my warnings seriously, but I have won a small victory today. He's agreed to tell me more about the search for my father, and that must be enough for now.

Hopefully, I will finish repairing Ripper soon and gain the freedom to explore the Undercroft. If my backup plan is to work, I must know how to navigate the labyrinth of tunnels so I can give directions to the Chief Inspector.

Muses grant that it does not come to that. I don't have any reason to believe the King is not holding up his end of our bargain, but if he doesn't find my father and I am forced to reveal his secrets to Scotland Yard, I am not fool enough to think he will not have me hunted, hung, and flayed for my betrayal.

Sleep tugs at my eyelids, and the rhythm of the King's breathing soothes something deep inside of me. Perhaps I am worrying for no reason, I think as I sink into the chair and the fire warms my face. He said to ask him his name again tomorrow, so I am determined to do just that.

But when I wake in the dying light of embers, he is gone.

# CHAPTER 13

*I nearly asked him today. I thought I had the courage to tell Papa I wanted to apply for an apprenticeship with the Artisan's Guild, but he was frustrated that the new coil for the Aetheric Charger did not convert as much energy as he hoped. And since it was the only day he could work on the invention this week, his temper was short.*

*I tried to bring it up over dinner once I coaxed him into a more receptive frame of mind, but when I opened my mouth, the words were not there.*

*—From the Diary of Willow Bowbriar*
*October 20, 1870*

HE DOESN'T COME BACK. NOT THE NEXT DAY OR THE NEXT. I TRY TO ignore his absence, to tell myself I am glad he isn't here to irritate and frighten me, but anger at his abandonment—especially when he promised me answers—simmers below my every thought.

Nothing in our arrangement required him to stay with me or answer my questions, but being trapped in the dark alone weighs on me far more than I realized during my first few days here. The lack of sunlight to guide my schedule turns every day into one long continuation of the day before it, on and on, like time doesn't exist.

The only way to stop myself from stomping around the room and throwing a few objects at the wall is to focus on repairing Ripper, who has quickly become my favorite person in the Undercroft.

Time slips by, I sleep and wake, but the minutes have no meaning as I lovingly recreate every rune and symbol, both on the outside of his brass skin, and on the inside. My awl and chisel, the tap and clink of the hammer, and little threads of curling brass fill my mind.

Soon or late, depending on how many days pass, the dented pieces and my replicas are mirror images. But as I begin replacing the panels, I hear a hiccup in the steady pumping inside Ripper's chest: Whump-whump-*wheeze*, whump-whump-*wheeze*.

"What is wrong with your heart, my darling?" I ask though he cannot answer. Scrubbing the back of my sleeve over the grease smeared on my cheekbone, I peer through the hole in his side. The hydraulic pump is the size of my joined fists and hums as the pistons keep pressurized fluid pouring through his limbs.

He turns his head to watch me over his shoulder, ears pricked.

"I don't think it's anything serious," I reassure him. "I see all the expected runes to reduce friction and so on, but"–my wrench taps the thick metal– "that is not the noise your heart should be making. No wonder we didn't notice, with all these noise-damp-ening runes in your hide. I wonder if the damage to your side also jarred something loose. But you're not leaking, so that is a good sign. Still," I sigh and let my fingertips graze the bridge of his nose, "I can't seal you up knowing your heart is broken, can I?"

Ripper tilts his head and wags his tail. He truly is the most lifelike construct I have ever seen. I suspect that is due to the runes I do not know, the fluid symbols I've been recreating for days. I can etch those neatly with the tools I have available. But I do not have the proper equipment for opening the hydraulic pump. And though I scoured the market, it does not cater to artificers.

"You'll have to wait a bit longer for me to fix that hole in your chest, boy."

I need to fetch my pressure gauge and a few other precision tools from the Mechaninca. As well as my acid etching box. Working with secondhand equipment is fine for disassembly and engraving, but Ripper's heart is a complex piece that will require a delicate touch, and I doubt anyone here has tools to match those in my shop.

A glance at the mantle clock says it is half-past noon. Lunch should be on its way. I sigh and roll my shoulders to loosen the muscles. The schedule of meals is the only thing I can rely on in this place.

So, when someone knocks on the door, I call over my shoulder, "Yes?"

To my surprise, Silk saunters in with a covered tray balanced on one hand. "Afternoon, Dove. I was in the area so I figured I'd deliver your–blimey, you are a mess!"

Gwil closes the door behind her, but she doesn't notice. Her eyes are fixed on me, and she barely seems to realize where she sets the tray as she frowns in my direction. "You don't look like the same person."

My old grey dress has become my work uniform and is now smeared with grease, stained with oil, and sports several burns and cuts. Not to mention that I've cut off the sleeves to keep them out of my way. I am also liberally smeared with grime, and my hair is tied back, though loose strands hang down to tickle my neck.

Compared to the way the King has outfitted me, this must be rather a shock.

"This is what I look like most days," I shrug and hold my arms out as if to present myself for inspection.

She tilts her head to the side in a mirror of the expression Ripper gave me a few minutes ago, but she can put her hands on her hips, and he cannot. "You know, I can't say it doesn't suit you. Though, just between us, I think you could do with a bit less grease. Might want to get some of that dirt out from beneath your fingernails before you tackle this, though." She jerks a thumb toward the covered tray.

"There's no getting rid of it entirely," I say, pouring water into the wash basin. "Once the grime sinks into your pores, it is nearly permanent."

"If you like the taste of grease, who am I to complain?"

I tell myself to ignore the fact that the cake of soap on the washstand is studded with rosemary. It is only soap and means nothing. But the camphorous aroma tells another story, one of consideration. Which only makes the contrast between these thoughtful gestures and the rest of the king's behavior harder to understand.

"Will you stay for lunch?" I ask.

"I should really..." she starts, then looks at my pleading expression and rolls her eyes. "Hell, why not? You probably eat better than I do anyway."

We tuck into the roast chicken and potatoes, our flatware scraping our plates as Silk makes little sounds of gastronomic pleasure, like a kitten with their first bowl of milk. To be fair, the food is rather good.

"Where does everyone else eat?" I ask before swallowing the last bite of vegetable pie.

"There's a dining hall. Well, it isn't much of a hall, but it serves well enough. The full-time servants and Ratcatchers eat there. And those too sick or old to make their way without help."

"But not you?"

"If I want to pay for it. But I don't take the Divvy, so my meals are my own affair."

My eyes widen. So many people took the Divvy that we spent hours waiting for the line to finish. Granted, the amount of money I'd seen collected had been mind-boggling, but providing for so many people must be expensive, not least in terms of paying enough staff to cook it. Unless cooking is a chore rotated like delivering buckets of hot water for the King's bath.

"Is it paid for from the coffers?" I ask.

"Of course."

That information drops into place next to everything I've seen since being in the Undercroft, and the resulting picture leads me to an uncomfortable conclusion. "That's why you all swear fealty, isn't it? The court is like insurance."

Silk snorts. "It's quite a bit more complicated, but yeah, that's part of it. It's good to know you'll have something to eat and a place to sleep if everything goes wrong. That's something we don't get on the surface."

"And he says he's not altruistic," I mutter beneath my breath, shaking my head.

"Did you just call the King a dirty name? If you did," she says with a conspiratorial grin, "I want to know what it was."

"He might think it's dirty," I laugh. "I was just thinking about how he claims to be pragmatic, but so much of what he does is kind."

Silk chokes on a potato. "Kind? Has this place ruined your common sense?"

"He provides a place to stay and food to eat when people can no longer contribute. You wouldn't call that kind?"

"Everyone contributes somehow," she replies in a mysterious tone. "Let me ask you a question, Dove. Is the King finding your father out of the goodness of his heart?"

That makes me want to laugh. "I'm paying for that with my freedom."

She stares hard at me as if I have just answered my own question. So I ask, "You aren't free?"

"In some ways. But we pay taxes, just like you, and you've seen the King's justice. He doesn't mete it out often, but when he does, it is brutal. I would think twice before you apply the word *kind* to that man. I don't think he's needlessly cruel." She amends when she notices my expression, "But he is hard. And you'd do well to remember it."

Maybe she's right, but I don't want to fight with her about it. I've never had a friend other than Ethel, and after days alone, her company is too nice to risk. "It's probably just the darkness making me hallucinate," I joke instead, glancing around the room. This place is never what one might call bright, not even when every lamp is charged and lit. "I feel like a gnome trapped in the side of a hill." And that is no joke at all.

"See if the King will take you Upstairs, then."

An idea–a wonderful idea–strikes me, and I sit forward with both hands pressed to the table. "Why don't we go Upstairs together? I need to get a few things from my shop to finish repairing Ripper, and–"

"No. Absolutely not."

"But–"

Silk pushes away from the small table and drops the flatware. "Do you think I'm stupid enough to disobey the bloody Cutthroat King? Didn't we just discuss what sort of man he is? If he wanted you Upstairs, he'd take you there."

"We have an arrangement, and nothing in it says I have to stay here all the time."

"I was there; I heard it. You agreed to belong to him. That means you must do what he tells you to do."

I try to sound both confident and reassuring. "He never said I couldn't go to my shop. He never ordered me to stay in this room forever. And he gave me permission to repair Ripper. I'm not breaking any rules."

She shakes her head and chews her lower lip. "I don't think it's a good idea. Not with all the troubles."

"Troubles? What troubles?"

"The kidnappings, for one."

My brows draw together. More than a year ago, several orphaned children were kidnapped, and some were killed. The entire city had walked on eggshells for weeks, certain Jack the Ripper had returned and chosen different targets. "I thought those ended?"

Silk shakes her head. "It's not children this time around. But that's not the point."

"That *is* the point. My father was kidnapped. Is it possible their kidnappings and his are connected?"

"Not unless your father lived on the street," she snaps.

I want to ask more, but her glower is intimidating, and I don't want to upset her further. But I do want her help, so I soften my tone and try to steer our conversation back to my question.

"Silk," I say, taking her hands, "I would never risk losing my chance to find my father by doing something that would nullify my agreement with the King. And I would never do anything I thought would get you into trouble. But the King isn't here, or I would ask him. And I cannot stay trapped down here forever. If I don't see the sky soon, I will tunnel straight up through the stones. With my teeth, if I have to."

She snorts and pulls her hands out of mine to fold her arms. Her expression is disapproving, but a hint of a smile hides in one corner of her mouth. "I'd like to see that."

"I'm not a hostage. My service lasts only so long as we both abide by the terms. If you don't want to help me, that's fine. I'll go myself."

"You'll get lost in the tunnels."

I shrug as if that is a small matter, but a chill of dread makes gooseflesh shiver down my arms. In truth, the tunnels terrify me. But if I am with Silk, who knows her way around, and if we have a light? The hope of seeing the shop, of watering my plants—Muses, I hope they aren't dead yet!—makes me almost as desperate as I had been to fix Ripper.

"We could be up there and back in a couple of hours. No one would know we are gone. Please?"

Conflict is written in the wrinkle between her brows and the lines bracketing her mouth. For a moment, I think she will give in, and hope soars in my chest. But her lips firm into a thin line, and she shakes her head. "I'm sorry. Truly. But I can't take the chance of crossing the King. Even if you're right."

If she hadn't taken the tray with her when she left, I would have hurled it across the room.

EARTHQUAKE! I gasp awake, my hands flying out to steady myself on the shaking bed. The only light in the room is the glowing coals and a single candle I did not light. It takes me a few panicked breaths to realize the whole room isn't shaking; it's only the bed and the man sleeping next to me.

The King is bare-chested, with sweat slick on his skin, and his forehead is creased in a grimace of pain. His arms strain as he grips the blanket like a lifeline, breath coming in hard and fast. Now and then, his legs twitch as if trying to run.

When he whimpers, my heart squeezes hard. That is the sound a terrified child makes.

"Not again," he pleads as his head turns from side to side, dragging his dark hair across his forehead where it sticks in sweaty strands. "Please."

He is normally so confident that nothing in the world seems to touch him, not even when he is injured. Seeing him this way is like looking at another person entirely. With as many times as he has caused and smiled at my discomfort, I should go back to sleep and let him suffer.

But I cannot see him in pain like this and do nothing.

"Your majesty?"

"Let me go. I'll do whatever you want," he slurs. "Please. Whatever you want..."

When I touch his shoulder, his skin is cold. "Your majesty. Wake up."

He flinches away and screams, "Don't touch me!"

Whatever nightmare has dug its claws into the King, it isn't letting go. Pushing the blankets away, I climb to my knees so I can lean over him and take both of his shoulders to shake him. "Your majesty! Wake up!"

"Graah!" He bellows, rolling into a sitting position and bowling me over before I can brace myself.

He pins me to the bed and straddles my hips, his eyes open but wild and unfocused. My heart leaps into my throat, blocking my ability to scream though my mouth is open and my lungs are fighting to force out some kind of sound.

Just like when the chandelier fell, everything slows as my brain processes what is happening. His teeth are bared in a grimace of hate, pointed canines gleaming, the candlelight making them look longer than they should be. Even his eyes are wider and darker. With another scream of hatred and pain, he presses my right shoulder into the mattress with bruising force and draws back his right fist.

*Oh, Calliope*, he's going to kill me.

His fist starts to fall.

I manage to gasp the word, "Please."

Consciousness snaps back into his eyes. I squeeze my eyes closed as he strikes. The bed gives a terrible squeal, my whole body jerks, and springs pop. When my eyes open, the King's face is inches above mine. His fist is buried elbow-deep in the mattress next to my head.

Though his dark eyes are wide with horror, a grimace is frozen on his mouth, and a bead of sweat drops from the tip of his nose to run down the side of my cheek like a tear, but I am too shocked to cry.

His Adam's apple bobs, and for a second, I think he might try to finish the job. But he jerks away from me, leaving my ears ringing and my shoulder throbbing. When I sit up, he has retreated to the other side of the bed. His elbows are curled around his knees, and his forehead is pressed hard into the crook of his forearm.

He shudders with every breath.

"Are you alright?" I croak.

He looks at me, and his eyes are so haunted that if I stared into them long enough, I would see reflections of the nightmare that was torturing him. I scoot forward and force myself to lay a comforting hand on his shoulder. "You're okay. It was just a dream."

He flinches from my touch, staring at my hand in utter disbelief, then surges off the bed. It takes no more than a few heartbeats for him to shrug on a shirt, slide his feet into his boots, and stride to the door.

"Wait!" I call, but he only growls, "Don't," and slams the door behind himself.

For a moment, all I can do is sit in shock, my heart thumping unsteadily. If he can strike with enough power to sink his fist through a mattress, that punch would easily have staved in my face. He might have killed me.

Anger bursts behind my eyes, and then I move, too, pulling on my long coat and slipping my feet into my boots. If that bloody man thinks he can show up after days away, attack me in his sleep, and then disappear without answering for himself, he is sorely mistaken.

My cheeks and chest are so flushed they burn, and my shoulder aches as I take the chamberstick from the bureau to light my way, slipping the silver coin into my pocket out of habit. Part of my mind screams at me to be careful, that he might respond badly or end our agreement if I chase and make demands of him, but I have spent far too much of my time trying to abide by the rules to be careful and considerate, and where has that gotten me?

I hurry across the room and jerk the door open. No one stands guard. Of course, no one ever stands guard when the King is in his rooms, which is the most backward nonsense I've ever—never mind, no time to think about that. I scan the shadows, trying to catch movement so I can follow him, but the King is gone as completely as if he never existed.

Standing in the corridor with my blood pounding in my ears and my whole body shaking from the aftermath of nearly losing my head, I admit the truth: this was a foolish bargain. It will never work. I shouldn't have put myself in this position, no matter what my father's note said.

I'll go to the Inspector and tell him what I know. I refuse to stay in this dark hole for another second.

Before I can talk myself out of it, I take a piece of chalk from the makeshift workbench, kiss Ripper on his cold head, and leave that room for the last time. Seconds later, I'm striding through the empty corridors, one fist clenched, the other holding my sputtering candle aloft. I know my way to the great hall now and that the King brought me in through the farthest door on the left.

It's as good a place to start as any.

When I enter the room, I catch my breath. People are sleeping there, curled on the floor in makeshift cots and blankets, and the room is warm and humid from so many resting bodies. I hesitate, then pick my way down the center aisle, careful not to make a noise. The door out yawns before me, opening into a corridor so dark it may lead to the center of the earth.

I take it anyway. My candle should last several hours, and I can mark each path with chalk to guide me back if I cannot find my way by the time the candle is half burned. If I made it through the dark the first time, I can make it now.

"Hold on, there," a voice says.

I swing around, ready to hurl my candle at whoever is accosting me but stop in time not to fling hot wax at Silk.

She's leaning against the wall, cleaning her nails with the tip of a dagger, one boot braced on the brick behind her.

"Thought you might not listen to sense," she says in a tired voice, shaking her head. "Though I expected you to try and escape a bit sooner, I'll admit. I've been waiting quite a while. You owe me the supper I missed." She pushes off the wall, tosses her dark braid over her shoulder, and retrieves a dwarven lantern from the floor. When she touches the rune at the base, stored sunlight glows gently, reflected by a dozen mirrors, and lights up the corridor far more efficiently than my candle.

"You really set on this?" she asks.

The King's face as I last saw it makes the cold sweat of terror run down my spine. If he had not woken at the last second, he could have killed me. My shoulder still throbs, and if I unbutton my coat, I suspect I'll find a bruise blooming there. He broke our compact when he touched me in anger, whether he did it in his sleep or not.

"Yes. I am."

She sighs and lifts the lantern. "Let's go, then."

# CHAPTER 14

*Mr. Boragard says I am a natural. I don't know what that means, but he is very happy I can make the shapes he showed me. He says they're called runes. And he says it's good Mama taught me to read and write. I already know that. But he is nice, and he lets me eat anytime I want to. And I have my own room. If drawing the shapes makes him let me stay here, I will learn to draw them all.*

*—From the diary of Willow Bowbriar*
*February 8, 1848*

I THOUGHT MY FIRST BREATH OF FREE AIR WOULD BE THE BEST THING I ever smelled, but after a few weeks in the Undercroft, I've learned one inescapable fact: New London smells awful. The cold winter air generally stops scents from traveling far, yet the stink of manure, garbage, and the distant reek of fish—and worse—makes my nose wrinkle.

Silk watches as I crawl out the sewage drain that isn't actually a sewage drain and says with a cheeky grin, "Undercroft ain't so bad when you get a whiff of the Upstairs, is it?"

I cough into my elbow, then dust my hands on my knees. The ladder we'd climbed hadn't been used in ages and left streaks of grime on my palms. Not that I wasn't used to grime, but metal filings, grease, and oil or charcoal are a clean sort of grime. This mess stunk like leftover mud smeared on the soles of old boots.

"I did think I would be a bit happier to breathe the free air," I admit.

We've surfaced in a part of New London far closer to the Mechanica than the old church had been, and it's nice to know the walk home won't take nearly as long.

"If we'd arrived in daylight," Silk says as she leads me down the quiet street, "you'd probably feel a bit different. The sun does wonders for a soul."

That makes me sigh. She couldn't be more right. But, I think as I lengthen my stride, it will all be worth it when I lay in my bed.

"Don't forget what I told you," she says as we start down the street. "Keep your eyes and ears open."

This part of town isn't as wealthy as the West Side, and now and then, we pass people sleeping in their clothes, huddled in doorways, and curled against the cold. One man is awake, at least mostly, and his arms are curled around his knees. His lids hang heavy over bloodshot eyes, and the expression of dazed hopelessness on his face sends a sympathetic arrow through my chest.

The pause in Silk's stride is barely noticeable, and at first, I think she will pass him by. But she sighs and steps lightly onto the stoop, pulling a few coins from her pocket.

"Get yourself something to eat," she says. "You can find shelter at the Rusty Nail on Understreet. Tell them Silk sent you."

He clutches the coins against his chest and scowls at Silk, but I think it is more fear and less bluster. "You're her, are you not?"

She shrugs one shoulder. "Suppose it depends who you mean

by *her*. But the King owns that tavern. And if you haven't sworn your oath yet, you can."

He goes pale. "I knew it. You are her."

"*Her* is giving you a chance to get out of the cold." She turns to walk away. "Take it or leave it."

As we leave the corner behind, I glance over my shoulder to see the man scurrying away into the shadows in the direction of Understreet. "Will he swear to the King?"

"Likely not. Not yet, anyway. Those who haven't sworn already are usually one of three types: those doing well enough on their own that they aren't scared yet, those scared enough to know what they're getting into, and those new enough to this life that they don't know any better. He's new," she says, jerking her head in the direction he escaped.

"How can you tell?"

"His clothes ain't worn in the way they will be after a year or so. His boots are new, which means no one more desperate, or meaner than him, has managed to steal 'em yet. So he's probably fast enough to outrun them. That means he's eaten regularly enough to keep up his strength. For now. But it's the expression that mostly gives 'em away, the new ones. Like they can't believe chance could be as cruel to them as it is to the rest of us."

I chew my lips. It had only taken one roll of the dice to drive the Mechanica out of business and force me to sell myself to the most dangerous criminal in the city. Others may have more dice to roll, but chance has unlimited throws, in the end.

"Do you proselytize everywhere you go?" I ask, skipping to keep up with her long-legged stride.

"Only to those who look like they need it. I didn't swear my oath lightly, and I don't expect anyone else to."

We pass through a pool of electric lamplight, a sign that we aren't in the poorest parts of town yet, but we are close, and the confident swing in Silk's stride makes me wonder what could have forced her to swear away her freedom for the promise of the

Unseen Court. She appears more than capable of caring for herself.

I venture, "Why did you swear? If it isn't taboo to ask."

"It is, but I don't mind saying. I have someone to care for, and there was a time I couldn't do it on my own. I didn't know enough about surviving, and I was desperate. See that sign there?" She jerks her chin toward a bunch of scratches marring the door of a rundown bakery.

Even with eyes trained to notice patterns, I would never have thought to look twice at symbol if Silk hadn't asked me to. "It looks like a house with a circle in it."

She raises a brow in surprise. "That's it. It's a bit of Thieve's Cant. It means you can stay the night there unmolested if you're in need."

"Thieve's Cant? Is that like a language?"

"Almost." She turns right, and the red brick of the laundry makes my heart thump hard. We are close to Penny Lane. "It's more like road signs, telling you which way to go, where to fence goods, who will give you a meal, and who will turn you over to the bobbies. Sometimes, they can tell you if the owner will help you run a con and which ones they're prepared for."

"I had no idea," I say, my eyes searching all the familiar doors and buildings, looking for patterns hidden in plain sight for years.

She chuckles. "That's the idea, Dove."

My steps slow. I'd lived on the street as a child long enough to learn the hard rules: who would hurt you for fun or profit, who was too slow to catch you if you stole from them, and which territories to stay away from. But my father rescued me before I found someone to teach me the language of the streets. My stomach clenches at the fact that I am abandoning the best chance I had of repaying him, of rescuing him the way he rescued me.

"Did they teach you all of this after you joined the Unseen Court?" I ask, hurrying to catch up.

"More or less. They gave me the tools I needed to care for my-myself, and that's what matters most."

Her hesitation over the word *myself* catches my attention, but I she won't appreciate it if I ask who she is caring for. That seems like information members of the court would guard with their lives. But I don't get to wonder about it long because the familiar whitewashed brick ahead makes my chest constrict.

Penny Lane.

My pace quickens until the cold air stings my cheeks and nose despite my scarf.

"Slow down," Silk says, catching my arm.

"The Mechanica is just—" I begin, but her expression stops the words before they hit my tongue.

"You are in the most danger when you're confident. Familiar surroundings trick you into thinking you're safe. Don't go rushing in like a fool. You told half the Court that your shop is in trouble. That makes it an easy target."

"But the King said—"

"Not everyone follows the code," she says, shaking my shoulders once and staring hard into my eyes. "Especially not whoever is kidnapping people off the street. Treat everyone like they'll betray you, and you'll never be taken by surprise."

That makes a trickle of unease slide down my spine, but I nod. "At least there is nothing left to steal. I sold it all."

"You'd be surprised what things can fetch a price," she says with a wry smile. "Trust me, will you? Just take your time and pay attention."

*Beauregard's Mechanica.* The wood sign hangs on a pole, swaying in the breeze. Time has softened the engraving until the gears and tools are barely recognizable. But the metallic whine of the chain swinging is a familiar lullaby I've listened to every night for so many years that hearing it now makes my eyes sting with unexpected tears.

The key never left my coat pocket, and Silk stands next to me as I slide it into the lock and turn. My hands shake with joy or fear, and I cannot tell which. The place hasn't changed.

Light from the street lamps casts a hazy glow through the front window, making shadows cut across the bare wood floor. The rows of shelves, my workbench, and the counter sit as if waiting patiently for Ethel to breeze through the door or my father to plunk a finished repair on the polished wood and say, "Another for the strongbox, Ethel."

But a fine layer of dust covers every surface, and our breathing echoes hollowly. The shop is as empty as a hungry belly.

"This is yours, eh?" Silk says as she steps inside next to me.

My words are so soft I barely hear them. "It belongs to my father."

A dam breaks in my mind, and a hundred memories flood out: sitting on the counter watching my father repair a dwarven heater as he explained the way the runes store and release sunlight while snow fell soft on the dirty cobbles outside; my first solo repair, where I skinned my knuckles and made myself cry; my father and Ethel dancing down the aisle when we thought everything would be alright at last.

The life that created these memories is one he gave me. Am I truly going to abandon my best chance of finding him?

"Is he looking for my father or just manipulating me for his own purposes?" I ask the silence.

Silk bites her lips as if she has something to say but isn't certain whether to let the words pass her teeth. The toe of her boot scuffs the dusty wood floor, and she sighs. "The King's reputation is built on trust... or maybe I should say proof; proof that he'll do what he says, whether that is allowing a gang to claim new territory or punishing someone for breaking the code. But how he goes about things and why he does them is a mystery beyond me. Either way, I wouldn't break an oath to him lightly."

Fear crawls up my spine on pointy little feet. I brush the goose-flesh away with brisk irritation; too much of my life has been wasted on fear. I didn't break my word, and I didn't break the code. In fact, I've done nothing wrong.

Jaw clenched, I pull a leather pouch from behind the desk and gather the tools I need to repair Ripper. My mind and heart whirl with so many disconnected emotions and contradictory thoughts that my hands shake.

Whatever I feel, I cannot make sense of it... but there are things I *can* do.

I can repair Ripper. And I can learn what the King has discovered about my father. He cannot deny that I earned that information, at least. If I leave the Undercroft, it should be my choice, not because he scared me away.

The satchel full of tools is as heavy as the constant worry for my father and the rekindled determination sitting like a burning coal in my chest. I am done merely accepting what other people give me. It is time to start taking what I need.

I sling the satchel over my neck and shoulder and cinch the strap until it sits snugly against my back. When I turn to ask Silk to take me back, a furtive rustling, barely audible, comes from the back of the shop.

The heat in my blood drains, leaving me cold. "Silk," I breathe, sliding slowly in front of her, "someone is in my father's office."

A knife leaps into her hands, and Silk edges around me, stalking to the back of the shop before I think to stop her. Her movements are smooth, liquid, and perfectly silent. No wonder they call her Silk. She stops short, listens for a moment, and reaches for the handle while keeping her body free of the door.

If there is an intruder in the office, I need to do something, find a way to help. The shotgun is behind the counter, but the drawer is locked, and only my father has the key. I don't know that I could shoot someone, anyway. But the tool drawer is still open, and the wrenches are heavy.

As silently as possible, I draw out the heaviest wrench. The cold weight of it is comforting–and scary.

Silk takes a deep breath, sets herself, and turns the handle.

The door flies off the hinges as if from an explosion, and smashes into the opposite wall with a crack that makes me gasp. Silk leans back in time to avoid the flying debris, pressing her body flat against the wall as a hand—and a dull silver pistol—

emerges from the broken door. Her knife flashes like a striking snake as she drags the blade across the inside of the arm where the biceps meet the elbow, where the tendons are close to the surface.

The arm flinches. Silk follows up with a sharp strike to the wrist that sends the gun spinning away. A man leaps into the hall, his face twisted in fury, and the air in my lungs freezes. He has the same grayish-waxy skin and a black bowler hat that has haunted my dreams.

Silk wastes no time. Her knife flashes in half-a-dozen strikes as she backs him down the hall. Less light reaches the rear of the building where our storeroom is, but the grunting, swearing, and dull smack of knuckles striking flesh echoes back to me with stomach-turning clarity.

With a cry of pain, Silk flies through the air down the hall to land hard on her back.

I dart toward her, but she rolls in a backward somersault to disperse the impact and comes to her feet in a fluid motion. Blood stains her collar from a cut on her left cheek.

Fury rises to meet my fear. The battle between my desire to attack the man who hurt her and the need to keep myself safe locks me in place. The bowler hat materializes from the shadow. A cruel, hungry smile carved into his face.

He blurs forward faster than any human should be able to move. Silk barely manages to dodge the first blow. It glances off her shoulder, and she follows up with a series of kicks and slashes, but she cannot match his speed.

And now that they are in the open with more freedom to move, the fight becomes a whirlwind of vicious strikes. And Silk is losing. He bats aside her punch, kicks her in the leg hard enough to turn her knee, and punches her when she wobbles.

His knuckles make a dull, fleshy *thwack* against her cheek. Silk crumbles, lost beneath the black coat as he crouches over her.

Anger roars to life in my chest, burning away the last vestiges of fear and making my ears ring. The blood is so hot in my face that the edges of my vision turn red. My father never taught me to fight, but I *am* strong.

My wrench swings in an overhand arc with the force of my whole body behind it. I brace for impact but hardly notice the blow. He crumples.

I think I am shouting, though I cannot tell what I say. It might be, "Get off her," or perhaps, "Where is my father?" Either way, it is warped with sounds of animal rage.

When I come to myself again enough to realize what I'm doing, I'm straddling his stomach with the wrench raised over my head. Blood runs in a sheet down the side of his face, and his eyes are dazed.

My muscles freeze in shock. If I swing this wrench now, it will kill him. I will have killed a man. If he dies, he cannot tell me where my father is. And he knows. I know he knows. The embroidered symbol on his lapel, the S with a diagonal line through it worn by the Bowler Hats, l tells me it is no coincidence he is here.

His pupils constrict, coming to rest on my face and lighting up with recognition.

"Where is my father?" I pant through clenched teeth.

He stares at me for what feels like several minutes but can only be a heartbeat. An inhuman smile wrinkles the corners of his flat, dead eyes. "Sneaky girl. We lost track of you."

Dread, cold as a chunk of ice, drops into my stomach. But I cannot let him see how much his words bother me. "Where is my father?"

"You'll see him soon enough," he says.

Before I realize what is happening, the world spins, and I hit the ground so hard on my back that the air rushes out of me. The tools jam into my spine and ribs, and the back of my head bounces off the floor. White light flashes, swallowing the world for a stunned heartbeat.

My fingers flex, but my hands are empty. The wrench is gone. And the bowler hat sits on my chest, crushing the air from my lungs as he smiles at me. When he clamps his iron fingers around my throat, my heart stops.

When the King held my throat there was a warning in his touch, but he was always gentle, as if he'd been taunting me, daring me to respond. But this man has murder in his eyes, and his grip is fierce.

A burst of desperation makes me flail, twist my hips and kick, but I cannot dislodge him. He squeezes, and the edges of the world darken. Blackness closes in until only a pinprick of light remains.

I hope Silk will be okay.

AIR SCRATCHES down my throat in a painful stream. Hands pull at me. I try to make my limbs move, to force myself to fight back, but a sharp voice scolds, "Stop scratching me, you bloody fool."

Silk?

I blink several times to bring the world back into focus, but my hearing sharpens first. Someone is still fighting. Fear strikes like lightning, and I gasp as air finally fills my lungs. The oxygen makes me lightheaded, but it also lets my eyes focus at last.

Two men circle one another in the center aisle of the Mechanica like stray cats with raised hackles. The bowler hat's pale bald scalp gleams with reflected lamplight, and his eyes are fixed with deadly intent on his opponent... the Cutthroat King.

Silk pulls me deeper into the shadows near the counter, one arm wrapped around my neck and shoulder, the other gripping the silver pistol.

"We've been looking for you," Bowler Hat says. The light from the street lamps outside makes it clear that he is not one of the men who took my father, but the resemblance is uncanny.

The King spreads his arms as if in welcome. "You've found me. Congratulations."

"You've killed several of my brothers. I think it's time we pay you back for that."

Bowler Hat turns his back to me as they circle, and the King's face becomes visible. His eyes are flat and cold, like the eyes of a snake, but his smile is sharp enough to cleave flesh from bone. "You're welcome to try. As you may have noticed, your brothers were less than successful."

Bowler Hat reaches beneath his coat and pulls a knife from the small of his back. "Yeah, well, I've got something for that. We learn from our mistakes."

The King smirks, and then his face goes unnaturally still, as if all emotion has drained from his body, leaving only the predatory desire for blood. His voice is low and flat and as dead as the grave. "Apparently not. Say hello to your brothers when you see them."

They fly at one another on some unseen signal, becoming a whirling, slashing storm of furious blows. Bowler hat is inhumanly fast, but the Cutthroat King is something else entirely. He dodges and strikes with the fluid grace of a hunting cat, always an inch outside Bowler Hat's reach, sliding away from the dark blade and counter-striking with devastating force.

But he doesn't have a knife, and Bowler Hat already recovered from a blow to the head that should have knocked him out cold.

"Can't you shoot him?" I ask Silk past the painful knot in my throat. Muses, it hurts just to speak.

"I'm a serviceable shot, but I'm not *that* good. Be quiet."

After a few breathless moments, when it becomes clear that the King is playing with him, Bowler Hat's expression darkens. He cannot reach the King with his blade *and* avoid injury.

As soon as his intent changes, my stomach drops and my palms break out in a cold sweat. His plan is clear in the lines of his face, the set of his shoulders, the way his lips thin, and his jaw clenches. I may not know how to fight, but I know how to endure pain, and that is the face of someone preparing to be hurt.

Maybe preparing to die.

A whimper escapes my throat, the King's eyes dart toward me, and Bowler hat strikes. He charges forward, unconcerned about the danger, and slams bodily into the King. The dark knife flashes. The King grunts. They look down at the metal jammed into the King's chest as if neither can believe it is there.

Bowler Hat smiles. "Recover from that, you bastard."

He is still smiling when the King rips his throat out with a wet, tearing sound. I roll away from Silk and vomit.

"Majesty," she says a moment later, her voice pained. "Are you—"

"Fine. Get yourself to the closest healer. Use your coin. Return to court as soon as you're able and find me."

"Yes, sir. Dove?"

"I've got her."

Footsteps retreat. The bell above the door rings. I vomit again. My stomach muscles tense hard, forcing bile to sting the damaged tissue in my throat. Tears blur the world and slide down my cheeks as my stomach heaves until nothing else comes up.

The King's arms slide beneath me, turning me until I am cradled against his chest. I want to tell him to put me down, that he is hurt, but only a sob escapes. My body spasms in reaction, and I cannot get hold of a single coherent thought.

He says nothing, only turns and leaves the Mechanica at a ground-eating lope. As we pass the front of the shop, I cannot stop myself from glancing at the corpse and the dull black knife he still holds. My home is now filled with gore and bile, and the King's warm blood soaks through the shoulder of my coat as he carries me into the darkness.

# CHAPTER 15

*Papa has finally listened to sense and allowed me to hire a shop girl. If we are to make enough to pay our bills and finance his damned invention, I must spend less time with customers and more time with repairs. I must admit, having another woman about the shop is comforting. I had not realized quite how alone I felt until I listened to her hum as she worked.*

*—From the diary of Willow Beauregard*
*March 2, 1900*

TOOL HANDLES DIG INTO MY BACK WITH EVERY STEP, THOUGH THE King's feet make no noise against the cobbles as he rushes me down the darkened streets. I try to speak more than once but nothing comes out, and every time I open my eyes I am staring up at some new place: the cloudy sky of New London, the rafters of a derelict warehouse, the blackness of the tunnels in the Undercroft. It feels as if my head is full of water, and whenever we move it sloshes to the side, dragging the whole world with it.

By the time I can keep my eyes open and focus, we are flying past parts of the Undercroft I recognize. And my shoulder and side are warm with blood.

"You're hurt," I mumble, trying to get my lips and tongue to cooperate with my mind.

He dismisses my worry. "A flesh wound. You are not much better. How is your head? Still dizzy?"

"A little," I admit. "But I think it's getting better."

"Thank your parents for their elven blood. It gave you more than adorable pointy ears. Anyone else would have had a headache for days."

"My parents are dead."

That wasn't what I meant to say, and hearing it come out of my mouth sends a shard of old pain into my heart. I meant to say something about how my head injury is less severe than his chest wound, but forcing my thoughts into coherence isn't easy. Besides, if he is carrying me and holding a conversation, perhaps it wasn't as bad as it looked. Maybe he does wear some form of armor after all, even if Tildie has never seen it.

"In that," he says as he kicks open the door to our room, "we are alike."

When the door swings shut he elbows the bolt into place and looks down at me. In the soft glow of the lamps and candles—which hadn't been lit when I followed him earlier—his dark eyes seem to glow and his expression is almost tender. "Can you stand?"

"I think so."

He releases my legs, his opposite arm still behind my shoulders holding our bodies pressed together. His lashes are unfairly long. For a moment they are the only thing I can focus on, the way the light catches the fine tips and how they shade his eyes, leaving a dark shadow on his cheeks.

An embarrassed flush makes me drop my gaze. "You saved my life. Thank you."

He tilts my chin up to study the bruises surely forming on my neck.

"And you have ruined mine," he says, his deep voice soft. But his eyes are hard and hot. "I wish I could kill the bastard again."

A shiver runs down my spine and my stomach threatens to revolt for a second time. I don't want to think about nearly dying, but it is impossible not to remember what the King did to Bowler Hat. The strength it took to do such a thing... and the sound, it... I cannot wash it from my mind. And to run so many miles carrying me after he'd been stabbed—the flood of my thoughts dies to a trickle.

I'd forgotten about his wound. For the first time, I notice how much blood stains my coat. It pools on the ground beneath our boots, spreading along the surface of the rug, gleaming dull red. I barely catch the King as he falls.

His knees give out, and I wrap my arms around his waist before he collapses onto the carpet. It takes all the strength in my legs to hold him up at such an uncomfortable angle, but I haul him to the chaise and drag his limp body onto it before slinging my pack into the corner.

As if the emergency is some kind of drug, my mind clears and my senses sharpen. The lingering pain in my back, throat, and head dull and shift to the background, like the hum of conversation on a crowded street.

I would love to fall apart and cry myself to sleep, but I don't have time. The Cutthroat King is dying. A deep breath to gather all the worries, and an exhale to release them. Focus.

His shirt tears easily, exposing a laceration two inches wide in the rounded muscle on the righthand side of his chest. Dark red blood oozes out in a steady flow, and though it makes cold pinpricks of unease run across my skin, I sigh in relief. If the blood were bright red and squirting, he certainly would have died.

The medical bag doesn't have enough linen so, after ripping

the sheet from the bed, I tear it in half and fold one side several times before pressing the cloth against the wound and leaning on it with all my weight.

His eyes fly open and he grips my wrists, still impossibly strong despite how much blood he's lost.

"I have to put pressure on the wound," I say, trying to sound calm.

"There's still... a piece," he grunts, his face white, "inside."

Oh hell. I may be competent enough with minor injuries but I cannot do surgery. "Hold this." I transfer his hands from my wrists to the fabric. "I've got to find you a doctor."

He grabs me before I can leave him, but his grip weakens as his eyes lose focus. "No. No doctors. Willow, you must dig it—dig it out. Then I'll... heal. Call Tildie. Have her clean the footprints. Have her..." His voice dies in a long sigh and his eyelids flutter closed.

Damn the man's slagging hide! I remain frozen for a couple of breaths, pressing on the wound so hard I can feel his heartbeat through my arms. I could ignore his wishes and run into the hall, shout for help, and ask someone to find me a doctor. But who knows how long that will take? And given how much blood he has already lost, he may not last that long.

Swearing, I dig through the medical bag with one hand, keeping pressure with the other, until my fingers slide across the smooth, cold shaft of a pair of forceps. All I must do, I tell myself, as I release the pressure and wipe the pooling blood away, is insert the forceps and remove whatever is still stuck inside. Hopefully, I do not make his injury worse in the process.

I search the bag again and find a bottle of alcohol spirits.

Tearing the cork out with my teeth, I pour the liquid liberally over both his wound and the forceps. That will have to do, as there isn't time for anything else. Breath held, I plunge the tip into the wound. He doesn't so much as flinch. Is that a blessing, or a sign that it is already too late?

My teeth grind together as I lock my jaw and fish for whatever is still inside the wound. All of my attention narrows to the subtle vibrations traveling from the tip of the forceps up to my fingers. He said he would heal if I removed whatever is inside. Likely he was only half-conscious with pain and blood loss, but I cannot stitch the wound with a foreign body inside, not without risking infection.

So much blood leaks out that any hope of seeing the forceps move is long gone; sensation alone must guide my hands. Something hard grates against the metal surface of the instrument. I freeze. Was that bone? Carefully, I repeat the motion and the sensation moves. Definitely not bone.

The handles open a millimeter at a time, my breath hitches, I close the teeth gently over the object, then squeeze, ratcheting the jaws in place. When the tip slides free of his skin, a triangle of dull, bloody metal is locked between the teeth of the instrument. The tip of the dark knife must have broken on one of his ribs. Whatever fool made knives of brittle cast iron should be dragged and prosecuted. I toss the forceps—shard and all—on the table, and replace the dressing, pressing hard to slow the bleeding.

After that, it is only stitches, which is easy enough if unpleasant.

Done, I stare down at the inert body of the man who just killed to protect Silk and myself, shaking with weariness and hollow with shock. The stitches are neat, at least, and the flow of blood has stopped. His skin is so pale, and his cheeks so white, that he may as well have been carved of chalk. But his chest rises slowly, and his heart beats visibly—if weakly—at the base of his neck.

He is alive.

And he is covered in scars.

With trembling fingers, I pry his shirt open further. The King's body is no stranger to me now, and before this moment I would take an oath that not so much as a freckle marked his skin. But the scars crisscrossing his body are impossible to miss. While there are a few jagged marks one might expect of a life lived dangerously, dozens and dozens of perfect cuts also mar his skin. It is as if they were made with surgical precision. And, between his ribs, is a recent scar still slightly pink and puckered around the edges.

As an elf, I heal relatively quickly, but nothing like this.

"What are you?" I breathe, filled with a mixture of wonder and fear.

They say that many more creatures used to populate the world, ones driven away or destroyed by advancing technology. Once upon a time, monster hunters captured and killed were-wolves and vampires. But nothing I've heard in science or stories makes sense of what the King has done, save perhaps being a vampire. And, so far as I know, none have been seen on the island in more than a century.

The Cutthroat King is a monster, they say. Maybe they are right.

Whatever he is, he cannot very well tell me now. And *I* cannot afford to let him die. After covering him with a blanket and rolling the stained rug against the wall, I turn to the construct. "Ripper, protect the King."

He trots over the King's foot and sits, tilting his head at me as if to ask whether he's doing it right. An unwilling, but welcome smile eases the strain in my face. "Good boy."

All I need now is a knife, and to move as quickly as possible.


A SLEEPY, swearing Tildie follows me back through the maze of corridors leading from the great hall to the King's room.

"I know the way well enough," she grumbles, "no reason to 'urry an old woman along so."

"He wants you to clean the footprints and I think it's urgent." Besides, I cannot escape the premonition that something will go wrong if I am not in the room with him, and finding Tildie amidst the sleeping bodies in the great hall had taken longer than I liked.

"Clean the footprints? What does he mean by that?"

We stop in front of the door and I point to the bloody footprints leading into the dark. He'd bled down his right leg for who knows how long as he carried me back. "Those."

Tildie pulls her scarf aside to look down, and her eyes widen at the sight. "Ah. Well, that is a problem, ain't it?"

"When this hall has been cleaned, can you send for Gwil?"

Her eyes narrow to slits as she examines me. "Let me see the King, first." I hesitate too long, unsure how to answer, and the uncertainty on her face ignites into suspicion. "You'll let me see 'is majesty now, or I will scream the Undercroft down on your 'ead."

My teeth grind together. He's in a vulnerable state, and I cannot prove I wasn't the one who hurt him. But he did ask for her, which means he must trust her at least a little. Lower lip clamped between my teeth, I nod and lead Tildie inside.

"See," I say, gesturing to the King as he sleeps near the fire.

She shoulders me out of the way and stumps up to him, conducting her own examination. It is pointless to stop her. One has only to look at his face to know he's lost a significant amount of blood. She peels back the blanket and gazes at his chest.

"That's clean work," she says in a professional tone.

"He was trying to save me," I say, and she snorts.

"I bet that don't cover 'alf of it. Very well, duck. I'll clean the 'alls. But the King will be here alive when I finish, and so will you. I've somethin' to say that you must 'ear."

When the door closes behind her, I slide the bolt into place, kneel next to the chaise, pat Ripper on the head, and fold my arms on the cushion. As soon as my head rests on my forearms, sleep claims me.

I AM groggy and dizzy when Tildie finishes removing the evidence of the King's mortality, and supremely grateful she's brought tea and a breakfast tray with her.

"Best to keep up appearances for now," she says, placing the tray on the table I haven't bothered to clean. "Besides, you look more like a walking corpse than he does. Drink up."

When my stomach is full, I feel less shaky and the grogginess wears off. She leans back to rest her teacup on her stomach and stares at me in a businesslike manner, white hair a frizzy halo around her head.

"Listen well, duck, for this matters more than anything else I have ever said to anyone still living: you cannot let another soul—save Gwil, per'aps—know what has 'appened 'ere."

My shoulders droop. "I had hoped to bring in a doctor."

She shakes her head firmly. "Not unless you kill 'im after 'e's done with treatment."

"Kill him? Why in Calliope's name would I do that?"

Leaning forward with her elbows on her knees, she levels me with a fierce gaze. It doesn't matter that she is feet shorter than me, her presence and intensity alone are enough to take seriously. "'Ave you been 'ere all this time and still do not understand what the King is? What part he plays in the Unseen Court?"

"He...rules it," I say slowly.

She rolls her eyes. "He ain't a mere ruler, fool girl. He's the god. The glue. The tiger in the trees that mothers warn their children about. Don't you see? If somethin' happens to 'im, all this"—she raises her hands in a gesture that encompasses the entirety of the Undercroft—"falls apart. And so do the lives of everyone in it."

Thinking back over everything I have seen since being here, I cannot gainsay her. The entire system was built on the foundation of a single stone, one pivot point... one point of failure. He must preside over the Unseen Court, over the Divvy, he must both give judgment and carry out the punishment. No government supports him; it is simply the King. Alone.

I am almost breathless at how much pressure that must be.

"Ah," she nods and sips her tea. "I see you begin to understand. And that means, if he ain't well enough to sit in court tomorrow, you've gotta do it for 'im."

"Me?" I squeak, my stomach dropping.

"He chose you, though the Smith knows why. You've got to make it work till he is healthy enough, or all this falls apart and none of us make it out of 'ere alive."

"They would kill us?" My voice comes out in a disbelieving whisper.

"What wouldn't they do, if no one stopped 'em? Most is loyal to the King, true enough. But not all. Not all."

We stare at one another, and ice steals into my bones. With it comes a sense of determination nearly as cold. I am well and truly stuck. My home isn't safe anymore. I have no relatives. And the King almost killed himself trying to save me. Tildie and the others like her don't deserve to have their lives overturned because I was seven colors of stupid and ran home despite Silk's advice. They don't deserve to suffer because I was hurt. Because I was angry.

Even if it was justified, what does that matter to them?

I straighten my shoulders. "I will handle it."

SHE GIVES me a wan smile and raises her teacup in salute before launching into a lecture on the politics of the Unseen Court.

Every time his breath catches, every shift and groan, makes me dart to the bed to check his pulse, his breathing. I try to keep myself busy by finishing Ripper's repairs, but just as I am about to tighten the coupling on his pump, I realize with sudden dread that it has been an hour since I made sure the King was still alive. My breath catches. What if I missed something? What if he has been bleeding while I have been absorbed in my work?

My tools clatter to the table and I rush to his bedside, leaping over discarded parts to check his pulse, his dressing. But the blankets over his chest rise and fall, and the dressing doesn't need to be changed. My heartbeat calms and I can take a breath without feeling like something heavy is sitting on my chest.

Before the fight, I was determined to force him to tell me about my father. I'd questioned whether he'd really been searching or not, if he made a false promise as a ploy to use me as a pawn or a shield... only to discover he'd been injured more than once and had killed several men to keep his promise.

Men responsible for kidnapping my father.

The blankets slide back up over his chest, and I settle them around his shoulders, my throat tight. My presence, even under the guise of a powerful White Lady, isn't enough to pay for this much sacrifice. I scrub my hands over my face and stare at the sleeping king feeling unspeakably helpless and confused. How do I reconcile the man who saved my life, who does kind things he claims are motivated by self-interest, with the man who mocks and belittles and intimidates? With a man I've seen kill with his bare hands.

Maybe it isn't a mystery I can solve. But I can, at least, nurse him back to health. He hasn't gotten any worse, and that is a good sign. Of course, he isn't better, either. Sweat beads his forehead in a fine sheen, and he is still terribly pale from blood loss. He may sleep for days.

I cannot do in the meantime but watch and wait. And, perhaps, help protect what he has built, if I must. I drop another log on the fire to keep him warm and return to Ripper, determined to finish his repairs. Working is the only thing that stops me from imagining a thousand ways everything might fall apart. And what may happen to my father, in the balance. Because if the King dies, I have no leverage to use in my bargain with the Inspector.

With tools in my hands, I finally take a deep breath and let my worries fade. Each new panel fits Ripper's chest with precision as I close the hole one rivet at a time. The process is painstaking, but soon his neatly repaired heart is enclosed behind layers of artifice. He is whole again. Ripper wags his tail as I drag a hand down his head and back. Petting a metal dog may be ridiculous but he seems to like it. In truth, so do I.

"There we are, my darling. Brand new, and with a tuned-up heart to boot. And the King said you couldn't be repaired."

Ripper lays at my feet and puts his head on his paws, revealing the keyhole at the back of his neck. I've never bothered to ask about it since it seems to be in perfect working condition and I doubt the King would answer my questions, in any case, private as he is. But I have suspicions. With constructs being so rare and expensive, most artificers build a sort of back door to let them access the interior of their creations.

Whoever built Ripper could likely insert the key and reach any part of the dog they needed to. Or shut him down if he malfunctioned. Had they seen me drilling rivets, they likely would have had an apoplexy. Then again, artificers spend their lives building things, not repairing them. That is for lowly repairists, like me.

I trail my fingertips over the elegant scrollwork that decorates the keyhole, marveling at the precision of the craftsmanship. Something inside Ripper makes a little clicking sound, and I jerk my fingers away just in time to watch the keyhole turn, split into separate pieces, and slide outward to open like the blades of an aperture, leaving a hole in his neck. From the hole rises a delicate little platform, turning like the inside of a music box.

I crouch to get a better look, watching in awe as it locks into an upright position. A needle pops up, the point so sharp it would have been invisible if not for the lamplight gleaming along its length.

"What in the Muses is this? One of your secrets?"

Ripper, of course, doesn't answer, only wags his tail.

And I know neither what I did to call it up nor how to send it back. On a level I cannot properly explain or examine, I *want* to touch it, want to touch it enough that I am already leaning toward the point before I realize what I am doing. What that means I do not know, but I cannot deny the impulse is there, and it is strong.

"There is only one thing to do, I suppose. Ripper, you wouldn't let me do anything foolish, would you? You are supposed to protect me, after all."

He wags his tail in an encouraging manner.

Quickly enough that I don't have time to reconsider, I prick the pad of my pinkie finger on the needle. A stab of sharp heat runs from the tip of my finger, through each consecutive joint, and up to my shoulder. I stuff my finger in my mouth and bite back a groan. That should not have hurt anywhere near so much.

A drop of bright red blood sits for a heartbeat on the tip, slides down a channel in the needle, and spreads in a circle along the base of the mechanism.

Designs in Ripper's neck begin to turn as swirl as the device lowers and the hole closes again with a final *click*.

"Ripper?" I say, breathless now that the urge to touch the needle has been satisfied. "What have I just done?"

He stands, looks into my face with those bead-black eyes, and opens his mouth in a doggy grin.

Hopefully, I have not done anything permanent. Or dangerous. "Perhaps best not to mention this to your master, eh? I'm in enough trouble already."

Ripper makes a noise I can only call chuffing, though I did not see any lungs in his chest, and tilts his head.

"Well," I shrug and look around feeling rather empty. "There's nothing to do now but clean up our mess. I don't suppose you clean?"

He trots, rather noisily, to the scrap brass on the floor and brings me back a piece. It is one of the damaged bits of his hide. My palm slides across the metal. "It seems a shame to throw this away. I wonder..."

Several hammers sit on the table, just waiting to be picked up, and an idea forms; shapes twisting and bending to the rhythmic tapping in my mind. Now and then, when I worked at the Mechanica, I would take the salvaged pieces of repaired gadgets, the bits that would otherwise have ended up in the bin, and resolve to give them new life.

Pieces of old lamp, toaster, and heater might become a sculpture or a little model ship. I sold them when I could, but people don't come to a repair shop for art. And there was never much time between repairs. But there are still several hours left before bed, the next court isn't until tomorrow, and I would rather not think about what I will be forced to do if the King isn't awake and capable of presiding over it.

The day bears its own burdens, or so the saying goes. So I lay the battered piece of old artifice on the table, pick up a hammer, and set to work, letting the metal beneath my fingers distract me from the possibility that, if the King does not wake, this may be the last bit of art I ever make.

# CHAPTER 16

*I have finally saved up enough money for the aspidistra I have had my eye on. Mrs. Wincombe promised to hold it for me, as I was so close, and her plants have not been selling as well as she hoped this year. The extra hours in the shop have paid off, though my hands are sore. It will be worth it when I bring the lovely thing home tomorrow evening. Some-day, I will have a healthy enough garden that the pixies will find their way through my window.*

*—From the diary of Willow Bowbriar*
*August 16, 1880*

WHEN THE KING MANAGED TO SNEAK COSMETICS AND GOWNS INTO the wardrobe without me noticing, I cannot say, but the variety is overwhelming for someone who only owns two dresses and my work apron. There are standard walking dresses with high collars and long sleeves, a few lingerie dresses covered in lace and ruffles perfect for a garden picnic, gowns similar to the satin dress I first wore (the fabric so fine it is almost-but-not-quite transparent), and one—one —that may be suitable for what I hope to accomplish today.

Who can guess what the King had in mind when he ordered it brought here? But I am glad he did because convincing the Unseen Court that I am both fit and powerful enough to preside over them in the King's absence will require every ounce of persuasion I can muster.

And some I must fake.

The King wears authority like armor, letting him attend court in nothing but shirtsleeves and trousers. But he earned his place and his power. The court knows him and what he is capable of. I, on the other hand, am an unknown quantity, so I need quite a bit more help.

With a sigh, I pull the white silk gown out of the closet and begin the laborious—and delicate—process of working myself into it. I wish Silk was here to help. Not for the first time, I whisper a prayer to the Muses that she is safe and healing. And that I won't twist off any pearl buttons as I press them through the embroidered button holes.

It is undoubtedly the most stunning gown I have ever seen. Ivory and silver threads climb up from the hem of the taffeta netting that covers the wide skirt, twisting into the stems and petals of embroidered flowers in an overgrown garden. Crystals and pearls scatter the skirt like frozen dew drops and fall from the curved neckline like snow.

The sleeves, too, are studded with tiny crystals placed carefully on a net of silk threads as fine as spiderwebs, gathered at the wrists with lace that looks like hoarfrost. In fact, the entire gown appears spun of winter, delicate and cold. And just as a blanket of fresh snow reshapes the landscape, the dress transforms me into someone entirely different—reserved and imperious, someone whose demeanor conceals their true intentions just as snow disguises dangerous ground.

Though it is unlike any gown I have ever seen in structure or style, it suits the person I must pretend to be, which must have been the King's intention. If the court believes I am a white lady, why not give them exactly what they expect?

The chill of the dress and the new identity seeps through the fabric and into my bones, lending me the confidence of being more removed from my emotions than I have been since making our bargain.

To complete the picture, I leave my hair loose down my back and swipe rouge across my lips until they are red as blood. The mirror confirms that the woman staring back at me is not the woman the King carried into the room last night. I am gone, and she is someone out of a legend.

With a deep breath, I drop the silver coin into a cleverly concealed pocket, set my shoulders, and raise my chin. I am as ready as I will ever be. "Ripper, protect the King."

He leaps onto the foot of the chaise, though there isn't much room for him, and circles twice before settling down to rest his massive head on his paws.

After a deep breath to steady myself, I open the door.

Gwil stands guard, thanks to Tildie, and eyes me with shock and respect. His expression says the woman he sees is not the same woman the King paraded through the market, not the same woman who piled his arms with tools and pots of flowers. He will be test number one.

He clears his throat and gives me a respectful bob of the head. "Lady. Where is the King?"

I draw myself up and try to slip into the role I think the Court has imagined for me. "You are loyal to the King, Gwil?"

"Of course."

"Loyal enough to protect his life with your own?"

His face goes blank, and he tries to push past me and into the room, but I throw my arm out, summoning every bit of command I imagine a white lady would possess. And, to my utter shock, he hesitates just long enough.

"The King is alive, but he is not well. He returned last night with an injury. I've stitched and dressed it, but he is not strong enough to wake, let alone to oversee the Court."

Gwil has arms like a blacksmith and a scowl that would terrify a vulture. He turns the full force of them both on me. But he does not try to push past me again when he warns, "I will see the King, lady."

For my part, I pretend not to be intimidated. "You may enter, but be careful not to approach too quickly. Ripper guards him, and I would hate to see what his metal teeth do to flesh."

When I lower my arm, Gwil hurries in. Ripper stands and squares his wide shoulders. A hollow growl rumbles in his chest, and Gwil stops a few feet from the bed, raising his hands.

"Ripper, down," I say, hoping desperately the dog obeys me.

He stares at Gwil a second longer, then resumes his position but never lowers his eyes. I pull the blanket back, then carefully peel the bandage away just enough to show the edge of the wound. It is already closed, though the stitches remain, and the other scars—the ones that crisscrossed almost every inch of exposed skin—have disappeared.

Gwil swallows and rubs his chin. "Who did this?"

How much do I tell him? Exposing the King's weakness this way is already a risk, and I do not know how much Gwil is privy to. Silk warned me not to trust anyone, but I do not have many options unless I leave him and make my way to the Chief Inspector. The idea of doing so while the King is too weak to defend himself makes me nauseous, and I still do not know the way out of the Undercroft alone.

"He was injured by one of the men who kidnapped my father."

Gwil folds his massive arms, his jaw working as if chewing over his thoughts. After a moment, he shakes his head. "Then you should not go to court, lady. Stay here, and I will guard the door until the King is well."

"If the King does not preside over the court, what will happen?"

He clenches and unclenches his hands. He must know, as I have learned, that if the King fails in his duty, it will sew the first seeds of distrust. That if the people don't believe he can protect them—or worse, carry out judgment—the fragile structure of power that holds the Unseen Court together will crack.

And if they believe the King can be hurt? It will crumble.

I am taking a terrible risk in assuming Gwil values his position and the power it grants him enough to protect the King. If I am wrong, neither of us will live through it.

He regards me down the length of his broken nose. "What makes you think I wouldn't be a worthy substitute to sit on the throne in the King's absence?"

"Because they know you and your relationship to the King. If you sit on the throne, they'll see it as usurping his power. They cannot possibly make that mistake with me. I can't be anything more than a placeholder. And he has already proven what lengths he will go to to protect me."

For a stomach-turning moment, I am certain he will refuse.

"This is a deadly risk," he says.

"I know."

"I'm offering you the chance to stay safe."

"I know."

He nods and relaxes. "If you're willing to risk it, I'm willing to trust you. But you'd better hope you're right, lady. For all our sakes."

THE GOOD-NATURED, respectful silence that greeted the King when he walked into the hall so many nights ago does not accompany my entrance to the Court. Thieves, murderers, gamblers, con men, and street toughs greet me with the puzzled stares and suspicion of spectators at a cheap side-show carnival.

Which makes me the spectacle, I suppose.

As I glide toward the throne, I can almost hear their thoughts: who does she think she is? Where is the King? Thanks to Tildie's lecture, I knew they would react this way, and I stayed up far too late last night puzzling over how to respond. But knowing a thing is not the same as experiencing it. Especially not when I spread the skirt of my gown to sit with all the grace I can manage.

Their confusion and suspicion darken into something near violence when I sit on the throne, filling the air with crackling energy. It is a experience I am familiar with on a much smaller scale. Unhappy customers, particularly those who feel they have been misused somehow, often come to the shop prepared to fight. They point, scream, slam their palms on tables, and, now and then, threaten.

One person's anger does not compare to an enormous room full, however, and despite my madly pounding heart, I force myself to remain calm and removed. If a powerful spirit would not be afraid, I cannot be, either.

Gwil takes position on my left and flexes his muscles as he glares at the crowd. Though he is silent, his presence signals that the power of the Unseen Court is behind me. I hope it is enough.

"Today," I say, my voice hanging in the silence like the first crack of thunder before a storm, "I act as the King's voice and speak in his name. Bring forth your offerings."

The crowd exchanges frowning glances as if asking, will we listen to her? And then glare at me, trying to unseat me by the force of their eyes alone. These people regularly risk imprisonment and death, and if they attack me, no one will stop them.

My proximity to the King, and their fear and respect for him, are likely the only things making them hesitate. I can barely breathe, but I force myself to stare back, to appear unbothered as I lock eyes with one Court member, then another, dismissing them afterward as if they are not worth my time. My father's voice blends with the King's in my memory: *Don't let them see you cower.*

So I don't.

"You heard our lady," Gwil says in a booming voice. "Bring forth the chests."

His voice breaks the spell, and the Ratcatchers carry the heavy wood chests up the aisle. The familiarity of the ritual asserts itself, and though they are still uncertain and unhappy, the queues form, and riches are deposited until the chests are full to overflowing.

I permit myself to take a few relaxing breaths before the court is opened for complaints and try not to remember Ambrose's fate. No one batted an eye as he strangled to death. They would be much less concerned for me.

The chests are closed and carried away, and an expectant hush fills the room. Will they bring their complaints to me? If I render judgment, will they listen? No one seems to know the answer, and none dares venture down the aisle. All I know is that to make this illusion real, I cannot break first.

Minutes drag by in a silence that grows more charged with every breath. My skin crawls with the desire to move, to hide from the pressure of so many glaring eyes, but I remain still. Composed. Until an elegant human woman with dark skin and braids held in a coil at the back of her head pushes through the crowd.

She wears men's breeches and a simple vest, but several knives are sheathed on her hips, and the scars on her well-muscled arms say she is no stranger to violence. Leonie Delacourt, according to Tildie. She leads the Whitechapel Wraiths, one of the largest gangs in New London, next to the Cogburners and the Hounslow Hounds. Aside from the King, she has the most right to rule the Unseen Court, and the intelligence that glints in her eyes tells me she knows it.

She stops short of the stairs to the dais, hands on her hips. "Where is the King?"

I prepared for this question, yet it still makes my stomach clench. "The King is keeping his word to me. He asked me to sit in his stead."

That is an outright lie, and I pray they do not catch it.

"He's never done anything like this before," she says with a glare.

"Has he ever made a public arrangement like mine before?"

She doesn't answer, and that is answer enough.

"All things change," I say, trying to sound as if I can see all the things that might. "But I swear that I will be fair in my judgments. And when the King returns to the next court, he will confirm all I say. Or I will deliver myself to the people for justice, and you shall decide on and execute the punishment yourself."

I can all but feel the tension build in Gwil's body, but this is a risk I must take.

Leonie narrows her eyes. Such a pronouncement before the court, one that gives her the ability to decide the fate of someone to whom the King has extended his authority, adds the appearance of his support to the power she already holds. It lends additional legitimacy to the Wraiths in the eyes of the people.

That is a serious temptation, particularly if, as Tildie said, the Wraiths are in conflict with the Cogburners for control of smuggling along the Thames in Tower Hamlets.

If she pushes me here or denounces me, she will lose the appearance of his support. But, more dangerously, her condemnation will carry the weight of her authority with the people. And their eyes tell me they are looking for any excuse to drag me off the King's throne, whether Gwil supports me or not.

A human man edges toward the center aisle behind her, his workman's shirt open enough to reveal the teeth of a cog tattooed on the pale skin of his upper chest beneath his black beard. His rather impressive forearm muscles ripple as he flexes his grease-stained hands and glares at me.

That must be Rufus, the leader of the Cogburners. He fits Tildie's description exactly, so the anger radiating in my direction is understandable. If Leonie accepts my offer, it will give his rival an advantage in the people's minds. It isn't a direct endorsement, but it would be one more weight on the side of the Wraiths on a scale that has balanced precariously in the Unseen Court for years.

Then again, if Leonie denounces me, there may not be an Unseen Court left to worry about.

I have to trust Tildie's judgment. "Leonie is hard," she'd said last night, "but clever and strategic. She cares for her folk. Rufus does, too, in his way, but he's like a guard dog who's been kicked one too many times. It's all brute force with that one."

If I must associate the throne of the Unseen Court with one of those two groups, a clever, strategic woman seems a much safer choice. Unfortunately, that may not protect me from Rufus, but what choice do I have?

Merciful Calliope, I am going to be sick. If Leonie doesn't accept my offer, I probably won't live out the night, and she knows it. She must also feel the malice of her rival because her eyes cut once over her shoulder toward Rufus, though her head never moves. He is tapping his fingers on a knife hilt at his belt.

Decision flashes in her eyes, and she raises her chin.

# CHAPTER 17

*Papa said he cannot protect me from angry customers and that tears will not help. He will not always be there to stop them from yelling at me, and I must learn to handle their tempers. But they are much meaner to me than they are to him.*

*—From the diary of Willow Bowbriar*
*November 19, 1875*

LEONIE NODS ONCE. "I SUPPOSE WE'LL SEE THEN, WON'T WE? DO THE Ratcatchers agree to this arrangement?"

Relief rolls over me with such force my knees would have gone weak if I wasn't sitting. Gwil, of course, has no choice but to nod, promising that the Ratcatchers will see that I hold up my end of the deal. I cannot tell whether that makes me feel better or worse.

When Leonie rejoins the crowd, her tacit acceptance of my power puts another pillar beneath me, another support for my temporary claim to the King's authority. When he wakes, I may just topple off that pedestal and break my neck, but I will worry about that later.

With her approval, the rest of the court seems to relax. Everyone but black-bearded Rufus, who glares daggers at me. When he eases back into the crowd, five or six other men and women of different races gather around him. Their collective fury radiates like an overheated teapot. Other court members shuffle away, giving the angry Cogburners plenty of room.

I shoot a look at Gwil, but he caught the entire byplay. He nods. All I can do now is get back to business. With a gesture, he urges the waiting Ratcatchers forward.

They drag the limp form of a man down the aisle toward the dais. The woman striding in front of them bears the black band on her arm and carries herself with the authority of someone used to taking charge. She glances once at Gwil, who gives her a subtle nod, before turning her attention to me.

"Mr. Coulter," she says. "We found him hiding in an expensive hotel on the other side of the river. Looks like he's been spending his money rather freely. Three of Charla's girls were with him."

Mr. Coulter. The man the King called out at the last court for not paying his tithe. The Ratcatchers haul Mr. Coulter to his feet, and the woman slaps him hard across the face once. I do my best not to flinch as he gasps and jerks upright, his eyes blinking in bleary confusion. I must become what the people think I am, what they need me to be to maintain the King's authority.

"Do you know where you are, Mr. Coulter?" I ask.

He struggles to focus on me, and I use the moment to let my mind race over how he should be judged. My heartbeat pounds in my fingertips.

"I'm... in the court," he mumbles.

"And do you know why you are here?"

He looks down at himself, at the expensive velvet vest with torn seams and popped buttons, and the fine wool trousers stained and torn at the knees. When he raises his eyes to mine, they are wide with fear. At least until he realizes I sit on the throne and not the King. His confusion quickly gives way to visible relaxation.

"It is only a small matter, Your—that is, my lady? Only a small matter. I was unaccountably detained during the last court, you see." He straightens his clothing and dusts off his trousers, giving the Ratcatchers dirty looks before smiling at me. He is a handsome man used to getting his way, to using his looks and charm to convince women to let him do what he likes. Those kinds of clients are not rare, and I have dealt with more than my fair share when Edith is not at work.

He separates himself from the Ratcachers and says, with humble contrition so false I can smell it, "I would have been here if I could have."

"Then I assume you have your tithe with you?"

"Well"—he opens his hands—"it just so happens that Charla's girls cleaned me out. But I will bring triple to the next tithe, my lady."

The way he says my lady makes my skin crawl. "Tell me, Mr. Coulter: does the King accept payment in installments? Does he extend credit?"

"Well, no, but—"

"Does he accept excuses?"

The charming smile falters. "My lady—"

"Does he?"

Panic enters his tone and tugs at the formerly confident expression. "Perhaps in this case, he would... be lenient."

"The money you squandered helps care for the most vulnerable among us. You failed in your responsibility, broke your oath, and abandoned them in favor of your own pleasure. And you believe he would excuse such action?"

"It's not... That isn't what I did, lady, if you just—"

"Judgement!" someone shouts, and their call is raised by others who stare at him with hungry eyes. They want violence, but I am not prepared to have a man killed. Hopefully, the crowd will find my solution acceptable.

I sit through their shouting, waiting as I have been doing, trying to seem unmoved, though just controlling my breathing is harder with every passing moment. I am a mere repairist; I don't have the skill or knowledge to do this. But I have no choice.

When the shouting dies, I announce, "Since you defrauded this court and its most vulnerable members, you will now serve them. You will wear only what they can afford. Eat only what they can afford. Sleep where they sleep. The value you stole will determine the length of your service, to be paid at the rate of the average dock worker, which is the only job I suspect you have the practical skills to attain."

The color drains from his face. "But that will take years!"

"Then I suggest you get started."

The Ratcatchers take his arms as he lunges away. Desperation carves deep lines around his mouth when he pleads, "Take my pinkie instead! Or a toe! Lady, please!"

I force myself not to blink or flinch as they drag him from the room to the cheers and jeers of the crowd. "See that the Ratcatchers are rewarded according to the King's terms," I tell Gwil, and he gives me a solemn nod, though his eyes shine with approval.

The next few complaints are simple compared to the first, and the crowd relaxes as I pass judgment. My decisions are gentler than I suspect the King would hand down, but as there aren't many and I must—hopefully—only do this once, I trust that I can't do too much damage.

When no more complainants approach, I ask Gwil for a glass of wine and swallow the whole thing before accepting supplicants. "Another, please."

"Yes, lady."

I do not drink generally, but the wine buzzes through my veins, and I settle a bit before the first supplicant approaches. It is a boy no more than twelve. A rope belt keeps his rags from falling off, and strips of dirty fabric are wrapped around his hands and bare feet. I swallow and fight back the tears. Now is not the time to cry.

He chews his lip and refuses to raise his eyes. "I... I come to swear to the King."

Tension springs to life in the air of the hall as people mutter and shift their weight. Several hands stray to the butts of pistols and hilts of knives. The hair on my forearms stands on end. I must walk carefully.

"Look at me."

When he raises his head, the leftover ink of a single tear is smudged high on his right cheekbone. "You were a member of the One Tear?"

He nods.

"They cast you out?"

Another nod.

I had run-ins with the One Tear gang when I was young. As the largest and oldest gang of street urchins in the city, the One Tear controls a substantial amount of territory in the Eastside Narrows. They have no authority over adults, of course, but most adults are not stupid enough to poach in that part of the city where the children swarm through the sewers and over the rooftops. A dozen orphans lobbing rocks at your head from the roofs of nearby buildings is not how anyone wants to spend an evening.

Besides, there isn't much to steal in that part of the city, anyway. But the One Tear is fiercely loyal. Until a child ages out— somewhere around fifteen, if I remember correctly—they are family. He must have done something unforgivable to be kicked out.

"What is your name?"

He sniffs and rubs the back of his sleeve over his cheek, removing the rest of the ink and the last trace of the single tear they use to commemorate their lost parents, their lost innocence. "Isaac."

"I cannot accept your oath, Isaac."

His face falls, and he presses his lips together hard to stop his chin from trembling.

"Only the King can accept an oath of loyalty. Do you have a coin?"

The hesitant hope in his eyes is painful, and I have to clench my teeth against the sorrow. "No, ma'am."

"Very well. Can you help in the kitchen until the next court, when the King will accept your oath?"

The tension that had been building sighs out of the room as the people finally believe that I am not here to usurp power. The expressions on their faces now are thoughtful.

"Yeah," he says, gaining confidence. Yeah, I can do that."

"Good. Gwil?"

"Yes, my lady?"

"See to it, please."

Gwil makes a lazy gesture, and one of the Ratcatchers appears as if out of nowhere to lead the boy from the room. His poor feet are purple with the cold. I don't think I can do this anymore. The remaining wine goes down as easily as water, and I hold the glass out. Someone refills it, though I don't bother to see who. This is almost over. I must last just a little longer.

With every supplicant, I repeat the phrase, just a little longer. A little longer.

My head is swimming by the time the last man approaches the dais. He is one of the most beautiful people I have ever seen: dark-skinned, with full lips, shining curls, and the slightly upturned eyes common to many elves. The tips of his pointed ears are red, and a bruise colors his high cheekbone.

He looks like a man more than uncommonly down on his luck, and his eyes have the look Silk described, like he is still in shock that the cruelty of the world touched him, too. But something about him, something compelling, makes it difficult to look away.

When he says, "I have a coin," and holds out his hand, a wave of desire to take it from him washes over me. I want to help him, to promise him anything he needs. Swallowing back the desire may only be possible because of the wine. But even other members of the court stare at him in admiration.

"Are you seeking the King's protection?" I ask, impressed I forced the words out.

"Yes."

"Very well, you may give the coin to me. I will deliver it to him. But you must wait to take your oath until he is present."

Worry creases his brow. "I was told to deliver my coin directly to the King."

I don't want this stranger to be displeased with me. I cannot help but think that he will smile at me if I drag the King from his bed so he can drop the coin into his hand. And when I imagine the stranger smiling at me in gratitude, it sends a little thrill of need down my spine.

"Are you questioning my lady?" Gwil demands, his voice hard. The sound of it stops me from rising to offer my assistance in whatever way the man needs.

The stranger blanches, but then his eyes lock on Gwil's, and something skips between them, like the current in a bit of artifice.

He shakes his head. "No, of course not. Forgive me, my lady. Please, take the coin."

When he drops it onto my outstretched palm, a wave of pleasure washes over me, one so strong I must bite back a smile. "You are welcome to stay in the Undercroft until the King calls for you," I manage as I stand. "This brings the court to a close."

I do not know whether that is the manner in which the King closes the court, but I don't care. I have to get out of the hall. My hurried stride is anything but graceful or stately, but if I don't get away from that man, from the stares, from the pressure, from the pain of those who are lost and desperate, I'm going to scream.

Halfway back to the room, I realize the wine glass is still gripped in my right hand. And when I shove the door of our room open, my head is swimming, and tears roll down my cheeks.

"You did well, lady," Gwil says as he pulls the door closed, and his voice is kinder than I've ever heard it.

My whole body is shaking, and the coin in my left hand bites the skin of my palm. I lean against the door and close my eyes, taking shaky breaths. It is over. My hope of finding my father hasn't been lost. It is over, and we are all still alive.

"Dove?"

The deep, scratchy voice from the other side of the room makes me catch my breath. My eyes fly open. Before I can think, I am kneeling next to the King. "You're awake! How do you feel?"

Some color has returned to his cheeks, which are still sharp but less hollow, and the bruising beneath his eyes is gone. The fact that he is awake after losing so much blood is a miracle in itself. Elves heal faster than other mortals, but we cannot replace so much lost blood in mere hours, and the King is only human.

His eyelids are heavy, half obscuring his irises, but he still manages to level me with his gaze. "What have you done?"

# CHAPTER 18

*A new boy delivered the mail today. He said he's taking his uncle's deliveries since his rheumatism has gotten worse. He has long lashes, and when he smiled at me, I thought my heart would stop. Papa asked me what I had done to bring so much color to my cheeks. I said it was just a difficult repair.*

*—From the diary of Willow Beauregard*
*July 21, 1883*

"DON'T WORRY," I SAY IN AS SOOTHING A TONE AS I CAN MANAGE under that glare, "I protected them. It's alright."

His hair has fallen in curling locks over his forehead, and something, a maternal instinct perhaps, makes me want to brush it out of his eyes. I was very young when I lost my mother, but those comforting memories are strong enough that I find myself reaching for him before I can stop myself.

But he jerks his head back and grinds out, "Don't touch me."

An echo of his nightmare.

I withdraw slowly enough not to alarm him and keep my voice soft. "You're safe. The court is safe. It's alright."

His eyes roll as if he is about to pass out, but he focuses on me with effort. "Tildie. The footprints—"

"Gone. No one knows, save us and Gwil."

"Gwil?" He falls back onto the cushion and sighs in relief, letting his long lashes rest against his cheeks. Within seconds, his chest rises and falls in a slow, steady rhythm, his lips parted slightly. The lock of hair still rests on his forehead, but I bite back the urge to touch him.

In sleep, he looks younger. Not boyish. I don't think a face so sharply carved could ever look boyish. But the razor edge forever in his eyes and the corners of his mouth has softened into something almost like peace. For a moment, I wish to the Muses, the heavens, and even the dwarven Smith that I was a painter so I could capture the way firelight caresses the planes of his face.

He came so close to dying. And to taking whatever knowledge he has gained of my father's kidnappers with him.

With a deep sigh, I begin peeling myself out of the gown and hanging it carefully in the closet. It would have been a joy if I hadn't been forced to wear it in such trying circumstances.

"You did your job well today," I tell the fabric, letting my fingers run over it one last time.

I didn't fail terribly, either, which is something. My hope of finding my father hasn't been dashed, and the court hasn't collapsed. But the King is still weak, so I may be forced to attend the Divvy tomorrow without him. After promising the court he would return quickly, I will need something more affecting than a dress to convince them he gave me the authority to sit on the throne.

I pace back and forth, striding from the bed to the work table, chewing on my lower lip. The King has cultivated a reputation for being invulnerable, and that belief has protected him, at least until now. I need something like that, some sign beyond merely a fancy dress and unusual hair that I, too, have a sort of armor.

Perhaps I can craft something. After a quick inventory of what I have to work with, a dangerous idea pops into my head and makes me stop and hold my breath. Most of the time, my work only requires me to repair artifice, but that doesn't mean I do not understand it. I passed the apprenticeship exam, after all.

"What if I can create a gadget, a tool that will protect me the way the King's reputation protects him?"

Ripper raises his head and wags his tail at me.

"If you like the idea, that's good enough for me."

While I sketch my ideas, I mutter my plans to Ripper. "I'll need a runic sentence strong enough to draw and hold the static electricity and a release mechanism of some sort to funnel excess energy out of the metal, as well as something to insulate my skin. Wool should do the trick. I hate to cut up my coat, but a bit off the hem shouldn't hurt much."

The sketch comes to life one frantic line at a time. If I make a mistake, I will electrocute myself, but if the bracelets work as planned? I may just pull this off.

\* \* \*

THE DIVVY IS only minutes away, I haven't slept, the King is still soundly unconscious, and I still haven't tested my new gadget despite staying up all night to craft it.

"I just need to finish this line," I tell Ripper, who has been watching me faithfully since yesterday. "My father always calls this rune the 'escape hatch.' It funnels excess energy from the metal in the form of heat so the piece doesn't turn into a small bomb."

The tip of the awl traces through the copper, leaving a thin, curling trail of scrap metal lying on the table. "There! They're finished! It took longer than expected," I say as I slip the twin bracelets on and fasten the clasps, "but they are ready. Unlike myself."

I practically dive into the closet and pull the white silk dress from its hanger. From my experience, the Divvy is less formal than Court, but if I really want to create this illusion, I must make it as influential as possible. And that means I must look the part.

A knock makes me jump and hold the open bodice against my chest with a gasp.

"It's time, lady," Gwil calls through a crack in the door.

Calliope's voice, I'm out of time. "One moment!"

My fingers fly over the buttons, and I pull out at least a handful of hair as I drag the brush through my tangles. Static electricity makes several white strands lift off my shoulders, and I have to dampen my fingers to calm them. After a hasty swipe of rouge and instructions to Ripper, I jerk open the door.

Gwil's fist hovers in the air just before my face. "Ah. There you are. You've company today."

Silk leans against the brick wall, her arms folded and her dark eyebrows raised. "Special occasion, is it?"

"You're alright!" I pull her into my arms, ignoring her squeal of protest and holding on until I'm certain I won't cry. "Muses, I was worried about you!"

She pries my arms off and steps out of reach. "I'm fine, but I'm not clean enough to rub against that dress. Good god, Dove. Have some sense. "

"Will you come to the Divvy with me?"

She shrugs. "Why not? So long as Gwil doesn't intend to chase me away."

He rolls his eyes, locks the door, and gestures at the hall.

Silk eyes me as we walk, and her examination makes me fidget until she finally asks, "Did you sleep at all?"

"A bit," I lie. I didn't, but I don't need more doubt cast in my direction. I have enough for both of us.

"It's a good thing you don't have to do more than stand there. Is the King waiting? He told me to present myself once I was healed."

Gwil's shoulders stiffen, which I take to mean it is better if Silk does not know why the King isn't present. "No. We are on our own today, I'm afraid."

My voice sounds suitably nonchalant, but Silk makes a choking sound. "What are you on about?"

"The King is keeping his promise, and he left me to oversee the Divvy."

The way she stares makes me tug at my sleeves. It was tricky buttoning the cuffs over my new copper bracelets, but as far as I can tell, they are invisible beneath the thick layers of lace.

She takes my arm and slows our pace until Gwil is far enough ahead that he cannot hear when she leans in and whispers, "Are you mad?"

"I don't have a choice."

"You always have a choice!"

I bite my lips together, frustrated that I cannot explain everything to her. And she isn't entirely wrong. Perhaps I am mad. "I know what I'm doing."

"Do you? That would be a nice change of pace. Look"—she grabs my shoulders and pulls me to a stop, her voice urgent—"If you're going to take your life in your hands, at least make it worthwhile."

"What do you mean?"

She glances over her shoulder, but these tunnels are far from the wider thoroughfare most members of the court use, and no one is close enough to overhear. "Don't reach for power unless you can actually grab it. But if you must, then hold onto it tightly enough to keep yourself safe."

Gwil turns and gives us a glare made threatening by slanting torchlight and heavy brows. There's no time to talk about this more. With one last, serious glance, the two of us hurry to catch up. I swing my arms as I jog along, letting the friction of the wool against my skin generate enough energy so the runes can absorb and store it.

I haven't had time to test them properly, so hopefully, I will not have to use them. If I haven't created the proper funnel and direction for power, activating the bracelets could blow my hands off. And I would rather not think about that.

My entrance today is nowhere near so dramatic, but the lines have already formed, and hungry people have more important things to worry about than who oversees the Divvy. I sit, and Silk slides off to the side, not in the shadows but clearly not part of the assembly. The Ratcatchers open the strong boxes, and money begins changing hands. The first hour runs so smoothly that I begin to relax.

Perhaps I will not need to use my gadgets after all. Perhaps I don't have to risk electrocuting myself, and everything will be—

"It ain't enough, I'm tellin' you."

The woman growling at the Ratcatcher looks too small for such a powerful voice. She is thin as a rail, with dirty brown hair falling out of her kerchief and smudges of dirt on her pale cheeks. The tiny, squirming bundle clutched to her chest makes a mewling noise.

A baby.

"It's right here," the Ratcatcher says, annoyed as he pokes at his list.

"But Emma weren't sick then!"

The raised voices make the baby let out a long squall of displeasure, and the woman pats the child's back unconsciously as she visibly fights to calm herself and lower her voice. When she bends over the table, the corner of the blanket falls away to reveal a pinched red face and fuzzy brown hair. "When I signed up, I just needed enough to get us through. But when she got sick, she stopped takin' my milk. I've 'ad to find a wet nurse. I can't see no gentleman on account of her cryin' and—"

"What I can give you is what's on this list. If I gave everyone more who asked for it, there wouldn't be none, see?"

"But—"

"Here, now." An elderly woman pushes her way out of the line and waves her arm. "Give her a bit of mine. I can do well enough till Divvy."

The Ratcatcher is growing flustered. He stands and puts both hands flat on the table. "People get what they get, you hear me? I won't be accused of not doin' my job. Now shut up and get back in line."

Cowed, the old woman edges back into the queue.

"Increase her Divvy," I hear myself say before I realize I've spoken.

Silk closes her eyes and sighs through her nose. Not a good sign. But it's too late now, and I do not care.

The Ratcatcher turns to me, his face red and his mustache bristling with fury. "I been charged by the King to do this duty. By the King, hear me? I don't know who you think you are—"

Gwil unfolds his arms and steps forward, but I hold up a hand to stop him. The baby continues to cry.

"—but I don't take orders from the likes of you!"

The other Ratcatchers are glaring at me, too, likely thinking I am overstepping my authority. If they revolt, there is nothing I can do. A few crowd members also send worried glances in my direction, likely wondering whether there will be enough left for them if I force the Ratcatchers to give away too much.

They would never question the King, but I am not the King. And this is dangerous ground. I should be careful, considered. But I'm no longer thinking about how to position or protect myself, or how to protect the King or the Court.

This child is hungry.

Elven women will carry few children in their lifetime, as our gestation is far longer than humans or dwarves. And most will only give birth once or twice. Our children are precious. Humans—who can and do sometimes have dozens of babies—take that for granted.

In fact, seeing an elf child on the street is so rare it is no wonder people turned me away when I showed up at their doors bedraggled and hungry. They must have wondered what was so wrong with me that my parents, who traditionally would have protected me fiercely, and the Artisan's Guild, which often fosters elf children, did not want me.

But this child has a mother who *wants* it.

The emotion expanding in my chest is too big to be called mere anger. I didn't have the chance to test the bracelets. And I do not know whether the motion of my body managed to generate enough energy for the artifice to work. A vision of what might happen if things go wrong crashes through my mind.

I would press the buttons, and static electricity would buzz through my arms instead of spreading across my skin. The metal would overheat. My skin would blacken as I tried to drag the metal over my smoking flesh. I could go up in flames, triggering the fire the witch warned me of. A shiver of fear makes gooseflesh break out down my arms.

But then I remember standing in the rain after my parents died, stabbing hunger pains in my belly, knowing I was unmoored, alone in the world.

And I press my wrists against my hips, depressing the button inside each bracelet.

Static electricity rushes out, tingling over my skin, making the hairs on my forearms rise. "You will address me as Lady," I say in a voice vibrating with emotion.

Electricity spiderwebs over the fabric of my skirt, lifting the fine white taffeta as if a phantom breeze has entered the chamber. Waves of electricity pass back and forth between the bracelets, and my hair rises and falls, the ends crackling with little blue sparks of energy. Frissons of electricity buzz from my fingertips like tiny lightning strikes.

A faint glow haloes my skin, and the crowd gasps and leans away, but they are too transfixed to move.

Just as quickly as it began, the electricity dies, my skirt falls, and a collective sigh stirs the still air. My heart pounds so hard in my ears that I do not hear my voice when I say, "Give her enough to care for the child."

The Ratcather's eyes are so wide the white shows all around his iris. His jerky nod makes the ends of his mustache wobble, and he digs a handful of coins from the box before making a mark on his list. He glances at me over his shoulder as if I will fly down the stairs and attack him.

"T-thank you... my lady." The woman offers a quick curtsey, but her voice betrays her fear. She backs up before hurrying out of the room with her child tucked against her chest.

All eyes are on me, but mine follow her until she disappears. Another collective murmur of surprise rises from the crowd, and I wonder for a moment whether the bracelets reactivated. But a barely audible scuff on the stone floor behind me says something worse has happened.

"I see our lady has taken good care of the court."

His voice is like velvet, soft and dark, and it acts on the room like a shot of whisky. Shoulders drop, hands relax, but their eyes are still trained on the front of the room. I've been sitting on the throne and now stand before it. What must he think, seeing me before the throne commanding his people? Worse, I just displayed unexplained power.

I expected to have the chance to explain it to him when he woke. But he's seen it now with no explanation, no context.

*Don't reach for power unless you can actually grab it*, Silk said. *But if you must, then hold onto it tightly enough to keep yourself safe.*

I have two options: try to hold onto whatever threads of power and respect I have just gained, or make a public show of submission. Power may give me some leverage, but it will make me an enemy of the King. If I give it up, I must trust the King not to make me pay for it.

As much as I hoped to trust him when accepting this arrangement, I know now that he could have taken what he wanted whether I agreed or not. Throat tight and hoping I am not making a terrible mistake, I turn, take a handful of my skirt, and give the Cutthroat King the most graceful curtsy I can manage.

When he takes my elbow, the heat of his skin burns through

the thin fabric. I let him raise me up but don't dare to look him in the eye or wait for him to speak. Instead, I turn to position myself again behind his chair to the left. My heart cannot tell whether to climb up my throat or stop beating altogether.

The King sits with an ease that makes even me question whether he was unconscious mere hours ago, and lounges comfortably as the crowd settles into the familiar rhythm. Everything is right, everything as it should be... except me. I fold my hands to stop them from shaking, knowing that a reckoning waits beyond the door to our room and praying I can withstand it.

The rest of the Divvy crawls by, and when the King finally rises and takes my arm in a firm grip, Silk gives me a resigned salute that says, *Good luck,* as her eyes say, *It was nice knowing you.*

# CHAPTER 19

*Everything that can be sold has been. I have enough to hold the creditors at bay, but there isn't much left. The Guild suspended our license since Papa was not there to renew it, so I cannot take more repairs without losing it. Ethel suggested I work for another shop, but they will not pay me half of what I need to maintain this place and look for Papa. More desperate measures must be taken.*

*—From the diary of Willow Beauregard*
*November 19, 1902*

GWIL FOLLOWS US OUT OF THE HALL AND THROUGH THE NOW-familiar labyrinth of tunnels. When we pass other members of the court, they bob their heads and stick close to the opposite walls but never speak. Our footsteps echo off the stone of the low ceiling in one corridor, then fade into the darkness beyond the high arches in another. It reminds me of New London in that different parts of the Undercroft have different personalities: narrow arched brick here, buttressed stone corridors there, but always the pervasive chill that seeps out of the stones, through clothing, and radiates into one's very bones.

Sometimes, we pass through pools of light lit with oil lamps, other times with dwarven ones. I bite my lip as we turn the corner that leads out of the central Undercroft where the great hall, market, and kitchens are and into the halls where rooms have been carved out of the earth. These I know well. Our room is thirty-five steps away.

"Who keeps the lamps lit?" I ask.

The King's fingers tighten. "You won't distract me so easily, Dove, so don't bother trying."

"I'm not trying to distract you."

"Is that so?"

"I'm trying to distract myself."

Twenty-seven steps.

"Are you worried?"

"Yes," I admit.

"You should be. Gwil?"

"Majesty?"

Twenty steps.

"Send Harris to guard the door. Get some rest."

"Yes, Majesty."

I pull lightly against his hold, but the King has no intention of letting me go. His fingers tighten around my arm in a velvet vice that could be either comforting or intimidating. "I hope you aren't planning to run."

"I tried that already. It wasn't successful. Besides... I have nowhere to go."

Five steps.

"How lucky for me. Get inside."

The lock snicks into place behind us, and though the sound is quiet, it reverberates in my chest like the clang of the prison door that separated me forever from my parents. My throat tightens. The King has been nothing if not unpredictable. Now that he knows I can usurp his authority, it's hard not to imagine him turning on me, clamping fingers around my throat, and squeezing until little white spots appear at the corner of my vision.

Perhaps he will dump my body in some dark hole where no one in the Undercroft will ever find it.

He doesn't release his grip on my arm until we are far enough from the door not to be overheard. When he lets go, I stumble to a stop and try to catch my breath. He strides to the table and pours a glass of wine, his back to me.

Ripper trots across the room and sits at my feet. We watch the King turn, lean his hip against the table, and salute me with his goblet. "You certainly know how to make an impression, Dove. I will give you that. Half the Court was ready to fall down and worship you."

His voice is cutting, but I cannot tell if the blade is aimed at me.

The inside of my cheek burns as I chew it while trying to decide how to respond: with the truth or with something he is more likely to believe. If he turns me out now, the only option I have left for finding my father is to tell the Chief Inspector the secrets I've learned about the King and the Unseen Court. It would hurt every member, the children and the elderly who shelter here, not to mention Silk, Tildie, and Gwil.

It would make me an enemy. And I do not want the King for an enemy unless I have no other choice. Perhaps I can diffuse the situation. I've managed my father's temper my entire life, after all.

"That wasn't my intention," I say in the most placating voice I can manage.

"I cannot decide if you are telling the truth or if you enjoyed playing queen enough to lie to me. After all"—he crosses the distance between us in three strides and takes my wrist in his free hand, exposing the copper bracelet through the lace—"You had a plan to manipulate them into submission, didn't you? And"—he rubs the pad of his thumb over the small white scar on my fingertip—"you managed to bond my dog without my help. You have been busy."

I raise my chin and meet his gaze, but I cannot stop my lips from trembling. "Ripper did that on his own. And you were unconscious for the Divvy. I didn't know if you would live or when you would wake. I was trying to protect the court. And you."

"Ah yes, my little injury. The one I received when you distracted me at a rather opportune time. Are you certain you weren't hoping I would sleep a bit longer?"

"Why would I want that?"

He drops my arm, then rolls the edge of the wine glass along his lower lip and takes a sip, not breaking eye contact. "Because you got a taste of power, felt the way it gets under your skin and makes your heart race and your body hum. You've been starved for power your whole life, and you wanted more."

Something inside of me, perhaps the dam I've so carefully constructed to control my emotions, breaks. After everything I have been through in the past three days, I do not have the emotional reserves to maneuver this conversation back to safe ground. Anger, frustration, fear, and grief come pouring out. I know he wants this reaction from me, that he's been pushing me, insulting me with accusations in the hope he would get it, and as much as I hate to give him what he desires, I cannot stop myself.

"If I wanted your power, all I had to do was let you bleed to death on that damned couch. Instead, I cleaned and stitched your wound—again—and watched over you for days without sleep. I put myself in danger to keep your court from doubting your authority when it might have cost my life. Rufus and the Cogburners likely want me dead! How dare you insinuate I did it to gain power I don't want!"

He grabs my chin and forces me to look into his eyes. "Everyone wants power, Dove. Everyone."

I slap his hand away. "I am not like you! I don't want power. All I want is to find my father and go back to our shop in peace."

Ripper maneuvers his big body between us like a wall, but we barely notice. The energy snapping in the air is too charged to ignore, and my emotions are raging like a river in flood.

"Oh yes," he scoffs, then downs the rest of his wine. "Your precious father. The father who forced you to work in his shop perfecting a trade you don't care about? Who abandoned you for a job he didn't need just to stroke his bruised ego and resurrect a dead career?"

"He didn't force me to do anything! I love repair work."

The infuriating sneer on his face lasts just long enough for him to stride to the table near the chaise and lift the brass rose from the vase I placed there. I created it from the dented pieces of Ripper's chest and thought, foolishly, he might like to see it when he woke. That it might bring him a bit of comfort, knowing someone was watching over him.

More fool I.

"No," he says, "you don't love artifice. You're merely good at it. Shockingly good. But you don't love it. You love this."

He spins the delicate stem between his fingers. Lamplight slides like water across the smooth, nearly translucent rose petals that still bear the faint trace of the runes once carved into the brass. They catch and hold light, glow. "No one creates art like this if the joy of making it doesn't live in their very bones. You work for your father out of duty. You do this for love. And you claim you don't want the power to decide for yourself which to spend your life doing?"

"This isn't about me, you selfish bastard!"

He shakes his head and lowers the rose. "No. It's never about you... is it?"

That statement punches me in the chest and forces the air from my lungs.

"You'll give up anything, risk anything for everyone but yourself."

I shake my head, unable to speak and unwilling to process his words. It's like having a mouthful of glass and trying to force myself not to swallow, like finally acknowledging the boulder that has been sitting on my chest for years but still being unable to breathe.

The King sits and places the rose back in the vase, turning it to catch the firelight, his brows knitted together. A lock of dark hair falls across his forehead, and the confused pain in his expression might have speared my heart to the back of my ribcage if it wasn't already hiding in my stomach.

"Desiring power is understandable," he says. "Power provides, it protects; deadly risks are simply the price one pays to gain it. I would not blame you for that."

Is he speaking to me or himself? I cannot tell.

Maybe it is my desire to justify myself, or perhaps it is his unexpected vulnerability and the chance, no matter how small, that I might reach some undefended part of him that makes me crouch at his feet. The skirt billows around my legs, and I wait for him to meet my eyes. When he finally looks up, and his jaw muscle flexes as if he's fighting not to speak, I find my voice.

"Power is a dead thing. Power doesn't protect. People do. People who choose to put the needs of others before their own."

The wonder in his voice is heavily laced with both disbelief and sadness when he says, "You truly believe that, don't you?"

"I do."

"It is a pretty myth, Dove. One that makes people trust too much. One that makes people risk things they would have been safer ignoring. Hope like that, trust like that, gets people killed." He turns away from me in a blatant dismissal and stares into the fire. "Go to bed."

What else is there to do but obey? When I emerge from behind the dressing screen and finally slide beneath the covers, he is still sitting by the fire and staring into the flames as if they hold the secrets to the universe. But I know better than most that the lessons fire teaches are painful and only make people more guarded.

"You lost a lot of blood," I venture, poking my head above the blankets just enough to speak. "You should rest."

He finally looks up, sad amusement carving deep lines around his mouth. "Giving orders already? I thought you might develop a taste for it."

"I didn't put all that work into your stitches just to see it wasted."

He runs a fingertip over the brass rose. "I suppose not. But there's something I must do first." He stands, and his customary bravado slides back into place as if the world-weary man sitting by the fire never existed. "I'll return when I'm finished. Sleep. You've had a long day."

"What needs your attention enough to risk your health?" I've never questioned him like this, but it was only hours ago he lay unconscious. The fact that he is capable of walking and arguing is something of a miracle. Part of the mystery of this man that I cannot puzzle out.

He stops with one hand on the doorknob. "I have an errand."

"If you overtax yourself, you'll just end up back on the couch. I'll be forced to do something stupider than this to find my father, and it will be entirely your fault."

"More stupid than selling yourself to the most dangerous man in the city? That would be something, even for you."

"Will you tell me about my father before you leave, at least?"

He glances at me over his shoulder. "I'll tell you everything I know tomorrow. I promise."

Before I can ask anything else, he slips through the door and leaves me alone with a million unspoken words crowding my throat and unshed tears stinging my eyes. Ripper settles at the foot of the bed, and I punch the pillow before settling against the cool fabric.

I stare into the semidarkness, and the moonlit lovers in the forest stare back from the tapestry, partially hidden by folds and shadows. Did that go well or terribly? Am I truly any closer to answers, or have I done nothing but maintain the power of a man I cannot trust? I have no choice but to wait until tomorrow to find out.

And tomorrow is a lifetime away.

# CHAPTER 20

*Mama's name was Rose. Papa said he married her because Rose Bowbriar was a faerietale name for a princess. He said her thorns made her flowers more beautiful. I don't want to forget that.*

—*From the diary of Willow Bowbriar*
*July 17, 1850*

According to the mantle clock, it is seven in the morning when I roll over and squint at the fireplace to see a dark shape outlined by the flames. His profile is cut cleanly by the light: a straight nose, high, hollow cheekbones, and an angular jaw sharp against the line of his neck.

Dark hair curls against his collar, and his long, elegant fingers turn the brass rose over and over, casting shimmering reflections against his chest and throat.

"Eat and dress," the King says without looking my way. "I've something to show you, and I'll answer your questions when we get there."

His voice and manner are devoid of their normally sharp edges. Even if I wasn't hungry for information, that would have intrigued me enough to climb out of the warm blankets and crouch behind the dressing screen to pull on a wool dress. After a few quick bites, he leads me into the wide central corridors with Ripper trotting behind us.

If he was a real dog, his tongue would be lolling out. As it is, his brass feet make bright clinking noises that echo off the stone, a rhythm for the melody of the skirts swishing around my ankles.

We turn past the kitchens, and the scent of buttery potatoes, sausage, cheese, and bread overwhelms the constant mineral stink of dank stone. The clatter of copper pots and the dull clang of iron skillets fills the hall with a homey noise that only lasts as long as the next turn. I close my eyes for a heartbeat and try to picture the Undercroft as I've begun to know it.

The central tunnels and corridors are easy enough to navigate once you know where you're going. They're laid out in a sort of interrupted spiderweb, with the great hall serving as the center. Our room lies toward the rear, where the lesser-used passages rest, mostly silent. And beyond that? Darkness. I may have followed Silk Upstairs, but there were so many twists and turns I have no mental image of the path.

So I begin noting turns, counting steps, and trying to add our route to the library of information I'm storing. Just in case. But it doesn't take long before the torches grow more staggered and soon disappear altogether.

"Ripper, light," the King says.

Two beams of warm orange flicker to life in Ripper's eyes, lighting up the corridor before us.

"That's what those runes were!" I exclaim, grinning at the dog. "They were similar to the runes I've used on lamps before, but they didn't quite line up. Ripper, you are clever, aren't you? Well done."

"He didn't engrave them on himself," the King says, but enough amusement colors his voice so I don't take offense.

"Well, I can't very well congratulate his maker, can I? Besides, Ripper is a good boy who deserves plenty of praise."

The King doesn't contradict me, but he does shake his head and turn us into a narrow passage that leads down at an acute angle. Unlike other parts of the Undercroft, where the ceilings appear to have been built separately from the walls, this corridor is heavy grey stone interspersed with pillars and arches.

I let my fingers drag along the smooth surfaces. "I wonder who quarried and carved these. The fit is almost seamless, despite all this time and pressure."

"Would it surprise you to know they were laid down with a sort of artifice?"

"After the last month, I'm not sure anything could surprise me."

The corner of the King's mouth curls. "Is that a challenge, Dove?"

"Absolutely not. A bit of blandness might be a nice change. Why? You aren't planning anything... exciting, are you?"

He chuckles at my wary tone, and the sound makes me smile. "If I told you, that would ruin the surprise. And I do love the look on your face when you're taken off guard."

I fold my arms and glare at him. "Yes, well, I could do without it, thank you."

"I'll keep that in mind."

"Only if it serves your purposes."

"You know me so well already, do you?"

A note of smugness enters my tone, though I don't believe myself at all when I say, "If I told you, that would ruin the surprise."

He barks a laugh, and the sound of it is everything I hoped, and feared, it would be. A spark of pride bursts in my chest. The Cutthroat King is human, after all.

Strangely, talking to him this way is natural and easy, as if we've been friends for ages instead of uneasy allies. Even that word gives our relationship too much credit. We are on anything but equal footing. The imbalance of power between us couldn't be greater.

That reminder sours my mood. "You said you would tell me about my father today?"

"And so I will. But I have something else to tell you first. This way."

We turn down a long flight of granite stairs with Ripper clanking along ahead of us. The beams of his eyes disappear for a heartbeat, only to soften into a diffuse glow that illuminates an arched doorway at least twelve feet high. Two ornamental waves meet and crash at the apex of the arch, and the pillars on either side are carved with fluid symbols.

Moisture clings to my cheeks and sticks in my lungs. "The air is warm down here."

"I told you about the artifice," the King says as he reaches the bottom and holds a hand up for me to take as I near the last step. "Let me show you what it does."

I follow him through the door into a huge room, larger than the market or the great hall, filled with humid air. Pillars of enormous size run in parallel lines down the center and edges of the room, and a pool of perfectly still water stretches out between them. The orange light of Ripper's eyes shines off the glassy surface like a mirror, lighting up our portion of the space, catching tendrils of steam that rise in lazy curls to disappear into a hazy fog above us.

My mouth hangs open. "It's a bath."

"Have I mentioned how impressed I am with your powers of observation?"

I snort. "Once or twice. It was never flattering."

"I do hope you'll see this as an apology, then. I thought you might like to see London as it used to be."

"What do you mean?"

"All this," he raises his hands, "is part of the city of London. London as it was before the war."

I pause and study his face. In the dim light, it's impossible to tell whether there is mirth in his eyes. "Before the war? You mean, like the old faerie tales?"

He strides to the pool and runs his fingertips through the water, sending perfect ripples dancing across the surface and making light cascade down the pillars in undulating waves. "Is this a faerietale? It's still warm."

"Underground hot springs," I shrug.

"Look at the tile work along the edge of the pool."

Blue tiles have been laid in a repeating pattern along the edge of the water, and each one shimmers with traces of metal laid in the glass. "Runes for retaining heat," I mutter and edge further down the pool. "For capturing condensation. And this one"—my fingertips trace the elegant arch of a rune I've never seen before—"it reminds me of the runes for gathering, but it isn't quite the same."

The King points to the ceiling. "This room is thousands of years old, Dove. And it still stands as if the last person left only minutes ago, wrapped in a towel. Any other building this old would be damaged by now. Just think of how much earth and stone rests above us."

A shiver makes me run my hands down my arms despite the warmth. "I've been trying very hard not to do that since you brought me here."

"The artifice in these walls, in these pillars, is older than anything you've ever seen. It's the prototype for the runic structures you use today."

"How do you know that?"

"Just look at them." He gestures to the closest pillar, and when I reach out to touch it, he places his hand over mine and guides it along the etching I assumed was only decorative but is, in fact, runes of a type I've never encountered. His voice is soft, wondering, and regretful when he starts to speak, making pictures spring to life in my mind.

"London was built by humans, elves, dwarves, and fae. Imagine the knowledge and skill of every race joined to create wonders like this." His palm is warm as he guides our hands over the curling symbols. His breath tickles the hairs on my neck. "In that time, knowledge was shared, not guarded. Each contributed according to their power. Magic and artifice joined."

"Artifice isn't magic," I say. My father taught me as much from the time I was old enough to wield an awl, and it was a prominent question on the entry exam to the Artificer's Guild. "It's a method to harness and direct natural energy, like a windmill or a power cable."

"Ah, yes, the dwarves are fond of that dogma. They're wrong, of course, but that's not important. What matters is that the citizens of this city used their abilities for the good of all. There were no starving children on the street. No power structures that celebrated some while oppressing others."

"A utopia?"

"Mmm." The sound reverberates in his chest and vibrates in the air between us, low as soft as a caress. "But it didn't last."

"The war?"

"The war," he agrees and releases my hand, which feels suddenly cold. "When faeries tried to dominate the world, mortal races joined forces to fight back. It destroyed... well"—he looks around—"almost everything. London was buried beneath the rubble of hundreds of years of fighting."

"How?" I ask, staring up at the arched ceiling, which is so high that light doesn't reach it. "How could something this big be buried so perfectly?"

"Magic. Magic capable of opening the earth, flooding the rivers, and making entire forests wither and die. For hundreds of years, the people rebuilt only to see the city destroyed again and again."

Now I know why the upper levels of the Undercroft have always reminded me of city streets, of why I keep looking up expecting to see the sky. Because they are city streets. Or they used to be if the King is right. "You believe the wars were real? Not just a myth to explain the dark ages? Doesn't it make more sense that plagues destroyed the population and drove the dwarves and elves into hiding because we were more susceptible to the illness than humans?"

He holds up his arms once more. "Explain this."

I can't. It is extraordinary. "I can accept this place is thousands of years old. But faeries? You might as well say giants built it. That would be just as easy to accept."

He narrows his eyes at me. "The woman who bends static electricity to her will can't believe in magic?"

"This," I say, holding up my arms so the copper peeks past the edges of my sleeves, "is science. Faeries banished behind a wall of magic with their evil king? That's mythology."

He grins and shrugs one shoulder. "It makes a good story, though, doesn't it?"

"You're impossible," I say, and, on impulse, reach down to cup a handful of water and splash it at him.

He slips aside, still smiling, but his smile has turned dangerous. "Are you trying to tell me you'd like a bath, Dove? The water is still clean and warm."

My stomach drops. I've seen him in the bath, watched beads of water glide over his skin, gather in the hollow between his muscles, and catch in the dark hair on his chest and lashes. The mental image makes my thighs clench. But the thought of him seeing me in the same state of undress makes panic bubble in my stomach. "I'm clean enough, thanks."

He eyes me a moment longer, then sighs in mock disappointment. "Ah, well. I tried. Come on"—he takes my hand and pulls me toward the far end of the room—"there's more to see. And I promised to tell you of your father."

Images of the King's nude body, of the city as it might have been hundreds of years ago, disappear. All I can imagine now is the black carriage disappearing down Penny Lane and the hastily scrawled words on stained paper, words that led me to take the coin and seek the King's help.

My mouth goes dry, but I manage to say, "Yes, you did."

We near the end of the room, where three separate passages leave in different directions: left, right, and up. Ripper hops up the stairs in the center path, and we follow.

Before he speaks, he squeezes my hand, not hard enough to hurt but enough to remind me that this knowledge comes at a cost. "Your father's employer is a collective calling themselves the Covenant of the Silver Dawn."

Hearing that name again makes my hand flex in shocked recognition. "That's it."

"But, much like the war between faeries and mortals, there are no official records of their existence. Only stories."

I'm not surprised, as that was my experience when searching for them. "What are the stories? What do people say?"

"That they've seen men and women in bowler hats with strange eyes," he says when we reach the top of the first flight of stairs and begin the second flight, turning right. "Men who lurk and threaten and promise and then disappear like smoke. Men who can make people do what they want just by looking at them. But no one has been able to follow them back to wherever they come from."

"I thought I saw one in the market," I admit, remembering for the first time since the event.

The King stops, and Ripper pauses ahead of us, turning the bright beams of his eyes at our faces. "In the Thieves' Market or the underground market of the Unseen Court?"

"The underground. I couldn't be certain, though. It happened so fast. And I thought I might have imagined it since I've been hoping to see one for weeks since my father left."

He stares at me for a moment as if trying to make a decision but finally pulls me on. "Tell me immediately if you see another. And never go anywhere without Ripper."

I swallow but nod. "Alright."

The flight ends and flattens into a wide passageway that looks like it used to be a main thoroughfare in a city, paved with broad, flat stone. Some buildings and parts of buildings still stand, others have crumbled, and still others were hastily repaired with wood beams and uneven stacks of dry stone. Rubble spills across the street in several places, forcing us to weave between the rock and debris.

Fallen roofs, makeshift pillars, and wood beams hold up the ceiling, and the white stone looks like it has been glassed over with crystalized minerals. Water drips from unseen cracks and echoes in the dark.

Swallowing hard, I ask, "Is this safe?"

"As safe as anything under the earth." He squeezes my hand, and this time, it is only comforting. "Thousands of years, remember?"

I nod, but a shiver still races down my spine at the thought of so much earth pressing down on us. "So we have a name," I say to distract myself, "but it isn't doing us any good."

"No. But I haven't exhausted my resources just yet. And I have a proposal for you."

My heart stops for a moment before rocketing into motion. "What kind of proposal?"

"It appears we have a common enemy in the Covenant. Let me ask you a question: Did you notice anything strange during your time in the Undercroft or when you sat for me at Court?"

I'd like to snort because everything about this place is strange, but when his attention is fixed on me, I want to squirm like a bug beneath a magnifying glass. I try to let my mind wander back over everything I've experienced since descending beneath the earth, but all I can focus on is his thumb making unconscious circles on the back of my hand.

"I can't think when you're touching me," I say, pulling my hand out of his, and trying to put a little space between us.

A strange look crosses his face, but I don't want to think about that when I'm having a hard time catching my breath. Once I have enough distance to ignore the way his gaze heats my blood, a memory itches the back of my mind, accompanied by a striking face. "A strange man brought a coin to court. I left it in our room for you. He said he wants to pledge his loyalty."

After a beat of silence, the King says in a subdued voice, "Strange how?"

"He was—compelling. It wasn't his beauty but something else. I think I would have sat at his feet if he'd asked me to. I told him he could stay until you received his oath yourself. Maybe he was a witch, too." I shrug. Strange how such possibilities are beginning to feel commonplace.

"And his coin is in our room?" A hard edge has entered his voice, and I don't miss the emphasis he puts on the word our.

"Yes. And Silk mentioned kidnappings," I hurry to add. Perhaps I can distract him from whatever I did wrong regarding the strange man. "That was one of the reasons she didn't want to lead me to the surface."

"Silk is clever. Too clever for her own good, most of the time."

We take a curving left turn, and a familiar scent enters the air.

"That touches the crux of our situation," he says, watching me instead of the path. "I have reason to believe the men who kidnapped your father are also taking members of my court from the streets. I was hunting them the night I discovered you in the Thieves' Market."

I stop and stare up at him. The Bowler Hat he fought in the Mechanica said, You've killed several of my brothers. "You've been hunting them?"

"Yes."

"Then... if you can take one alive, we can question him!"

He exhales through his nose and tilts his head. "In case you didn't notice, they're rather fierce fighters, nearly suicidal, and completely zealous. That hasn't made capturing one alive easy. When I get close, they either fight to the death or kill themselves."

"...kill themselves?"

"And, if you've seen one in the Undercroft, then they've managed to get their hands on a coin."

"Do they need a coin? Can't they just sneak down?"

"No. They'd never find the Unseen Court without either a coin or my permission. Unless they planned to swear fealty, which I doubt they would risk."

"How do you ensure—"

"And that means a member of my court is likely in collusion. Whoever is trying to kill me is connected to the Covenant. I suspect they've been trying for several months."

He turns and continues walking, drawing me along in a daze. Everything is connected, after all. The familiar scent distracts me for a heartbeat, and light grows in the distance, though it isn't the fiery glow of Ripper's lamp eyes.

"That is partly why I agreed to your scheme," the King continues.

I know he protects me for his own purposes, but it still hurts to hear it; it hurts to know that I will only ever matter for how I can be useful. My lips sting when I bite them together and wrap my arms around myself. Despite my intentions, my voice drips sarcasm, "It's so nice to be useful."

"Usefulness isn't the only measure of value," he says as we turn a corner into a beam of sunlight so bright it blinds me. "Nor even the most important one."

Those words stir something deep inside me, something dark and jagged that scrapes against the walls of my heart. But I ignore the sensation and hold up my hand to shade my eyes. "Contradicting yourself isn't the best way to convince me."

The scent of earth and living things rises up as I blink into the light.

"I don't have to convince you of anything. You already believe it. I have only to show you the proof."

As soon as my eyes adjust, a vision solidifies before me, one that cannot be real.

I stumble forward with my hand flattened against my chest as if the pressure can calm my beating heart. Rows and rows of wooden and stone boxes and dozens or hundreds of pots fill what was once a market square with ferns, flowers, and broad-leafed plants; so many I can't count them all as they blur together through a lens of tears.

After the dark chill of the Undercroft, this is a golden dream of spring; it is waking to the sunrise after a nightmare, and I lurch toward it as if it might disappear at any moment. Dwarven lamps supplement the beam of light, and heaters interspersed between the planters keep the moist air warm enough for the plants to thrive.

"Where?" My fingers run over waxy leaves, lightly furred stems, and rich black soil, all while the earthy scent fills my lungs and the pillar of sunlight warms my head and shoulders. My knees give out, and I sink to the ground next to a planter, holding the edge to keep myself from tipping over.

I bury my face in the feathery fronds of a fern. The tips tickle my cheek, and my tears fall onto the soil. "Where did you get these?"

He clears his throat and stuffs his hands in his pockets. "I had them brought down after our trip to the market. I considered bringing you earlier, but I wanted to be certain they would live."

The hesitation in his voice makes my breath catch. My small bedroom garden—a few plants by the window—is a place I built for myself by hoarding one coin at a time. This garden amongst the ruins of an ancient city is glowing with light in the darkness, life amongst the rubble.

Finding sunlight in the dark, bringing light to such a place, must have cost more than I can imagine. And if he is not lying, the process began shortly after I arrived when he saw me descend upon the purveyor of rare plants like a locust. No one has ever done anything like this, nothing close to this, simply for my sake.

A small voice whispers that this may be just another tactic to manipulate me, but I squash the thought ruthlessly. The last month has been drawn in strokes of fear, stained by grief, pain, and uncertainty. So, I will hold on to the joy and peace of this moment with both hands. And I will make certain he knows how much this gesture means to me.

I climb unsteadily to my feet, cross the space between us, and throw my arms around his neck.

He is stiff with shock. I don't care that he is the Cutthroat King and I am nothing but a tool he uses to protect himself. This thoughtfulness, though colored by self-interest, is a blessing I have rarely received and never on a scale like this. I press my face hard against his neck to muffle the sob trying to escape.

"Thank you, your Majesty."

A moment later, his arms slide around me in a tentative embrace, one hand cradling the back of my neck. When he answers me, his voice is rough and low, as if just speaking hurts. "Raeth. Call me Raeth."

# CHAPTER 21

*I try to be content. I know the Muses will bless me so long as I create and appreciate beauty wherever it lies, but sometimes I cannot help believing I was meant for more than Penny Lane and repairing toasters.*

*—From the diary of Willow Beauregard*
*February 30, 1899*

"IF WE ARE TO MAKE THIS WORK," THE KING—THINKING OF HIM AS Raeth is still a novelty—says, "we must both play our parts. I will continue hunting the Covenant on the surface while you draw them out here."

I slide the last handful of fresh flowers I carried back from my garden into a vase and position them next to the bed, where their sweetness will reach us in sleep. "How am I meant to do that? What do I look for aside from bowler hats and waxy skin?"

Raeth leans his hip against the bed frame and folds his arms casually as if asking me to use myself as bait is nothing to worry over. "If I am right, so long as you are available, they will approach you. None of their other efforts have worked so far."

"But I share your room," I say, understanding at last. He did take quite a bit of trouble to make people believe we are romantically involved rather than merely business partners of a sort.

He inclines his head. "Your proximity makes you the easiest and most likely path to me. Especially if they believe I am fond of you."

"Then why haven't they tried to use your...ah, that is"—my cheeks burn when I remember the woman who accompanied him into our room weeks ago— "your paramours, instead? Surely they would have, if they believe your bed is the key to your heart."

Wicked amusement lights his eyes like burning coals. "I have been assured on more than one occasion that I do not have a heart." When I scowl at him, he relents. "I am very careful never to show interest in any one person for too long. It would make them a target, if not for these assassins, then for ambitious social climbers seeking power."

"Like the gang leaders."

He nods.

Having seen Rufus's ruthless eyes, I have no doubt he would use the King's—Raeth's—paramour to gain an advantage for the Cogburners. So Raeth is careful to protect his partners, but it doesn't seem to bother him that this scheme makes me a target. The thought makes a bubble of resentment burst in my chest. Part of me wants to hang on to that sense of injustice—after all, I doubt any of them have stitched his unconscious hide—and the other part wonders how lonely it must be to carry such weight without the benefit of a partner or a confidant.

Normally, this internal struggle would result in burying my own frustration in favor of empathy, but I cannot dismiss my feelings with such ease. After all, why should I be more expendable than they? I turn back to my flowers, frowning. "If they're willing to kill you, they must also be willing to hurt me. How am I to protect myself?"

"Ripper will be with you."

"Ripper cannot stop a bullet."

"He can, actually. Besides, attacking you would be counterproductive. They cannot use you against me if you are dead."

"Well, that's a relief."

Raeth turns me toward him with one hand on my shoulder. "I do not make this decision lightly or without consideration." My raised brow makes him roll his eyes and sigh. "Allowing you to be hurt after so much time and investment doesn't serve our purpose. It would be a waste of resources and effort. Are you willing to believe that much of me, at least?"

"Of course. You are nothing if not practical."

"Moon and stars be praised. Was that a sneer, gentle Dove?"

I turn away from him and try to master my expression. The King already has too much power over my life. The last thing he needs to know is how much power he has over my emotions. But he is still standing close enough that the heat of his body radiates against my back, which does not make ignoring him any easier. "Not at all. I was simply marveling at your pragmatism."

"How disappointing. You will, however, be gratified to know that I also prepare. That's why we are going Upstairs this evening." His footfalls are silent on the carpet as he strides toward the door. "Get dressed."

I shouldn't be angry. I shouldn't be disappointed that the hesitant tenderness I glimpsed in my garden has disappeared behind the familiar mask of mocking self-confidence. It was bound to happen.

I saw through the cracks in his armor to some considerate, tender part of him, but the cracks have been neatly welded shut again. Not that it matters. We did not make this arrangement so I could dig the man out from behind walls he built around himself, no matter how intriguing the glimpses of his softer side are.

I am here for help finding my father. Raeth is providing it.

What right do I have to complain or care about his loneliness? Besides, my emotional response to his coldness isn't his fault. Forcing him to deal with the fallout of my nonsensical disappointment is not only unfair, it will probably make him resent me.

I KNOW THIS LOGICALLY, but the anger still simmers, suppressed beneath the mask I wear to keep the peace.

Left after the kitchen. Right at the Y junction. Up a flight of worn stone stairs. Past the rooms used as barracks for the Ratcatchers who live and work in the Undercroft.

The map in my mind grows as I follow Raeth through the labyrinth of tunnels, trying to memorize the twists and turns that will lead me to the surface. Imagining turning over an Undercroft map to the Chief Inspector shouldn't give me a little glow of satisfaction, especially as the result would be as devastating to the denizens of this dark world as it would be to Raeth. Still, as I watch him stride gracefully through the dark and remember him describing my potential death as a waste of resources and effort...it does.

And that frustrates me even more. Especially when I think about the warm, stylish dress I wear, the rosemary water in my bath this morning, the chocolates, Ripper, and the garden.

*My* garden.

"Where are we going?" I ask. If I dwell on every confusing aspect of his behavior, I will drive myself mad and explode. He is what he is. Hoping for more won't help anyone, least of all my father.

"To the House of Bywater."

My steps falter. Since I spend most of my time working, my lack of fashionable clothing has never bothered me much. But even I, uncultured as I am, know of the House of Bywater.

I have to jog to catch him up. "What? Why? They would never make an appointment for someone like me."

"Ah, but they will for someone like me."

TWO RATCATCHERS GIVE us respectful nods as we leave what appears to be a rather nice house in the center of town. The sheer number of entrances and exits to the Undercroft is mind-numbing. Even if I gave the Inspector a rough map of the passages and tunnels as I know them, the Ratcatchers could keep the constables out by simply destroying a passage or blocking a tunnel. They could trap dozens of constables in the dark and forget about them.

Would the Inspector help me search for my father, then?

The thought makes a chill unrelated to the winter air run down my spine. I entered the Undercroft in late November. It must be January already. Sunset light still glows on the scattered clouds along the horizon and reflects in the tallest windows of the grey stone buildings on either side of us.

Frost has turned the perpetual mud that crusts the gutter and sidewalk into icy traps waiting for a careless boot. I lift my skirt to skip over the slippery muck, but Raeth takes me by the waist and easily lifts me across. My boots never so much as skim the frozen wagon tracks.

IT IS full dark when we reach the House of Bywater a quarter of an hour later. There are no lights in the downstairs windows, which are wide and styled with gorgeous walking dresses, plumed, wide-brimmed hats, and other accessories, the cheapest of which would cost me several month's wages.

I pause at the door, but Raeth continues and turns left into the next alley. No one is on the street to notice, as most people have sense enough to hurry indoors on bitter winter nights. He knocks in a pattern that itches at my memory, and the backdoor opens a crack before swinging wide.

A beautiful elven man stands in the open doorway. Dwarven lamplight cuts across his handsome features in sharp angles, making his dark skin glow. His house robe is more finely made than anything I own. "Your majesty, please, come in."

He leads us up the servants' stairs and into the second-story apartment. Unlike my obsessively clean and organized workstation, his home is a nest, a cluttered hive of creativity; bolts of cloth stand against walls in stacked disarray, half-finished skirts lie draped over the backs of chairs, needles poke out of stuffed armrests, and bits of thread are stuck to every surface.

"I would beg you to forgive the mess," he says in an airy tenor, "but that would suggest my home is clean most days. I regret to say it is in a perpetual state of disrepair. Such is the life of an artist."

We stop in the center of a drawing room filled with mannequins instead of guests, the table covered in scissors, measuring tape, and pins rather than platters and tea cups.

"I have the dress," he says and turns to lift a gown from the back of a chair. "If the lady will stand here?"

He gestures with his chin, as his arms are full, and Raeth gives me an amused glance that seems to say, *you heard him.*

I dutifully take up a position in the clean spot on the floor and he holds the gown up to my shoulders. "Are you Mr. Bywater?"

"At your service, my lady. What would you like me to call you?"

I nearly tell him my name but remember at the last minute that names are dangerous, and if I ever make it out of the Undercroft, I may not want mine associated with this version of me.

So I say, "Dove," instead.

Mr. Bywater smiles at me, his blue eyes wrinkling at the corners. "It suits you. I must say, your coloring is extraordinarily beautiful. Dressing you is a rare pleasure. And your majesty," he adds over his shoulder, "you were spot on with her measurements. I will only have to make a small adjustment to the hem."

"How long will that take?" Raeth asks.

Mr. Bywater makes a tipping gesture with one hand. "Less than a quarter of an hour, certainly. Shall I bring you tea while you wait?"

Raeth shakes his head, and Mr. Bywater doesn't seem to take offense to the short reply despite his elegant manners.

"Please make yourselves at home then."

He whisks the gown to the next room, where the homey sound of a treadle sewing machine makes quiet music. He must have enough money to commission a dwarven machine, but his home makes me think he enjoys the physical aspect of his art the way I enjoy the drag of the awl or the vibration of a well-struck hammer blow.

"Why do I need a dress?" I ask. "And how did you convince the most sought-after fashion designer in the city to create me one?"

Raeth picks up a measuring tape and winds it around his finger. "Mr. Bywater is a rare artist who specializes not only in fashion but in more...unusual garments."

"Unusual, how?"

"I'll ask him to give you a demonstration."

I sigh and fold my arms. "Must you always be so cryptic?"

"I enjoy your expressions of consternation."

"That is less than comforting. But I suppose I should be happy to be of service."

He places the neatly coiled tape back on the table and advances until we stand a breath apart. "I am less interested in your comfort than I am in keeping you alive. And I very much doubt you have ever been happy to be of service."

Everything about him is tailored to goad me: his beauty, the smooth, mocking timbre of his voice, the full bottom lip curled so slightly his expression cannot be called a smile. But it is the probing insight I resent most. "You are not qualified to make such a judgment about me. I enjoy helping others."

"Am I not? Do you know why I have maintained control of the Unseen Court for so long?"

"Your charm?" I throw the sarcasm in his face as if it could hurt him, but he only smiles and picks up a lock of my hair, twirling the strands around the tip of his finger.

"I watch. I observe. I learn the nature of mortals so I can use it to control them. And I have watched you most carefully of all."

The rhythmic hum of the treadle and the click of the needle from the next room are loud in the silence. I force myself to raise my chin and maintain eye contact. "And what have you learned?"

"That you are a bird in a cage," he says, his voice caressing the words as if he's been waiting ages to release them. "That you've learned to justify the bars. You believe if you sing prettily, someone will open the door."

My heart throws itself against the back of my breastbone as if it, too, wants to escape the bars his words are building.

"But the truth is," he drops my hair and lowers his voice until it is a whisper, "the idea of the empty, endless sky terrifies you. So you sing and tell yourself you love the sound, that you prefer the safety of bars even though you deserve to fly."

Every word is a well-placed arrow shot into the darkest parts of my heart. And each one strikes its target. The pain of it wells up and spills into my chest, making my voice shake. "I have not kept my eyes closed, either, King of the Unseen Court. And I say that we have both accepted our cages. But you built yours one brick at a time."

He flinches and pulls away from me just as Mr. Bywater returns.

"Here now," the elven designer says, holding up the gown, "let's try this on."

I force myself to swallow the lump in my throat and appear unbothered, though it is hard to breathe. "I'd like to see what it does first, if you don't mind. I've been told the design is unusual in addition to being lovely."

Mr. Bywater smiles. "I will happily show you. Here." He lifts the skirt over a mannequin's head, adjusting the fabric until the dress lays smooth against the form. He disappears beneath a pile of remnants and emerges a moment later with a dagger as long as my arm. "Will you do the honors, your majesty?"

Raeth accepts the weapon with customary grace. "Gladly."

The impact of the blow and the sound of metal sliding across fabric makes me shudder. I have seen the power and violence the King is capable of. The garment should be shredded, but the blade did not so much as scratch it.

"A veritable suit of armor," Mr. Bywater says with deep satisfaction. "Not even a bullet will penetrate."

"Is someone likely to shoot me?" My voice comes out in a high-pitched warble.

"Not unless they're ready to take on the nearest constables and attract every spectator in listening distance," Raeth says. "And, given their behavior, I do not believe they are interested in drawing that sort of attention."

Somewhat relieved, I crouch to examine the fabric, fascinated despite myself. It appears to be fine brushed wool, light but dense and very sturdy. Still, wool could not withstand a blow like that, no matter how well made. Mr. Bywater is a member of the Artisan's Guild, highly trained in his chosen art as so many elves are. But their carefully guarded trade secrets cannot turn fabric into steel.

Pinching the material between my fingers, I ask, "How is it done?"

"Come, my lady, an artist must have some secrets."

Though his tone is good-natured and warm, it is clear this is a mystery I must solve on my own. He shows me several hidden pockets in seams or folds, some on the outside garment and some close to the skin, accessible via cleverly disguised plackets. When he is satisfied that I can find and access them all on my own and that the fit is just right—he pays particular attention to the seams —he folds the dress into a box and gives me a serious-eyed look.

"The dress will protect you from most mundane injuries, like slashes, penetration, and blunt force, up to the partial impact of a small auto. But it cannot displace energy forever or too quickly. Fabric is a much more delicate medium than metal, after all. So if it is overloaded too fast and you do not give the dress time to dissipate the energy into the air in the form of heat—"

"It will catch fire," I finish.

He inclines his head, sending the earrings running up the length of his pointed ears dancing.

MR. BYWATER SEES US OUT, kissing my knuckles at the door. "Go with the grace of the Muses, and keep yourself safe."

"May inspiration find you," I reply, squeezing his fingers in thanks.

He bows to Raeth with a hand on his chest and closes the back door with a soft click.

The box containing my new dress is far lighter than it should be, though it is large enough to be awkward to carry. "I would not have expected the city's finest designer to be a criminal," I say as I tuck the box beneath one arm and step onto the sidewalk.

"He isn't."

"Do you mean to say you paid for this design?" I cannot imagine the cost.

"I did not."

"You evade the simple truth as if it will make you ill."

Raeth looks at me over his shoulder, and the light of the dwarven street lamp makes his eyes glow. "I always tell the truth. And it is never simple."

A derisive laugh escapes. "Of course you do. Who would expect the Cutthroat King, ruler of criminals, to tell lies?"

"People are quite good at lying to themselves without my help."

I sigh and rephrase my question. "Why would Mr. Bywater give me a free dress of such value?"

"Because I asked him to."

Would the dress box break over his head if I smashed it atop his crown, or would his head break instead?

"Do you remember the strange man who gave you the coin at Court?" he asks as we take a righthand turn into a wide, well-lit street.

My gruesome imaginings disappear, replaced by that

compelling face. How could I forget him? I'd nearly knelt at his feet. "Yes."

"He did not come to swear fealty to me, not entirely. In fact, he came to me much like you did. He is a refugee trying to build a new life in the city, and he needs help. I will fund his business venture. It is an investment of sorts. One that pays long-term dividends."

"I see. Then you gave Mr. Bywater a loan for his shop and he still owes on it?"

"Something like that."

I shift the box to the other arm. "Was he fleeing when he came here as well?"

"That is his story to tell, not mine. Here." He takes the box and tucks it comfortably beneath one arm. "I want you back underground before the moon rises. Things have not been particularly safe Upstairs."

I let him drag me through the streets, but despite missing the wind, fresh air, and the sky so much that I dream about them, I cannot slow my mind enough to appreciate being outside. All I can think about is how bloody confusing this man is.

At least until a shadow cuts silently through the growing mist at the end of the street. Something about the unnatural way the shadow moves, quick and predatory if not graceful, makes my muscles freeze.

"The Covenant," Raeth swears beneath his breath. He tilts his head to the side as if listening.

Though fear locks me in place, a flash of hope makes me whisper, "We can follow him! Trail him back to wherever he comes from!"

Raeth is in front of me one moment, and the next, he is behind me with a hand pressed gently over my mouth. His breath is hot on my ear. "It's not safe for you. Come on."

But the tendrils of mist curling beneath the light of the street lamp, the proof of disturbed air, are slowing. Soon, the growing fog will hide all traces of the Covenant member's passage, and whatever he knows of my father will disappear with him.

I pull against his grip, frantic, but Raeth ignores my struggles and hauls me down a side street, rasping into my ear, "Be quiet."

He shoves the box into my hands, unlocks a door, and drags me through. It all happens so fast that I freeze in the darkness to try and get my bearings. "Where are we?"

"A safe house. The Ratcatchers have hundreds of them throughout the city. Whenever we travel on the surface, we choose paths that keep us close to them."

A scratching sound followed by the sour bite of sulfur fills the air as a match flame springs to life. Raeth lights and trims the wick on an oil lamp, revealing a narrow, unadorned passage.

"If you leave me here, you can still follow him," I press, taking his forearm. "I'll be quiet. I'll wait."

"Covenant members are never alone. It's not safe."

"But I've seen what you can do; you recover faster than any mortal has a right to. You can—"

"If something happens to me, they will come for you," he growls, pulling his arm out of my grasp and turning to lead me away from the windows that may reveal our light. "I'm not going anywhere until you are wearing that dress. I should have made you change in the shop, but knowing how modest you are...I was stupid."

I hurry to follow him, but a scent catches my attention, and my leg muscles lock up. Raeth stops, too, his body going dangerously still. That stench only comes from one place. Fear forces my eyes wide and makes my jaw tighten.

"It's probably an animal," he says, though his voice isn't as comforting as I think he means it to be. "Something probably crawled down the chimney and couldn't get back up. Stay behind me."

The sweet stink of rot makes my throat close and my stomach turn over, but I hold my wrist over my nose and follow Raeth to the back of the house. The light of the oil lamp slides across cracked plaster and discolored wallpaper. The mouth of the drawing room opens wide and black before us. Anything could hide in those shadows.

Firelight shows bare floorboards, a scarred wooden work table, and—my stomach heaves, and I turn away, gasping, just as Raeth blocks my line of sight with his body. But it's too late. I've already seen the rug stained with blood and, worse, the leathery skin tightened against stark bones, the gaping holes left in the softest parts of the bodies where maggots fed.

My hand flies up to cover my mouth.

"Tom and Kumar," he whispers. "Now we know where the Covenant got their coins."

The names are familiar. Weren't those the Ratcatchers an old woman mentioned my first night at Court, the ones who went missing?

"We aren't safe."

# CHAPTER 22

*It has been a week since he left for L'Exposition des Merveilles in Paris, and Papa has not sent word. I'm certain he is simply busy, but a voice in the back of my mind says he is probably relieved, at last, to be rid of me and everything it costs him to feed and house and care for me. After all, he would have much more money for his invention if he had not taken me in. Perhaps he could have found a wealthy benefactor or patron. Instead, he has to care for me.*

*—From the diary of Willow Bowbriar*
*September 8, 1876*

RAETH HURRIES ME BACK DOWN THE HALL AND INTO A SIDE ROOM and eases the door shut behind us.

"Get into the dress as fast as you can," he urges in a low voice.

I dig the dress out of the box with shaking hands but freeze when Raeth holds out one hand and cocks his head toward the window. He motions for me to get down, then blows out the light. I sink into a crouch and wait for my eyes to adjust to the dark.

Seconds later, a figure passes by the window; no more than a man-shaped shadow, but I know instinctively it is a member of the Covenant. Raeth was right: they're hunting us. Cold sweat beads on my upper lip.

We wait, breath held, for one minute. Two. But no one else passes. Raeth slides behind me and whispers, "Change," in my ear.

This room is not as dark as the Undercroft. Faint light from the street lamps filters through the fog and glows between the gaps in the drapes, enough to warn us if someone passes but not enough to see the delicate buttons and hidden plackets of the new dress.

I strip out of my clothing easily enough—Raeth's body heat on my back in the chilly house is so distracting I stumble over the skirt—but fastening the buttons on the unfamiliar garment when I cannot properly see them is impossible.

I bite back a squeal when his hands brush mine away, as he had done so long ago, only this time I would be a fool to stop him. His fingers are sure as they fasten button after button. His arms are wrapped around me, his chest presses against my shoulder blades, his breath is hot on my neck, and the tips of his fingers slide fabric across the tops of my breasts. Heat flushes from my navel to my cheeks. I'm a fly caught in a spider web, unable to move or breathe.

When the last button slides through with a soft pop, his hands linger at my throat, fingertips grazing my jaw, my earlobes, the sensitive skin at the nape of my neck, and the fine hairs curling there. I want to lean back against him and rest my head on his shoulder, which is an asinine thing to do, but his gentleness weakens my knees.

And when his lips graze my skin between the top of the collar and just below my ear at the corner of my jaw, a shiver of pleasure makes gooseflesh run up my arms. We are in active danger, and I do not even like this man, yet I cannot stop a whimper from escaping my lips.

"Damn you," he says into my hair. His fingers tighten on my shoulders momentarily, and then he pulls me toward the door. "I have to get you back to the Undercroft."

As we ghost back through the building, I try not to think about the fact that the Cutthroat King just pressed his lips to my neck. If I can't focus on the danger we are in now, I'll probably do something stupid...like ask him why on earth he would do such a thing. And why did my body respond?

Raeth pulls me to the back room, motions for me to wait, and pulls the dark cloak he wore when I first met him from his pocket. How so much fabric folded into such a small parcel is another mystery. When the cloak conceals his form, from hood to hem, he blends into the night, becoming as invisible as the moon-cast shadows on the ground.

He slips through the rear door and into the night air. I flatten myself against the wall and hold my breath to ward off the rotten stink of dead bodies in the room next to me. The scent would be faint, practically non-existent to humans or dwarves, but it is still strong enough to turn my stomach. I find myself praying Raeth will return quickly.

When his hand appears through the open doorway, I take his fingers gratefully and let him guide me into the alley. He doesn't slow as we navigate the maze of streets. Obscuring fog dampens my footsteps and turns the buildings into inky smears. The mouth of every street is wide open and dark as a scream.

Anything or anyone might lurk in those dark corridors. At least in the Undercroft, you can see exactly what is in front of you.

My muscles relax as time passes, and no shadowy figure leaps out at us. We must be nearing an entrance to the—Raeth's grip tightens, grinding my knuckles together before he spins and flings me to the side. I stumble over the curb but right myself as a figure slams into Raeth directly where I had been standing. They crash to the ground in a silent rush, rolling and twisting until it is hard to tell who is who beneath the swirling cloak.

They roll to the side, the force dislodging Raeth's hood. When they pass beneath the lamplight, the King takes hold of the Bowler Hat's arms above the elbows. He plants his feet against the other man's stomach and kicks. Bowler Hat flies through the air and hits the building feet from me with the dull thwap of soft flesh. He crumples to the ground as if he was struck by a speeding wagon.

Raeth doesn't continue attacking him. Instead, he turns and glares into the fog, every line of his body tight with coiled power. He said the Covenant does not hunt alone. A thrill of fear runs up my spine, and I turn, too. Was that a shadow moving through the fog?

An arm snakes around my throat, followed by a cold hand that clamps over my mouth so fast I do not have time to scream.

"Don't move, King of the Unseen Court," says the dead, rasping feminine voice just behind my ear.

Raeth freezes, holds his hands out to his sides, then turns slowly in place. In the fog his eye sockets are dark and hollow as a skull, and his voice sounds like it echoes out of a grave. "Release the woman."

"You ain't in a position to make demands, Your Majesty."

The Bowler Hat Raeth flung against the wall staggers to his feet and lurches forward with a knife held low. Raeth doesn't move. When the Bowler Hat grabs a handful of his shirt and presses the blade hard against the side of his neck, drawing a trailing droplet of blood down the pale column of his throat, he doesn't fight back. His eyes are on me.

"Be a good lad, now, and I won't have to hurt this frail creature. And make no mistake, King. I'll strangle her and make you watch. Now do as I say." Her arm tightens, and my eyes flare as white sparks dance at the edge of my vision. My dress might protect my torso, but my throat is bare, and her arm is a vice.

Cords of muscle stand stark in his neck, and his knuckles and tendons press white against the backs of his hand. "Your eyes don't work on me, so don't bother," he growls but doesn't move. Calliope's voice: he's going to let them take him. Take us. They said they'd been hunting him, they've tried to kill him before, and he won't stop them.

Because of me.

Fear that has nothing to do with my own safety races through my veins like an electric charge, and the answer comes to me in a violent flash. I grab the woman's forearm as anyone might when it's pressed against their neck, but as I do, I shove my wrists against my chest.

The buttons on my bracelets depress.

Static electricity isn't very dangerous for the most part; it might give you a jolt when you wear socks on a carpet or brush your hair too quickly. But when it has been charged over days and stored in a capacitor, the release can be...well...shocking.

The crack and sudden burst of light make all four of us flinch. Electricity races from the bracelets in a visible blue-white spiderweb of energy that crawls over my fingers and into the woman behind me. She screams. The sharp, rotten-egg stink of burning hair makes my eyes water as she releases me and flails, trying to put out the fire on her head.

Raeth wastes no time. When the woman releases me, he spins with one forearm raised. The motion drags the blade across his neck, but the force of his forearm striking Bowler Hat's wrist breaks bones with a meaty crunch. The knife hits the cobbles and clatters into the fog.

Bowler Hat ignores the broken bones and throws himself at Raeth, but the move is foolish. Fury rides The Cutthroat King like lightning rides a thunderstorm, and he attacks with the same implacability. He kicks the outside of Bowler Hat's knee, which breaks inward with an awful sound, followed by a vicious punch that snaps the man's head so hard to the side it must break his neck.

I want to look away from the violence, but I am transfixed. As distasteful as it is, watching Raeth fight is like watching a hawk pluck a pigeon out of the sky, terrible and beautiful all at once. And over just as quickly.

The Covenant recovers from injuries that would incapacitate, if not kill, humans. But no one gets up after having their face staved in. The sight makes my already unstable stomach heave, and I turn to look away from the gruesome sight, only to see the woman staring at her dead partner with a snarl curling her upper lip.

She succeeded in putting out the fire, and I expected her injuries to cause so much pain she wouldn't have the will to fight. I was wrong. She screams in rage and launches herself at Raeth as if she is unbothered by the bald, blistered scalp that shows bright red between patches of burnt hair.

Unlike the other Bowler Hats, she isn't silent and calculating. She is an angry cat, all claws and teeth and unremitting rage, lashing out with total disregard for her own safety.

And she is fast. Mind-numbingly fast. Too fast for a mere human.

They swirl around one another, hands and feet flying, pushing the fog away from them in tendrils that curl and twist. When Raeth breaks her arm, she keeps fighting. When he tears a chunk out of the side of her neck, she ignores the blood and the pain and leaves nail marks across his cheek in ragged, bloody stripes.

Still, he is clearly the better fighter. She may be fierce, but he is going to kill her, and all of us know it. Her only chance is to do something desperate, to land a parting blow that won't make her death easy.

So, when his heel comes down on the discarded knife and his balance wavers, she seizes the slim chance of victory and tackles him.

Off balance, their combined weight makes Raeth hit the ground on his back. She lands atop him, grabs his left wrist, twists her body for leverage, and wrenches his arm out of the socket with a muffled pop.

My vision goes white with fear. He cannot defend himself if

he doesn't have the use of his arms. Her lips curl back from her teeth in a rabid snarl as she raises a knife above his unprotected face.

"No!"

My ears are ringing, and my mind is blank as I spring at the two of them. Neither expects me, so she doesn't react soon enough to save herself as I place my hands on either side of her head and release the rest of the energy stored in my bracelets.

Electricity buzzes hot down my fingers, through her skin, and into the bones of her skull. A shock of heat makes my palms tingle and then burn. I jerk my hands from her head and stumble backward, panting. I may someday be able to forget the feel of her shaking flesh beneath my hands. But I know I will never, ever forget the sound of her eyeballs boiling in her skull.

Acid burns the back of my throat. I want to crawl into a dark hole and vomit until my stomach is empty, but Raeth is still on the ground and hurt. Dropping to my knees, I reach out to take his arm but jerk away before I touch him. How can I help anyone with hands that just burned a woman to death from the inside? Blisters are already forming on my fingertips and the base of my thumb, pale white circles with flushed red edges that stare back at me like condemning eyes.

When hands grasp my upper arms, I start so violently that I topple to one hip and throw a hand out to catch myself. Rough stone scrapes against the tender blisters, and pain hisses through my teeth.

"I've got you, Dove. Shh, I've got you. Come on."

The ground drops away. My feet are moving in a steady rhythm, pounding vibrations running up my legs. Cool air is a relief on my palms but burns my cheeks and nose. I try to peel the bracelets off my wrists, but grabbing the copper hurts my fingers too much.

I pull the mineral and mildew scent of the Undercroft into my lungs, breath after breath, but it isn't enough to rid me of the stench of burning hair. And the quiet, dark tunnels cannot replace the dirty cobbles, the inky sky, the swirling fog, the bodies lying broken on the ground.

"Drink this."

I have to blink several times to focus. Raeth is crouching before me, backlit by the fire, holding a cup of tea between two hands. Numbly, I reach for the cup, but as soon as my fingers brush the handle, I jerk them away with a wince. The firelight gleams off the polished surface of my bracelets, and a wave of disgust curls through me hard enough to make me gag.

For years, I've repaired gadgets and artifice designed to improve people's lives. When I etched the runes into these bands, I thought I would only ever use them as a sort of theatre, a way to protect myself with a mirage.

Instead, I murdered someone with them.

"Get these off of me," I grind out, rubbing my wrists together as if I can grind the metal away and free myself.

"Calm down—"

"Get them off of me!"

"Drink this, and I will. I swear it. It will help with the pain."

My eyes unwillingly focus on his face, on his dark eyes framed by long lashes, and the concern evident in the tightness at their corners, in the warmth I'm not sure I've ever seen there. When he raises the cup, I let the liquid slide past my lips, becoming a comforting heat in my chest. Brandy?

"Drink a bit more. It will help."

I do. And then a little more. And a little more until the cup is empty. The room has taken on a hazy glow that softens the edges of the table and edges the firelight with subtle rainbows. Raeth takes my hands and turns them over until the angry red skin is exposed.

"Shit," he says, his voice low.

My lip trembles, and I can't stop it.

"One thing at a time, then." He releases the clasps and opens the bracelets before sliding them gently over my hands and laying them on the table. An afterimage follows his motions, the way the forge burns your eyes if you stare at the coals too long.

"There was more than brandy in that tea." I intend the words to be accusing, but they come out as a soft statement.

"You're going to want a bit more than brandy when I bandage your hands," he says.

His fingers are gentle, so delicate that I barely feel it when he smears lavender oil from the medical satchel on the blisters. The scent, the heat of the fire, and the comfort of his hands combine to lull me into a sort of dreamy numbness that isn't at all unpleasant.

Until he begins wrapping the bandages around my hands.

The linen is clean, and he only wraps my hands lightly, but they burn and throb enough to make me pull a sharp breath in through my nose. I grit my teeth against a whimper and try to stay still as he ties the bandages off. Cold sweat beads my brow, and my breath comes in shallow gasps.

Raeth brushes my hair out of my face and tucks it behind my ear. His fingertips linger on the side of my neck, precisely where his lips had been mere hours ago. "The pain will ease soon."

The gentleness in his voice, his touch, and most of all in his eyes, makes my vision blur. A month ago, I would have told you gentleness was as alien to him as compassion. He might care for my wounds purely to keep me healthy, the way one cares for a horse, but not with concern tightening his expression and drawing his lips into a thin line.

"Doves aren't meant to cry," Raeth says, brushing his thumbs across my cheekbones.

"But maybe they should. Maybe sometimes they should."

A frown draws his brows down but he doesn't respond, only unlaces my boots.

"I can do that."

He snorts. "That would be quite a feat with your bandaged hands. Are you hiding some healing magic you haven't told me about?"

The laces slide out of my boots with a hissing sound, and the memory of taking off his boots on the first night we met careens into my mind. The sense of deja vu must have touched him, too, because he looks up at me through long lashes, and one corner of his mouth quirks in a roguish grin. "Revenge is a boot best removed. Would falling on my arse make us even?"

An unwilling laugh bubbles in my throat but never makes it out.

With my boots set aside, Raeth slides an arm beneath my knees and lifts me easily. I could ask where we are going or what he thinks he is doing, but just summoning the will to speak is hard. I would rather not speak, or think, or feel right now. And somehow, he knows it because he sits me on the bed and begins working at the buttons on my dress, buttons he fastened not long ago.

Should I stop him? Probably. After all, he was the one injured in the fight. I should be helping him. If he is forced to care for me, it won't be long before he tires of the effort. But I cannot dredge up the will to stop him, and the oblivion of sleep sounds like heaven.

So I let his capable fingers slide the pearl buttons through the wool, enjoy the cool brush of his knuckles as he works the skirt over my hips, watch lamplight slide across the sculpted planes of his face as if it worships every contour and angle of him.

Soon, nothing but my chemise stands between my skin and his eyes. But he doesn't look. Instead, he works off his boots, locks the door, turns off the lamps, and removes his shirt before climbing into bed next to me. The mattress dips beneath his weight.

"Come here."

He lays back against the pillows on the headboard, his chest and abdomen carved by firelight, and opens one arm to guide me toward him. But I can't move.

"Sometimes," he says, his eyes serious and his voice gentle, "death comes to visit us in nightmares. We can't control when he appears or what he does. But the warmth of a living body can keep him at bay for a while."

A chill makes gooseflesh run down my legs. I'd only considered sleep a release from the images burned on the backs of my eyelids. Would I be tortured with them in sleep, too? My breath comes in hard.

"I'll keep the dreams at bay. Come here, Dove."

I let him draw me down, let his hand slide across my waist to pull me flush against the side of his body till we fit together like peas. His palm brushes across my cheek, my temple, curling around the back of my head until my cheek rests against the curving muscle of his chest, just beneath his collarbone.

His other hand glides from my shoulder blades to the small of my back and up again. There is nothing passionate in the touch, just the warmth of his skin, the sound of his heart beating, and the comforting rush of air in and out of his lungs, in and out, in and out.

I should not find safety in his arms, but I do. And my brain is too fuzzy to bother denying it. Whatever he used to lace my tea makes my limbs grow heavy. The burning in my hands dulls. And his hand continues the soothing motions, up and down, up and down.

I am so tired. But the words, "I killed someone," come out anyway.

He swallows, but his hands never stop moving. "I know."

I am glad he doesn't try to excuse it. Glad that he didn't turn away from me in disgust. Instead, he's holding me. We are both killers now.

And the Cutthroat King is holding me.

The tears start, then. They sting my eyes, pool in my eye socket, run down over the bridge of my nose, and slide down my cheek onto his chest.

# CHAPTER 23

*Ethel has been ill with summer flu. I brought her family a basket of groceries and tea, but her mother was unhappy to see me. The look on her face made it clear she only accepted my gift because I am her daughter's employer. I like to think of Ethel as my friend, but relationships are hard to build without the support of a family, and hers was quick to close their door in my face.*

*—From the diary of Willow Beauregard*
*August 27, 1901*

"I CAN FEED MYSELF."

Raeth raises a gently mocking brow and pauses with a spoonful of steaming porridge halfway between us. "The way you dressed yourself this morning?"

His voice is both satisfied and amused, and the sound of it

makes my stomach flutter almost as much as the memory of his hands. I'd stood as still as a frightened doe while he pulled the cloth up over my hips and fastened ties above my breasts, holding my breath so his fingers wouldn't brush my skin. Letting him remove my clothing while stunned with shock had been one thing, but feeling his eyes on my skin through the thin chemise had been quite another.

I can't let him slip the spoon between my lips without breaking out in a nervous sweat. With a determined set to my jaw, I hold out my hand for the spoon. He positions it to rest between the middle joints of my thumb and forefinger, avoiding the stinging blisters.

I manage to take the bite—cinnamon, sugar, butter, and slices of late winter apple so sweet the flavors make me groan—and give him a triumphant grin. I may be injured, but I am not incapacitated. My sense of accomplishment fades, however, when I try to take another bite.

Controlling the spoon while scooping up the porridge is impossible. I can't exert enough force to stop it from slipping without pressing the metal into a blister. When the handle slides sideways in my tenuous grip, I grab for it instinctively, and my palm bursts into fiery pain that shoots up my forearm. The spoon drops into the porridge with a splat.

Raeth cleans the spoon with a napkin while I blow on my stinging palm, tears standing in my eyes.

"Do you need something for the pain?" He asks. No trace of mocking colors his voice or expression.

I bite my lips together.

Raeth scoops another bite and levels me with a serious expression. "Is it so hard to let someone else care for you for a change?"

Yes. Yes, it is. "It's just...every good thing I have—every good thing I *had*—is because of my hands. Not being able to use them makes me feel useless. I cannot even dress or feed myself."

"For the record," he holds the spoon out and wiggles it enticingly, a mischievous glint in his eye, "I'm rather enjoying it."

When the spoon slides between my lips, his eyes follow.

~

THE NEXT TWO days proceed in the same manner. My blisters grow as fat as well-fed pigs, and though I heal faster than humans, I still rely on Raeth to help me dress, eat, put up my hair, and—most embarrassing and humiliating of all—use the chamber pot. My face is so hot I might as well use it to light the fire as he raises my skirt. When his long fingers brush my thighs, I bite back a gasp. Never in my life did I expect to rely on a man to help me sit on a commode. Especially not this man, who delights in my discomfort.

As soon as I am seated, I say, "You can leave now."

"What if you need help?"

"I won't."

"But what if you do?"

"Then I'll help myself!"

He looks pointedly at the loose linen bandages that protect my blisters and folds his arms. "How?"

My back teeth grind together so hard it hurts my jaw. "I'll figure it out."

Instead of leaving, he stands by the fire, the back of his head visible above the top of the dressing screen, and turns on the gramophone. A waltz floats through the room. "Better?"

"Cover your ears."

"Come now, this is loud enough to disguise the sound of your—"

"Cover them!" I scream. Then glare at Ripper and order, "You, too!"

The dog, who has been patiently watching us, obediently jogs to the other side of the room and sits near Raeth's feet.

I cannot hold back the flow of nature any longer and the idea of him hearing me—I didn't think my cheeks could burn hotter, but I was wrong.

~

WE ARE READING after breakfast when the door opens, and a line of servants troop through with pails of steaming water. I look up from the book balancing precariously on my knee. Raeth has been turning the pages for me, since I declined having him read to me. Poetry read in that voice would likely be my undoing.

My eyes widen when I realize why they are here. "No."

Raeth shrugs. "We have court this afternoon."

"No."

"You haven't bathed in days."

"No!"

A man glances at me from the corner of his eye, then jerks his gaze back to the floor and hurries out. I don't care. Sleeping next to Raeth, being cared for by him as if I am an infant and not seventy-five years old, has worn control of my temper to a thin veneer that is close to cracking.

"What about the baths by the garden?" I ask, desperate.

"If you'd like me to dress and undress you twice more for the journey, that is a chore I am happy to submit to."

"I would not," I growl and nudge the book onto the table. "A spit bath will be fine, thank you. If you wouldn't mind wetting a washcloth for me."

When the door closes, Raeth leans his hip on the lip of the tub and folds his arms. "Have you forgotten your oath of obedience, Dove? Shall I tell the Ratcatchers to stand down and stop hunting?"

Gentle Calliope, good Calliope, give me patience. "No," I grit out.

His smile is sunny. "Good. Because I cannot drag you before the court smelling like that."

"I don't smell!"

"Having slept next to you for the past few days, I can assure you—"

"Fine! Fine." I rub the back of my hand across my forehead and close my eyes. "You tell me what the Ratcatchers have discovered in the last few days, and I will..."

I cannot say the words, but Raeth revels in them. "Allow me to bathe you?"

Words will not come, so I nod.

"If it is to be another bargain, then I accept. You allow me to bathe you, and I will tell you all I know. Agreed?"

I make an unhappy noise of assent.

"Let's get you out of those clothes, then, shall we?"

Luckily, I am wearing an ornate robe, something like a tea gown, though I have no idea where he got it. More requests of Mr. Bywater, perhaps? But that question withers when he approaches me, his dark eyes intent and sparkling, moving with the lazy grace of the predator I know he is.

My throat closes up, and I stand to fumble at the ties. If I can get the robe off before he reaches me—but I can't, which leaves me standing, trying to control my breathing when he stops in front of me, his finely carved mouth curled into a crooked grin.

"May I undress you, Dove?"

I cannot speak past the lump in my throat, so I give him a shaky nod instead.

His long fingers slide beneath the tie, and one jerk loosens the knot, making me stumble half a step closer to him. He hooks his thumbs beneath the shoulders and slides the fabric off. It puddles on the floor at my feet, leaving me in my corset and chemise.

And he is right, as much as I hate to admit it. Wearing the undergarments for three days hasn't left me smelling like roses or rosemary. He steps around me, then slips his fingers beneath the laces of my corset. The cotton chemise is no barrier to the heat of his touch.

"I'm sorry for the smell," I mumble, my cheeks hot.

After a moment of silence and the loosening of laces, he says, "I like the scent of you, Dove. Though, it is safer for you if I don't."

A little thrill of heat rushes from my breastbone to my toes. When we first made this arrangement, I feared he would require bed service of me. But this is different. He told me he had no intention of taking me to his bed. And when he said it, I was relieved. Now? I cannot tell what I feel.

The corset slides down to catch on my hips, and his hands circle my body from behind to loosen the busk. The posts pop free one at a time, and he pulls the heavy fabric away.

My voice comes out breathless. "That was fast."

"I've untied my share of corsets," he says, bending to take the hem of my chemise and lift.

"I can bathe in this!"

He stops. And no wonder. I shrieked at him.

"It needs a wash as well," I insist.

"You cannot wear a wet chemise, Dove."

I frantically wrap my arms around my chest. "When I'm done, and the towel is around me, you can pull it off over my head."

For a moment, I think he will argue, but he only says, "After you."

I stomp toward the tub with his gaze hot on my back. My chemise is thin, and I know he sees more than I wish he could. Before I can step into the tub, he says, "Wait. If you slip, you'll never be able to catch yourself."

So, instead of quickly dropping beneath the safety of the water on my own, Raeth swoops down to lift me. His arms hook beneath my shoulder blades and knees, leaving the sharp line of his nose and jaw and the elegant line of his neck inches away from my lips before he lowers me into the water, soaking his shirt sleeves.

The heat of the water is nothing compared to the fire burning in my cheeks...and other parts of me. This isn't safe. In fact, it is more dangerous than creeping through the city. The way my heart pounds, you'd think I just fought for my life, not settled into a hot bath.

He crouches behind the tub just over my right shoulder. "Shall we wash your hair first?"

That seems safest, but I still have to swallow before I say, "Yes."

Luckily, the water is dark enough that my body is only visible in glimpses when I shift to make room for his hands.

He dunks a glass into the water above my belly with one hand, then cups the back of my head. "Relax, Dove. I've got you."

My stomach muscles tighten in a flutter, but I slide further into the tub, let my head fall back, keep my elbows resting over the lip, and close my eyes so I don't have to look up into his face or see where his eyes rest. Water sluices over my forehead.

"I sent the Ratcatchers out when we returned the other night," he says in a low, conversational voice as he rubs rosemary soap into my scalp in a circular motion. "The bodies of the Covenant were already gone. They tracked them as far as possible, but it was another dead end. The next night, they found something interesting."

No one else has washed my hair since I was very young, and my mother helped me bathe in a small wooden tub. A shiver of pleasure run from my scalp down the back of my neck and out along my arms.

"What did they find?" I ask.

"A recently vacated warehouse with several bodies inside."

I stiffen. "Not—"

"No," he says, pausing, "no sign of your father. They were members of my court."

Sadness overwhelms my relief. "I'm sorry, Raeth."

He pauses a moment before his fingers resume their gentle massage. "Thank you. However, we do suspect the Covenant was using it. If your father was ever there, they found no trace of him. I am inclined to think it was a temporary hide or perhaps a safe house of the sort we also use. But it is the closest we've come yet."

My eyes fly open. "Did they find any hints of where to look next?"

"Close your eyes," he orders, then rinses the soap from my scalp. "Yes. But I haven't much to tell yet. They'll go out again tonight, and I will join them. I'll tell you what I discover. You can sit up."

With his hand on my back, warm and slippery beneath the water, I pull myself upright but stop before the water can reveal anything it shouldn't. He lifts the length of my hair, pale and heavily waterlogged, and rubs soap into the strands.

"I'm sorry you have to do this," I offer. I have a lot of hair, and washing and drying it is a chore that usually takes me most of a day. "I will understand if you regret your willingness to help."

"I've wanted to get my hands into your hair for ages," he says, watching the lather slide through the lightly curling tendrils.

"Really? It's never been more than trouble to me."

"Have the fashions shifted to find fair complexions out of vogue? Weren't milkmaids popular recently?"

"I wouldn't know. But I doubt milkmaids have skin you can practically see through, no matter how fair they are. One woman told me I was cursed."

"She was a fool. Your hair reminds me of spider silk the morning after a freeze."

I'm tempted to argue with that, but the compliment makes an unfamiliar ember of pride glow in my chest, so I don't. Raeth lets my clean hair fall out of the tub with a towel beneath the dripping strands and kneels by the right side of the tub. I cannot bring myself to look at his face and know how much of me he sees beneath the soapy swirls and eddies.

"Arm or leg?" He asks.

Hardly daring to breathe, I raise my right arm.

"Sit up a bit."

I shift until the water barely covers my nipples, my skin hotter than the steam rising from the surface. Before he takes my wrist, he says, "May I?"

Breath held, I nod. He dunks the rag into the water above my legs, rubs fragrant soap into the fabric, then cradles my wrist in one hand while dragging the cloth across my forearm. Up the underside of my biceps. Over my shoulder to my collarbone. Across the upper swell of my chest above my chemise.

"Lift your arm."

I do. The rag travels down along the underside of my arm, his fingers pressing into my skin through the cloth, brushing my ribs and the outside swell of my breast. My nipple hardens in a rush, and I suck in a surprised breath.

If he heard or saw, he ignores it and dunks the cloth to rinse the bubbles and set them sailing across the surface. They gather where the water meets my chemise, which clings in transparent wrinkles to my skin.

Fire and lamplight make the surface of the water dark, trailed by the rainbow sheen of rosemary oil and pale soap bubbles. Raeth soaps up the rag and says, in a low voice, "Leg."

Bracing myself on the edges of the tub, I raise my right leg. My skin is flushed pink from the heat. Raeth stares down at my exposed limb, dark eyes roaming from sole to knee, then locking on a bit of white chemise floating in the water above my hidden thigh.

His Adam's apple bobs before he takes my foot gently by the arch. The soapy cloth slides along the inside of my ankle, my calf, brushes across the front of my knee and the sensitive skin beneath. When he reaches the boundary of the water, he stops and raises his eyes.

I stop breathing.

His pupils are blown wide, and the muscle at the corner of his jaw flexes. "May I?"

A vice is clamped around my chest, squeezing my lungs and forcing my heart to beat hard to avoid being crushed. I must nod because he takes my knee in one hand and plunges the cloth below the water.

The rough fabric slides along the outside of my thigh to my hip, back to my knee, and along the top of my thigh. His grip tightens. If I could clench my fists around the lip of the tub, I would. Jaw locked, his hand and the cloth slide along the inside of my thigh, and we both hold our breath.

Raeth drops my leg. It hits the water with a splash. He shoots to his feet and snarls, "Fuck," while rubbing his palms on his thighs as if he can rub the feel of my wet skin away.

He turns and stalks across the room, muttering, "Maybe if I turn the lamps down."

When he disappears behind the dressing screen, I drag in a deep breath, then another, trying to calm my heart. The lights dim, a cork pops, and the sound of swallowing is loud in the silence. Either I am seven colors of stupid...or the Cutthroat King wants me.

The novel idea careens into my chest like a runaway train. I've never had a romance. Work keeps me too busy, and I am only around men who are not customers when I pick up or accept deliveries from our suppliers. There was a boy, once. But we were young, and my father put an end to things. He said I was too talented to waste my attention on fruitless relationships.

But Raeth and I don't have a relationship; we have an agreement. And the power has always been on his side of it. I've heard being wanted is a kind of power. At least, according to Ethel, it is. But I have no idea how to wield such power. And I doubt it would work on him, anyway.

My thoughts are a storm of confusion, swirling faster than the water and just as impossible to keep hold of.

The lights dim until the room is lit by firelight alone, and when I look up, Raeth stands over me. I can clearly see every breath as his chest strains against his shirt. He kneels on the left side of the tub.

His voice is calm when he says, "Arm."

Our gazes don't meet. His eyes are locked on the progress of the washcloth, moving with brisk, businesslike efficiency. When the cloth slides across the upper swell of my chest, I take a reflexive breath, one that drags the tips of my breasts out of the water. The cool air makes my nipples pebble.

The cloth slips, Raeth's palm slides across my bare skin, and he snatches his hand back as if I've burned him. But his eyes stray to my breasts and stay there like a bee circling a flower.

"I don't think lowering the lamps helped," I say, but my voice doesn't sound like me. It's low and husky, thick with the tension building in my body.

His eyes stray to the water as if his gaze can penetrate the swirling shadows. "I think you're right," he says hoarsely, then clears his throat. "But we are nearly finished. Leg?"

I have never seen him this flustered. Is that sweat on his upper lip? He handled mortal danger with more composure than this. Is it possible, even a little, that I have this effect on him? The question burns into me, a promise of power I have never considered.

I raise my left leg. He stares for a few heartbeats, then takes hold of my ankle. The cloth slides across my skin, and a languor steals over me. He washes my calf. I lean back, bracing myself on the tub, exposing my torso. It is the single boldest move I have made in my life. But I cannot help myself. The heat of his regard has lit a fire in me.

When his eyes darken, and he hesitates, I know in the pit of my stomach that I am right. The washcloth floats away. With a muttered curse, he retrieves it and viciously rubs the bar of soap against the fabric until a trail of bubbles drips onto the water.

I lift my leg higher, offering it to him. His eyes narrow until they are dark slits in the harsh planes of his face. When he finally meets my eyes, the hunger in them is physical, hot enough that my stomach tightens in reaction.

"You are playing a dangerous game, Dove."

He is right. And I don't even know what the stakes are. But I've never felt this heady combination of fear and power. Of desire. And something tells me that if I ignore this moment, it will not come again.

So I say, "I've only done what you asked me to do."

A sardonic smile graces his face. "So you have. Do you expect to be rewarded?"

An answering smile curls my lips, and I am amazed to hear myself say, "I expect to be washed."

This time, when he takes hold of my leg, his fingers dig into my flesh, and I don't mind. The washcloth plunges below the water line, sliding up to my hip, pushing the clinging chemise to the side. My hips shift instinctively, but Raeth draws his hand away.

When the washcloth slides up the inside of my thigh, only to stop inches from the juncture between my legs, I suck in a deep breath. His fingers flex, testing the resilience of my flesh, and my hips respond in a helpless roll.

"I never saw a dove so hungry for the fox's mouth," he says, his voice between wonder and anger.

The washcloth slides free of his hand and floats to the surface. His skin on mine makes a longing I've never known blossom in my core. I can't control my breathing, and I cannot drag my eyes away from him.

"You want me to touch you." He said those words to me once, and I denied them. "Say it."

The words are a mere whisper. "I want you to touch me."

His fingers dig into my thigh, pulling my knees farther apart. A strangled sound escapes my throat.

He shakes his head. "Obyrron's beard, do you have any idea how wanton you look, spread for me in the water, your breasts pink-tipped and hungry? I knew this bath would tease you. I didn't know it would torture me. Seven gods, you will be the breaking of me, and it will be my own fault."

With that, he bends and scoops me out of the water.

I gasp and cling to him as much as I am able, the water sliding from my skin onto the carpet and soaking his clothes. "What are you doing?"

"Giving you a chance to reconsider," he says, sitting on the chaise with me on his knee. He wraps one towel around my torso before taking another and grabbing a handful of my hair. "If you still want me when I am not the only man who has ever made you wet, tell me again. In the meantime, let's dry your hair."

Confusion swamps me. I saw his expression, the strain in his body when he looked at me. "I don't want to reconsider."

His focus remains locked on my hair as he towels the water from the dripping ends. "You don't know any better."

The need is still thick inside me, tight and hungry, and being wrapped in his arms isn't making it better. But that statement ignites anger along with it. "I am not ignorant."

"That's not what I mean. You are passionate, Dove. And you want to spend that passion. But I—"

"Don't want me," I breathe.

How could I have been so stupid? He told me the first night that he wouldn't take me to his bed, and I just threw myself at him. Do you know how wanton you look, spread for me in the water? In the moment, those words had felt like praise, but now? A lump forms in my throat as shame makes my blood sting and my hands go numb.

He takes my chin between his fingers and searches my face. "Don't want you?" He leans back so that his hips press against his trousers. The hard length of him is visible, straining the fabric in the firelight.

He clearly does want me, and badly. How had I not noticed that his hands were shaking and the pulse at the base of his neck was hammering? "Then you...then why?"

He shifts me off his lap and stalks toward the door, fists clenched and shoulders tight as if expecting a blow.

"Raeth..." I begin but don't know how to continue.

He pauses with one hand on the latch and takes a deep breath. When he looks back over his shoulder and sees my face, his expression hardens.

And when he speaks, his voice is as cold as granite. "I am using you as bait. You know that. I am a murderer, a racketeer, and a thief. I have frightened and mocked and intimidated you. Yet you sit there with honesty in your eyes and offer yourself to me as if I am a man worth trusting with a gift as precious as your body.

"You have not learned yet that trust is a weakness. It is a trap. Anyone will betray you if and when it best serves them, and if you survive long enough, someone will teach you that lesson. But it will not be me."

When Silk enters less than an hour later, she finds me crying.

# CHAPTER 24

*I finished my first repair without Papa's help!*
*He examined it and tested it, but I already did that.*
*He thinks I am ready to begin unsupervised repairs*
*on smaller gadgets and appliances. That means I can*
*save money for more plants and art supplies.*

*—From the diary of Willow Bowbriar*
*December 20, 1863*

WE WALK TO COURT ARM-IN-ARM, BUT EVEN THAT SMALL CONTACT makes me want to retch. I cannot touch or look at him without remembering his censure and the shame of expressing what I wanted for the first time only to be rejected.

But worse is the memory of his words. Anyone will betray you if and when it best serves them, and if you survive long enough, someone will teach you that lesson. But it won't be me. Who taught him that lesson, and how painful was the learning of it to have left such scars? He still experiences it in nightmares, in memories that remain so sharp they cut not only him but everyone around him.

Ripper trots ahead of us, his gait smooth. He had once been damaged, too. And I wasn't without bruises to show for life's cruelty. But Ripper had me, and I only fixed him because I had my father. We healed one another.

Who did Raeth have?

The contrast between empathy for his pain and anger at his rejection leaves me unsettled and sick, more alone than I have since stepping into the dark. So, when we enter the great hall, and I take up position behind the throne, the last thing I expect is for Raeth to bow at the waist and kiss my knuckles before sitting. The show of affection makes the crowd murmur in approval, but it makes my stomach turn over.

I fight to keep a neutral expression as the line forms and tithes are deposited into the coffers, complaints are made, and judgment is rendered. Thankfully, no one dies today. But my pretense of calm is impossible to maintain when the handsome elven man approaches the throne.

Somehow, between the last court and now, I'd forgotten his charisma, but it is palpable, and every eye in the room follows him as he kneels at Raeth's feet. Luckily, everyone is so busy looking at him that no one notices how impossible it is for me to control my expression.

"Your majesty," the man says, "I have come to swear fealty and ask your protection."

Raeth dips his chin. "Rise. Have you brought a gift for the court?"

"Indeed," the man says, and his smile is like the sun rising. I clench my fists in their loose white gloves just to let the pain of my mostly healed blisters stop me from doing something stupid, like sitting at his feet to bask in the glory of that smile. And I am only catching the edge of it. I pray he never aims it at me.

The man produces a polished but uncut emerald teardrop pendant the size of my thumb. It appears opaque, but as it spins on the end of the silver chain, it catches and holds lamplight like inner fire. Silver vines make up the setting, the leaves holding the stone captive and curling up to clasp the chain.

"An impressive gift," Raeth approves. Then he addresses the audience. "But is it worthy of our lady?"

A shout of approval goes up, and Raeth motions me forward. When he reaches to clasp the necklace behind me, he whispers, "Don't look at his face; look past him. And when he speaks, let his voice fade into the background."

His breath is hot on the side of my neck, making gooseflesh spread across my arms. When the heavy stone hangs against my breast, he presses a kiss to the side of my neck, and my knees wobble. "Steady, Dove. It's all for show."

All for show doesn't account for the unwelcome heat in my stomach.

"What would you have of the court in return for this gift?" Raeth asks the man after resuming his seat.

"I plan to open a jewelry shop," the man says. "Though, I have no connection with the"—he hesitates as if trying to remember something—"the Artisan's Guild. I hoped you might intercede on my behalf."

Did he forget the Guild? Not likely. The Artisan's Guild is the center of political power for our people, just as the Artificer's Guild is for the Dwarves. It is a central pillar of our community. This necklace required extraordinary skill. If he isn't already connected to the Guild, the reason cannot be benign.

"You will pay your tithe and ensure the Court has a place to fence goods?" Raeth clarifies.

The man bows, one hand on his breast, the motion so graceful it makes my chest hurt. Look past him, Raeth said. I let my eyes unfocus as if trying to see through him to the people on the other side. Immediately, the influence fades to something I can control, and the urge to prostrate myself disappears.

I let the rest of the conversation fade, too, trying not to hear the smooth tones or musical cadence of his voice. When the oaths are spoken, however, it is impossible not to notice because the air rings with compulsion.

"And in return," Raeth intones, "to you, I give the protection and might of the court in your need, and Guestright in the Undercroft in your want, so long as you live and abide by the night code, so long as the Unseen Court survives, and no magic is performed in these halls."

The man blinks as if surprised.

"Do you accept these terms?" Raeth asks, his tone formal, as if this is a ritual or ceremony.

After a swallow and a deep breath, the man says, "I accept the terms."

At those words, my bracelets spark, and electricity runs along my skin until the hair on my forearms stands on end. The jewel on my chest glows like cat eyes in the dark and the air crackles with energy.

Cheers erupt as the man bows to Raeth before melting back into the crowd, and they accept him as easily as if his promise didn't just light the air on fire. Why does no one notice?

Raeth stands, nods to Gwil, and holds out his arm. His eyes repeat the earlier sentiment; it's all for show. This performance was meant to protect his power and to keep me safe. So why do I want to turn my back on him and stalk out of the room?

I manage to keep my expression neutral when I take his arm, but he isn't fooled. His grip is tight as he leads me out of the hall with Ripper behind us and Gwil taking up the rear.

"Must you hold so tightly?" I ask between my teeth.

"If I loosen my grip, you'll slap me."

"You're fast enough to dodge."

"It's the principle of the thing."

"You don't have principles."

"I believe I've proven otherwise."

"You also have a history of deluding yourself."

We turn the corner from the main corridor into the hall outside our chambers. Raeth glances at me, and the corner of his mouth twitches as if he can't decide whether to smile. "I didn't know you had such a sharp tongue."

Neither did I. "It only appears when I am provoked beyond measure."

"And I provoke you?"

"Exceedingly."

"Good."

I drop his arm and turn to face him, my cheeks and neck hot. "Why is that good?"

"Because you are honest when you're angry, and you spend far too much time lying to yourself."

I jerk the white gloves off, wincing as they slide across my blisters but too mad to check whether I've popped one. "You don't want my honesty."

"Oh, but I do."

A sharp smile carves across my face, and the anger feels good. "I believe you've proven otherwise."

"Majesty?"

We both freeze, and I blink in surprise. When did we enter our room? I don't remember walking through the door.

"Close the door, Gwil," Raeth says without taking his eyes from my face.

The barrel-chested man looks about nervously before following orders.

"My restraint was a kindness," Raeth says once we are alone, "not a rejection."

"It was kind to provoke and then leave me? To push me, over and over, to pursue my own desires, and, when I express them at last, to reject them? And then, when it suits your public persona, to kiss me? That is not kind. It is confusing!"

"I am trying to keep us both safe."

"You're trying to keep yourself isolated!" The words come flying out of me like thrown knives. "You think if you are never vulnerable, you'll never be hurt, but refusing to trust people and refusing to care *also* has a price." His eyelids flinch as if I have slapped him, and his expression makes me lower my voice. "Would it truly be so terrible to let someone in?"

"Yes!" He roars. "It is the foolishness of trusting that made me what I am! Do you think I lurk here like a spider for my pleasure? That I chose the Undercroft for its beauty?" He flings an arm at the door. "You've seen the wretched fucking masses. They trusted in the lie society told them they would be rewarded if they were good people who worked hard. But do you know what happens to them as soon as tragedy strikes? As soon as they are no longer so easily exploited? Society turns its back on them."

He stalks away from me, every line of his body taut and humming with furious energy. When he faces me, his eyes are entirely black, wider than human eyes, and his canines noticeably sharper. "Do you think it is easy for me to lie next to you? To balance your safety with my hunger? To calculate and guard every word I say while they pile up behind my teeth like a river in flood?"

"You think I would use your words against you?"

"Haven't you already?" He demands with a cutting sneer.

My first instinct is to apologize and smooth things over until our relationship is mended, at least enough for civility. But angry tears fill my eyes, and I find that I cannot. "I am not a perfect person. I can be pushed beyond my ability to measure my reactions. But I don't hurt people on purpose or for pleasure. And the last time I hurt someone, it was for your sake, not mine."

"Oh yes," he says, his voice lowering, "and there is the rub. Your selflessness is disarming. Charming. Lovable. But it is just as much a mask as my indifference; only it is more dangerous. Because I don't hide what I am. If I must be a monster to protect myself and the people who come to me for help, then I will not apologize for it or wallow in useless guilt for becoming what survival requires of me."

We stare at one another, chests heaving, and the weight of deep tiredness slides over me, slipping into my muscles and bones and dragging me toward the earth.

I sink onto the chaise and deflate. "I don't want your guilt. I know what you are. But have you ever wondered if being monstrous is not the only way to protect people?"

"If I wasn't a monster, you never would have sought me out. You refused to do what was necessary, so you found someone willing to do it for you."

He flings the words at me as if they will hurt, but as I stare at my palms and the blisters healing on my fingertips, I find I can feel nothing. "True. I have neither the resources nor the shrewdness to find my father, if he's still alive. Society failed me, too, you know. But there is a difference between us."

"Oh, there are several, I think."

I look up at him. His expression is guarded and sneering, but sadness lurks behind his eyes. "I know I cannot do it alone."

DAYS AND WEEKS slip by in an uncomfortable state of tension. We sleep in the same bed but do not touch. We break our fast in company but do not speak, save when it is necessary. The delicate web of growing trust and respect built one catastrophe at a time has been torn apart by a few angry words.

The freedom I enjoy now would have looked like heaven to me when I first arrived, but it is wearing me down like a rasp on a bit of metal, teeth filing away at my nerves with every drawn-out silence and avoided moment of eye contact. But it is a good reminder that I am here to find my father and not to build a comfortable working relationship with the man who forced me to exchange my liberty for his assistance.

When my blisters heal, I begin circuits of the Undercroft with Ripper and Silk at my side, whenever she is willing to join us. Gwil follows as I catalog every twist and turn of the central tunnels, watch Ratcatchers replace the dwarven lamps and candles when they run low, dust rugs in the great hall, carry boxes, and wheel cartloads of supplies to the kitchens.

Now and then, the little ones scamper down the passages, black with soot from being sent up and down the chimneys. They carry wire-tipped sweepers and bags of alchemical powder to stabilize the creosote that builds up inside the chimneys. It prevents fires but leaves the children with stained fingers.

When storms ravage the Upstairs, instead of drawing smoke up and out, the wind pushes it back into the kitchen, sending everyone running and waving their arms to clear the air. And since ventilation in the Undercroft is poor, the smoke lingers in the tunnels.

On those nights, we eat cold sausage, bread, and cheese.

After a particularly bad storm leaves the kitchens unusable for days, I retreat to my worktable and emerge a week later with a prototype to capture the smoke. A few revisions (and a small but memorable explosion later) I install the new artifice to the kitchen staff's applause.

My growing popularity does not endear me to Rufus and the Cogburners, who send baleful glares my way whenever I cross paths with one of them. Luckily, the Wraiths seem to have adopted me as a mascot and put themselves between the Cogburners and me as often as they can. For my part, I try to ignore the rivalry and keep my mind focused on business.

Every day, I greet people, learn their names, and try to make myself as available as possible, hoping that whoever is plotting against Raeth will seek me out. And every night, I wait to see if he will return so I can ask him for news. Most times he doesn't come home until well after I am asleep.

"The kidnappings are getting worse," he says one rare early night, but he says it while peeling off his shirt. I try not to let the lean muscles of his abdomen distract me, but dragging my eyes away is impossible.

"They aren't only targeting my people anymore. And we found another abandoned house filled with corpses."

"How are these kidnappings connected to my father?"

He slides beneath the blankets, and the familiar sound and

feel of the mattress sinking beneath his weight shouldn't be so comforting, but it is.

"Only that the same people are responsible. If we could track them back to their base of operation, that would solve half of our problems."

"Why can't you?"

"I suspect the Covenant is using magic. Even my elven Ratcatchers cannot track them reliably, and I would say they are the best in the city, with perhaps one exception."

"Who is the exception?"

An unwilling smile curls one corner of his mouth as he leans against the pillows and folds his arms behind his head. A little needle of pain reminds me that, for a short time, that smile appeared when he spoke about me.

"A woman. A lady, in fact."

My stomach drops. "A lady?" I try to keep my voice neutral, but my dismay is clear.

"Yes. A rather extraordinary woman."

"Why haven't you pressed her into service if you admire her skill so much? I'm certain you could find some way to manipulate her."

Raeth makes eye contact with me for the first time in days, but his thoughts and emotions are well concealed by a mask of indifference. "Don't think I haven't tried."

"And failed?"

"As I said, she is extraordinary. And dangerous. She dislikes being manipulated. But I expect I will convince her in time."

I bite the inside of my cheek. "You sound as if you like her."

It wasn't meant to be an accusation, but that is how it sounds, and he raises a sardonic brow before leaning a little deeper into the pillows. "Oh, I do. We are similar creatures, she and I. Likely to kill one another, but the journey there is certain to be invigorating."

I roll over and yank the blankets against my chest, tightening my fingers until my knuckles hurt. The tapestry of King Obyrron and Queen Titania peacefully joining hands in the moonlight stares back at me. The fact that I could be distracted by whatever interest he has in another woman when my father is the only reason I am here in the first place makes guilt and shame blend with jealousy.

Why should I care about the affection of a criminal? A thief, murderer, and racketeer, as he called himself? Have I experienced so little affection that the scraps of false kindness, doled out solely for his benefit, are enough to touch my heart?

My garden comes to life in my mind, glowing in unlikely sunlight. I spend every hour I can there, escaping to the silence and letting the peace seep into me. No. No, it wasn't all selfish. His concern, the way his body responded to me, those weren't lies. When he sat before the fire with my brass rose in his hands as if no one had ever given him a gift, that, too, had been honest.

*Anyone will betray you if and when it best serves them, and if you survive long enough, someone will teach you that lesson. But it will not be me.*

Sleep comes slowly and uneasily, accompanied by hazy dreams like watercolor paintings that slide in and out of one another, blending with reality as I shift and roll, trying to coax sleep back to me. Moonlit forests and dew-laden grass overlay my garden in my mind, only now stars are suspended in a velvet sky above, rather than earth and stone.

Raeth also weaves through my dreams, sometimes as a shadowy figure moving through the trees, and other times so clear his face is indistinguishable from reality. I lay in the grass or in our bed, staring at the canopy, and Raeth leans over me, watching me with eyes dark as the sky. His fingertips glide across my cheek with the delicacy of a pixie lighting on a leaf.

When I wake up, he is gone. And I cannot tell what was a dream.

"You are about a month away from making yourself Queen of the Unseen Court," Silk says, saluting me with a croissant.

Her dark curls are pulled back on one side and cascade over the opposite shoulder of her cream-colored blouse. If she weren't wearing a leather corset and a pair of men's trousers, she could have been having afternoon tea with a duchess instead of breaking her fast with me.

My teacup halts before touching my lips. "I am no such thing."

"If you don't think so, you haven't been paying attention."

The tea is hot and sweet, and I let it burn down my throat before answering. "Doing a few useful things to make the Undercroft more comfortable doesn't deserve that sort of recognition."

"Isn't it?" She raises a dark brow. "You seen anyone else trying to make life better for these people?"

I stare at the untouched porridge and bacon, at the blackberry jam pastry Lucinda, the cook, made because I mentioned I liked it, and bite my lip. "Is that what the people think? That I am trying to curry favor?"

Silk snorts and drops a cube of sugar into her teacup. "No one suspects you of anything. Your face is too honest, which is a bit of trickery I'd like you to teach me when you have the time."

"It's not trickery!"

"I know, don't get your knickers twisted. The point is, you're in an enviable position if you can hang onto it. Half of the Undercrofters think you're a spirit, and the other half stare at you like you just walked out of Buckingham Palace. If you sent out the call, they'd show up armed to the teeth."

My stomach does an uneasy little flip. That hadn't been my intention. When I created my bracelets, I did it to protect myself long enough for Raeth to recover. But it appears to have had a few unintended side effects.

A napkin sails across the table and hits me in the face. "Hey. You alright?"

I fold the napkin and try to smile, but the expression isn't genuine. "My stomach is a little sick, that's all."

"No wonder. You haven't touched your food. You're too thin anyway; your stomach is probably trying to eat your backbone."

"Neither have you."

"I ate before I arrived," she says airily. "I had a date. Eat a bit, and I'll tell you about it."

Maybe she's right. So much tea on an empty stomach probably wasn't a good idea. The porridge is still warm, but barely, and the combination of maple, cinnamon, and walnut makes my mouth water. Lucinda has included something else in the spices this morning, but I cannot place the flavor.

"Tell me about this date," I say around my mouthful, and waggle my brows at Silk.

She starts speaking, but I can't concentrate on what she's saying because the flavor lingers in my mouth; it is bitter but not quite unpleasant. It makes the insides of my cheeks tingle.

"Dove?"

The tingling sinks into my tongue and runs down my throat and into my lungs.

"Dove? Are you alright?"

My throat tightens, constricting until I can barely breathe. My eyes snap wide, and my fingers dig into my throat as horror sets in.

"Dove? Dove! Gwil!"

I stand, jerking away from the table as my throat closes around the last bit of air. Plates and glasses crash to the floor as I flail and fight to breathe. Calliope, I can't breathe! The door slams open, and Gwil rushes in. Ripper is barking and growling, but the metallic ring of his voice is drowned by the pounding rush of blood in my ears.

"Find the King!" Silk shouts as she catches me when my knees give out. "The white lady has been poisoned!"

# CHAPTER 25

*I begin training for the Guild Apprenticeship test tomorrow, only it will not be the Artisan's Guild, as I hoped. Papa is confident the Artificer's Guild will accept me, though they'll never grant me membership. He says it will guarantee my future at the mechanica.*

*I cannot keep pretending my dreams of being an artisan are realistic. If I succeed, I can take over the shop, and he can return to inventing full-time. I can repay him for everything he has done for me.*

*—From the diary of Willow Beauregard
January 6, 1900*

SHOUTING. SHAKING. PANICKED FINGERNAILS SCRATCHING MY throat. I'll dig a hole through my flesh if it will let me breathe! Fading light. A sense of empty, welcoming peace. A brief flash of pain in my shoulder.

Raeth's face above me, carved in furious lines, his eyes burning. "Don't you fucking die! Not for me, you hear me? Hold on, Dove."

Hands on my mouth, around my wrists as I struggle, my mouth full of dirt and ash, choking and heaving. Heat on my face, burning in my limbs.

Darkness.

∾

"CALL IN THE RATCATCHERS. All of them."

"But, majesty, what about–"

"Nothing is more important than this. Do you understand me?"

"Yes, majesty."

"Have them close all the passages until further notice and assemble everyone who has had kitchen duty in the last week. I want them in the hall by this afternoon under full guard." The cold, hard voice drags me out of the depths of sleep just far enough to hear people speaking. I understand the words but I can't make any meaning of them.

"Yes, majesty."

"Silk, fetch the items in this receipt. Be certain every ingredient is of the highest quality. And see Goetrid is paid well for her trouble."

The vaguely familiar voice that replies sounds as brittle as old paper. "I don't want payment. I want to come home."

"You can return if she lives. If she doesn't, you die with her."

"I will accept that bargain."

"And send Tildie to me," the cold voice continues as if the other hadn't responded.

My eyelids twitch in an effort to open, but my body won't respond to my commands. And I cannot cling to any thought long enough to haul myself into wakefulness, so I float in a tepid pool of half-conscious thoughts and memories. People speak, but their words ebb in and out as the undertow of sleep tugs at me, pulling me deeper... deeper.

～

I CAN'T BREATHE! Air scratches down my raw throat as I bolt upright, coughing in great racking spams that make me double over. White spots float across my vision, and every cough makes pain flare between my ribs.

Hands lock around my upper arms, and when the worst of the coughing has passed, someone presses a glass into my hands.

"Drink this slowly."

The authority and compulsion in that voice are so potent that even though I want to drink the liquid in great swallows, I take several careful sips instead. It tastes like cold, bitter tea, but it soothes the scratchiness in my throat, and when I take my next breath, it doesn't make me cough.

I don't need to wipe the tears from my eyes to know it is Raeth by my side. The sound of his voice and the feel of his hands are enough. But when I do wipe the cough-induced tears away, it is to see that the breakfast things have been cleared, and my friend is gone. But more than that, half of the room lies in ruins; tables overturned, chairs broken, and glass shards scattered across the carpet.

Was there a fight?

"Where is Silk?" I ask. My voice is scratchy, as if I haven't used it in days. More tea helps but doesn't entirely mitigate the dryness.

"She is gathering the herbs for your antidote."

My stomach drops, and like a flash, I remember her scream, "The white lady has been poisoned!"

My free hand presses hard against my chest. "Antidote?"

Raeth takes my face in his hands, examining my features like a man exploring the landscape of his youth after returning from a lifetime away. "You weren't breathing. I—" He clears his throat. "I gave you a chemical. It is called atropine. It is sourced from the

Belladonna plant but can be used as medicine,"—he hurries to reassure me when my eyes and nostrils flare in panic. Why is it so bright in here?—"when used in small enough doses. You will have a dry throat and mouth for a while, but it won't last."

It takes a moment for that to sink in. I have been in danger many times since agreeing to this arrangement, but those affairs were over quickly, leaving me panicked and shaking, but not so close to death.

My voice sounds small when I say, "I wasn't breathing?"

Raeth takes my free hand carefully in both of his and rubs his thumbs across the backs of my fingers. "Your lips were purple. So were your fingers. I didn't think I could save you. But then the atropine set in, and I got a bit of charcoal and water into you to soak up the rest of the poison in your stomach. I had to force you to swallow by holding my hand over your mouth and nose. I'm sorry for that."

"Sorry? You saved my life."

He is looking at my face but not quite into my eyes. "You were poisoned because of me. It was the least I could do."

"Ah. Duty, then." I pull my hand from his and wrap it around myself instead. "I see. Thank you."

Raeth curls both his hands into fists and stares down at his knuckles. His skin is stretched tight, white across each peak, and his mouth is a thin line that looks like it has never smiled. "I have gathered the kitchen staff. I think your presence may be helpful when I question them. If you feel strong enough, that is."

My throat is tight, but this time, it is not poison, merely emotion. But I release a slow breath and hand him the half-empty glass before scooting off the bed. It takes a moment to regain my balance, so I brush my hands down the front of my robe to disguise my discomfort and keep my voice neutral. "Of course. We must discover who attempted to poison you."

Raeth leaps from the bed and is before me in a heartbeat, his long fingers engulfing my wrists to pull me against his chest. "I have been poisoned a hundred times," he growls, "a thousand. But

I never felt fear till I saw you limp on the floor. I will not take that chance again. Whoever hurt you will know the depth of my vengeance, I swear it."

"What if the person is one of your own?" I ask, suddenly remembering the look on Rufus's face when I offered Leonie the chance to punish me if I was lying about Raeth returning.

"That changes nothing."

An hour later, we enter the hall where a dozen men and women, dwarves, humans, and elves, stand in a line before the throne. I know their names now. Lucinda stands at the center, her round cheeks pale.

Ratcatchers guard the doors, weapons in their hands, their expressions stony. Even Raeth is armed, though I have never seen him carry a weapon openly. My bracelets hide beneath the sleeves of my dress of armor but practically hum with energy. He insisted, though the thought of using them makes my stomach sick.

I stand behind the throne and to the left, both hands clasped to stop them from shaking. It takes every ounce of my will to stay still and quiet as Raeth paces back and forth down the line of suspects like a tiger stalking the bars of his cage. Twelve sets of confused, frightened eyes follow him until he stops and turns on them.

"Which of you poisoned my lady?"

A series of gasps accompanies the exchanged glances of shock. "Majesty, we would never! Lady Dove is so kind to us."

Nods of agreement.

"Then explain to me how a deadly dose of fly agaric happened to slip into the porridge she eats almost every morning." His voice is cold, low, and hissing, like snake scales sliding across themselves. "If you do not, I will hurt you. One at a time while the others watch. Until my lady is satisfied justice has been done."

My stomach roils and twists as I stare at their faces. These are people I have laughed with and teased. I cannot imagine any of them being hurt in such a way. If I have to contradict the King in front of them, I will. But when I open my mouth, Lucinda bursts into sobs and slams both hands over her mouth.

No. Not Lucinda.

Raeth prowls toward her, every line of his body a promise of violence. He stops in front of her. "Explain."

She shakes her head and opens her mouth, but nothing comes out. Frustrated, she tries again, her face reddening with effort. Nothing. Raeth grabs her by the sides of her face as if her head is a melon and his hands a vice, but he doesn't put any pressure on her. "Is this a geish?"

Lucinda's entire body shakes in reaction, but she says, "I don't know what that is, Majesty."

"Look into my eyes." The compulsion in his voice is so strong that every pair of eyes turn in his direction, but Lucinda closes hers for a heartbeat, a line of strain between her brows. "Now."

She opens them, and within instants of making eye contact, she relaxes.

"Did you poison the porridge?"

"I did."

"Why?"

Her voice is dreamy and eager, as if nothing would make her happier than pleasing Raeth by giving him answers. "The man with yellow eyes made me do it. He gave me a little envelope and told me to speak nothing of what was said."

Raeth's fingers flex, but he releases her. "And you poured the poison into the porridge?"

She nods. "I did. I didn't want to, but it was like I was watching myself do it. And when it was over, I was back in me body. I tried to tell Sarah what I'd done, but the words wouldn't come out. I tried to take the porridge away, but my hands couldn't touch it. Like there was invisible glass between us. So, I made the lady a blackberry pastry and hoped she'd eat that instead."

Tears run openly down her cheeks, and she turns to me. "I'm so sorry, my lady. I never wanted to hurt you."

"The man with the yellow eyes," Raeth interrupts. "Describe him."

Lucinda opens her mouth, but again, no words emerge. Helpless frustration carves lines into her face, and her hands ball into chubby fists.

So Raeth uses that voice again, the one that seeps beneath the skin and sinks deep inside. "Describe the man."

Lucinda's eyes soften, and her expression relaxes. She would look just like that if she sank into a warm bath. "If it were only his face, I couldn't tell you nothin' about him. But yellow eyes he had, and skin that didn't look right. Like it belonged on a dead man. I didn't like him one bit, but when he looked in me eyes, I couldn't say no."

Raeth's jaw is clenched, his eyes hard, and I think he would have hurt someone if he wasn't tightly controlling himself. "Did you not think to report the presence of a stranger in the kitchen?"

"But he—but you only allow—he told me not to tell."

"From now on, you will taste every bit of food that leaves the kitchen for my rooms."

Her face pales, her lips tremble, but she clasps her hands and nods shakily. Turning on the rest of the staff, Raeth says, "No strangers in the kitchen. And if any of you see a yellow-eyed man with waxy skin in the Undercroft and do not report it immediately, I will put out your eyes and abandon you on the streets. Am I understood?"

Terrified nods follow the question.

"I'm so sorry, my lady," Lucinda cries, her eyes filled with tears. "I never wanted—I never would have—"

"Get out," Raeth growls.

The staff turn and flee the hall.

"Gwil, escort the lady back to my room and guard the door," he says before stalking out.

～

267

Ripper waits by the door, his metal tail wagging with barely audible creaks.

"You need a bit of oil, don't you?" I say, but it's only to hide my nerves. When the door clicks shut, I shudder and sink to my knees. Ripper chucks me under the nose with his chin, and I take his face between my hands. His dark eyes are expressionless, but I swear true personality shines beneath the artifice. "What are we going to do, boy?"

He doesn't answer, but I throw my arms around his wide neck anyway and hold on, pressing my cheek against his shoulder. The metal isn't cold, as one might expect, but room temperature, and the steady thrumming of the pump in his chest is almost as comforting as a heartbeat.

"His majesty ordered it," Silk's voice floats through the door. "So unless you'd like to tell him why his lady ain't drinking the antidote like she's supposed to, you'd better—"

"Open the door!" I shout, standing and turning.

Silk saunters in after giving the guards a look somewhere between smugness and irritation, a cloth bag in one hand while the other rests on the hilt of a dagger. She eyes my face and nods. "You're looking a sight better than when I saw you last. I see someone cleaned up the mess in here. I hope it wasn't you."

I hadn't noticed, but she's right. The tables have been righted, the glass cleaned, and the chairs replaced. "Someone must have done it while we were out."

"Here," she extends the cloth bag. "It's already blended for tea. A teaspoon for a glass of water, Goetrid said. Twice a day till it's gone."

"Who is Goetrid?"

Silk raises a brow and stuffs her hands in her pockets but jerks her chin at my wrist. "The witch who gave you that scar."

"Oh. And we trust her to medicate me?"

"King's orders."

"I see. Would you like to sit? I'd offer you tea, but…"

"I'll pass, thanks," she laughs. "Besides, I'd rather not be here when the King returns. He's been on a rampage for days."

My hands clench the fabric of my skirt. "Days?"

"You weren't in a good way, Dove. And when the King finally arrived, neither was he. He's the one who destroyed half the room. Thought he was going to smash me with a chair for a moment."

"Calliope's voice," I say, closing my eyes. "I'm sorry."

"Who? That's a curse I've never heard before, and I've heard most."

I stare at her, trying to shift my mind from imagining Raeth destroying his room to the heritage of my people. "Ah-Calliope. She's the most powerful of the Muses, known for eloquence and poetry."

Silk rolls her eyes. "Leave it to the elves to have the least offensive curses in existence. At least dwarves have a bit of spirit in their swear words. You should give something more creative a try. Like pox-ridden tosspot or obnoxious gobshite."

"I'll pass, thanks," I say, but my cheeks are hot.

Silk smiles, and by the mischief in her brown eyes, it's clear she was trying to distract me. But her expression turns more serious and she leans in, catching my hand. "You alright? He didn't hurt you, did he?"

I start to say no, of course not, but realize there is no *of course* about it. He threatened to put out the eyes of innocent people less than an hour ago. And while he may have promised not to touch me in anger, that doesn't account for accidents. Or nightmares.

Yet I find, for some incomprehensible reason, that I do trust him. How many times has he put himself in danger to protect me?

"No," I say at last. "He didn't hurt me."

She nods, but I don't think she believes me. "If he ever does, you let me know. I'll get you out."

Lip trembling, I pull her into an unwilling hug.

～

IT IS NEARLY time for dinner, and I am still bent over the workbench in the back, with my coat acting as an apron to protect my dress. I thought making a bit of art from scraps would distract me from the nervous energy and leftover effects of the poison, but it was a temporary fix. My hands are still shaky, and the closer dinner gets, the more upset my stomach becomes.

I was apparently unconscious for days, and while the tea has helped, I am both ravenously hungry and terrified to eat. A hundred disjointed thoughts fly through my head in a whirlwind, and at the center is Raeth, and everything about him I cannot make sense of.

"I don't know what I'm doing," I tell Ripper, who waits patiently with a wrench held between his metal teeth. "We are a little over two months away from the deadline, and I don't have my father back. We haven't stopped the Covenant from trying to kill Raeth, and I share a bed with a man who will not share my bed. He cannot be human, but I don't know what he is, why I haven't demanded he tell me, or why I haven't given up and run for my life. I cannot make sense of any of it."

He only tilts his head and wags his tail.

I sigh and push my tools aside, leaving them in an uncharacteristic pile. "It's like I keep seeing these bits of him, these charming or tender parts that make me think there is so much more to him than he wants to show. And then I have to ask myself if I am absolutely mad to care. But I do, and I cannot keep lying to myself about it."

Ripper nudges my hand with the wrench as if saying, *Take this. It will help.*

I laugh and pet his head, though I am certain he cannot feel it like a real dog would. "No, my darling boy. I'm afraid I cannot repair this situation with a wrench. People can't mend relationships or people the way they fix clever dogs like you. People must generally fix themselves. The question is, is waiting and hoping worth the pain? Or are we better off cutting ties?"

The door slams open, and I fumble the wrench. Ripper lets out a deafening bark, and Raeth says, "You've sadly neglected your garden for the past few days."

It takes a moment to process everything and respond. "I believe I was unconscious."

He waves that away. "Poisoning is no excuse for laziness. Come. I'll take you."

When he holds out his hand, I merely stare at him.

"I haven't grown a second head, have I? Come. Consider it an order if that makes you feel better."

Glancing down at Ripper, I mutter beneath my voice, "You see what I mean?"

The dog huffs but follows us out of the room as I take the King's arm and let him lead me once more into the bowels of the earth.

We take a different path this time, one that doesn't detour through the ancient baths but leads through older and less-used corridors. The dark is oppressive but not as uncomfortable as the manic energy radiating from Raeth.

"Are you alright?" I ask, at last, unable to take another moment of charged silence.

"No," he replies cheerily, "but we can discuss that later."

The combination of false bravado, a mask I have never seen him wear, and agitation make me wonder what he is hiding. "Raeth?"

"Hmm?" His eyes remain fixed ahead.

"Are you...afraid?"

"Terrified, Dove. Terrified."

When he doesn't explain further, I bite the inside of my cheek and tell myself I don't care. Which is, of course, a lie. But I am very good at lying to myself, as he has pointed out more than once. So, I ask what I have been trying to avoid thinking about for the last few hours. "Did you discover who the man with yellow eyes is?"

"Unfortunately, I have not. But the Ratcatchers are on full alert."

"Is it—could it be someone tied to the Cogburners?"

"What makes you ask that?"

My lip stings as I worry it with my teeth, and I have to force myself to speak. "When you were recovering and I took your place at Court, the Wraiths challenged me. I told Leonie that I would turn myself over to her for punishment if I was lying."

"Ah," he says. "That."

"I should have said something sooner, I know, but—"

"You cannot possibly think I did not learn everything within hours?"

"In truth, I hoped you would. I didn't want to bring it up. But if anyone had cause to hurt either of us, Rufus makes sense. He was more than a little unhappy that my pronouncement gave Leonie and the Wraiths a political edge."

Raeth waves that off with his free hand. "It would take more than that for Rufus to risk incurring my wrath."

"Unless he was certain the poison would kill you."

"Poison cannot kill me."

That pronouncement makes me hold my tongue. Despite his current easy attitude, I am not stupid enough to ask him what manner of creature he is, no matter how much I want to. I am not stupid enough to risk that thornfield. But it does force me to acknowledge a logical conclusion. "But it can kill me."

His voice comes out in a low growl. "You think Rufus targeted you?"

"I did side with his rival using authority that wasn't mine to take," I admit.

The muscle in Raeth's jaw works as he considers how to respond. "I generally refrain from supporting factions within the Court. Whoever wins will be strong enough to control their territory and protect themselves without my help. But I cannot say you chose wrong. Rufus is strong, but Leonie is smarter, and the court cannot afford stupidity."

"I doubt Leonie would have tried to poison me if I had chosen the Cogburners, instead."

"Remember what I said about her being smarter? But this scheme is a little too elegant for Rufus's mind."

I snort. "I wouldn't call getting poisoned elegant."

"Whoever poisoned you either chose to do it directly or hired someone else, someone with yellow eyes capable of enthralling others. That is a skill held almost exclusively by vampires."

"Vampires?" I squeak, tripping over my own shoes in surprise.

He shrugs. "I cannot rule it out. The kidnappings Upstairs are indicative of vampire behavior. And only a vampire can enthrall someone long enough to plant long-term instructions in their mind."

A chill makes gooseflesh run from my shoulders to my ankles. "If it was a vampire, why not send it to kill you? Are they not as fast and dangerous as the stories say?"

"Oh, they are. Vampires are among the most dangerous of monsters."

If they are so dangerous, and they are not sending vampires to kill him, then I can only assume they believe Raeth is capable of defending himself. Against a vampire. I would really like to crawl into a hole and hide. I can only sigh, "As if we didn't have enough to deal with."

"I'm hoping this will distract you," he says, squeezing my hand.

The unmistakable scent of growing things soon overrides the constant stale musk of the damp air this far down, and my heart speeds in anticipation. The garden always steals my anxiety and soothes my worries.

We turn a corner, and, as it had the first time, the garden catches at my soul in a way that few things ever have. Only this time, it is for an entirely different reason.

# CHAPTER 26

*Mr. Beauregard took me to Kensington Gardens. I didn't know any place could be so beautiful. I even saw a pixie! He said they only live in the healthiest gardens. He said I could have a plant for my room, I liked it so much. We ate blackberry tarts and drank ginger beer. Some day, I will have a garden of my own.*

*—From the diary of Willow Bowbriar*
*July 30, 1857*

A TABLE SITS AT THE CENTER OF THE GARDEN BATHED IN THE WARM glow of candles—hundreds of candles perched on stands, on the sills of nearby windows, the edges of planters and garden boxes, and standing candelabra. In the still air of the Undercroft, they burn with steady light, like a spark of pixies hovering over their chosen flowers.

A veritable feast has been laid on the table, and the scent of roast chicken, herbs, potatoes, bread, and pudding mixes with the dusty sweetness of night-blooming flowers. And all of it surrounded by the memories and silent bones of a city long dead.

My grip tightens on his arm until my fingers dig into fabric and muscle alike. "What is this?"

"I thought you may find eating rather...discomforting after your experience. But," he pulls me toward the magical tableaux that cannot be real, "you need food. So I made this myself. It is safe. You have nothing to fear, save perhaps the burnt rolls."

He pulls a chair out and hands me down onto it. I cannot quite believe what is happening. I glance at Ripper, who sits at my feet, but he doesn't seem surprised in the least. Raeth sits across from me and proffers a glass of wine. A sense of unreality steals over me as he raises his glass in salute and takes a sip. I only stare at the red liquid and try to wrap my head around what is happening.

"Can I cut you a bit of chicken?"

When I look up to answer, Raeth has finished his glass and is pouring himself a second while watching me, one brow raised. Struck dumb, I nod. But when he has half piled my plate with food, I find my voice, though it is weak. "I don't understand."

"You haven't eaten properly in days," he says as he forks green beans onto my plate, "and you need fuel so your body can process the last of the poison."

He says it as if it is simply good common sense and sets the plate before me. Numbly, I fork a piece of chicken into my mouth and chew. My body catches on quickly, and I eat half of the plate before I realize how hungry I am.

"Not too fast," Raeth says over his third glass of wine. "You don't want to make yourself sick."

"You've had three glasses of wine and barely touched your dinner," I point out.

"Ah, but that is because I am absolutely terrified."

"Lies. I have never seen you scared."

He sighs and shakes his head. "How many times have I told you that I do not lie? I may be mistaken now and again—though the occasion is rare, I grant you—but I do not lie."

My stomach is comfortably full, and the wine has loosened both my nerves and my tongue. It is empowering to sit across from Raeth with confidence warm in my chest for once.

So I rest my elbows on either side of my plate and fold my hands into a hammock for my chin. "Prove it."

"How?"

"With a truth you don't want to share," I say, flinging the challenge at him like a gauntlet. He is too careful, too guarded to tell me anything he doesn't want to. So, I add an addendum certain to prove I am right. "Tell me something that will give me power over you."

"Gentle Dove," he says, leaning back in his chair though his eyes are quite serious. "If you cannot already see how much power you have over me, then you are a fool."

"There," I say, vindicated. "Misdirection already. I should have known."

He looks down and shakes his head. "I suppose the curse of being the fox is that no one believes you even when you tell them you've come to raid the hen house. Very well," he meets my eyes, and his expression is entirely unguarded, his eyes opaque, as if I could stare into them and see every corner hidden within the darkness. "I will bear my soul to you. I trust you will handle it with care. As you do all things."

I roll my eyes, feeling like seven colors of fool for taking him seriously yet again. I should know better.

"Fifty years ago, I fled my country," he says. "I was the apprentice to a renowned artificer. They don't call them that where I come from, but it is the closest I can get to a word you'd understand. The constructs, weapons, and tools he made were the stuff of legend. The best European artificers can't come close to the wonders that left that shop.

"But the King of our country planned to invade another nation, and he coveted my master's skills. He offered riches, and my master refused. He sent soldiers, and we fought them off. But when he sent fire, there was nothing we could do. If the King could not own my master, he would be certain no one else could."

A napkin is clenched so hard between my hands that the fabric creaks in protest, but I hardly notice.

"He did not survive the blaze, but I knew that if the King discovered I did, he would hunt me to the furthest reaches of our land. So I fled to the north and the court of the Queen. She was kind. Perhaps even good. But she wanted to protect her people as much as my King wanted to subjugate them, and I..."

"You wanted freedom," I say.

"I found the closest border crossing and fled once again. I came to England and the estate of a wealthy nobleman. I did not speak the language, but I needed sanctuary, at least long enough to find my bearings and learn to make a life here. He offered me a place to stay."

Dread sinks its claws into my stomach, and I swallow past the lump forming in my throat. I hope my intuition is wrong; I am terribly afraid it is not.

"He taught me to speak English," Raeth says, swallowing the rest of his glass in a single gulp. Mine follows. "He became, in a way, a father to me. I learned much of this place, of the structures of power, and what motivates mortals. He was cunning, and since I wanted nothing more than to survive on my own, I swallowed every lesson he was willing to vomit up."

Raeth pours himself another glass of wine, and I hold mine out as well. I want to speak, but I don't want him to stop talking, and I don't know what to say in any case.

"Over time, I grew comfortable...and stupid. I thought, in our months together, he'd grown fond of me. So when I told him the truth, I was too foolish to expect him to use it against me. I woke one night to find myself in iron chains, dizzy and sick. I didn't understand what was happening. I screamed his name into the dark until he walked in with a lantern and told me what he wanted of me."

Another glass of wine disappears.

I can barely breathe, and I am terrified of the answer, but I still whisper, "What did he want?"

Raeth gestures at my feet with his wine glass. "The fruit of our relationship sits there at your feet. A beast who will protect with unflinching loyalty, one who cannot be killed. And the proof of it," he tears open his shirt with a casual tug, sending the top few buttons popping and dancing across the table, "you've likely already seen."

In the candlelight, scars crisscross every inch of exposed skin; perfect, careful incisions, delicately made.

"I won't bore you with the rest of the sordid details of our acquaintance. Suffice it to say, valuable lessons have been carved into my very flesh."

Tears fill my eyes, and my throat swells with pity and grief that threatens to choke me.

"Don't you dare," he growls, sitting up and leveling a hard glare in my direction. "I was weak. I didn't understand the full extent of the cruelty that exists in the world. I do, now. At least I wasn't stupid. I built a trap into our little metal friend. And when he was ready, Ripper helped me escape. I couldn't take him with me, unfortunately, so he was lost to me for years. I only recently recovered him."

He downs the last of the wine, and I suck the dregs from my refilled glass, wishing I had more. I've never been drunk, but it sounds like a good idea right now.

Raeth folds his arms over his exposed chest, eyes locked on the empty wine glass. "I built my empire from the Undercroft to the halls of Parliament, brick by brick, using every ounce of power that stealth, cruelty, money, and death could bring me. I was a thief, an assassin, a smuggler...all to accumulate enough power to revisit pain on the bastard who made me one cut at a time.

"And I did it all believing I cared nothing for those who pledged their loyalty to me. People who had been used by fate as badly as I. They were merely tools in my quest to gather enough power that I would never again find myself beneath the thumb of men like Lord Rutledge."

Holly slagging hell, Lord Rutledge? The Lord Rutledge whose water heater I repaired after my father went missing?

Raeth leans forward so that I can see every candle flame reflected in his eyes. His Adam's apple bobs. "Then you came along and neatly tore down wall after wall, exposed lie after lie, until I found myself naked and alone with nothing left to protect me from the man I'd become. I haven't a scar now that you have not uncovered. And the worst part is," he pops a grape into his mouth, "you didn't even do it on purpose. You have destroyed my entire life merely by existing."

I cannot breathe or move. I'm fairly certain that if I tried to speak, no sound would come out. The coincidence of the man who tortured him being the same Lord Rutledge I worked for is too convenient. Part of me wants to call him a liar, accuse him of using the guilt of my connection to the lord to manipulate me for some purpose I cannot understand.

And the other? That part of me wants to cry. To cry for him, myself, and every other soul used and abandoned by those meant to protect us.

Sometimes, an abused dog cowers and fawns, and sometimes, it bites. Why shouldn't Raeth use his teeth after such an experience? No. Empathy cannot drive me now. Raeth must live with the consequences of the life he chose. I cannot blame either of us for what we have become under the cruel hand of fate. But maybe neither of us has to stay as we are.

"There," he says with a self-mocking smile, leaning back to kick his feet up on the table. "Does that truth put me far enough in your power, or do you require more?"

Guilt worms into my stomach. My challenge wasn't meant to force him to dredge up the most painful memories he has and sacrifice his peace on the altar of my pride. I shake my head. "No. I'm sorry, I didn't—"

"Don't," he says, his voice hard. "Don't you dare apologize.

This"—he gestures at the room with both arms—"was meant to be my apology. Poison should never have reached your lips. I should have been with you, should have been more careful, especially knowing the Covenant is trying to kill me. But the longer I spend in your presence, the harder it is to stop myself from saying or doing something that will shatter the illusion that keeps everything from falling apart. And rather than stay near you and watch the illusion crack, I fled. That wasn't your fault, so keep your apologies behind your pretty lips. I don't deserve the comfort of your guilt."

So he is honest, after all. This is an apology. If he knew of my connection to Rutledge, it doesn't seem to matter to him. Why would he reveal such pain if he suspected I was connected to the man?

Chewing the inside of my cheek, I try to think of the right thing to say, the thing that will put him at ease and assure him I will honor the truths he's shared with me. But how does one begin to do justice to a speech like that? It is too heavy a burden to treat lightly, yet I find myself saying, "You are a rather good cook. Did you know that?"

Raeth stares at me for a few heartbeats, then throws his head back and laughs. The sound is rough and merry, and it warms my insides more than wine does.

"God's breath, Dove. You are an unexpected light in the darkness. It is no wonder you terrify me."

"Me?" I demand. "Between you and I, you are by far the scarier."

"Ah, that is because you have never seen yourself angry," he says. "You even tried to hit me once."

My cheeks flame, but I cannot stop myself from grinning. "You did deserve it."

"That goes without saying."

We stare at each other for a long time. I cannot reconcile this man with the other version of him, the one I know all too well. Or, perhaps, never knew at all. "Why tell me this now?"

He drops his head and looks at me through his lashes like a shy little boy. "Can we have pudding first? And more wine? I don't think I'm up to another confession without a little sugar and bottled courage."

I cannot help but smile and gesture for him to continue. The pudding is sweet and sticky, and the molasses compliments the wine so well that I say, "You did not make all this. Tell me the truth."

With one hand on his heart, he says, "I would swear on my honor, but I don't have the privilege, so I will simply remind you that I do not lie and hope you believe me."

The wine has settled nicely into my blood, making it warm and fizzy, making me brave enough to ask again, "Why? Why now?"

He downs the remaining wine, eyes the bottle, and then pushes it firmly away. "If this is to be my penance, I'd better be at least partially sober."

"I don't want your penance."

"And yet you shall have it because if I don't get it out of myself, I'll be insufferable."

"How will that change things?"

"If you don't hold your sharp tongue," he says, leaning forward and tilting his head like a hawk, "I will do it for you."

I bite my lips between my teeth on reflex and wish I'd been brave enough to speak and find out whether he would fulfill his threat...and how.

He closes his eyes and scrubs both hands across his face. "Moon and stars, I am not suited to this shit."

A surprised snort escapes despite my best effort, and he opens one eye to stare me down."None of that, madame, this is serious. And if you don't stop, I won't have the courage to continue."

After a few moments of silence, his jaw muscle works as if chewing over the words. "When Gwil found me, I was trying to convince myself I did not care what happened to you so long as you served your purpose and upheld your end of our bargain. Then he told me you'd been poisoned. I've never run so fast in my life. When I saw you on the floor in Silk's arms, my heart stopped. I didn't think I could save you.

"Building the Unseen Court took dozens of years and more blood than I have the time to recount. And I spent three days willing to shovel all of it into the fire for the slightest hint that you'd wake. Do not mistake me, Dove," he holds up one hand as if to ward off my pained expression, "and don't look at me like that. I have used and discarded more people than you have seen or known, and felt not an ounce of guilt for it. When I say I do not deserve your guilt, pity, or forgiveness, I mean it. I know what I am. But you have made me wish I was something else. You trusted me when I did not deserve it. And I cannot leave the scales so unbalanced between us.

"So, here you are," he sighs. "As much of an apology as I am capable of; for the poison...for all of it. And a promise that no one will ever hurt you again so long as you are under my protection. And sweet bloody gods under the mountain, don't ever expect me to speak so much again."

His head falls into his hands as if he has finished a herculean task, and his fingers dig through his dark curls and into his scalp as if he can pull his head apart in two pieces, neatly as a melon.

"I would like to remind you that I expected none of this, and you did it all on your own."

He peeks at me between his fingers. "See what you've done to me? I should have tossed you on the ground and ravished you, and instead, I've made supper and admitted my darkest secrets."

Heat rushes from my stomach to the tops of my thighs at the suggestion, though it wasn't serious. "I think it's rather an improvement."

"Yes, well, don't get used to it. I have a criminal underworld to rule and a reputation to maintain."

Where do we go from here? Should I accept his apology? He doesn't seem to expect one, and in truth, I don't know that he deserves it. As much as I empathize and understand what drove him, I cannot excuse his actions. Then again, he doesn't seem to expect me to.

"If you could do anything," he asks suddenly, "what would it be? How would you choose to spend your days?"

"Sculpting." The word comes out so fast it shocks me. "I mean...I do find true joy in fixing broken things. And a sense of pride knowing that what I fix improves people's lives. And when I can combine the two, that's best. I enjoy being a repairist."

"But you don't love it."

I shake my head, a little dizzy at the subject change and guilty for admitting the truth. "People like me don't have the luxury of doing what they love. We do what needs doing and learn to be content with that. I can repurpose some old scraps in my free time, but it can never be more than a hobby. I cannot sell art from the mechanica, and I can't imagine leaving my father. I owe him too much, and he needs me."

"If the only thing I accomplish in our time together is convincing you to value your own needs as much as you value the needs of others," he says, "I'll count that a victory."

This isn't a conversation I want to have. My secret desires, the things I've only written in my diary, fall too easily from my lips when we talk like this. I don't like that the first person I've ever spoken to about my selfishness is the only person who will not chastise me for it.

"And you?" I ask, gulping more wine. "What would you do?"

Raeth stares around the cavern as if he can see through the walls to the tunnels and halls beyond. His eyes are far away, and a wistful expression softens his features. "When my people are no longer forced to flee and hide, to either bow their heads in subservience or rely on men like Rutledge...then I may be able to imagine a life other than this one. Until then, I shall make myself a thorn in the shoe of men in power, a wrench in their carefully crafted systems of exploitation. I'll protect my own as they steal food from the mouths of those who already have more than enough, and I'll do it with a fucking smile on my face."

How can I blame him for that? He knows firsthand what it means to be betrayed and abandoned by those who should have protected him. But crime isn't without victims, and the people hurt the most are often those just doing their best to live. Like my parents.

Biting my lip, I let my eyes roam across the candlelit garden, searching for a topic of conversation less fraught than the one that has dominated the last half-hour. Something hidden in the ferns catches my eye, the dull gold gleam of brass. "You brought down the gramophone?"

He glances over his shoulder. "Ah, yes. If I failed in my attempted apology, I thought I might distract you with music."

An idea strikes, and though my initial reaction is muscle-locking fear, the wine has eased my inhibitions, and the mental image that popped into my head is so compelling that I swallow my misgivings, stand, and cross to his side of the table.

My voice doesn't even shake when I say, "Will you dance with me?"

A strange expression crosses his face, something like wonder mixed with hesitant desire. Then he smiles, and I am struck again with how beautiful, how perfectly made he is. Another man might use his looks to his advantage at any opportunity, but Raeth never has. Thank Calliope for that, or I would have been ruined.

He shakes his head and says in a wondering voice, "The dove asks the fox to dance. I'm afraid the only music I brought is a waltz."

"I don't know how to dance anyway," I say, my cheeks heating. "So it doesn't matter."

Raeth stands, and though he is only a few inches taller than me, his presence dominates the space. Our chests are within inches of touching. He gives me a gentle, crooked smile, and the warmth of it tingles in my blood, stronger than the wine. But when he offers me his hand, something in my chest tightens so fast and hard it feels like my ribs might break.

"I'll teach you."

He holds my hand while cranking the lever and setting the delicate needle on the record. Static pops and music warbles to life, filling the space with the tinny sound of strings filtered through the brass trumpet. My heart is beating so fast it must sound like a hum when he turns and pulls me gently against his chest, one hand on my waist with our joined hands outstretched.

"Is the hold supposed to be this close?" I ask breathlessly.

His smile is unrepentant. "No."

We swirl into the lane between flower boxes, Raeth turning us easily, candles and flowers blurring past as Ripper follows, the metallic clink of his paws punctuating the music. Muses, I am dancing by candlelight in the rubble of a destroyed world with the most dangerous man in the city, and I cannot stop the smile that tugs at my lips.

"You are rather good for someone who has never danced," he says when we reach the end of the aisle and turn away from the encroaching darkness to spin back toward the candlelight.

"You are supporting me," I laugh. "My legs are still a little uncertain."

He tightens his grip until I can feel his heartbeat against my chest through the layers of clothing. "Then hold onto me. For I do not mean to stop any time soon."

My toes skim across the ground as he lifts me lightly into a turn, one-two-three, one-two-three, and the world breaks into momentary impressions: the powdery scent of flowers; one-two-three, one-two-three, the blurring candlelight; one-two-three, one-two-three the heat in Raeth's eyes as he looks at my lips. The cinnamon scent of his breath. The rapid beat of our hearts. The warmth of his hands.

I feel like a flower when I turn my face up, hoping and hungry, as if I have been aching for the sun for a thousand years. And for a moment, a breathless moment, I think he will pull away again. But a line forms between his dark brows; he leans toward me with a groan that sounds like pain and—

"Ah!" I scream.

Ripper yelps.

"Shit!" Raeth swears as we trip over the dog.

We'd been too distracted to see where Ripper was, and he'd managed to get behind our legs in the middle of a turn. Raeth tries to right us, but we are moving too fast and are too close to the table.

Ripper bolts from under our feet, and we crash into the beautifully prepared setting with squeals of surprise and protest.

Raeth turns, taking the brunt of the impact as the wood splinters.

# CHAPTER 27

*I did it. I passed the entrance exam. Mr.
Irons said I will be the first elf ever accepted into
the Artificer's Guild apprenticeship program. Papa is
over the moon, and treated me to dinner at Royal. I
have never seen him so proud. My chest hurts
with it.*

*—From the diary of Willow Beauregard
September 15th 1902*

RAETH BLINKS UP AT ME, AND I THINK WE ARE BOTH EQUALLY
surprised to find ourselves on the ground covered in food and
wine with the tablecloth beneath us. Ripper trots over as if
nothing is amiss and shoves his face between ours.

"What madness induced you to fix this worthless pile of
rubbish?" Raeth says as he frees one hand to shove Ripper's face
away. The construct merely sits and continues wagging his tale as
if everything has gone according to plan.

And all of this would be very funny if I wasn't lying atop Raeth with one of his arms around my back and staring down at the face that has been haunting my life for months. He looks back at me, all traces of amusement gone, his lips so close I could—

His mouth tastes of cinnamon.

I thought it would. How can lips capable of such cutting words be so soft, so tender? When he cups my face and deepens the kiss, sliding his tongue along my bottom lip with a little sound of need, delicious warmth steals over me, loosening my muscles and dulling my inhibitions far more than the wine has.

What is it about this man that makes me capable of saying and doing things I would never dare to try? How am I sliding my hands up his chest, letting the silk of his hair slip through my fingers, pushing myself against him and letting his hands roam over my back, my hips. Muses, when his tongue glides over mine, I cannot stop the moan in my throat.

And when the heat of his fingers sinks into my naked thigh, my entire body clenches with need.

*Woof!*

Is that smoke?

Another metallic *woof.*

I lift my head to see that not all the candles were extinguished when the table broke, and one is lying on its side above Raeth's hair, happily burning the tablecloth.

"We should probably put out the fire," I say, but my voice doesn't feel like it comes from my throat.

With a growl, Raeth rolls us until I am beneath him, and his hips are pressed between my legs. Delicious, shimmering heat blooms in my stomach and makes my legs so weak that I cannot bring myself to care whether my hair is caked with gravy.

"For another taste of you," he says against my lips, "I'd let the whole damned place burn," and kisses me again.

*Slagging hell*, I am lost. I was afraid I would be.

When he pulls away and yanks me to my feet, the motion makes me so dizzy I'm forced to hold onto his shoulders for balance. He taps the candle with the toe of his shoe, leaving a trail of smoke rising to disappear into the darkness.

"Well," he tilts my chin with his forefinger. "You are a rather delicious mess, aren't you?"

I swipe a bit of pudding from his shoulder. "You aren't much better."

"I suppose it's good that the baths are so near then."

IT IS one thing to follow my body's natural reaction to Raeth when his hands are on me and wine sings happily in my blood. It is quite another to stand in the enormous stone baths and stare at the perfectly still water, knowing I will have to remove my clothes while he watches.

The only light we have to see by are the candles we've carried from the garden, and Ripper's unusual eyes.

"You," Raeth says to the dog, "can lie over there until I call for you. You've been quite helpful enough for one evening."

Ripper trots happily to the side of the room farthest from the water, lays down near the arched doorway, and rests his huge head on his paws.

"Does no one else ever come here?" I ask, my gaze drifting from Ripper to the door.

"Not often enough to bother with. Only a few people know of the deeper parts of the undercity, and it is generally more trouble to walk here than it is to bathe Upstairs or carry water from the kitchen or wait for a heat stone to become available."

He peels off his shirt, then stops and tilts his head. "Would you like to go first? I can watch the stairs if it makes you more comfortable."

I nod mutely and wait till his back is turned, one shoulder leaning against the door frame, his ankles crossed, before unbuttoning my jacket. I'll have to scrub the worst of the food from my clothes before I put them back on.

"How long will it take for our clothes to dry?" I ask. I don't have to raise my voice for sound to carry across the vaulted room.

"Remember when I told you this civilization was advanced? There are drying racks down there," he gestures with a tilt of the head. "The marble slabs standing straight up like an open deck of cards. They will dry our clothes within minutes."

Then I have no excuse not to step into the pool. Knowing I cannot delay longer, I bite my bottom lip and remove my garments. My jacket, blouse, and corset cover are easy enough. I've taken those off in his presence before. But the corset and, finally, my chemise, are harder.

After a quiet internal battle, I am fully nude, with gooseflesh covering my skin, and Raeth is no more than twenty feet away.

I hurry into the water and bite back a hiss as heat closes over my feet, ankles, calves, thighs… "It's only waist deep!"

Raeth's laugh floats through the room like a mocking ghost. "I'm sorry the thousand-year-old baths aren't up to your specifications."

"Shut up," I mutter as I sink to my knees.

He hears me anyway, and chuckles as I tilt my head back, letting the heavy length of my hair soak up enough water to scrub the food away. The bits and pieces rise to the surface, then float toward the far end of the pool, carried by some invisible current. There must be a grate or something on that side. I try to see what becomes of the particles, but the darkness defeats my eyes.

It doesn't take long to clean myself and my clothes. I stand in the waist-deep water afterward, unsure what to do next. Do I carry the garments to the drying plates or hide until Raeth is clean? Putting distance between us seems like the safest plan.

"I'll bring my clothes to the other side of the baths if you want to take your turn," I offer, wading to the dark end of the pool.

Raeth pads toward the bath, his soft footsteps a counterpoint to water rushing around my hips. I am far enough away, deep enough in the shadows, that my torso should be nothing more than a pale smudge in the dark.

As I hang my outer garments across the drying panels and let my fingers trace the invisible runes carved into the marble, the sound of Raeth's clothes sliding over his skin, and then the water following, filter toward me. I know just how his body looks in candlelight, the lines of muscle on either side of his spine, the swell of his buttocks, the lean curve of his hips.

I try not to imagine him in the water we share, but it's impossible to scrub the memories from my mind. And once my clothing is arranged, I have nothing else to do but wait and wrestle my imagination.

"You're awfully quiet, Dove. You didn't drown, did you?" The acoustics of the place make his voice sound shockingly close.

I bite my lips together to stop myself from saying I'm just imagining you naked, that's all. "I'm fine."

"I need to hang my clothes to dry as well. I'm afraid we didn't think the mechanics of this through."

My mind races for answers. "Give them to Ripper. He can carry them to me, and I'll hang them for you."

"Clever. Ripper, to me."

Seconds later, the dog sits at the edge of the pool and waits for me to retrieve the dripping clothes. I arrange the fabric over the stone slabs, feeling the contrast of the warm, wet cloth against the cool, smooth marble, and force myself to admit that stone and fabric are not what I wish I was touching.

I want his skin beneath my fingers, the flat, hard muscles of his chest and abdomen beneath my palms. And I don't know if I will ever be brave enough again to admit it. A little voice in the back of my mind reminds me that he's turned me down before, and when I was so drunk with unspent passion, I would have given him anything.

But wanting that from him is foolish. Despite his honesty in my garden, Raeth is still a villain. Any relationship beyond our current arrangement can only hurt me in the end, only put me and my goal of finding my father in danger. I shouldn't want that.

But Muses help me, I do.

*There is power in admitting what you are, what you want,* he said to me once. On the heel of that memory comes another, words spoken while we glared at one another. *No. It's never about you...is it? You'll give up anything, risk anything for everyone but yourself.*

I've done everything I can to find my father, tried for months to bend myself into a shape that fits this place, helps these people, protects Raeth. Would it be so terrible to have this one thing for myself?

If he is willing?

Lip between my teeth, heart pounding so hard he must be able to hear it from the other side of the pool, I walk toward the light. Raeth is easy to spot standing in the candlelight. His arms are above his head as he runs his fingers through his wet hair. The waterline hits him low across the hips, exposing the deep ridges of muscle above his hip bones, the flat space between, and the dark trail of wet hair disappearing beneath.

When he hears the sound of water moving, he turns, and freezes. His arms lower slowly. He is barely breathing. His eyes are fixed on me as if I am some goddess from a vision, and the heat in them gives me the courage to keep walking.

Candlelight carves every ridge of muscle on his abdomen, picks out the crystalline droplets caught in the hair on his chest. As if by magic, his scars appear, silvery and covering every inch of exposed skin from his collarbones to his wrists, from his neck to his hips.

"Dove..." he speaks the name he gave me like a warning, a curse, or both. His pupils are so wide that meeting his eyes is like staring into the night sky.

Less than ten feet separates us.

"What are you doing?" his voice is raspy, as if he had to force the words out.

"I'm going to kiss you."

"That's not a good idea."

Seven feet.

"Why not?"

He tenses as if to retreat. "I'm not a safe person for you, for this."

"I don't want someone safe."

Five feet.

"I'm not a good man, damn you. How many ways will you force me to say it? Maybe...maybe if I was—"

"I want who you are now," I say, and I cannot deny that it's true. Raeth is anything but an angel. He is no hero. He is not even a good man, not really. But I want him anyway, and I can no longer deny it.

Three feet.

I stop. Every inch of my skin tingles with heat, with how much I need him to touch me. "I want you."

"Don't say that to me."

"Why not?"

Frustration tightens his expression. "A few months ago, I would have taken your offer and let you live with the consequences. But things have changed. You don't deserve someone like me in your memories. You deserve—" he swallows, and his hands flex as if he'd like to rend and tear, but there is nothing to hold besides water and air. "You deserve someone better."

I raise my hands to touch him but hesitate. When he makes no move to stop me, I rest my palms on his chest over his heart. "I don't want a good man. I want you." His heart pounds as hard against my palm as mine does against my ribs. And he is shaking. "Are you scared?"

His hands rest over mine, pressing them against his skin. "I have never been more terrified of anything than I am of you."

"For once, our positions are reversed." I close the distance between us until our hands are trapped between our bodies. "And I am not scared."

Slowly, his hands slip from mine and he takes my face between his fingers, as he has so often, only this time they barely touch my skin. His voice is a low rumble that makes my stomach tighten. "If you knew all the things I wanted to do to you, you would be."

A thrill of danger runs down my spine, and my breathing hurries to catch up. I let my fingertips glide across the ridges of his muscles, down to his hips. "Then tell me. I promise not to run."

One corner of his mouth curls into a smile so sinful it makes my stomach drop in anticipation. His grip tightens. "Is that a challenge?"

"Let's call it an arrangement."

He growls and drags me against his body. This kiss is not quite as tender, but I throw myself into it with abandon as his arms wind around me, crushing my breasts against his chest. His skin is hot and I am hungry for the taste of him.

But he pulls away and swallows, holding me captive when I try to close the distance. "You don't have to do this. I will help you find your father. You don't owe me your body, no matter what I made you promise."

I want to laugh. Does he truly think I am trying to pay him with sex? Or has it been so long since anyone gave him something without expectation that he cannot fathom the idea that I want him for myself, agreement or no?

Arms wrapped around his neck, I turn our bodies and push until the low steps at the edge of the water butt up against the backs of his knees. He sits in a rush, leaving me standing before him with his hands on my hips. If I didn't know any better, the way he stares at my breasts would make me think he had never seen a pair before. But something about that makes me bold.

I climb onto his lap until I am sitting astride him. "You told me there is power in admitting what I want. And I want you to touch me."

His fingers tighten on my hips. "Far be it from me to deny a powerful spirit." With damnable slowness, he leans forward until his lips brush my throat, making a shiver of pleasure run down my arms. "But we had an agreement." He releases my hips, and his hands slide up my waist to my ribcage, resting just below my breasts. "I'm supposed to tell you what I want to do to you, and you're not supposed to run."

I shiver. "I remember."

He kisses my throat, and my fingers dig into his shoulders. "I want to bite you." His teeth lightly graze the sensitive skin where my neck and shoulder meet. "I want to bite you hard enough to leave bruises that others will see, so they know who marked your skin."

But his teeth are gentle, instead. Nipping and teasing until my head is thrown back to give him more access. His hands slide up my back, his fingers locking in the hair at the base of my neck. "I want to hold a fistful of your hair and force you to watch me when I take you. I want to see your eyes widen and hear your gasp when I fill you."

But he kisses me instead, our lips meeting like magnets drawn together.

"I want to kiss you hard, until your lips are swollen," he murmurs against my mouth, then bites my bottom lip.

A shudder runs through me.

And when his eyes drop to my breasts, every muscle in my body tightens. I've never wanted anything so much as I want him to touch me there. When he releases my hair, I kiss him again, pulling myself toward him with every thrust of his tongue against mine.

But he wrenches his mouth away with a groan and shapes my breasts, letting them rest in the curve between his thumb and fore-finger, his other fingers splayed across my ribcage. "I want to suck on your breasts and bite your nipples until you are writhing and crying and dragging at me for more."

His thumbs flick across my nipples, and a jolt of electric plea-sure makes my back arch. I grab his wrists and force his hands, leaning hard into him as he palms my breasts. But when he dips his head and sucks one nipple into his mouth, the bright burst of sensation makes me dig my fingers into his hair and trap him against me.

"Moon and stars you are sweet," he mutters before lavishing

the other breast, pulling the nipple deep into his mouth and holding me captive with both hands.

My throat is dry, my head is spinning, and every inch of me is on fire even as lazy hunger steals through me. I may be losing my mind, but I don't care.

"I thought you were going to scare me," I tease, but my voice is low, husky, and too breathy for teasing.

"I'm trying to be gentle with you," he says, wrapping both arms around me and gripping the back of my neck. "You have no idea of the restraint I am exercising. I deserve an award."

Before I can answer, he bucks his hips, forcing me to slide down the hard length of his thighs until—my eyes go wide with shock. He is pressing against me, the shaft of his cock between my legs as my hips trap the length of him between our bodies.

I brace myself with my hand on his neck, and he rocks his hips against me. Heat blossoms and pools between my legs in a rush that makes me gasp. He rubs against the most sensitive parts of me in a slick glide that makes tingling pleasure throb at the apex of my thighs.

"Have you ever touched yourself here," he asks, using one hand to shift my hips so the gliding motion makes me shudder.

I swallow hard, and more heat rushes to my cheeks, but his gaze holds me riveted. I nod. His hand slides between us, his long fingers tracing up my thigh, across my stomach, down—my body jerks, my back arches, and my fingers dig into the tight muscles of his arms.

"I want to kiss you here," he says, two fingers tracing the center of my pleasure as his words conjure an image in my mind. "I want to bury my face between your legs and suck on you, lick the sweet wetness waiting for me, slide my fingers into you until you scream."

My hips roll against him helplessly, trying to increase the pressure of his fingers. With a hungry sound, he pulls my breast into his mouth, and the combination of sensations makes my core tighten impossibly.

"Raeth," I sob as the tension grows.

I can't find the words or make myself say more than his name as I desperately pull at him. His fingers increase in speed, matching the rhythm of his tongue and teeth, and I am burning, shivering, flying apart, everything tightening until—

"Come for me, little dove," he says against my skin.

Pleasure bursts from my center in wave after wave, and I hold him as I shake, riding each peak until nothing is left but shimmering, like the trail a falling star leaves in the sky.

When I lift my head from his shoulder, his expression makes my breath catch. His eyes are hot, black, and hungry; predatory. "We aren't done yet, Dove."

My brows rise.

The smile he gives me makes heat pool low in my belly. "Oh yes. But for now," he takes my hand and flattens it on his stomach, then pushes our joined hands below the water, guiding me until the shaft of his cock presses against my palm.

He sucks in a deep breath, and wraps our fingers around him, his eyes narrowing. Our hands glide up and down the hard, smooth length of him. And when we reach the base, he flexes his hips.

My breath catches. I repeat the motion, watching his lips part, his lids flutter closed. His free hand locks around my thigh. As I stroke him, he groans, "I want to sink into you, Dove. I want to feel you hot and tight around me. I want to spread your thighs and ride you until your legs shake and you scream."

My mouth falls open, the combination of his words and the hard length of him in my hand making breathing impossible.

He releases my hand and grabs my hips, lifting me easily until I'm forced to release him. His cock brushes against my entrance. "Look at me."

I can't look away. His lips, his eyes, his long lashes, the flush on his cheeks, his pulse beating like a drum at the base of his throat, the strained muscles of his neck and shoulders.

"I want to have you in every way. Your breasts, your hands,

your pretty mouth wrapped around me," he flexes his hips and lowers me, and the tip of his cock slides into me just enough to make me want more. When he speaks, it is as if the words are being dragged out of him. "But this time, this first time, I want you to take what you want. Do you understand me? This way"—he sinks a bit deeper, and a line of strain forms between his dark brows, as if controlling his need to bury himself inside me is a physical battle—"or not. Fast or slow. Hard or soft. It's up to you. I'm yours in any way you want me."

And he lets me go, releasing me to retreat if I want to. My thighs catch my weight, and I remain hovering as he cups my face and our gazes lock. Muses, how can he be so beautiful? So perfectly dangerous and lovely and dark?

"When you look at me like that," he says, "every bloody thread of my life unravels."

His eyes close, and his Adam's apple bobs, but he doesn't move. The decision is mine. And I am balancing not only on the edge of joining my body with his but of something else, something bigger, and if I give it to him, I will not get it back.

Ripper barks, and this time, it isn't gentle or playful. The metallic boom rips through the room and bounces off the stone ceiling like a thunderclap. Raeth drags me off of him and pushes me behind him, hiding my body with his as the sound of running feet reaches us.

"Majesty!"

"It's Gwil," Raeth says and nudges me toward the dark end of the pool. "Get dressed quickly."

I sink to my neck in the water and begin slinking to the dark side of the pool, but my legs shake, and my heart is racing. Raeth and I had been a heartbeat from—I swallow hard and try not to think about it. But Raeth turns to face the doorway, the light of our candles outlining his profile.

His jaw muscle flexes, and he rolls his shoulders as if he'd love nothing more than to tear someone apart with his bare hands. But by the time Gwil barrels into the room and skids to a stop in front of Ripper, hands up, the King looks as relaxed as he does when sitting on the throne...with one very notable exception.

"Ripper, down," he says, his voice calm and unbothered.

The dog sits but doesn't take his black eyes off the burly man.

Gwil's chest rises and falls in great gasps, his face red and sweating. "The Covenant, Majesty. The Ratcatchers have 'em cornered at a warehouse by the docks!"

Raeth remains utterly still for several heartbeats as I push myself faster through the water, desperate to retrieve my clothing. "Good. See the lady back to my room once she is dressed. Ripper will accompany her. Don't let her out of your sight. Am I understood?"

Gwil's gaze rakes over the pool and I sink beneath the water just to avoid him, but he spots me anyway, then drags his eyes away as if he's seen more than my hair floating pale atop the water. "Yessir."

Raeth's voice is soft and intense when he says, "Protect her with your life."

"Of course."

With that, Raeth springs naked from the water and disappears through the doorway at a lope. Hands shaking, my stomach echoing like a drum to the pounding beat of my heart, I struggle into my dry clothes and follow Gwil back to my room, where I can only wait, alone and aching.

# CHAPTER 28

*Mr. Boragard has all sorts of old things on shelfs and in trunks. He says his parents left them for him when they died and they're very preshus. Even his grandparents. I wish I had anything from Mama and Papa. I miss my old room and my toys.*

*—From the diary of Willow Bowbriar*
*September 2, 1848*

RIPPER WATCHES AS I STRIDE BACK AND FORTH FROM THE UNMADE bed to the workbench where a bouquet of silver Cala lilies lays forgotten next to the planishing hammer. The mantel clock clicks to three am, and I throw myself onto the chaise with a huff, then stand up again when the fire makes my left side too hot.

"I'm not worried," I snap at the dog as I begin my second lap of the room. "I just want to know if he's discovered more about my father."

Ripper tilts his head as if to say, *oh, really?*

"It's not a lie," I insist. But it is, and I know it.

Wanting to explore the passion Raeth stirs in me is one thing, but worrying for him—not for his position or the negative effect his death might have on the citizens of the Undercroft but for his *safety*—says something about my emotions I have no interest in exploring; especially when my first concern should be for my father.

All the plants in our room have been watered and pruned. My sculptures have been dusted and polished. Even Ripper received a good buffing, making his tail wag and his back hunch like a cat. He glows now as he must have when he was first created.

Even the tapestry has been stretched and dusted, but now that I pass it, the way the King and Queen of faeries stare into one another's eyes grates on my nerves. When I release the tie holding the fabric taut, it billows into folds that hide the design.

"Serves you right," I mutter. "Displaying such a private moment. Not everyone is so lucky, and you shouldn't flaunt—"

The door clicks shut. Raeth.

My heart leaps into my throat as I spin toward him, then plummets back into my chest. Blood stains his shirt and smears his hands, visible even beneath his shadow cloak. I don't have time to wonder how he always manages to sneak up on me because I am too busy searching him for damage.

But the way he stands, weight casually on one hip, arms folded, says the blood isn't his. "Worried, Dove?"

"No." The irritated word slips out before I can stop it, followed quickly by, "Are you alright?" Just to be sure.

One dark brow arches, suggesting that he expected my first question to be about the Covenant or my father, and the fact that it wasn't is both amusing and gratifying. But not to me. I lock my jaw against the guilt of caring so much when my focus should be on other matters.

"Well enough." He tosses his black cloak over the back of a chair, then gestures at his chest. "Will you help me out of this? It's bloody, and my hands are sore."

He doesn't need help. I've seen him manage quite well when hurt more. But I still pull the hem of the black shirt out of his trousers and work the fabric up his chest and over his shoulders. His stomach muscles clench and shift beneath his skin, and I have to tear my eyes away to ease the collar over his head.

When he's free of the fabric, Raeth pulls me into his arms and kisses me so soundly that the floor tilts and the room spins. His mouth is sweet and hot, and he smells of salt and sweat. When he releases me to toss the shirt into the fire, I have to hold the back of the chair for balance.

"I never thought I would care if someone worried over me," he says, crossing to the basin to wash his hands. "But I find that if it is you, I rather like it."

A warm little ember crackles in my chest, but I ignore it and try to salvage what I can of my dignity and morality. "Did you capture anyone? Anyone who could tell us where my father is?"

He sighs. "No. By the time I arrived, only two were left, and they fought like demons. But I did confirm something." After drying his hands, he tosses the towel onto the table and digs a scrap of cloth from his trouser pocket. "The Covenant is using magic."

Embroidery catches the light when he tilts his palm, and my fingertips fly to my mouth. "That's the symbol I saw! The slanted S!"

"It appears to give them some form of physical protection."

"Like my dress?"

"Not quite as sophisticated as your dress," he admits, "but yes."

That makes sense, given how much damage they appeared to withstand. "But...how do they heal so quickly? When I—" bile climbs up the back of my throat at the memory, but I swallow it and press on, "when I struck that man with a hammer, he just shrugged it off. And his head cannot be protected by his coat."

"That," Raeth raises one finger and sits on the bed to remove his boots, "is the mystery. We have examined their bodies, and apart from the strange quality of their skin and puncture scars on the insides of their elbows, we haven't found much."

I begin pacing again, letting my forward motion drive my mind. Witches were outlawed in New London hundreds of years ago, and since witches are the only creatures capable of magic, magic has *also* effectively been outlawed. So even those who believe in it, few as they may be, would have no way to study its use.

But Raeth said the Covenant uses magical symbols on their clothing, and if my dress is doing the same thing to protect me... I pull my jacket out of the closet and scour the outside, then turn it inside out and search the seams. There: embroidery in a matching thread so delicate it is difficult to see, are rune-like symbols. "Is Mr. Bywater a witch?"

Raeth laughs. "No. Not at all."

"Are you certain he has not helped the Covenant?"

"Absolutely."

"Well, this," I stab one finger at the exposed seam, "is not artifice. And if the Covenant uses magic the same way Mr. Bywater uses these symbols, then he is almost certainly using magic in his designs. Which means magic can be done with symbols. Just like artifice."

His amusement fades, and he regards me with narrowed eyes and bare feet. "Go on."

Well," I say, walking faster, "artifice works by channeling and controlling natural forces. And if these two forms of symbol usage work in a similar fashion," I hold up the jacket and look pointedly at the scrap of embroidery, "then magic may also be a force like electromagnetism or gravity. And if artifice can harness and detect natural forces, why can't we use it to use and detect magic?"

"The dwarves would call that blasphemy."

I wave that away impatiently. "They can call it whatever they like. If it works, we can use it. The Covenant can't disappear into the shadows using magic if we can detect magic in the air!"

My heart is pounding as my mind rushes through logical

connections, just as it does when repairing complex artifice or helping my father with his inventions. I am onto something; I can feel it. "If we can create a sort of magical compass, we can use it to follow traces of magic back to their lair. Or...hideout? Whatever villains call their base of operations."

"It's a good theory, Dove, but artifice doesn't respond to magical forces."

"How do you know that?" I demand, then pause and slap my palm against the side of my head. "Ripper! No wonder I wasn't familiar with so many of those runes. They aren't runes at all, are they? They're magical symbols!"

Raeth looks supremely uncomfortable, and I remember that *he made* Ripper. When he admitted it over dinner, I'd been so focused on him, on the truth he revealed and his pain, that his artistry hadn't registered properly. I hadn't thought to ask who pioneered this style of artifice.

"Calliope's voice, you're a master artificer! Raeth," I grab his forearms, "do you know how brilliant you are? How visionary your work is?"

He clears his throat and politely disengages my hands.

"With your knowledge, we can create a tool to help us detect magic! It will take a bit of trial and error, but if we can do it, the Covenant cannot hide from us. We could find my father!"

"No."

My stomach drops. "You cannot deny this is a good plan."

"I don't deny it."

"And you have the knowledge to help me."

He doesn't deny that either, but the familiar mask of indifference slips over his features. Which means he's hiding from me.

"Raeth," I begin and try to school my tone to be as inoffensive as possible despite the hope fluttering against my ribcage like the wings of a trapped bird. "I'm not asking you to do the work yourself. I'm happy to create and test the experiments. If you'll just teach me which symbols do the—"

"No. And stop trying to manage me by swallowing your emotions."

That brings me up short because it is exactly what I was doing. When my father would lose his temper and fling tools about his office or storm out of the Mechanica with a handful of banknotes, a careful voice and a gentle demeanor were required to coax him to sensibility. If I yelled at him, as I often wanted to—especially when I was young —he would only have yelled louder or ignored me altogether.

I pinch the bridge of my nose until I am calm enough to respond. "I don't understand, I'm being perfectly sensible. Would you rather I screamed at you?"

"I'd prefer an honest screaming match to being coddled like a spooked horse."

"Fine," I growl, "then help me! You promised to help me find my father if I held up my end of our agreement, and I have. I know this will work, and we are running out of time!"

His jaw muscle flexes, and he stalks to the other side of the bed, putting yards of mattress between us like a shield. "After Ripper, I swore I would never touch artifice again."

Lessons carved into my very flesh.

That memory silences me. If Raeth was tortured into creating Ripper, is it any wonder he doesn't want to revisit such pain? Then again, so much is at stake, and my father's life hangs in the balance.

"I understand if you don't want to dredge up those memories," I say softly, though he refuses to look at me. "But you chose to build a world where people rely on you for safety, and the Covenant is threatening them. Isn't a bit of pain worth their lives?"

Worth my father's life?

He doesn't answer, but his eyes are haunted. He climbs into the bed with his back to me. Have I pushed too hard or not hard enough? I cannot coax or cajole him like I can my father, and if I tried, he would only resent it. And no wonder, given his past. Have I been unfair?

Stomach in knots, I strip to my chemise and climb into bed. For several minutes I lay there, staring at the shadowed canopy above, but I cannot stand to know he is curled to protect himself from memories, ones he chose to be vulnerable and share with me.

Slowly enough not to alarm him, I scoot across the mattress and curl against his back. He's cold. I slide my hand over his ribcage, the ridges of scars beneath my fingertips, and he takes my hand and holds it against his heart.

When I wake hours later, his side of the bed is cold and empty. But a note lies in the indentation his head left on the pillow: a scrap of paper with neatly drawn symbols inked in a line.

"I HAVEN'T SEEN you in weeks."

Blowing an escaped strand of hair out of my eyes, I glance over my shoulder at Silk lounging on the chaise with a line between her dark brows. "I've been busy."

And I have. I've barely left this room, sinking every spare moment into creating the compass that will lead me to my father.

"I can see that. But the court is starting to talk."

The best I can give her is a one-shouldered shrug as I finish the curve of the second-to-last symbol on the compass. If I don't etch this line cleanly, I'll have to discard the face—again—and start over. "Let them talk."

The chaise cushion squeaks as she stands and pads across the carpet toward me. "You don't understand what happens when the court talks. It's not something you can shrug off."

"I'm building something that will help keep them safe. They got along for decades without my presence." I hold my breath as the awl scrapes away metal to complete the last bit of the curve. "They'll be fine."

There. I let out a long breath and smile at the finished line. This sentence was so close to working that the needle twitched yesterday when I brought Ripper close. But it overheated and nearly burned my fingerprints off. If I got everything right today, I—

"Listen to me, Dove," Silk interrupts my train of thought with a voice like a razor blade. "You've done something no one else in the Court has done; you've gained respect and power not expressly given to you by the king. I understand you don't plan to stay here, but—listen to me!"

She's been curt and pointed in the past, but the anger in her voice now shocks me into dropping the compass face. And it is worse when I realize that I did to her what my father has done to me so often: focused on his own work at the expense of our relationship.

I fold my hands together and nod. "I'm sorry."

Silk rolls her eyes. "Don't be sorry, just listen. I don't talk just to hear myself, even if I have a lovely voice."

"You do have a lovely voice."

"Thank you."

Unwilling smiles tug at the corners of both of our mouths in an unspoken truce. She sighs and pins me with a serious glare. "Power is the most useful tool you have at your disposal. It will protect you when other things fail. It's not foolproof, of course, but it multiplies your ability to get things done. It's foolish to take that for granted. But more than that," she gestures at the door, "those people like you. Don't take that for granted, either, because it's rare. It's a power, too, in its way. You say you want to find your father. Well, you may need them before the end. Especially if the King can't manage it.

"And if you don't care to preserve your standing for your own sake, do it for them. The kidnappings are getting worse, and...it's more than that now. There are murders, too. People are afraid. It would do them good to have some comfort."

Biting my lips together, I nod. She has a good point, and it would be foolish to ignore her. "Thank you, Silk."

She shrugs. "I like you, Dove. Can't say why, but I do. And I like to see a woman getting ahead down here. Gives hope to the rest of us, you know?"

"Don't act like you don't have a fair share of power. I've seen the way Gwil looks at you. He's half-convinced you're going to knife him when his back is turned."

"That's 'cause he's smarter than he looks. Now finish that thing, damn. Why is it taking you so long?"

She leaps out of the way before I can swat her.

"Lady?" Gwil leans into the room. "Court in an hour. Will you be going?"

Silk raises a brow at me. I'm so close to finishing the compass that my fingers itch to grab the awl, but I squash the desire. "Yes."

Silk grins. "That's my girl."

THE TITHE LINE is shorter than usual, and the court members are more ragged, their expressions tighter, their eyes narrow and suspicious. Their collective fear billows out of the crowd and washes over me where I stand behind the throne. The sharp stink of it makes the hair on my forearms stand on end.

Raeth doesn't lounge this time; he sits erect, like a cat listening to the hidden scratching of a mouse. The people may not know it, but that is as much a performance as the lounging. When Raeth is lounging he is at his most alert, his most dangerous. But the appearance of being primed for action means he is worn down.

And no wonder. Trouble Upstairs has called him away more times than I can count. If I sleep poorly with the empty space his absence creates stretching endlessly around me, he must not have slept at all. And when he does return to sleep fitfully, knowing he is there, feeling the warmth of his body and the sound of his breathing, makes the loneliness worse.

I wake from dreams of him touching me, of me touching him, sweating and aching. But he may not share my struggle. He certainly behaves as if my presence is of no more note than a lamp or chair. Perhaps he sleeps well, and I'm only imagining things.

When the tithing chests are carried from the hall and Raeth announces complaints, shouting erupts from the back of the room. Ratchatchers with their black mourning bands rush down the center aisle with a man dangling between them. He hangs limp, and blood smears the ground where his legs drag behind them.

It isn't until they stop that I get a good look at his blood-smeared face. It is the handsome elf man, the one meant to be opening a jewelry shop. His clothing hangs from him in torn rags, and the skin of his exposed neck is shredded where it meets the line of his shoulder, but he is still alive.

Raeth calmly stands. "Gwil, send for the doctor immediately."

After a quick half-bow, Gwil turns and bolts from the room.

"Take him to the infirmary. Light every lamp and then guard the door."

The Ratcatchers drag the limp man out of the room.

"What happened to him?" Someone shouts.

Before the murmur of agreement can catch on, a woman pushes her way forward. "It's the monsters! They killed Tom Jefferson two days ago. Tore him up until I could barely tell whose body it was."

"It ain't monsters, you crack-brained fool," a man shouts. "It's Jack the Ripper come back."

"No," someone else yells above the growing racket, "I seen one! Dogs big as horses, I swear it!"

"The real problem is folks keepin' their doors and windows locked," Rufus says, pushing his way forward, his black beard bristling. "They're staying in at night. Not buying a pint at the pub. Not visiting knockin' shops as often. Rich folks got extra security on shipments, too. My take ain't half of what it usually is."

"That's because of the monsters you bleedin' eejit!"

"Or," Rufus says, glaring at me, "it's because the King is too distracted to protect us as he ought."

"Aye, what is our money good for?" Shouts one of his gang, a dwarven man with his tattoo on display.

Leonie elbows forward and levels a finger at Raeth, but her eyes have Rufus pinned like daggers. "Have you any idea what he's done the last few weeks? No, because you're busy hiding in your bleeding warehouse while the rest of us—"

"Enough." One softly spoken word silences the entire room. They stare hopefully at Raeth, their King, with set jaws and clenched fists. Desperation makes the air thick.

"Everyone will receive a share of the Divvy and a plate at supper."

"But majesty," someone short enough that I can't see their face through the crowd whines. "It's gettin' bad Upstairs. One share ain't enough to—"

"Enough!" Raeth's voice echoes through the room like thunder, and everyone cringes. He seems to have grown at least a foot, and the compelling aura surrounding him is irresistible, just like the elven man now being tended to. "Believe me when I tell you that every resource at the Court's disposal has been put to work. My blood has been spilled in the service of your protection. Even your lady has worked her fingers to the bone to create tools we can use to find and destroy those responsible for harming us."

Their hopeful gazes land on me with physical weight and a fervor that heats my skin. But it is the expectation of help I cannot escape. "The tool is nearly complete," I say with more confidence than I feel.

A sigh of relief fills the room. Muses, have I truly earned such trust that a simple reassurance would convince them their hope in me is well founded?

"Grievances must wait," Raeth says, holding his hand out to me. "Have food and drink brought in for those who need it. The Undercroft is open this night. Remember the Night Code."

"The Code!" They respond in unison.

We exit to the chatter of relieved voices and hurry through a series of tunnels I've never used.

"Are you truly close to finishing," Raeth asks with a backward glance. Does he think someone is following us?

I try to ignore the sudden fear that sits like ice at the base of my spine when I remember the hatred in Rufus's eyes, and take comfort in the solid warmth of Raeth's arm under mine. If anything happens, he will protect me. I know it. "Yes. I think so."

"Good."

Ratcatchers nod us through as we turn into a room I've never visited. The light makes me squint and blink. A dozen dwarven lanterns hang from hooks in the ceiling, illuminating the man lying atop a sturdy wooden table. Gwil stands in the corner, burly arms folded as he oversees the affair.

"Call in all the ratcatchers to keep peace in the Undercroft overnight," Raeth says without preamble. "I want them here until after the Divvy tomorrow."

Gwil nods and slips out before the door closes.

Raeth turns to the small, mouselike man hovering over the figure on the table, his spectacles perched low on a narrow nose, a cloud of white curls making his dark skin more prominent. "How is he?"

The little doctor wipes the back of his hand across his forehead before pulling his glasses off and gesturing at the prone man with an irritated flick of his wrist. "Fine, as far as I can tell. His vital signs are strong, and I cannot find any injuries. But he's all over blood, and his clothing has been torn to shreds! I can't make sense of it."

Raeth nods at the Ratcatcher near the door, then gestures the doctor out of it. "Very good, Doctor. Double your usual fee."

That mollifies the little gentleman, who gathers his things and allows himself to be escorted out. When the door closes again, only the three of us are inside.

"Aren't you afraid he'll tell someone what he's seen?" I mutter beneath my breath, remembering Raeth claiming there was no doctor in the Undercroft he'd trust with his own care.

"No. The good doctor's primary motivation is greed. And I pay him very well." He turns to the unconscious man. "You are safe."

Raeth tightens his grip on my arm when the man opens his eyes. The tension in his hand is the only signal I have to maintain my composure because otherwise, I would be sputtering and demanding answers. I've never seen anyone heal so fast save Raeth himself. Which must mean these men are connected in some way. Perhaps they are refugees of the same country.

The man sits up and grimaces. "Thank you for that. If I had to allow him to prod at me for another five minutes, I'm afraid I might have lost my temper."

"What happened?" Raeth asks, not bothering to offer any comfort.

"To be honest," the blonde man sighs and rubs a hand across his face, "I think it was a vampire."

Shock buzzes up my spine despite Raeth's earlier guess. "A vampire?" The word doesn't sound real. "Vampires haven't been seen in England in hundreds of years."

He gives me an apologetic smile. "Beg pardon, Lady, but Vampires are terribly adept at hiding."

What can I say to that?

"Why didn't you have the coin on your person?" Raeth asks.

The man flinches. "I forgot it at the shop."

"If my Ratcatchers hadn't stumbled upon the fracas, you would be dead. The injuries must have been severe for you to still be wounded by the time you reached my court. Forgetting your coin was a stupid mistake. Don't make it again."

Looking properly chastised, the man nods.

They have a short, terse discussion about whether it was a vampire, how it discovered him, and several other topics I can't seem to pay attention to because Raeth was right. There are vampires in New London.

And they are hunting people.

Are they connected to the Covenant or an entirely separate problem we must solve on top of everything else?

I need to finish the compass, and I need to do it now.

# CHAPTER 29

*I held off the creditors again today. Papa is late on the mortgage, thanks to a new development with his invention, but the bank is not interested in how his Aetheric Charger could change the world. They only want to know where their money is.*

*—From the diary of Willow Bowbriar*
*April 31, 1880*

"THE COVENANT AND A CONSPIRATOR IN THE UNDERCROFT," I SAY, ticking things off on my fingers one at a time, "the kidnappings, and now vampires and possibly werewolves?"

"That sounds right," Raeth replies.

Ripper lights the way as we stride down the unused corridors behind the central tunnels. The compass sits lightly on my palm, the cover closed to protect the delicate mechanisms inside until I am ready to use it. "Has anything like this happened before?"

"Something is always amiss; politics, a disease, or something else. But no, this combination of catastrophes is unusual, even for the Unseen Court."

"They must be related, then."

Raeth looks down at me, but his eyes are shadowed beneath the black hood. "Hopefully, we will find out before long. We're far enough; this ought to do."

We stop, and Raeth backs away from me several paces, leaving Ripper and me in the center of the narrow hall. The air is colder without him near, and I want to hurry back to his side, but we are too close to finding the Covenant to let the fact that he hasn't touched me in days distract me now. I shouldn't be worrying about romance when lives are at stake.

This prototype (the last one caught fire, though how that is possible with bronze, I cannot say. Magical artifice is far more fiddly than the traditional kind) took two days of work before I was willing to risk testing it. And if it works now? A shiver of anticipation makes the hairs on my forearms rise.

We could trace the Covenant back to their stronghold and find my father before the week is out. Before six months have passed, just as I prayed for. This compass alone is both worship and a prayer to the Muses, perhaps the most complex thing I've ever made.

With their grace in my favor, I'll rescue my father, and we will return to the surface and try to save the Mechanica from the bank if they haven't already reclaimed it to pay off our loan. Perhaps we can salvage what is left of our lives.

I'll have everything I've hoped for...as long as he is still alive. The thought makes a lump form in my throat.

"Are you ready, Dove?"

A deep breath gathers all my distracting thoughts, and a long exhale releases them. "Yes."

"Good. My cloak is thick with magic. You should be able to track it. If you do not find me, order Ripper to bring you back to our room."

He's only a few feet away, still within the reach of the light, but already, the cloak makes him look more like a shifting shadow than a person. But I trust my instrument. "I'll find you."

"You sound certain."

"I am."

His face is shrouded, but I can hear the velvet smile in his voice. "Care to make that a wager?"

"What are the stakes?" I ask, a little thrill arrowing through my stomach.

"If I elude your artifice, you will spend every winter with me in the Undercroft. Not because our contract binds you, but because you want to."

His condition hits me like a sledgehammer in the chest, forcing the air from my lungs. "And if I win?"

"I will fund your art shop."

Tears sting my eyes, but I refuse to let them fall. Do I want to give up the sun again? To say goodbye to my father for months every year and surround myself with this silent, never-ending dark? A vision of Raeth as I remember him in the pool, his gaze clear and hungry, his hands tight on my hips, sears my mind like a brand.

And next to it, a golden, glowing possibility: my own shop. With sunlight streaming in the windows, glowing off the petals of metal flowers, useful sculptures, and my name on the sign hanging outside.

"I accept your terms."

He retreats until his cloak melds with the dark, and his smooth, teasing voice drifts back to me. "Then I win, either way. See you soon, Dove."

A faint rustle of his cloak and Raeth is gone.

For a few heartbeats, the wager swells in my chest, filling it until my ribcage might burst. Because either way, I win, too, and he arranged it that way. To find another way to give me something he can pretend is no more than a clever game, a way to maintain control.

But it is so much more than that.

The tears fall anyway, and I ignore the tickle as they trail down my cheeks. Until I remember that, for any of this to matter, my compass must work. And Ripper and I are alone, far from the central tunnels I am familiar with.

The air feels like a held breath, and if I were to scream, the silence would swallow my voice long before it reached friendly ears. All that stands between me and hundreds and thousands of tons of earth are stone arches shaped and laid by ancient hands. If I think too much about it, I'll run screaming.

No, I can do this. Focus.

Heart beating wildly, I flick the cover open and stare at the compass. It stares back up at me. The bronze is thin and light, hammered and polished into a shallow circle housing a delicate gold needle. Carefully inscribed symbols adorn the face surrounding the needle, adding a much-needed decorative flair, though they are purely functional.

"Time to find out if you work." Inching closer to Ripper, I hold the compass on my palm in front of me and watch the needle. The symbols glow with faint blue light as soon as I am within a few feet. Just as it did in our room, the needle swings around to point directly at him.

Now, I need confirmation of my theory.

"Okay, that's you sorted, boy. The easy part is over. Let's see if it can pick up the leftover magic of the King's cloak."

As I turn, the needle stays locked on Ripper, but with every retreating step, the blue light fades from the symbols. "That looks to be about five feet," I murmur, shifting back and forth to watch the light grow and fade. After five feet, they go entirely dark. But when I reach the last place Raeth stood, the blue light flickers back to life, a bit dimmer than before.

Excitement fizzes in my veins. I've done it. "Magic does leave traces in the air!" I crow. "Just like scent chemicals or radiation."

Practically humming with excitement, I follow the needle's direction, inscribed to orient on the strongest traces of magic.

Perhaps someday, I can fine-tune it to specific signatures, like Ripper or Raeth's cloak.

Ripper stays behind me so his presence doesn't divert the needle, and we begin a series of winding twists and turns with the needle and blue light to lead the way. I imagine Raeth hurrying down this path on silent feet, amused at the idea of leading me on a merry chase. Picturing what I might do when I find him distracts me enough that I almost miss the needle jerk to one side at a four-way intersection.

I turn left, then right, but the needle swings in both directions, and the magic-detecting symbols continue to glow blue. So magic moved in both directions, then. Raeth must have completed a circle to throw me off. I turn right and chuckle. "Nice try, Your Majesty, but circling back won't save you."

Only the trail doesn't circle back.

It winds into unused tunnels, through crumbling arches, past broken pieces of ceramic pots, and the rusted remnants of tools so old I cannot tell what they used to be. In the Undercroft, maintaining a sense of direction without landmarks is impossible. Still, the arrow points steadfastly ahead despite it feeling as if Raeth is leading us farther from the central tunnels.

We angle upward, and the air warms as the older stone gives way to modern brick. Now and then, corridors open at oblique angles, sometimes leading down wooden steps so rotted a stiff breeze would topple them, and other times dropping suddenly into pits so dark the light of Ripper's eyes doesn't reach the bottom.

We have been walking for what seems like hours, but without the sun or a pocket watch, I cannot tell how much time has passed. I stop in the center of a rough-hewn tunnel, frowning. Something isn't right. The damp mineral scent has faded, and I swear there are hints of manure in the air. And...is that light? Are we so close to the surface? Raeth would not have led me Upstairs, would he? Icy dread slides down my spine.

"Ripper, light," I whisper and close the compass just in case, slipping it into my hip pocket.

The lamps behind Ripper's eyes fade, leaving us in utter darkness...only it isn't utterly dark. A brick and earth tunnel stretches before us, so indistinct that I don't trust even my keen sight. But after a few more steps, I cannot deny that light is leaking into the Undercroft from somewhere.

I sneak forward with Ripper creeping behind me. The light grows. A surface opening must be nearby, so there should also be a Ratcatcher somewhere inside the tunnel, guarding the entrance.

We make a righthand turn onto a set of stairs that lead to a distant door outlined by broken light. But no one waits inside. Raeth would absolutely not be waiting for me in the daylight. I know enough of him to know that. Which means I have been following a magical signature that does not belong to him.

Sudden light blasts down the corridor, blinding me. I stumble backward, blinking, and catch myself on one of the passage doorways. Fear closes my throat, though I cannot say why, and I slide into the door, motioning for Ripper to follow me into the dark.

The passage curves away to the left before taking another sharp turn, and I follow it around, thinking to hide in the shadows, but the floor has fallen into darkness, and I skid to a stop before my feet cause any loose stones to topple in. Heart pounding, I lean against the wall and flatten my arms, pushing all my weight away from the hole.

Controlling my breath requires concerted effort. The last thing I need is for whoever used that door to hear me panting and investigate. Slowly, I ease away from the hole and back toward the door.

Footsteps and muttered conversation drift toward me through the dark, the words too distant to make out clearly. But as I inch closer to the main corridor, the voice–and the unmistakable smell of late spring in New London–becomes clearer.

"I don't care how delicate the situation is. We're on a timeline, you understand? We can't finish this unless we have resources, and the fucking King is cocking it up. So you'd better stop worrying about stealth and start worrying about what happens to someone's ability to walk when they have one or two fewer toes."

Slagging hell, is that the conspirator? If so, whoever they're talking to must be Covenant.

Footsteps again. I flatten myself against the wall and try not to breathe while motioning for Ripper to stay still. Over my left shoulder, a shadow passes silently before the open door. Seconds later, the light disappears.

Do I follow? And if I do, should I follow the shadow or whoever closed the door? One may lead me to my father; the other is the key to keeping the Unseen Court safe. But which is which? And how would I recognize the speakers when I've never seen their faces?

Breath held, I slide sideways and peek first into the dark and then toward the door. When the figure standing silently a foot from my hiding spot snatches me by the front of my dress, I even don't have time to scream. I grab his wrist as he jerks me into the hall, but I don't have the breath to scream.

"I thought I smelt someone." A match scratches, and a flame springs to life. It lights up the yellowish sclera and waxy features of a Bowler Hat. "You," He says with a cutting smile before pulling me close enough that his smokey breath washes over my face and makes me gag. "I've been wanting to get my hands on you."

My mind screams at me to fight back, to run, to scream. But I am wearing my bracelets, and Ripper is at my back. I'm not out of options. I pull in a shaky breath instead. "Me? Why?"

"You'll find out soon enough," he says, his voice bored, as if he has already dismissed me.

Wrenching my body away with all the strength of my legs does nothing to break his grip. Beneath my fingers, the muscles of his forearms are as tight as steel cables. He only smirks and turns to drag me toward the light.

I can shock him into releasing his grip; my bracelets have stored energy for hours. But the sound of the woman's eyeballs boiling scalds my memory like a flash burn, and I cannot force my hands to move.

"Ripper!" The word squeezes out of my lungs, high-pitched and terrified.

The dog roars out of the concealment of the shadows and barrels into the hallway like a dull gold blur. He slams into the legs of the Bowler Hat, who crumples with a howl, dragging me to the floor with him.

I curl to the side to pull my legs beneath me and push myself away, but I needn't have bothered because he releases me to try and fend Ripper off. The construct is no flesh and blood animal to be easily frightened away, and the blows that beat him about the head and shoulders don't deter him.

He sinks his teeth into Bowler Hat's thigh and shakes him like a rag doll. The Bowler Hats may be inhumanly strong, but Ripper cannot feel pain or fear, and he attacks the man with single-minded ferocity.

"Stop!" Bowler Hat screams. "Call him off! Call him off, and I'll take you to your father!"

I scramble to my feet. "Ripper, stop!"

Ripper lowers his head, a bass growl rumbling in his chest, and retreats just enough that one quick lunge will bring him back within range.

Bowler Hat grabs his injured thigh, trying to hold the pieces of his mangled leg together, but the damage–the damage is...my stomach rolls over. I've never seen so much blood. It spurts between his grasping fingers like a leak in a dam, the stream reaching halfway across the tunnel.

"Shit," he growls. "Help me! Bind this!"

But he is panting, and his already waxy skin has gone grey, his lips blue in the dim light. I drop to my knees and press a handful of my skirt against the wound, but the fabric soaks within seconds.

Bowler Hat's head lolls to the side as he flails at his leg. I've seen them heal so fast that it can be nothing other than magic, but magic can not connect ripped arteries fast enough to replace so much lost blood. The pressure of my hands isn't enough.

I fight his belt off, yanking hard enough to jerk his body to the side, then slide the leather beneath his thigh. My fingers are slick with warm blood, and when I try to force the end of the belt through the buckle, it slips through my fingers.

"Calliope, help me," I growl, finally shoving the end through the metal buckle. But when I try to wrench the leather tight, it slides free. "Dammit!"

Wrapping my hands in the folds of my skirt for purchase, I grip the leather again and pull, tightening the tourniquet. But it's too late. He slumps to the side, his head hanging loose upon his neck, eyes wide and staring. I could not save him.

But I can find out whether it was *his* magic that affected the compass. Hands shaking, I slide my fingers into my pocket only to pull the mangled brass from inside. My dress protected me from the impact of the metal, but the compass face and the all-important inscriptions that detect magic were warped and smashed.

How could I have been so stupid? I focused on perfecting the symbols to detect magic, but I'd been in such a hurry to test my work that didn't add the standard runes for hardening the metal. My fingers close around the bent artifice hard enough to sting my palms, and my muscles bunch and tighten with the desire to hurl my stupidity at the wall.

Ripper buts his head against my thigh and whines.

"You're right." I drop my arm in defeat, ignoring the frustrated tears blurring my vision. "We must tell the King."

Ripper leads me back with unwavering certainty, winding through the rarely used tunnels like a rabbit in a warren. I follow him, but numbness has settled over me, and my feet move on their own. If the Bowler Hat can be believed, my father is alive. That alone should have my blood running hot.

But I am now responsible for multiple deaths. I've destroyed a tool that took me weeks to make. I never saw the other party, the one who must be a conspirator. And my hope of tracking the Covenant, of saving my father by the end of the week, is as dead as the man in the tunnel.

If I had more sense, I might have cataloged the twists and turns Ripper took that led me to the surface, but the idea of turning Raeth over to the Chief Inspector for help now is unthinkable. Besides, I can't seem to keep track of anything. Every time I grab for a thought, it slips through my fingers like smoke.

"Dove?"

I blink and try to bring the tunnel into focus, but all I see is a shadow flying toward me out of the dark.

"Dove?" Warm hands on my face and shoulders, sliding over my ribs and stomach. "Is this blood yours? Dammit, speak to me!"

"No," I manage to say and swallow to clear my throat. "No, it's not mine."

Raeth scoops me up, letting his hood fall back so I can see the anguish in his eyes as he rushes me back down the corridor.

"You really can't be carrying me everywhere," I say nonsensically.

"Third time is the charm, isn't that what they say?"

"I can walk."

"I know."

"There was no guard at the surface," I say after a moment, knowing there are several important things to tell him but struggling to decide which to start with. "The conspirator must be using it. And my father is alive, I think. But I broke the compass." The last sentence comes out with a sob. "Ripper killed him and broke the compass."

"Shh," he says, pressing his lips against my temple.

"I didn't mean for him to die."

"Of course you didn't. Hold on, Dove, we're nearly there."

I turn my face into the space between his neck and shoulder and squeeze my eyes shut.

# CHAPTER 30

*Sometimes, my youth feels like it happened to some girl in a story. I'm looking at my history written in spidery ink on the yellowed pages of an old book. Other times, when I see her favorite color or smell rosemary, I can still see Mama sitting by the window with embroidery in her clever hands. Those memories make me ache for the safety of sitting at her feet and watching her needle dance. I wonder: will I ever feel that way again?*

*—from the diary of Willow Beauregard*
*June 9, 1901*

"WHERE IS YOUR COIN?" HE ASKS AS SOON AS THE DOOR CLOSES behind us.

"What?"

"Your coin." He sets me on the chaise near the fire. "Where is it?"

My palms slide numbly across my torso. "I forgot it when I changed clothes."

The muscle in his jaw ticks, but he begins undressing me with deft motions. "I told you to keep it on you at all times, didn't I?"

"Yes, but—"

"I cannot find you when you are in danger if you don't do as I say."

"I...the coin is magic?"

Raeth's dark hair falls across his forehead as he bends to loosen the final button on my bodice. "Never leave this room without that coin on your person. Do you understand me?"

I can only nod.

"Fuck, you're all over blood. Let's get this off you."

He pulls me to my feet and undresses me with brisk, impersonal efficiency. When I am in nothing but my chemise, he wraps a blanket around my shoulders and sets a steaming bowl of water on the table next to me. "Give me your hands."

Numbly, I hold them out. Dried blood flakes from my knuckles, leaving dark stains beneath my fingernails. The thicker stuff sits in sticky pools along my cuticles. My stomach heaves.

"Tell me what happened," he says gently as he lays my hands in the bowl.

I do, in as much detail as I can remember, grateful for the fire that keeps my blood from condensing to ice in my veins. I shiver anyway and drag my gaze from the coals to watch him wash my hands.

"I shouldn't have left you alone," he says, not raising his head. "I thought I stayed close enough for you to track me, but it did not cross my mind that you might stumble across another trail of magic." The cloth scrubs violently against the stubborn blood dried in the creases of my palm. "How does your very presence disrupt every sensible thought? I have only to look at you, and my mind is chaos."

How am I meant to answer that?

When my hands are clean, he goes to work on my face, gently wiping away the traces of my encounter with the Bowler Hat, his dark eyes intent as they scan my features. "You're still shivering. Come on."

With that, he lifts me into his arms and carries me to the bed.

"But what about the—"

"I'll investigate tomorrow."

"But—"

"Tomorrow, Dove."

He scoots into bed behind me and pulls my back against his chest, wrapping his arms around me as his leg curls over my thigh. My bottom nestles in the cradle of his hips, and his breath is warm on my neck.

"Your feet are like ice," he says, sandwiching my cold toes between his feet.

The blankets warm with our body heat, but it is Raeth who chases away the cold. With a sigh, I settle back against him, shifting my hips until we're pressed tightly together.

"Don't do that."

I freeze. "What?"

His arms tighten around me. "Don't wriggle against me like that."

What had I done wrong? "I didn't mean to...I was just trying—"

"I know what you were trying to do," he growls. "But I won't be able to maintain my chaste intentions if your bottom keeps rubbing against me."

That makes me laugh unexpectedly. "You? Chaste intentions?"

"Don't make me regret it. I'm only trying to warm you and help you relax. You were shivering like a marble statue in an earthquake."

His distracting presence, the scent of cinnamon on his breath, the warmth of his body, and the strength of his arms around me are a welcome reprieve from the pressure of my thoughts and memories. He warned me not to, but I snuggle backward anyway, as if he is a warm blanket I can burrow into.

He groans and buries his face in my neck. "You are a cruel woman."

"I'm cold."

Raeth wraps himself tightly around me, tucking the blankets beneath our feet. The fire plays a comforting symphony of little pops, crackles, and hisses to the rhythmic beating of Raeth's heart. Warmth and a profound sense of safety chase away the shock of the last hour, leaving me no defense against sleep.

WHEN I WAKE, Raeth's chest is pressed to my back, one hand wrapped around my ribcage to keep me close. His hot breath tickles the hair at the base of my neck. I must have slept several hours because the fire is mere coals, and only the lamps are left to chase away the darkness.

Raeth murmurs in his sleep and shifts his hips against my backside, and unexpected heat pools in my belly. If I only wiggled my hips a bit, the length of him would press against me. The thought makes my mouth dry. He is sleeping, and after what I've been through today, the last thing I should be thinking of is how it would feel if he slid into me from behind.

*Muses*, what sort of a person does that make me? Perhaps living in the Undercroft has corrupted me more than I thought. Or maybe it's just Raeth. Being around him brings parts of me to life I did not know existed, and it would be useless to pretend I don't want him.

I cannot stop the frustrated sigh that escapes.

"Are you alright?"

"I thought you were asleep."

He nuzzles my neck. "I was. And you didn't answer my question. Are you alright?"

"Yes? No." I was honest with him about what I wanted before, and his response was more than I could have hoped for. I still dream of his fingers, his mouth— "Why haven't you touched me since...since the baths?"

His breath catches. "Did you think I was lying when I said you terrify me?"

"I thought you were exaggerating."

"Am I given to exaggeration?"

"Now that you mention it, no."

He slides his bicep from beneath my head and turns me onto my back so I can look up at him. "Emotions are dangerous things. They sing comforting songs and make tempting promises about the future. They spin dreams thin as cobwebs and just as fragile." His fingertips dance along my cheekbone, delicate as a butterfly lighting on a flower. "But emotions are not truth, no matter how badly we want them to be, and dreams do not keep their promises, no matter how badly we wish they could. They are ephemeral as smoke on the breeze and so sharp that if you manage to catch one, it slices deep before you let it go. I learned that lesson."

His scars reappear, as they often do when we are alone, and he is distracted. I reach up to trace the sharp line of his cheek and watch his eyes darken, pupils so wide they look like windows to an empty house, one desperate to be filled with firelight and laughter.

"But when I look at you," his voice is raw and heavy, "I forget what I thought I knew. Or I convince myself that another scar won't hurt so much if I can just hold the dream for a few moments. Only," he withdraws his hand and his Adam's apple bobs, "I know I'll wind up bleeding when I let go. Holding onto dreams is too dangerous."

I cannot stand to let him withdraw from me, not when I can see through his eyes to the man beneath, to the traces of who he was hiding inside of the person he was forced to become. I push myself into a sitting position, and he retreats from me, leaning back as I advance. But I won't be put off so easily, not now.

I climb over his legs, pinning him in place until he lies beneath me, and I can cup his face between my hands. "Then let me hold your dreams for you. Just for a little while. Just for tonight."

He searches my face, fear and hope mingled in his eyes. I know he has been with other lovers, probably many before me. But I wonder if he has ever looked on any of them with such honesty. "Let me hold then, Raeth. Just for tonight."

When I bend to let my lips slide along his, gratitude wells inside me, gratefulness that I can give him this intimacy, this one thing he is so afraid to reach out and take for himself. When our lips touch, he shudders, and his arms wind around my waist to hold me to him.

"I thought I lost you again. I've tried to give you as much freedom as I can allow, but every time I turn around..."

I silence him with another kiss, letting my hands roam across as much of him as I can touch. "No worries tonight. This is a night for dreaming."

He hooks a leg around mine and rolls us to the side so fast I squeal and wrap my arms around his neck. The catlike smile he gives me, a slow, pleased curve of his finely caved mouth, sends a jolt of pleasure through my core.

"If tonight is about dreaming," he nuzzles the side of my neck, "then you must allow me to do something I've been dreaming of for months."

A frisson of anticipation makes me shudder. "What?"

He kneels between my legs, his eyes hot. The purring rumble of his voice is possessive as he cups my breasts through the thin cotton of my chemise. "I told you once that I wanted to taste you. Will you let me do that, Dove?"

Calliope's breath (and voice and soul and every other holy part of her) how can I say no when he looks at me like that? But I cannot force the word out while he's kneeling between my thighs with his hands on me. So I nod.

Raeth bends and draws my nipple into his mouth through my chemise. His tongue swirls around the pebbled tip as he sucks. Bright sparks of pleasure dance across my skin, and my hands fly to his hair to hold him tightly against me. When he withdraws, the sight of my skin pink through the wet fabric is so erotic it makes me shiver.

"If there are gods," he says, tugging the hem of my chemise up my thighs, "they have my thanks for letting me see you like this."

My skin is burning beneath his eyes, his touch, tingling as the chemise slides up my body. When he works the cloth over my head and shoulders, he twists it in his fist, binding my wrists together. My eyes widen and he smiles at my expression, a predator enjoying the captivity of his prey.

But when he kisses me, nibbles my earlobe and the length of my neck, buries his face between my breasts, struggling against the bond to touch him feels almost as erotic.

"Is this," I breathe when he releases my hands to slide lower, kissing my stomach and the inside of my hip, "is this what you dreamed of?"

His chuckle is low and sensual and makes gooseflesh run down my legs as his cheek drags across my stomach. "Not nearly."

Propping myself up on my elbows, I watch in disbelief as he hooks his arms beneath my knees, his dark head... *oh, holy Calliope.* He kisses my thigh and takes hold of my hips, whetting his lips with the tip of his tongue as he positions himself. I can't breathe. And when he looks up at me with a hungry smile, my heart stops, only to catapult against my breastbone when he lowers his head and parts my sex with his tongue.

Shock and pleasure make my back arch as his name rips from my throat. His purr of pleasure against my sensitive flesh steals the air from my lungs and every conscious thought from my mind. The slow, rhythmic pace of his tongue makes my hips flex in help-less rolls, pressing his mouth more firmly against me.

"I knew you would be sweet," he says, then slides a finger inside of me.

The sound I make would have made me blush if I wasn't so wanton with desire that I've lost control of my faculties. All I know is that I want more. More of him, of this, of the pulsing pleasure expanding in waves from the center of my body. And when a second finger joins, stretching me gently while his mouth—oh Muses, I cannot take it.

"Yes," he growls, his free hand taking my breast in a none-too-gentle grip and rolling my nipple between his fingers. "That's it, Dove. Let go."

The sensation is too much. I squeeze my eyes shut and bury my hands in his tousled hair, my hips rocking helplessly against his mouth as the pleasure surges, retreats, surges again, and then breaks over me like crashing waves that make my legs shake. But Raeth doesn't let me go. He doesn't stop, only settles in as if my pleasure is a challenge.

"Raeth?" I breathe, dazed, as spasms wrack my body.

"Once more, love," he says, and somehow, the threads of pleasure snap back into place, winding and twisting around one another as if they've never broken. His pace increases, and my inner muscles tighten around his fingers again and again. When they break this time, I scream, and the world goes white, then collapses into languid, liquid blackness.

I barely register him kissing his way back up my body, paying particular attention to my breasts.

"I've been dying to do that," he says, sounding entirely too pleased with himself.

"I didn't know that was possible," I breathe and raise limp arms to wrap around his neck as he positions himself above me, taking most of his weight on his elbows. How can he continuously show me that I am capable of more than I believed?

He settles between my thighs with a wicked smile. "We aren't close to done yet."

Despite the way his smile makes my stomach flutter, my limbs barely move. "I don't...think I can."

He leans down and lets his lips slide over mine in a slow, leisurely rhythm. "I'm patient. And we have all night, remember?"

"Mmm."

He rolls us again, the world spinning in a dizzy kaleidoscope until Raeth's back is leaning against one of the bed posts, and I am sitting astride his lap. Luckily, his knees are drawn up, giving me enough support so that I don't simply topple over.

"This," he says, tracing his fingertips from my collarbones to the tips of my breasts, "is a view I will remember till the day I die."

My skin is so sensitive that those delicate touches make me shiver in delight. But I want to touch him, too, and to taste him. My palms run up the ridged muscles of his abdomen, over his chest, and my lips and tongue follow. When I reach the column of his throat, he groans and tightens his arms, arching his neck against my mouth.

"Bite me," he says.

I've never considered such a thing, but I can't deny that the idea of testing the resilience of his flesh with my teeth has a certain appeal. So I kiss the curve of his neck where it meets his shoulder and bite down. He shudders, his hips rocking in reflex, which drags the shaft of his cock against my already sensitive skin and sends needy heat pooling once more between my legs.

A whimper escapes my lips, proving that I am still hungry for him despite being as weak as a newborn kitten minutes ago. And I remember too clearly the feeling of him pressing into me in the pool, the promise of being filled, being stretched, of having him inside me.

Raeth captures my mouth, one hand threaded through my hair at the base of my skull, the other slipping between our bodies to drag two fingers up my center, making me shudder. My hands follow, sliding over his stomach until the hot, hard length of him fits against my palm.

When I stroke him, his jaw locks, and the kiss deepens. The taste of him, and of me on his tongue, is wild and sweet, but it isn't enough. I raise myself to my knees and guide him to the center of me, but he holds me still.

"Slowly, Dove. I don't want to—I don't want you to hurt yourself."

My heartbeat kicks because Raeth doesn't misspeak. He

doesn't mince words. Everything he says means something, even if it is only deception. And even his deceptions are revealing.

"Say what you mean," I breathe.

His jaw locks as he struggles against what he wants to say, his chest heaving. "I want you to know you're in control. I don't want your first time to be painful."

I sink just enough that the head of his cock presses into me. The delicious stretching, the fullness, and the heat of him inside me makes my eyes widen as my breath catches. He watches my face, sweat beading his brow, his jaw clenched.

I search his eyes for the truth, but his evasions have already told me the answer. "But you do want to hurt me. Don't you?"

Raeth grips my waist as if he is afraid I'll leave. His jaw muscles flex, but he swallows audibly and releases me, bracing himself on the mattress. He is letting me go in case his answer scares me. "Yes. I want to hurt you."

The growling admission makes gooseflesh run down my arms. The idea of pain shouldn't excite me, but the hungry growl in his voice does. I repeat the motion of my hips and moan at the pleasure of him sliding deeper inside. "How?"

Every corded muscle in his upper body strains as he forces himself not to move. "God's breath, you're so wet. I want..." He growls and swallows. "I want to tie you down, spread your legs, and hold you impaled until you arch off the bed like a drawn bow. I want to see the marks of my fingers, my teeth, red on your skin—I want..." his breath catches as I slide onto him, and a hot spear of burning pain makes me whimper and clutch him to my chest.

He wraps his arms around me as I shake and buries his face in my shoulder, letting his hands run up and down my back in soothing motions. The soft sounds of comfort he makes wash over me until my body relaxes.

"Pain can be pleasure, too," he says gently and flexes his hips.

Pain rears again, but this time, pleasure rides with it, and I moan. Raeth holds my hips and pushes me, then pulls me against him, retreating, then filling me in a rhythm like a heartbeat.

I cannot stop my head from falling back or my mouth from falling open. I pick up the rhythm, eager for more. Every roll and flex of my hips brings him deeper, and I cannot think, cannot imagine anything better than being filled by him, his lips on my skin, his fingers finding and circling the center of my pleasure again.

Raeth groans against my neck, urging me faster. "Come for me one more time, love."

Tension grows in my core, my arms tightening, my toes curling. I want him deeper, touching me everywhere, filling every hollow place. I never knew I could hunger like this but *Muses, I want*. I bite his neck in frustration, tasting the salt of his skin and drinking in the groan that tears out his throat.

My muscles are too tight, the tension too hard, and it is too much to bear. Raeth growls and I am on my back. He is forcing my legs farther apart. Our hips meet in rhythm, our hearts pounding, foreheads pressed together as his breath becomes mine, and my body becomes his.

The whimper that escapes his perfect lips as he buries his face between my breasts tells me the Cutthroat King is entirely at my mercy, and the thrill of that truth, of my power and his vulnerability, sends my need spiraling out of control.

"Raeth," I cry, wrapping my legs around his driving hips. My muscles clench so hard that stars burst at the corners of my vision.

My breath hitches as I squeeze my eyes shut, every fiber of my being focused on the slick length of him and the bright, spiraling pleasure of his fingers. His body is tight as a coiled spring beneath my hands, his muscles clenched and slick with sweat.

We shudder and pant, riding the very edge of self-control. Raeth grabs the back of my neck and forces me to look at him. Our eyes lock. A spark of incandescent heat rockets through my chest.

"I want to see your eyes," he pants. "I want to watch you realize the moment you become mine."

The tension cracks, then breaks like a dam in flood. I spiral out of myself, losing sense of everything but Raeth between my legs.

He holds me steady through the tremors, rocking his hips as pleasure breaks inside me and over my body so hard and fast that my vision tunnels. But I cannot look away from Raeth's eyes, from the dilated pupils that blow wide as completion overwhelms him.

His mouth drops open. Muscles locked, he bucks against me, pushing deeper inside, brows low and pinned together as if he is in pain. I drag his mouth to mine and drink every cry and whimper, pulling his panting breaths into my lungs.

When he stills, his lips tremble against my cheek. My legs are shaking. My joints have given up trying to hold me together, but more than that, the threads that used to tie all the separate parts of me into one cohesive person have been cut, and I am left unmoored, unmade. The sensation of it wells in my eyes and spills across my temples and into my hair.

Our bodies are still locked together when he kisses me, holding my face as gently as if I were made of glass, his thumbs wiping away my tears. A little sob wrenches free from my chest and pushes past my lips, though I try to swallow it. I don't want him to think I'm crying for the wrong reasons, even if I can't quite pinpoint why I'm crying in the first place.

"Shh, love," he says, kissing my forehead. "It's okay. Cry. Cry for me, too."

Something inside me breaks, and I lock him against me, inside of me, as every bit of emotion I've swallowed or hidden away comes pouring out.

Raeth rolls to his side and pulls me against his chest, cradling my head, curling around me as if his body is a shelter. I don't know if I will be able to find and weave all of the snapped threads of my soul back into place.

Even as exhaustion and the comfort of his arms pull me into sleep, I know the person I was before he touched me no longer exists.

∿

TUCKED against Raeth's side hours later, I yawn and run the tip of my finger along a scar that trails from beneath his collarbone to the edge of his shoulder; one torturous mark out of hundreds. They are delicate threads of silver in the lamplight, perfectly healed and clearly intentional. Whoever made these knew what they were doing. Looking at them as his chest rises and falls, I cannot help thinking it is a miracle he survived.

But his scars run far deeper than his skin, as evidenced by his nightmares.

Not for the first time, I'm tempted to ask what he is. Raeth is faster than any elf, far stronger than the dwarves, and he heals at a rate I have never heard of outside stories of vampires and were-wolves. And since I have seen him stand in sunlight in my garden, he is clearly not a vampire. Then again, the stories may not be true.

"What are you thinking about, Dove?"

I glance up at him through my lashes, still amazed we are lying here so intimately. Still shocked his handprint is on my bottom and that I actually like the warm, comfortable way it stings. And now I wonder, how honest can I be with him?

I've risked trusting him with my body, which I must admit is foolish though the payoff made my toes curl. And we may have pushed our cares far enough away to allow a moment of connec-tion—and pleasure—but the world has a habit of shoving in where it's not wanted.

I've been avoiding this question for months, and I may never have another chance, so I decide to risk it anyway. "I'm wondering what manner of creature you are."

A slow, approving smile curls his lips, and the sight makes warmth gather in the pit of my stomach. My reaction to him has always been problematic, but now that I know what my body is capable of in his hands, controlling myself may become a prob-lem. Which is not a worry I thought I would ever have.

"I wondered when you would ask me that." He brushes hair

from my cheek and tucks it behind my ear. "What took you so long?"

I shrug one shoulder. "If Undercrofters are hesitant to share their names, asking what someone is seems far more taboo."

His fingers curl into my hair, and he pulls me up his body to kiss me. Conscious thought spins away at the first touch of his lips, the gentle probing of his tongue. The fingers of his other hand tighten on my hip as I open for him, and bloody hell, how did I not know being kissed could feel this good?

He leans away just enough to let me see how hot his gaze has grown. "Exploring taboos with you promises to be very enjoyable."

I intend to respond, but the only sound that escapes me is a gasp when he rolls us over and seats himself between my thighs in a single, breath-stealing thrust.

He groans in pleasure, and my legs wind around his hips to lock him in place.

"I've been trying to tell you for weeks," he admits, framing my face with his hands. "I'll have to rely on your clever mind to suss out the details. I'm a bit distracted at the moment." His stomach muscles flex, curling his hips into me, pressing him deeper. "God's breath, you were ready for me with just a kiss, weren't you? How am I going to let you go?"

I don't want him to let me go. My fingers dig into the rounded curve of his buttocks, urging him to move. We can answer those questions when the driving need for tightening my insides has been satisfied.

"Who knew my gentle dove would be so demanding in bed?" He teases, only for a breath to hiss through his teeth when I bite his chest. "Very well," he thrusts hard enough to make our bodies slap together, hard enough to sting, and the sound that slides past my lips isn't gentle at all. "No more talking."

# CHAPTER 31

*I saw a member of the One Tear Gang when Papa and I ran errands today. The boy slipped through the crowd like a fish through water. I only noticed the ink on his cheek because he happened to look up as I passed. He was achingly thin, with hard eyes that belonged on a man, not a boy. I dropped a few coins, because he would never take charity. I hope he finds them.*

*—From the diary of Willow Beauregard*
*May 29, 1899*

WHEN I WAKE, A SPRIG OF ROSEMARY LIES ON RAETH'S PILLOW NEXT to a quickly scrawled note: *gone hunting, have taken Ripper. Gwil at the door.*

Gone hunting? For the body of the dead Bowler Hat, I suppose.

Hopefully, he learns something from the body so the man will not have died in vain.

I rub the rosemary leaves between my fingers, letting the pungent scent fill the air before forcing myself out of bed. I pad toward the table near the fireplace, where a tray of breakfast is steaming, but I have to stop halfway and wince at the soreness between my legs. A hundred little memories from the night before flash across my mind–a hand on my hip, my leg over his, the warm water as he helped me wash. My cheeks burn, but the embarrassment is tempered by wonder.

Not only had I seduced The Cutthroat King, but I'd fallen apart in his arms, and instead of dismissing my emotions or, worse, being disgusted by them, he held me as if my breakdown weren't a burden.

The relief makes me feel lighter than I have in ages. At least until I catch sight of the bent compass sitting on my worktable. The weight of my mistake lands on my shoulders, especially heavy under the knowledge that I was right: my father is alive, and they have him.

But I will get him back.

Even working at my best speed, it will take several days to fabricate a new compass, and we aren't that far from six months.

"He said he would still help me find my father," I tell the hammer as I begin pounding a sheet of brass thin enough for the compass.

But a little voice that has grown stronger over my months in the dark reminds me that trusting everything Raeth says just because we've shared a bed would be foolish. And neither I nor my father can afford foolishness.

For hours, nothing disturbs the silence but the ping of my hammer and the scratching of my awl. The compass begins to take shape, the shallow cylinder of a body waiting for a heart, when someone knocks on the door.

"Lady?"

Gwil. I set my tools carefully back in their places and slide the bolt open. "Yes?"

The lantern-jawed man gives me an apologetic half-smile. "The King calls for you. He says it is urgent."

A thrill shoots down my spine. He must have news about the Covenant. "Do I have time to change?"

"Quickly."

It takes minutes, though my buttons aren't even, and my hair lies in a simple braid before I follow Gwil through the back tunnels. "Where are we going?"

"The Hall," he says over his shoulder.

"I've never gone this way before."

He shrugs but offers no explanation.

We stop in front of a bare wall of brick. This corridor is shorter than the other tunnels and square. Gwil's head nearly brushes the low ceiling. He raises his lamp to search the wall and presses one brick. It shifts backward about an inch, and an entire section of the wall follows, mortar and stone grinding until a narrow door opens.

Gwil hands me the lamp and gestures at the room with his chin. "The King asks you to wait in here."

I stare into the dark and swallow hard.

"Lady," Gwil rests one enormous hand on my arm, "it's only a secret room. I'll be outside. If I were to lock you in somewhere, his majesty would skin me alive."

Perhaps that is true. I have to force myself to remember everything that has happened since I've been here. Even when I was poisoned, Raeth did not try to cage me, not since the witch attacked me, and then it was only temporary. Swallowing hard, I step into the dark with the lamp in one hand. It is a small room, no more than six by six feet, with a bench and nothing else.

"Dim your light," Gwil says as the hidden door crunches back into place.

My heart stops, but I fight through the rising panic and turn the dimmer switch on the lamp. A faint light shines through cracking mortar on the left side of the room. Frowning, I press my cheek to the narrow slit and peer through. A large room opens before me. I am viewing it from above eye level, closer to the ceiling. And what I thought was a crack in the mortar is more purposeful than that.

It is a peephole, and I am looking down on the great hall. Raeth lounges on the throne, with the silver crown of spoons tipped lazily to one side of his brow, Ripper sitting next to him. His attitude is one I've seen him adopt countless times before the court: confident to the point of insouciance.

The hall is empty, which is unusual. Setting the lamp on the floor so no light will leak through the opening, I carry the bench to the hole and sit so I can watch comfortably. An aristocratic woman strides into the room with a huge raven on her right shoulder.

People born into wealth and power have a way of walking and holding themselves that tells everyone exactly who and what they are, even when they're dressed as plainly as she is: shoulders down, chin up, chest forward, with a gait trained from birth to appear elegant. She stops in the center of the room. With regular features, clear skin, and fine, dark eyes, she is pleasing, if not pretty. But the confidence in her carriage and grace of her movements make her compelling.

"Ahh, Lady St. James," Raeth says in a tone full of disingenuous graciousness, "I wondered how long it might be before you graced me with your presence once more. And is that the Raven I see sitting so tamely on your shoulder? Come, Assassin of the King, do me the honor of appearing in your true form." He raises his hands to either side. "We are all friends here, after all."

Assassin? A chill runs down my spine.

The Raven leaps from Lady St. James's shoulder, and the air around it shimmers like heat waves rising from the pavement. An instant later, a tall man stands where the Raven had been, his sharp features devastatingly handsome but cold and hard. His flawless black suit is the height of fashion, but my instincts tell me this is a wolf in sheep's clothing.

I take in these details through the haze of shock that has already stopped my breath and made my heart pound hard enough to hurt. I know now that magic exists, and that it is not so rare as I once believed. But seeing a man change his shape makes me blink and rub my eyes in shock. Gracious Muses, what is he?

Raeth claps his hands, delighted. "I hoped we might meet. I have heard so much about you."

"Most of it is likely true," the man Raeth called the Raven says with a long-suffering sigh. His voice is deep and resonant and so cultured it hurts to listen to. "The bad parts, anyway."

Raeth smiles with a joyous sort of madness, and the unpredictability in his manner suggests he might do or say anything, no matter how deranged, and enjoy it. "How delicious. Now, do tell me, lady, why have you brought a notorious assassin into my court? You do not have designs on my life, do you?"

A malicious smile curls the woman's lips. "My dear King, I do not require such as the Raven to kill you. No, I have come to propose a temporary alliance."

A deadly serious expression replaces the mad amusement in Raeth's eyes. "Have you, indeed?"

"Indeed, I have."

"Speak on."

"I imagine the appearance of monsters in the city has been as bad for your business as it has been for ours."

She knows of the monsters? How?

Raeth raises a brow. "You know how I feel about locked doors and windows."

"So I do," she says. "I have several leads that may expose how monsters are getting into the city, and why. And I also believe I may have a way to destroy them. All of them. But to make my plan work, I need manpower and eyes on the street."

"And here I sit with a city full of minions at my disposal."

"The first night of the full moon cycle is in two days," she says, tilting her head, "and the violence we have seen so far will be nothing compared to the damage of rampaging werewolves, particularly to those members of your court who rely on night work to fill their coffers."

Raeth runs a finger along his chin. "And if I loan you my minions, you believe you can prevent the abuse of my people as well as destroy the monsters plaguing the city? Forgive me but, are you not overestimating your capabilities?"

"What does it cost you if I am? You only stand to gain by this alliance."

Raeth surges to his feet and stalks toward them with predatory grace. The Raven slides in front of Lady St. James, a pair of iron knives appearing in his gloved hands as if by magic. He holds them low and casually, as if he is so familiar with them that they are mere extensions of his body.

"Control your pet, lady," Raeth says, amusement coloring his voice. "I mean you no harm."

"Swear it," The Raven demands, his voice flat and dangerous.

I can barely breathe. None of the normal Ratcatchers are in the hall. Will anyone respond in time if the Raven attacks? I know firsthand how dangerous Raeth is, but there is a cold violence to the taller man that makes my instincts scream.

Raeth, of course, doesn't seem impressed, which likely means he also recognizes exactly how dangerous the other man is. He holds both arms out in a gesture of innocence, fingers open and palms up, but he doesn't stop walking. "I mean Lady Gwen, no harm, Raven. I swear it."

"Do you extend us guestright?"

Raeth freezes. One corner of his mouth twists, but his eyes are cold. He hadn't intended any such thing, and he isn't pleased about it. "Very well. I extend guestright to you both for so long as you remain in my presence."

As long as you remain in my presence. That qualifier is telling. Raeth never makes agreements without loopholes of some sort embedded in them.

He reaches out to rub a fold of Lady St. James's skirt between two fingers. "Is this the armored coat I have heard so much about?"

"Is answering that question a requirement for our alliance?" Lady St. James asks.

"It is. If I invest the time and effort of my people, then they cannot earn their wages or pay me a proper tribute. I must care for them from my own coffers. I want to know my investment will be well protected. And effective."

"You have seen my effectiveness, yourself. I believe your guards still carry the scars."

"How about a little demonstration? Just to—"

The woman spins and lashes out with a kick, faster than any human, if not as fast as Raeth. He could have caught or avoided that kick if he chose to. Instead, her right foot collides with his chest, and he flies through the air, catching himself in a crouch.

I swallow a cry, but Raeth appears unharmed. When he stands, there are gouge marks where his fingers—his *fingers*—dug into the stone floor. Lady St. James opens the canopy of her umbrella toward him as if the fabric is a shield. Runes glow along the shaft.

Artifice! Of what kind? I peer at the device, but from this distance, my eyes aren't sharp enough to make out which runes were used. Is it truly a shield? I find myself hoping she will use it, if only so I can see what it does.

The Raven lowers his knives, Raeth smiles as if he wasn't just kicked more than six feet across the room, and Lady St. James says, "Was that enough of a demonstration, or would you prefer we continue?"

"Consider me convinced," Raeth says with a respectful tilt of his head.

She nods. "Are we agreed on this temporary alliance?"

"We are, if we can agree on terms and timeframe."

"For one week or until all the monsters are found and destroyed, we will cease hostilities against one another, vassals or our extended allies, and aid one another in freeing New London from the monsters plaguing it."

"Very well, ally," Raeth says, "What do you want of me?"

"First, a question: are you or any of your vassals involved in smuggling monsters into the city?"

I stifle a snort. If she thinks he would purposefully put his own people in danger, she doesn't know as much about him as she appears to think she does.

"You wound me, lady," Raeth says, echoing my thoughts. "Do you believe I would endanger my people so?"

"Answer the question."

"You already know the answer. I prefer my crime organized, neat, and by the books. Monsters only complicate things unnecessarily."

"Answer. The. Question."

He grins as if her doubts please him. "No, neither I nor my vassals are involved in smuggling monsters into the city."

"I need your people to find a man, find but not approach. They can send a signal up for Aris. Three lights from a dwarven torch will be enough. He wears a dark frock coat with embroidery at the collar, a symbol that looks like this." She shows Raeth a drawing, but I cannot make it out. "He was seen down by the Twisted Eel, wearing a bowler hat. Spot him, and signal for help."

My hands clench into fists. A bowler hat. Then, she is engaged in this affair as well. She is clearly competent. Is she the dangerous lady Raeth mentioned? She certainly fits the description.

"That can be arranged," Raeth says as if that isn't exactly what we have been doing for months. "What else?"

"Discovering how the monsters are entering the city may be instrumental in finding the source. So far as I can tell, cargo shipments into the city are one of the most viable routes of access, particularly as your men are so susceptible to bribery."

"Do you mean to say you are not? For that shall be a great disappointment to me."

The Lady grins at his sally. "Not with anything you have to offer."

"Touché. All shipments will be inspected. How shall I communicate the results with you?"

She gives Raeth an address and suggests methods for passing along information. The longer they fence with one another, the more her intelligence impresses me, and the more I envy what it must be like to have such power over one's own life.

At last, she says, "If we are in agreement, Aris and I will be on our way."

Raeth, who returned to his throne earlier in the conversation, sits up and trains his gaze on the Raven, a speculative tilt to his head. "And here I thought you had bestowed your favor upon the honorable erstwhile inspector, lady. But it appears you use your favor as purposefully as I use mine. Be careful with that one. Even I have heard rumors of his deeds."

My stomach drops. *As purposefully as I use mine.* Was that an allusion to me, to our relationship? If so, why let me hear him say it?

Lady St. James raises her chin defiantly. "There is not a creature on earth I trust more. And my favor has nothing to do with it."

"Are you so certain of that, lady? Perhaps you do not understand the power of your...affection. What about you?" he asks the Raven. "Does she speak for you, pet?"

The taller man laughs but the sound is more insulting than amused. "Has the mortal world filed the edge from your tongue that your insults cut so shallow? Yes, if the lady called, I would come to her heel like a happily trained hound. Perhaps one day, you will be blessed enough to know what it is to trust someone blindly...but I doubt it."

Whether the Raven knew it or only suspected the King's weakness, his arrow strikes with a force that makes Raeth freeze. His face becomes a mask, his voice flat and dangerous. "Do take care as you leave. It would be a shame if you got lost in the dark."

The two of them stride out of the hall without a backward glance, and I am left with a racing mind and uneven breath. I turn and lean against the wall to stare sightlessly at the ceiling, uncertain whether I can process everything I've just seen.

Raeth became an entirely different person, one just as believable as any of the versions of him I have seen. And the Covenant may be connected to the monsters, only no one knows how, but more people than us know of it and are trying to stop it.

They suspect the monsters are being hidden in cargo shipments, which directly implicates both the Wraiths and the Cogburners. That means I may have given the support of Raeth's crown to someone responsible for the death and kidnapping of dozens of people, if not more.

And a raven turned into a man.

More than that, or worse, Raeth knew who he was and spoke to him as if they shared a history of some kind. *Has the mortal world filed the edge from your tongue that your insults cut so shallow?*

Mortal world.

Hundreds of bits of information swirl through my mind, memories flashing like lighting: Raeth being stabbed but showing no wound, then being injured by the cast-iron chandelier. More stab wounds not healing until a bit of metal was removed from his body, then healing faster than any human, elf, or dwarf. His scars appearing and disappearing. The way his eyes sometimes darken or his canines appear to grow.

His speed and strength.

*I've been trying to tell you for weeks.*

*I never lie.*

*Fifty years ago, I fled my country.*

Raeth hadn't lied. He told me about himself in a hundred small ways, and I never put it together. My people grow old so slowly that I did not think to question it when he said he left his home fifty years ago, far too long for a human to still appear in his mid-thirties.

When the bricks grind to open the secret door, and the warm yellow light of Ripper's eyes spills into the room, they illuminate me where I sit frozen on the bench, my chest heaving. The dark figure in the doorway steps inside and kneels in front of me. Concern pinches his brows together, but his jaw is locked as if preparing for a blow.

"You," I pant, clenching my hands. "You're a faerie. Aren't you?"

Raeth takes both my cold, shaking hands in his and looks down at our joined fingers with a sigh. But is it a sigh of relief or frustration?

He looks up at last, his voice raw. "Yes."

Though I expected it, the truth is a sledgehammer that shatters my understanding. *Raeth isn't human.* He is a member of a race long believed to be nothing more than myth. Humans and elves can mate and produce offspring, but it is incredibly rare, as elves carry children far longer than humans and become fertile far less often.

But what of faerie biology? I am not currently fertile, but stranger things have happened, so I must force myself to ask the question clawing at my insides. "Am I...could I be carrying a faerie child?"

Raeth flinches but doesn't let go of my hands. His voice sounds torn from his throat. "No. I cannot give you children."

I close my eyes and shudder in relief. Not because I wouldn't want a child, though I never gave much thought to the idea of being a mother. But because of what I suspect his words mean. "The lord? He did this to you?"

His grip tightens. "Yes."

My heart aches for all that has been taken from him. Pulling my hands from his grip, I trace the lines of his face, lines I once thought harsh, a face capable of so much depth and complexity. One that has suffered so much.

It would be easy to feel betrayed, lied to, and manipulated. But who he is and what he has suffered are his secrets to share as he sees fit. And he found a way to tell me, even if he could not say the words himself. He shared the truth, and his pain, with me. Would I do the same, unprovoked? Tell someone the painful story of how my parents fell into debt gambling, how they took out usurious loans to save their business? How they died in prison, leaving me to scrape a life from the streets long enough for my father to take pity on me?

No. I have no wish to share that painful truth, to relive it. But he did. Which means he must see some value in my knowing what he is. The man who trusts no one, trusts me.

My thumbs glide over his brows, the curve of his cheeks, the line of his jaw. He is such a painful, beautiful contradiction. "I am so sorry."

That seems to shock him more than anything else. "You've just learned a truth few people in the mortal world know," he says with wonder, "and your response is pity and empathy. You should be angry with me."

"I think I am too shocked to be angry," I admit. "But if I were, that would not stop my heart from hurting for you."

He shakes his head and touches my cheek once, softly, as if the barest touch might shatter me. "You are a wonder." He shakes his head again, but this time to clear it, pulls me to my feet and clears his throat. "Well. We haven't time for pity. Events are in motion, and we must speak."

# CHAPTER 32

*I often forget how tender-hearted Papa can be. He is so intensely single-minded in pursuit of his goals that it is hard to remember what a gentle soul he is. We found a wounded cat in the alley today, a poor, scraggly beast with a torn ear. Papa carried it inside with tears in his eyes. He cannot stand to see things in pain. The cat and I have both benefited from his kindness. Strange to have a kindred spirit in such a ferocious little beast. When I tried to pet him, he took half of the skin off my forearm.*

*—From the diary of Willow Beauregard*
*February 2, 1902*

❀

"THAT WAS HER, WASN'T IT?" I ASK AS WE STRIDE DOWN THE corridor.

The halls are full of people, far more Undercrofters than usual, hurrying about carrying boxes, bags, and baskets, their expressions distracted.

"Ah, Lady Gwen, yes. She is my favorite adversary. I find her endlessly entertaining."

"She kicked you across a room," I say, looking at him sidelong.

"I would have been disappointed if she hadn't."

"I do not understand you."

"That's part of the fun." He winks, and I shake my head.

"You are impossible."

"For everyone but you. But yes, I have had my eye on that woman for quite some time. Her upbringing hasn't damaged her independent mind, and she has put herself in danger more than once to protect those who needed it. More than that, she rescued a pair of rather important children. I think she may be of particular use to me."

"It sounds as if she thinks the same of you."

His smile is wolfish. "That is what makes our game so stimulating. The Raven is a variable I did not account for, however."

"Who is the Raven?"

"You remember the King I fled from?"

I wait to answer until a string of people file by, passing in and out of the lamplight, each nodding their heads to Raeth respectfully. "Yes."

"The Raven was the King's assassin. Lady Gwen appears to have him on a leash, but if she were ever to release him, well. I have heard stories that make even my blood cold, and that is saying something."

"It sounds like he may be a useful ally as well," I say, thinking of how furiously the Covenant fights.

"If I could trust him, perhaps. But I do not."

We turn back into the central corridors where Ratcatchers have gathered to pass out weapons. "What is happening?" I ask under my voice, knowing he will hear me.

"We are mobilizing."

When we reach our room at last, I move to the hearth and

shiver, letting the heat drive away the constant chill of the Undercroft. Raeth pours himself a glass of brandy, throws it back, and pours another before joining me by the fire.

"Things have been dangerous," he says, "but I think they are about to get worse. I suspect the monsters are tied to the Covenant somehow. And we know the Covenant has been kidnapping my people for months. What I did not tell you," he glances at me from the corner of his eye, "is that all of the people they kidnapped are also fae."

I stop rubbing my arms and stare at him. "Then the elven jeweler is a faerie? Where did he...how did you—" I don't know what to ask. When myths reveal themselves as facts, where does one begin? It is as unlikely as Thor descending on a cloud to say that he has been taking tea with the Queen for ages.

Raeth rubs his forehead with his fingertips. "A quick bit of history, then. After the war, mortals and the faeries who allied with them—those who survived—agreed that living separately was safest for both parties. They married fae and mortal magic to create the Sunset Lands, a realm where magic creatures might live without being a danger to mortals. I believe many died creating it. The result was a sort of wall between realms. You may have heard it called a veil."

"Samhain, when the veil is thinnest," I murmur, thinking of a book of faerietales my father gave me when I was young.

He raises his glass in a mock salute. "Even so. But the wall isn't foolproof. Those without much magic, such as myself, can sometimes slip through the cracks in places where the veil is weak. But it is a dangerous proposition. The wall kills more people than it allows through."

"That seems like a terrible risk."

"The only souls mad enough to try it are those willing to die to escape the Sunset Lands." He swallows another mouthful of brandy and sits on the chaise. "You can imagine that finding oneself here after crossing the wall is a bit of a shock. We have no homes, no family, no culture. And the mortal world is a confusing place. Mortals and faeries do not even share a proper morality."

"So when Lord Rutledge found you and offered you safety," I say slowly, imagining Raeth traveling through a strange countryside alone, "it must have been a relief."

His laugh is hard. "In faerie culture, offering someone hospitality is a sacred thing."

"Guestright," I say, remembering what the Raven had requested.

"Here, it must be given explicitly. In Faerie—the Sunset Lands —it is implied. But mortals are not bound by it as fae are. And mortals can lie."

My mind races over everything I remember of faerietales, and smashes it together with what I have seen and heard. "So your coins are a promise of guestright. You are protecting fae refugees, setting them up to live safely here."

"And whoever the Covenant is," he growls, "they are targeting my people specifically. That is why they want me out of the way."

"Are all of the Undercrofters faeries?"

"No," he shakes his head, "not a tenth. But, none of them fit into the machinery society has built to benefit the privileged. They are not neat little cogs happily turning the wheels of industry; some because of the bodies they were born in, others because of the indifferent cruelty of fate. But all have been abandoned."

"And you protect them," I say, a lump rising in my throat.

"I expect them to protect each other, even if it is a brutal sort of protection."

"But there are...murderers and—" I struggle to name the extent of the criminal populace, to reconcile my idea of morality with extending protection to murderers as well as those who simply do not fit the mold of society. How does one phrase such a question?

"I am a murderer," he says softly. "And so are you."

My mouth falls open in shock. "But I—I was trying to save you, and I...we were in danger," I finish weakly.

"Can you prove it? If Scotland Yard questioned you, would they believe you?"

I swallow hard. Would they? "I don't know."

"Would you have me monitor everyone who enters the Court? Interrogate them about their pasts to decide whether their crimes were justified? To judge the morality of their actions by my standards? I am not even a mortal, Dove. When they give me their oath, I do not ask for or consider their pasts. All I ask is that they keep the code."

"And if they don't," I begin, but let the thought hang in the air because we both know what happens to someone who does not keep the code.

"What is that old Christian saying?" He murmurs. "Something about living by the sword?"

A deep breath will not settle my stomach, but I take one anyway.

He downs the rest of his brandy and sets the glass aside. "I do not expect you to agree. And I will not apologize. Circumstances forced many of these people to become dangerous, and the only way to protect them from one another is to be more dangerous than they are."

"Are you certain? Raeth, are you certain of that?"

He considers me for a long time, his gaze searching mine as if the answers lay somewhere behind my eyes. "Problems may be solved by many different answers. But this one works. Until I have a more compelling answer..."

I bite my lips together and close my eyes merely to release myself from the intensity of his gaze. "I think we've gotten off topic."

"Yes." He stands and carries his glass back to the cellarette for another pour, his manner businesslike. "Lady Gwen is correct. The full moon is in two days, and if werewolves are in the city as my folk claim, and our new ally fails, things will get significantly more deadly. Unless we discover the source of the monsters."

"And the Covenant is our only lead."

He turns to face me. "Precisely."

I flex my fingers and shift my gaze to the unfinished compass on the table. "Then I had better get to work."

HAMMERING, turning, drawing, welding, etching, shaping, the hours bleed into one another as the new compass takes shape beneath my fingers. Gwil comes in to replace the fading lamps with freshly charged ones, Tildie clucks and shakes her head as she delivers and removes trays of uneaten food, and Raeth comes in and out as he organizes and manages the Undercrofters.

All the while, my mind and heart play tug of war, trying to make everything I have learned about Raeth, all of his contradictions, fit into a of cohesive picture of his character. Trying, if I am honest, to decide whether I want to fit in that picture beside him.

But when he wraps his arms around my waist and kisses the side of my neck, I think: I would carve myself a place in his life even if I had to do it with a blade made of my own bones. Even if I had to cut bits of myself away until I was the right shape.

And then I think of my father, of what being criminalized cost my parents, of the violence that is an inescapable part of life in the Undercroft, and I want to scurry back into the sunlight.

Though I never come to any firm conclusion, my hands never stop working. I do not know how much time passes as the compass comes together one piece, one runic symbol at a time, but when my hands start shaking, and my knees wobble, I look up to find Ripper whining and wagging his tail, his head tilted to the side.

"You're right," I say weakly. "I need a break."

But Tildie has gotten irritated with me wasting food. I seem to remember her saying something about my going to the kitchens if I was hungry. So, I pull on my armored skirt and jacket and wobble into the hall.

"Just headed to the kitchen," I tell Gwil. "I'm taking Ripper." But he follows me anyway.

I glance at him once or twice over my shoulder, wondering whether he, too, is a faerie. He is incredibly loyal to Raeth. But I cannot know without asking, so I stay silent.

When I step into the kitchen it is fuller than I have ever seen it. Several people are bent over the long wooden worktable, kneading enough bread to feed an army. Two others lean in and out of the massive hearth to stir a cauldron of soup the size of a washbasin, move pottage, pull out loaves of baked bread, and add more wood to the iron stove in the corner.

Another table on the left wall is full of chopping knives, raw meat, and vegetables in big pots.

Several sweating faces turn toward me with smiles, but it is Lucinda I look for. When she looks up, a huge smile creases her face, only for the expression to wobble and disappear.

"Welcome, lady," she says, looking away as she cleans her hands on her apron. "Can I get anything for you?"

Closing the distance between us, I take her hands in mine. "Lucinda, please. I know it wasn't your fault. I am so sorry for the way you were treated, and—" she pulls her hands out of mine, not ungraciously.

"Not at all. I was the one who—well, in any case," she picks up a wooden bowl. "You look a bit peaked. Can I get you some stew and fresh bread? Maybe some cheese?"

I nod and try to smile, but the expression sticks on my face. "I'm glad to see the chimney functioning well," I offer to fill the uncomfortable silence.

"Never better!" She says, but her enthusiasm is strained. "You really should give it a name and sell it."

"Mmm," is all I can manage when I take the bowl and plate.

She dismisses me with something about how she'd better get back to work, and I head to the Great Hall with sadness weighing me down.

"Don't take it personal," Gwil says as we enter the room.

"Hard not to."

"It's guilt, not resentment that makes her push you off."

I plop my food on one of the scarred tables. "That's ridiculous. She had no control over what happened."

Before I can answer, he tears a bit of the loaf from my bread, dips it in the soup, and tosses it in his mouth, then says around the mouthful, "I think maybe that makes it worse, lady."

He leaves me with that thought, turning to fold his arms and look intimidating so no one bothers me while I eat. In truth, I would welcome being bothered so I did not have to sit here with so many dissonant thoughts clanging around in my head, like the fact that he just endangered his own life by testing my food for poison.

With a sigh, I scoop up a spoonful of stew. My stomach realizes how long it has been since I fed it and growls with a ferocity even Ripper hears. The food is gone in minutes, and my mind is less fuzzy.

"Cor, Dove, isn't the King feedin' you?"

Silk slides in next to me with her own plate.

"This was my fault, I'm afraid," I admit, but smile. "It's good to see you."

She bumps my arm with hers. "You too. How've you been?"

"Good and...less good. You?"

"Busy," she says before tearing off a piece of bread. "The court is gearing up for something nasty. Monsters, sounds like."

"You say that so casually."

"Getting worked up don't change it. You finished already? You must want something sweet."

It takes a moment to realize she's talking about me. I frown down at my plate. "I don't really—"

"Oi, big lad, the lady wants something sweet. Be a dear, will you?"

Gwil looks over his shoulder at Silk, and she gives him a cheeky grin.

"I've got Ripper," I remind him. "And the kitchen isn't far."

Gwil sighs and stomps out of the great hall.

"What was that about?" I whisper, leaning in.

She shrugs me off. "Don't do that, you look suspicious."

"Fine. Why did you want to get rid of Gwil?"

"Because he's too loyal to tell you what I'm going to tell you."

A sick feeling twists my stomach. "What do you mean?"

She continues eating as if we are chatting about the latest fashions over lunch. "I'm worried about you."

I am, too, but I don't say it. "In what way?"

"I've seen the way you have started looking at the King."

My back stiffens. We've been playing this game for months now, appearing affectionate in public to cement our relationship enough that no one will question his desire to protect me. "What do you mean?"

"Don't treat me like I'm stupid, Dove. I survive on my instincts, and I know the difference between a game and what I see in your eyes. I'm worried you've forgotten who he is."

"How could I?"

"Because he's handsome, and he can be charming when he wants," she pops a piece of cheese into her mouth. "Because it's easy to forget what he's capable of when he's not doing it to you."

"But...but you," I stutter, "I thought you were loyal?"

She rolls her eyes. "That don't have jack shit to do with this. Look, I like you, Dove. I think you truly are a good person, and those are rare, I can tell you. I know you made the deal you thought you had to make. Can't say I wouldn't have done the same. We'll all do stupid things for the people we love. But if you're going to take risks, you should do it with your eyes open."

I rub the back of my hand across my lips, thinking about the last time Raeth kissed me. The way he held me against him as if he wanted to absorb me, and the way my whole body went molten. "You don't think my eyes are open?"

She turns toward me, meal forgotten. "Let me ask you a question: do you think he's really trying to find your father?"

"Of course he is. I've seen him come back injured."

"Oh, yeah? Can you prove that's how he got injured, or is that just what he says?"

I don't respond because I can't.

"Mmhmm," she nods. "Now, how many times has he had a Covenant bloke within his grasp only to kill them before he can force them to tell him where they're hiding your father?"

"He—" I start, intending to explain the way they fight and how capturing one is nearly impossible, but Raeth is faster and stronger than they are. And with the entire Unseen Court at his disposal, it does seem unlikely that he wouldn't have been able to capture anyone in months.

"Look," she says, glancing around to make sure no one is listening, "I'm just trying to get you to stop trusting so blindly and think. How does the King benefit from letting you go? He loses his White Lady, the person who makes gadgets to improve the Undercroft, who helps him keep people in line. You're a symbol now, not just a person. A valuable one. I might follow the King," she stacks her plates, "but I know what he is. He didn't become the King of the Unseen Court for no reason. He will always serve his own best interests first, if they align with yours or not."

"He's protected me; he's done so much," I begin, but I can't finish because the suggestion makes too much sense.

My heart sinks back into the familiar spot in my chest, whispering that, of course, he wants to keep me around for my usefulness. That is all I am, all I have ever been: a useful tool in whatever hand wields me. A devotee of the first person who shows me the smallest kindness; first with my father, and now with Raeth.

He saw the truth about me from the beginning; of course, he would take advantage of it. Why wouldn't he? Power helps him protect his people and himself, and I help him secure that power. My throat closes, and I try to swallow, but it hurts too much.

No.

My fists clench, and I force myself to breathe deeply. I refuse to let doubt creep in now. Raeth has shown me trust. He's put himself in my power, taken risks for me, and told me truths that could destroy him. I can't deny that he is self-serving, but I also can't believe he is lying to me about this.

Silk must see the growing conviction in my eyes because she shakes her head and stands. "If you want proof, try following him sometime. See what he's up to. If I'm wrong, my hats off to you. But I don't want to see you hurt. Not if a simple warning can help. Do with that what you like."

She pats my shoulder and leaves, passing Gwil on his way back with paper-wrapped pastry.


I WALK BACK to the room and my workbench in a sort of daze, trying to weigh everything and come to some conclusion, but the only certainty I feel is in the metal beneath my hands, the ring of the hammer, and the way the runes glow when Ripper steps close.

I cannot prove anything one way or another, not yet. But I can finish this compass. I can help find my father.

That is all I ever wanted, anyway.

# CHAPTER 33

Thus begins a new diary. I found it while perusing the goods at the Undercroft Fair. It isn't much of a fair, but it suits the place well enough. I think I have been here nearly a month, though it is hard to judge as no one here tracks the passage of time.

Despite that, the place does not seem as strange now as it once did. I no longer smell the mineral and mildew of the far tunnels.

It remains perpetually chilly, but the King keeps the fire always burning, so this room is warm enough that it is easy to forget the cold outside. It's not as easy to forget the lack of sunlight. Or the witch's pronouncement. Even when I am distracted, I hear her voice in the back of my mind, promising betrayal, fire, blood, and death.

I would like to think she was merely taking some sort of obscure revenge upon the King by discrediting *his lady, but her words feel like more than that. Since I cannot do anything about them, I should ignore it and try to make the next few months more bearable. Hopefully, this diary will accomplish that without the King noticing.*

*—From the diary of Willow Beauregard*
*December 1902*

~

A WRENCH IS CLUTCHED TIGHTLY IN MY FIST. THE SIDE OF MY FACE IS smooshed against something hard. Shooting pain arcs down my spine, and my eyes are so dry I can barely blink them.

"Ugh," I mumble, smacking my lips against the sour taste in my mouth as I sit up and rub the back of my hand across my eyes.

I don't remember falling asleep, but I must have because the compass is on the table before me, glowing a dull gold. Finished. It is far more elaborate than the last one, with runes for strength and flexibility engraved decoratively along the outside. Does it work? Did I test it before I fell asleep on the table?

I force my fingers to uncurl from the wrench handle and flex them before I pick up the compass and flick the cover open. As soon as I do, the little arrow swivels to point behind me to my right, where Raeth sits with Ripper at his feet.

"Good morning," he says with a crooked smile.

For a moment, I just stare. He looks as tired as I feel, with disheveled black hair curling over his forehead, purple smudges beneath his eyes, and lines bracketing his mouth despite the smile. Still, he is so beautiful it makes my chest hurt.

"It works," I say, holding out the compass.

He stands and approaches, and I wonder how I failed to notice that he is shirtless. His britches are slung low on his hips, and the slide of muscles across his torso is fascinating. Calliope's voice, I am too tired to control myself.

He gestures to the compass with his chin. "I was afraid to reach around you to inspect it for fear you would wake and stab me with that wrench."

"No stabbing today." I yawn and pass him the compass. "Is it really morning?"

"Afternoon, but morning as far as you are concerned. I attempted to carry you to bed, but you growled and flailed, so I left you at the table."

"I did not!"

Raeth puts one hand on his chest. "I swear it. You know I cannot lie. Ask Ripper."

The dog opens his mouth and wags his tail enthusiastically.

"Fine," I sigh, standing to stretch. "I was a sleeping monstrosity. Any news?"

But when I look at Raeth, he isn't examining the compass. It sits forgotten in his fist. He watches me with his lips parted, eyes dark, and muscles tense. Is he about to spring at me? Heat rushes between my legs, and I swallow audibly.

He blinks, and his eyes focus as if he's just woken from a dream or surfaced after a long swim. I half expect him to shake his head and rub his eyes. Instead, he lifts and turns the compass, watching the light play over its surface. "This is beautiful work, Dove."

A glow of pride flames to life in my chest. "Coming from the maker of this little miracle," I pat Ripper on the head, "that's quite a compliment. I'll take it, even if it is an exaggeration."

He lifts my chin with one finger. "I don't lie. And I don't exaggerate. You are an extraordinary artisan."

Such a compliment shouldn't bring tears to my eyes, but the backs of my eyelids sting just the same. A little voice whispers that he only compliments me to make me more malleable, more susceptible to his influence, but I shove it aside.

I deserve to have one thing for myself, even if it turns out to be a lie in the end. Raeth leans in and kisses my cheeks where my tears have fallen, his lips soft and warm. And when he kisses my mouth, the salt of my tears is on both of our lips, a contrast to the cinnamon taste of him.

"Before I get carried away," he says, stepping back, "you need to eat. I'll answer your question while you break your fast."

I plop gratefully onto the cushioned chair near the table and roll my neck to loosen the cramped muscles. I try to make my tone as nonchalant as possible when I speak, but I don't quite succeed. "Does that mean you intend to get carried away later?"

The look he gives me is half desire, half something else, something intense and disarming, like I am chocolate that will poison him to eat, but he is considering it anyway. I start to ask if he is well, but he interrupts me.

"Ratcatchers spotted a Bowler Hat outside a tavern called the Twisted Eel and sent up a signal. When Lady Gwen and her Raven followed him, they found him opening locked warehouses to release monsters."

"I *knew* the Covenant was responsible. But why unleash monsters on the city? To cover up the kidnappings?"

"Eat."

I scowl at him, but he is unimpressed by my ferocity. With a sigh, I pull the lid off the tray, and my mouth waters immediately from the scent of sausage, egg, bread, and apple confit. Raeth waits until I bite off a piece of sausage to continue.

"Perhaps," he admits, pulling on a shirt. "But it is a rather convoluted way to go about things and far more effort than a simple coverup would require. My contacts in Scotland Yard think the missing persons were related to some territorial dispute between rival gangs, so the Covenant wasn't in danger of being discovered. It is more likely they have some other reason for releasing the beasts. To distract from whatever business includes your father, perhaps."

As he talks, I continue shoving food into my mouth, trying to subdue my stomach while my mind works.

"All that matters is that the Covenant is responsible. And they made the mistake of tangling with Lady St. James and the Raven. They managed to identify one of Bowler Hats as the driver of a wealthy lord who travels in her circles—a wealthy Marquis with very bad habits. He has been in hiding since last year, but one of the young witches was apparently able to locate him."

"Witches?" I ask, lightheaded despite the food.

"Mmm." He slips his feet into the soft leather boots. "Found him hiding in plain sight. They plan to apprehend him tonight. Lady St. James has requested Ratcatchers to assist and asked that I be the one to question him."

A bite of egg sticks in my throat. "Why you?"

"Because people believe I am mad, my darling," he says, smiling like a shark.

"Only because you convince them of it."

"It is a useful fiction." He shrugs. "If the lady can pull this off, we may learn more about the Covenant in several hours than we've discovered in the past six months."

My stomach clenches. Has it been six months? I'd rather not think about how much time we don't have left. "Why were the lady and the Raven able to discover so much when you have more resources?"

Raeth tears off a piece of bread and pops it into his mouth. "The information I gather is generally of a different sort: political secrets, cargo shipment schedules, that sort of thing. As much as I hate to admit it, the lady has access to information I do not, particularly with the Raven at her side. It is difficult to compete with someone who can fly. Of course, I am about to haul the truth out of the puffed-up Marquis, so that will even the score somewhat."

"Then you are going tonight?"

Raeth nods. My eyes glide over his features: his long lashes, the sharp line of his nose, a stubborn chin softened by the fullness of his lower lip, and eyes so dark I could disappear inside them.

We could learn where my father is tonight.

It's almost over.

I should be elated, but my stomach is sick. Eating was a bad idea.

"I am." He holds the compass out, though I stare at it numbly. "And I will bring you back whatever information I learn."

"I didn't expect my work to become obsolete before I finished it."

"It isn't," he reassures me as I pocket the device. "We may still need it. And if we do not, you will be the best prepared and protected woman in the city."

Protection doesn't seem so important compared with everything I stand to gain...and lose. "How long until you leave?"

He looks down at his hands. "A few hours."

A few hours may sever the bonds between us forever. I will return to the life I have fought for, and Raeth will stay here. I will be in the sun, and he in the dark. And I will never know his touch again. Unless he chooses to enforce the six month visits he won from me in our bargain.

The idea of spending months without hearing his dark chuckle or feeling his hands on my skin makes my throat close with sudden grief.

Silently, I stand and take his hand. He frowns at me in confusion but follows me and doesn't argue. Ripper's brass feet clink softly as I lead Raeth down the corridors I have walked so many times I could follow them in my sleep.

Down and down, with Raeth's warm hand in mine, the trip feels as if it takes hours, though perhaps only fifteen minutes have passed when the glow of my garden lights up the cavern ahead of us. He never told me who keeps the lamps lit.

The last rays of natural sunlight break through the rock above in shifting beams, turning the little paradise into a faerie grotto. Somehow, pixies have found the garden, their small, softly glowing bodies bobbing above the flowers and leaves I have tended so lovingly for months.

They say pixies only inhabit the healthiest plants, and knowing they thought my garden a worthy haven makes my heart swell with joy and grief. We stop in the center near the fountain that has been empty and quiet for hundreds or thousands of years and is now filled with life.

"What are we doing?" Raeth asks at last.

But I don't answer. Instead, my fingers find his belt buckle and the buttons of his britches beneath.

"Dove," he begins, his fingers curling around my wrists as if he would stop me. I don't know what look is in my eyes, but when our gazes lock, he releases me.

My chest is tight, my heart hammering as I unbutton his fly. Muses, he is already hard. A single hand on the flat of his stomach makes him sit on the fountain's edge, the ferns spilling around his shoulders and hips.

Our gazes lock as I kneel between his legs, wrap my fingers around him, and tug him free. His stomach muscles clench when my hair slides over his thighs. And when my lips part and my tongue glides over the head of his cock, his entire body goes rigid.

A little sound of pleasure hums in my chest. He tasted me, and ever since that day, I have wondered what Raeth tastes like. I could not stomach the idea of leaving the Undercroft and never knowing.

His skin is smooth and soft, stretched tight, his pulse beating against my tongue as his hands gently cup the back of my head.

He groans. "Dove. God's breath."

When I release him, he is wet and shining, throbbing with every heartbeat.

I trace his length, base to tip, with the flat of my tongue. "My name is Willow."

His hands cradle my face like he fears holding me too tight. But he told me once what he wanted and how he wanted it, the violence he craved, though he was gentle with me. And the idea of giving it to him makes my blood run hot.

So I place my hands over his and thread our fingers through my hair, lowering my head again. "I don't want your gentleness, Raeth," I murmur against his sensitive skin. "I want you to leave marks on me. To hold me tight and use me hard. When I leave the Undercroft, I want proof of exactly where you touched me."

His moan, the way his fingers tighten in my hair, makes a bolt of pleasure shoot through my body, and I draw him into my mouth again, this time sucking hard as I withdraw. A breath hisses through his teeth, and his hips shift. He thrusts into my mouth with a tortured noise.

I hum in pleasure, letting the sound and vibration tell him how much I like this, how much I want it. And when he growls and thrusts again, sliding to the back of my throat and retreating, a whimper escapes.

"Willow," he groans, and my name on his lips for the first time almost breaks me. "Fuck, you feel so good."

He thrusts again. I respond by opening wider, sinking my fingers into his hips, and pulling him deeper. Though I imagined this a dozen times, the erotic pleasure is dizzying. The experience of being filled by him this way, of the most intimate part of him sliding into and out of my mouth, of hearing my name moaned in his velvet and honey voice, is far beyond anything I imagined.

Raeth, for all his strength and cunning, cannot stop himself from letting me give him this, letting me take this, from being vulnerable and at my mercy. And when I look up to see him watching me, brows knit together over eyes heavy-lidded with desire, his mouth open–when I know *I* make his self-control break, I only want more. Faster. Harder. Deeper.

Sweat slicks his skin and beads on his upper lip as he traps my face and thrusts into my mouth, pulling me to him until my nose touches his stomach and my lips reach the very base of him. Every panting moan is like music. He tightens beneath my hands, in my mouth, as his body cries out for release.

"Wait," he says, and tries to pull me away, "you don't have to— Willow—oh fuck, you don't—"

But I want to. And when he bucks under me, when he groans, and his hands tighten in my hair, when his hips flex hard, and he shoves himself far enough that my throat swells with him, with the salty taste of him on my tongue as he moans my name, I think I might die of the pleasure.

I hold him in my mouth as his flesh softens, fascinated by the changing feel of him.

When I finally release him and meet his gaze, he is staring at me in wonder, his chest heaving as if he was mortally wounded, his voice raw and ragged. "What have you done to me?"

\* \* \*

I AM PACING AGAIN. Raeth is dressed, strapping knives to himself as he prepares to assist Lady St. James. I try to hang onto our brief time in the garden, to remember his determination to reciprocate pleasure despite my intention to focus on him.

I can still see his face above me, surrounded by leaves and flowers, the pixies darting over his head. I still hear the purr of pleasure as he slides between my legs. Still taste him, still feel the slick heat of him between my thighs.

The pain of my heart breaking when he called my name with raw, soul-deep need as he found a second release in my arms washes over me still.

But those memories cannot stop my stomach from sinking or my hands from shaking as I imagine him leaving. Not because he will be in danger; I have learned to accept that part of his life.

But because this may be the last time he leaves.

"Gwil and Ripper will stay with you," he says as he slings the belt of the last sheath around his waist. As usual, he is in all black, wearing a hooded greatcoat.

"You aren't wearing the cloak?" I ask, eying the shadow garment tossed over the back of a chair.

"I have no need of it. Questioning is to be held in the basement of the Triumphant Sisterhood, and there are tunnels from here to there."

"The Triumphant who?"

"Sisterhood. The witches I mentioned. They are the only coven in New London and not to be trifled with. If I stroll into their stronghold with the stink of magic about me, they may get the wrong idea. No reason to make them fear I am more dangerous than they suspect."

"But you are."

"That, Dove, is a secret best kept between us. If I must expose myself, I would like to choose the time and place to my advantage."

His tone is flippant, but there is a sort of manic energy about him that makes me nervous. He carefully guards his emotions, even around me, but they seem to be bubbling out of every crack in his armor.

"Are you alright?"

He slides the leather strap through the buckle, then adjusts the sheath to fit flat against his lower back. "Of course."

Of course.

Raeth finishes his preparations and pulls me into his arms. "Stay here tonight. It will be dangerous above."

"I don't relish the idea of stumbling across a monster."

His arms tighten, and he smiles wryly. "Evidence strongly suggests you do."

"You are not a monster."

Our gazes lock. "Yes, Dove. I am."

The intensity of his regard would have made me retreat months ago, but now I simply wait and ignore the uneasy churning of my stomach. When Raeth is certain he's made his point, he kisses me.

It is a lingering kiss, not the kind that makes promises, but the kind that wishes promises had been made. My body melts, molding to every swell and hollow of his. When his fingers slide through the hair at the base of my neck and tighten, I know this moment is a tipping point, a ledge leading to the cliff of some unknown future, and he is holding me like a man dangling by bloody fingertips.

The empty dark stretches beneath us, I feel the danger of it in his body, though I do not know why. He breaks the kiss and strides toward the door without looking back.

"The monsters are bad enough," he says over his shoulder, "but it is Lady St. James's influence that worries me. She is clever, but reckless, and her plans often cause collateral damage. If you go Upstairs, you will likely be caught up in the mess."

I fold my hands, swallow hard when he opens the door, and try to give him a reassuring smile when he says, "I'll tell you everything when I return."

Then he is gone, and I am alone with nothing but the empty ache in my chest and an uneasy feeling in my stomach. After a few heartbeats to calm my nerves, I pull the compass out of my pocket, open the cover, and—with a deep breath—turn the face to realign the symbols.

The outside ring turns with faint clicks until the symbol facing away from me is a curve with a half-moon pointing upward. In the center of the compass, protected by tempered glass, the gold arrow spins to point to Ripper. I turn the outside ring again, this time to a different symbol. The needle wobbles, then swings around to point at the cloak. Barely breathing, I turn it again to a symbol that is all hard lines and acute angles.

The arrow points at the door. No matter where I move, the arrow follows Raeth.

"And now," I tell Ripper as I sling the shadow cloak over my shoulders and ignore the pit of guilt opening in my stomach, "we wait."

Minutes drag by, and I swear I can hear the mantle clock tracking the hours. But less than ten minutes pass when the door swings open, and Silk pokes her head in.

"If you're going to go," she peers down the hall, "do it now. I can only give you about five minutes."

Stomach churning, I slip out the door, leaving Ripper inside. Shouting echoes from a nearby corridor.

"What about you?" I ask.

Silk shrugs. "It's not much of a distraction, but it will have to do. Go."

I pull her into a quick hug and turn to peek through the crack in the door. "Ripper, stay."

He drops his ears and whines, his tail barely twitching.

But I don't have time to feel bad about that. I take the small lantern from Silk, give her a weak smile, and tighten the shadow cloak before trotting down the corridor, following the golden needle as it tracks Raeth through the dark.

# CHAPTER 34

The bins are a success. The Undercroft doesn't have ventilation capable of dispersing odor, so the slightest smells are more intense and linger.

I managed to fabricate a liner for the bins that traps scent. Some of these do exist on the surface, but they're generally too expensive for the average customer, and since they only have a small area of effect, they're seen as a waste of time by most artificers.

But the Undercroft is an entirely different situation, and the bins have already cut down on the smell so much that it almost smells good down here. Almost. Knowing all the time I've spent waiting will at least benefit the Undercrofters is some comfort.

—From the diary of Willow Beauregard
March? 1903

~

New Londoners know there are sewers beneath the city, the bellies of old buildings, ruins of past fires or natural disasters, and catacombs beneath the churches and temples of various gods. But they do not know how deep the tunnels reach—that there is a honeycomb, a labyrinth, a human anthill of tunnels that spiderweb deep beneath the earth and reach for miles.

Raeth unknowingly leads me through parts of the Undercroft that are so old they are not much more than crumbling ruins. Twists and turns take us down and down until the air is cold enough to make me shiver despite the cloak. Several times, I turn sideways to squeeze through the narrow space between fallen stone blocks so large that only a fraction of their bulk is visible in the tunnel.

I refuse to consider that the compass may be wrong, that I am wandering deep into the bowels of the earth with no idea how to get back and limited energy in the small dwarven lamp. Managing my anxiety takes all of the attention not being monopolized by paying attention to the compass and not tripping over old rubble.

Before long, the winding trail winds into an upward climb. When warmer air twists through the tunnel, signaling a larger room is somewhere ahead, much closer to the surface, I try not to sob in relief. But I do turn the dimmer on the lamp until it is so low only elven eyes could see by it. Raeth must be close.

This is not a betrayal of trust, I firmly tell my whispering conscience. He told me not to go to the surface. And how many times has he kept secrets from me? I'm only trying to protect my father, to learn as much as I can since the time of our agreement is coming to an end and I may be forced to seek him again on my own if this plan does not work.

Following Raeth has nothing to do with my fear that Silk may be right, that he hasn't told me everything and has only kept me around for what use he can get from me.

The heavy, stale scent of mineral-rich air fades, and more

familiar smells work their way into the tunnel: wood smoke, manure, and the sour bite of body odor. My pace slows further, and when dim light enters the tunnel, I thumb off the lantern.

The rough floor gives way to brick and then slate as the tunnel opens and branches into several paths. Barely audible voices float toward me from the righthand tunnel. Barely quietly, I ghost toward the sound until the words are clear.

A decisive feminine voice with a posh accent says, "This ends Tony's commitment to you."

"So it does." That is Raeth. My heartbeat speeds, and I sink deeper into the shadow of the cloak. "And now begins the enjoyable part of our association. Unless...you would like to engage in other pleasurable activities."

My throat squeezes closed. This is the voice he used on Lady St. James in the great hall, and while I don't think he is serious, Silk's words needle the back of my mind; *he didn't become the King of the Unseen Court for no reason. He will always serve his own best interests first...*

"The only pleasurable thing you will do for me is keep your commitment to our alliance," the female voice snaps. At this, I am certain it is Lady St. James.

"But it doesn't have to be the only thing," Raeth says, "I could—"

The dull, fleshy thump of a body against stone is barely audible, as is Raeth's chuckle. "This could be fun, too, Raven. No need for jealousy."

The Raven responds in a tone that is all the more chilling for how conversational it sounds. "If the woman says no, she means it. If you try to convince her when she doesn't want convincing, I will let her watch while I cut your eyes out and eat them."

"My, my," Raeth says. "Possessive, are we?"

"Unfortunately," Lady Gwen interjects, "we don't have time to stay and chat. And the King has a job to do. I'm certain he will remember your warning."

"I will," Raeth assures them. "I remember everything."

That has an ominous sound.

The Raven's voice is dismissive. "What you remember is your business. So long as you keep your word, and keep your hands to yourself, you won't become mine."

After the sound of shuffling of feet on stone, Raeth calls, "I await your signal, Lady Gwen."

"One day," The Raven says, his voice far away, "you should let me kill that creature."

Lady Gwen's voice is barely audible when she replies. "You know, I just might. By the by, please never call me pet."

"On that, we are agreed."

I only dare to move after several minutes of silence. The last thing I need is for Raeth to hear me fumbling in the dark. Once I am certain both parties have moved on, I creep forward. There is barely enough light to see the compass needle, but I follow it through several more corridors, these clean and well-used, suggesting they are part of the greater complex of the Sisterhood's basement. The grey stone was laid far more recently than that of the Undercroft, and the neat lines of mortar and clean joints suggest someone keeps the place up.

I turn down a long corridor, stopping to peek around the corner. Warm torchlight flickers off the stone at the other end, and I pull the cloak tightly around myself to cover every bit of skin before continuing. Raeth's shadow cloak is the next best thing to invisibility, but that doesn't mean I want to risk anyone seeing me, especially not if this is the basement of a coven.

Since I do not know enough about witches to guess whether they can see through magic, I ease toward the light and listen with every ounce of concentration.

Someone with a deep, flabby voice complains nearby.

"Do you know who I am? I will have every one of you arrested and flayed for this! You will lose everything. Everything, you hear me?"

The tunnel splits as a second passage runs through it at a right angle. It resembles a colonnade that circles a central room with a domed ceiling. If I edge to the left, I should get a decent view of the room while staying in the shadows of the outer circle, separated from the inner room by a wall with arched openings.

Herb smoke makes the room fragrant and fights off the musty scent of stale air. Women in flowing white dresses stand in a circle, their hair loose down their backs, hands at their sides, palms facing the center of the dark room.

An enormous chandelier hangs from the highest point of the domed ceiling, the flickering candles illuminating an older gentleman's broad sloped shoulders, keg-like belly, and white hair. His thick arms suggest he was once quite strong, but whatever strength remains in those arms is not enough to break the ropes that bind him, wrist and ankle, to a wooden chair.

His cheeks are soft beneath a walrus mustache, and his skin is deathly pale aside from furious red staining his cheeks and nose. Several bruises color his arms and face, visible even from here. This must be the lord Raeth mentioned, the one whose involvement connects the Covenant to the monsters ravaging the Upstairs.

Movement in the dark catches my eye, and I flatten myself against the wall, barely daring to breathe.

A figure stalks the shadows on the outskirts of the rotunda, barely visible, circling, circling. Though he is nothing but a smudge in the dark, I instantly recognize the way Raeth moves. He prowls, sometimes coming close enough to the light to be almost visible.

Whenever he does, the restrained Marquis flinches and his demands grow louder, panicked. "Release me, and I'll see that every one of you is given a title. Whatever you ask, you will get it. I swear. I have power you cannot guess at. Connections of the highest order!"

None of the women answer or bother looking at him. Their attention is turned inward, their eyes distant and vacant, muttering something so low their voices are only a background susurrus, a hum that fills the space like the buzz of bees fills a meadow.

"They cannot help you, my lord." Raeth's voice floats out of the darkness, seeming to come from nowhere and everywhere. "Only I can do that."

"I will not speak to you!" The man begins struggling anew, fighting his restraints with wrists already rubbed bloody.

"Oh, I think you will." Raeth steps into the candlelight across from the man, holding a silvery knife in one hand and turning the tip delicately in his opposite fingers.

"Ladies," the Marquis pleads, his voice rising an octave as a bead of sweat slides down the side of his face. "Anything you wish! Anything you dream of! You want power? I can give it to you! Money? It's yours."

Raeth stalks forward, and all traces of the man I've come to know–the one who smiles unexpectedly, who is beginning to laugh more, who feeds me when I am injured–are gone.

This man is hard and cold, devoid of any emotion.

So quickly his hand blurs, Raeth strikes the lord. The smack of his open palm echoes through the room, a counterpoint to the spell the witches mutter in unison.

The older man's head snaps to the side, his grey mustaches flying. "Don't lie, my lord. You don't share power, and we both know it."

Another blow, this one to the body with a fist.

The older man tries to double over as he wheezes, "Don't let him—do this to me!"

But the witches are no more responsive than rustling trees in a wood. Their hair lifts from their heads and blow around their faces on an unseen wind.

"I am going to ask you questions," Raeth says, circling the man again. "And you will answer them. If you refuse, I will hurt you. I will hurt you until I am satisfied with your answers."

Bile climbs up the back of my throat. I know Raeth is a violent man. I have seen it. But he isn't defending himself against an attack against or protecting a member of the court; this is the threat of torture.

"Release me, you monster, or I will have you hunted to the ends of the earth!" the bound figure says.

"Now, now, Lord Rutledge. You are not in any condition to make such threats. As I told you, all you must do is answer my questions, and I will release you."

My knees go weak, and I wobble to the ground, barely catching myself before I fall. Lord Rutledge: the man responsible for the scars covering Raeth's body, for his inability to father children. The man tortured him until he became capable of ruling a city of criminals. Until he believed love was a weakness.

Fury lights my blood on fire as I fight to control my breathing; if he has done what Raeth and Lady St. James think he's done, then he is also responsible for my father's kidnapping. A metallic taste fills my mouth, red tints my vision, and my hands shake. Is this what hate feels like?

"You lie!" Rutledge shouts.

"You know better. I cannot lie. No faerie can."

Muses. He just admitted his heritage in front of the witches. Why? Does it have something to do with the spell they are casting? The one making my skin burn?

"You'll find some way out of it," Rutledge says. "You always do."

"So suspicious," Raeth chides. He scrapes the tip of the knife over Rutledge's belly, making one of the buttons on his waistcoat pop off. Rutledge squeals and curls his upper body as blood blooms red on the fabric.

"Don't," he begs. All the angry color drains from his face.

Raeth's smile is chilling. "Calm down, pet. I shall give you my word. Answer my questions, and I will release you."

"Swear it."

"I swear it," Raeth promises, and my head spins. He just promised to release the man responsible for so much pain and death? Even I cannot stomach the idea. He deserves a trial and prison, at the very least.

Rutledge shakes with fear and relief as his head falls limp on his shoulders. "Very well, damn you. Ask your questions."

"How long have you been working with the faerie King to help him invade mortal lands?"

The air rushes out of me. No wonder Raeth was so anxious to come here. A faerie invasion? The one he mentioned when he told me of his history? I assumed he meant the king wanted to invade some nearby country, not New London. How is such a thing possible?

Rutledge sighs. "Close to ten years, I suppose."

"What did you do on his behalf?" Raeth asks, letting his fingers trail along the back of Rutledge's shoulders as he circles him.

"I helped elect certain people and placed them in positions of power. I made deals with the vampires on his behalf."

"Then it was you who helped the monsters enter New London?"

"You knew it was me. Stop wasting my time."

"Your time belongs to me right now, Rutledge," Raeth says in a low, dangerous voice. "Answer the question."

"Yes," Rutledge says in a sullen voice. "It was me."

"How?"

"On the river, of course. By night."

There are miles and miles of Riverfront and docks up and down it from one side to the other. It would be impossible to search them all, especially under the cover of night. The Wraiths and the Cogburners control a decent stretch of the river. The idea that some of them may be involved makes a chill run down the backs of my legs.

"Clever man," Raeth congratulates him. "But tell me truly: how could you betray all mortals in favor of their long enemy?"

"Quite easily."

"But why? Why side with the invaders?"

Rutledge snorts. "Power, you fool, why else? Don't act as if you don't understand. You've cultivated power yourself."

Power. It always comes back to power. I cannot get enough air. All of this is too much to understand, too much to cope with.

"But don't you care about your people?" Raeth asks the question as if setting a trap.

"What a stupid question. Why would I? There will always be more of them, new coopers to replace the old, new washerwomen, and farmers and...oh, whatever else they do. One dies, and another springs up to take its place, like rats or fungus. They'll die and be forgotten, easy as trampling a flower."

"Then you only care about power?"

"Power is the only thing any sensible man cares about because it is the only way he can order his own life as he sees fit, free of control by other men."

Those words are so close to phrases Raeth has said that nausea curls in my belly and crawls up my throat.

Raeth grimaces. "Have any other members of Parliament helped you in these schemes?"

"You think I could have done all this on my own?"

"Where there is a will, they say there is a way," Raeth says, not without a trace of amusement. "When will King Obyrron invade mortal lands?"

"He hasn't told me that, only commissioned me to prepare the way."

"And what do you get in return?"

"Power," Rutledge says, his voice tired. "What else?"

"Just one more question before I release you."

Rutledge has deflated, but his eyes remain defiant. "Ask it, damn you, and be done."

"How many innocent lives have been taken by your collusion with the faerie king?"

Rutledge snorts and tries to shrug but winces. "Who knows, man. Hundreds? Thousands? What does it matter? Now keep your word, and release me."

"Very well, Lord Rutledge. I am a faerie of my word, after all." Raeth kneels in front of his captive and cuts the ropes binding his feet. Their respective positions remind me forcibly of our moment in the garden mere hours before.

Raeth is gentle as he releases Rutledge, and the last rope falls away from the older man's mangled wrists. His chest heaves as if the promise of freedom has let him breathe again. But Raeth touches his cheek delicately, and Rutledge shrinks away from the terrible, hungry light in his eyes.

"I have kept my word," Raeth purrs. "I have released you."

"Yes...now—now let me go."

He climbs astride Rutledge's lap fast enough that the man has no time to push him away or shift his weight. Wrapping his fingers around the man's jaw like a lover–like he has done to me more than once–Raeth says in a velvet voice, "Oh, that was not part of the bargain, my lord."

Rutledge's face turns green, his eyes widen, and he swings his fists wildly. "Help!"

But Raeth wraps his legs around Rutledge's hips and rides him to the ground while the larger man flails, knocking the chair aside to skitter across the stone floor.

"You remember what games we used to play, my lord?" Raeth asks as he raises his knife.

"No!"

"Now it is your turn. And my turn."

"By the gods, no!"

I squeeze my eyes shut as the razor-edged blade bites into Rutledge's flesh. He screams.

"I thought this was your favorite game," Raeth growls. "I thought you enjoyed pain, my lord? You certainly loved inflicting it."

The heels of my hands press so hard against my ears they burn, but the screams are too loud to drown out. I crouch with my eyes closed, hiding from the sight, the metallic bite of blood filling the air, the whimpers and cries making my gorge rise for what feels like hours. But one scream is so high-pitched my eyes fly open on reflex.

Raeth traps Lord Rutledge beneath him. The older man's shirt is open, revealing a soft white chest and belly smeared red.

These cuts are not the surgical wounds Raeth received; they are jagged, uneven, evidence of shaking hands.

"How many other faeries did you torture?" Raeth snarls. The knife flashes in the light. "How many did you betray?" Another cut.

Rutledge cries and pleads as he tries to shove Raeth off, but his hands are slick with blood, and he finds no purchase. The knife continues its grisly work.

Tired of the struggles, Raeth presses both knees into Rutledge's elbows, trapping his arms as he sits atop Rutledge's chest. But Rutledge is in too much pain to fight back effectively. He only turns his head from side to side to avoid looking his torturer in the eye.

"Mercy," he sobs weakly. "Mercymercymercy."

Raeth's hand locks over the crying lord's mouth, fingers digging into his cheeks. When he speaks, his whisper vibrates with fury. "You forfeited your right to mercy when you betrayed guestright. When you betrayed your people."

The keening whine that escapes Rutledge is such a human sound of pain and despair that sympathy wells up in my chest, even as horror and disgust twist my stomach.

Raeth leans down until his mouth nearly touches Rutledge's ear. "I promised I would release you. And if I was like you, I would twist my promise and make it hurt, make it last, until you gave up begging. Instead," his voice softens, becoming almost tender as it trembles. "I will extend the mercy you never gave me. Not because you deserve it, but because I did."

This time, the knife slides delicately across Rutledge's throat, the movement like a caress, parting the skin, muscle, and cartilage with the ease of a surgeon. His body convulses, arms flopping, legs kicking as a pool of blood stains the stones beneath him, spreading along the lines of mortar in a macabre design.

The witches end their spell, their hair and dresses falling as the magical wind dissipates. One by one, they turn their backs to the awful sight. A few retch. I cannot blame them. I wish I could vomit the scene from my mind as well as my body.

But I don't think I will ever forget the sight of Raeth's eyes locked on the dying man, his hands stained and his cheeks spattered with blood, chest heaving as the man beneath him dies, gurgling.

Here is the monster they whisper about, the one who can murder a dozen men and disappear into the night, who rules a continent of criminals with cunning ruthlessness.

Now, after all this time...I finally believe them.

My knees wobble as I push myself to my feet. For a moment, all I can see is the mangled carcass of someone who used to have a heartbeat and breath in his lungs. His eyes stare sightlessly at the ceiling, staring into nothingness.

I pray my legs will hold me as I turn away from the carnage and flee into the dark with my hands clamped over my mouth to stop the sobs from escaping.

# CHAPTER 35

*Tildie and I played a game of chess today. She is absolutely vicious and cornered my king with her pawns before running him to ground and pinning him with her queen. I think she was trying to teach me something.*

*—From the diary of Willow Beauregard*
*April 1903*

"WILLOW!"

The echo of my name rumbles through the tunnels like far-off thunder. Adrenaline jolts through my veins, breaking past the grief and sorrow to force more speed from my burning muscles. I must find a place to hide.

The tunnel opens into a cavern that must have been an intersection at one point but now looks more like a cave. Several tunnels exit in branches, and I lift the lantern, my eyes flying over each one for the least likely escape.

"Willow!" The bellow is closer this time, and loose stones and dust tremble on the ground.

My heart hitches and then gallops onward. There's no time to escape. So I squeeze myself between the remains of a fallen building and the rough wall of naked stone, then thumb the lantern off. Complete darkness engulfs me. Running footsteps join the traces of my name that seem to linger in the air.

Closer.

Closer.

I bite my lips together against a sob and hold my breath. The running footsteps skid to a halt, sending dust and rocks rattling across the ground. Hard breathing. Though I know it does not matter, I squeeze my eyes shut and sink deeper into the cloak, willing myself to disappear.

Silence.

Silence, but no retreating footsteps. Surely he cannot see?

"I smell you, Willow."

His voice is raw, and the words come out between ragged breaths, but I do not dare respond. I cannot bear to see him. If I do, I will either scream or pull him into my arms, and the thought of either scenario makes my throat close in panic.

A rough scratching sound and orange light flames to life. I see the bright burn of it red through my eyelids.

"I'm sorry, Dove. You were not meant to see that."

I cannot respond. I won't. I am still invisible inside the cloak despite his profession of smelling me. But questions claw at my throat anyway, and when they pry my lips apart, I hear myself grate words I never intended to say. "Why not? So you could continue to hide what you were really after all this time?"

Hands settle on my upper arms and drag me to my feet. Hiding is useless now. There never was much point in avoiding him, as much as I wanted to believe otherwise. Raeth never let me hide.

When I open my eyes, his well-known face is before me—only it's not. His eyes are larger, dark with no whites showing. His lashes are thicker and longer, and his canines are more pronounced. Even his body is slightly altered. He is the same height, but his shoulders are a bit more rounded, his body lithe and agile. A fine furring of hair rims his delicately pointed ears, limned by the taper left burning on a rock behind him.

The breath wooshes out of me. He is still Raeth, though infinitely stranger and more beautiful; his true self, not the one he hides behind a glamour or only lets slip when he cannot control his emotions.

Another side of himself he hid from me.

"I never hid myself," he says, and it is only then I realize I spoke the words aloud. "I warned you. I told you what I was."

"But you—" I begin and stumble over the words. Every thought and emotion I have ever had is fighting to climb out of my chest and up my throat. "It was never like that. You killed people, but it was a matter of survival, not revenge."

He advances, and I skitter back, keeping out of his reach. Pain at my retreat makes his brows draw together and his mouth tighten. For the first time, I can see the signs of it all over him: the strain along his shoulders, the locked jaw, and his hands curled into fists.

"The people you've seen me kill made the mistake of attacking the wrong person, and they paid the price for it. But he"—he flings an accusatory hand back toward the tunnels, his eyes intense— "chose his victims carefully. He did not merely inflict as much pain as necessary to further his goals; he did it because he enjoyed the power it gave him. This wasn't just revenge, it was justice."

"Justice isn't reveling in the pain of others!"

"You think I am a monster because I enjoyed hurting the man who tortured me?" He stalks forward, a growl entering his voice as he rips open his shirt to reveal the scars crisscrossing his skin. "The man who chained me with iron so I could not heal and cut me day after day, even when I did what he commanded? Who forced me to swear I would not seek him out myself and kept my people at bay with the construct I created? Who loosed monsters on an innocent city, stole priceless artifacts, exploited people like your father, and profited from their hard work while they rotted in the streets? That bastard forced me to live in a world where he was allowed to continue hurting those weaker than himself and profit from it while I bided my time in the shadows, waiting like a spider, able to do nothing."

My stomach flips over as my ribcage tries to crush my heart. I want to shout at him just to release the storm of emotion boiling inside me, but my words come out soft and sad. "But you did to him what he would have done to you. Raeth, you cannot fight them by becoming what they are."

He flinches, but anger replaces the flash of pain in his eyes. "And you think because your hands are clean, you aren't like them?"

My hands are clasped painfully in front of me, hands that have killed. My breath hitches. "I'm not."

"Right," he scoffs, "because your complicity is invisible, you think you are absolved from the guilt of participating in a system designed to exploit people. When children freeze to death in the streets, when mothers cannot work enough to feed themselves, and their babes starve because their milk goes dry, do you beat your breast? Do you march on Parliament and demand reform? Or do you keep your head down and your eyes shut and just be glad you have enough?"

"I was them!" I scream, the dam broken at last. "I watched them haul my parents away for unpaid business loans. When they repossessed the luthier shop, and I had nowhere to go, I starved on the street unless I could steal enough to eat. And I carried every spare penny to the prison to pay against my parents' debts." I am panting raggedly, and my cheeks are burning, but I have to get the rest out, no matter how painful it is. "I stole and scraped until fever took my mother and father. So don't you dare scold me for working hard to ensure that will never happen to me again."

"The people who left a child on the street to starve don't deserve to live safe and painless lives. They deserve to pay for what they've done."

"They don't deserve to be cut slowly to bloody ribbons!"

He closes the distance between us in a single rush, his face mere inches from mine. "Don't they? It is a faster death than your parents were given. You find my violence distasteful because it is bloody and visible. But men like Rutledge live on mountains of broken bodies and the only reason you ignore it is because they built the system to hide it. They criminalize my violence and write laws to protect their own. Their violence is so big you cannot see it for what it is, even as you participate in it. Think of what you may have become without your precious father."

He points up, beyond the rock and earth, to the world above. "They create monsters and then punish them for it. So, I will spend my life making them fear the monsters they've created. And if it ends in the bloody death of men like Rutledge, so much the better. I can live with that."

"I can't."

We are only inches apart, panting and furious, but my words make Raeth jerk upright. His glamour snaps back into place, and the guarded expression turns his face into a mask. "We haven't found your father yet."

My chin is trembling, but I force the words out anyway. "If torture and death is the only path to finding him, I don't want to walk it. I'll find another way."

Raeth retreats a step. His Adam's apple bobs. "No one is forcing you to stay. If you no longer require my help, say so."

His eyes are hard, and the line of his jaw is set. Was it only hours ago we were wrapped in each other's arms? Part of me wants to ask him to hold me, to swear this sort of violence won't be our future if I stay and accept more of his help. Whatever he says will be the truth, but no one is better at twisting words to sound like one thing and mean another.

And the other part of me cannot stop seeing Raeth staring down at Lord Rutledge's bulging eyes, cannot stop hearing the man's gasp as the blade parted his flesh.

Silk's words return once more: *he will always serve his own best interests first.* "You never asked Rutledge about my father or the Covenant."

His jaw works. "You have the compass. And I was—distracted. Would you rather I kept him around and tortured him a bit more for answers?"

Disgust curls my lips and sours my already unstable stomach. I press my hands over my abdomen as if pressure can force it to calm. "No."

"What do you want, Willow." He examines my face. His hands are coated with drying blood, and when he flexes them, little flakes break free and float to the floor like a macabre snow. "What do you want?"

I want everything to go back to the way it was. I want to forget what I saw and live next to Raeth, believing the violence is justified. It is a horrid, selfish desire, an impossible wish, but I cannot pretend it isn't there. And I cannot pretend I will forget what I saw. As much as I wish it were otherwise, a gulf now yawns between us, deep and hungry and too far to cross.

"I want to go home."

Raeth closes his eyes, and it is like the lowering of a curtain separating him from me. Pain flashes across his face, in the tight line between his brows, and then disappears.

When he opens his eyes, the King stares out of them. He tilts his head to one side in a courtly nod that has the appearance of good-natured acquiescence but none of the sincerity. "Very well. After court tomorrow, I will have Ripper escort you home."

With that, he turns and walks into the dark, leaving me to follow and wonder whether I have a home to return to.

THE SILENCE of our walk back is heavy with recrimination and thick with everything I cannot force myself to say. When we arrive in the central tunnels of the Undercroft, folk are running down halls, shouting to one another, and—once they spot us—staring in mute surprise.

Gwil turns a corner, leading a handful of Ratcatchers, only to stop short. "Majesty!" He says, then gives me an accusatory glare. "She—"

Raeth waves it off without speaking, passing everyone as if they did not exist.

I send Gwil an apologetic half-smile but hurry to follow Raeth. "Shouldn't you say something? They're in a panic."

"Because Lady St. James and her crew of madmen killed dozens of werewolves and vampires tonight. It drew a rather large crowd." He continues speaking as if that statement alone isn't worth gawking over. "The witches cast my...interview with Lord Rutledge onto the clouds for everyone to see and hear. Now they know exactly what the bastard was up to, and they can hold the government accountable themselves. At the least, they can protect themselves from the invasion however they see fit. Not that it will do them much good."

The door of our room slams closed behind me. Ripper barks and waggles happily, dancing at my feet, but I cannot take my eyes from Raeth. He strides to the liquor cabinet and does not bother with a glass. He takes the bottle in one blood-stained hand and tips it, drinking several guzzles before drying his mouth on the back of his forearm.

When he notices me staring, one quizzical brow raises. "Haven't had enough of judging my actions today? Here, let me give you more fodder." Several long swallows later, he salutes me with the bottle. "If I am a monster, I may as well be a drunk one."


Silence smothers the rest of our evening routine. Raeth fills the tub, whisky bottle still in hand, but I feel his eyes on me as I disrobe and climb into bed. Neither of us had the stomach to eat anything.

When he tosses his stained clothes into the fire, it blazes up, gorging itself on the fabric and sending black smoke up the chimney. Raeth stands and stares for a long time, watching the blood-soaked material char and crumble, firelight reflected in his eyes. When he settles into the tub, I cannot take my gaze from his skin and the scars that mark him.

"I don't need your pity," he says before finishing off the last of the whisky and tossing the bottle into the fire.

So I turn over, close my eyes, and pray for sleep. But it doesn't find me. Instead, I float in an uneasy haze surrounded by sharp-clawed memories that attack every time my back is turned. A knife flashing. A door opening. My father's hand on my shoulder. Raeth's lips on mine. Hands that once touched me with reverence and passion covered in blood. The crackling sound of my bracelets as I burned someone alive from the inside. Runnels of blood on stone. Weeping.

Weeping.

Only the weeping isn't in my drowsy memories. Pushing the blankets off my legs, I sit up to see Raeth naked on the floor with his back against the side of the fireplace. One leg is bent, and his elbow rests on his knee, fingers threaded through his hair as his head hangs.

And he is crying.

Every emotion I have been suppressing hits me like a storm front. I am halfway across the room by the time he looks up and stops me with his eyes. "Don't."

But I know something now that I didn't allow myself to see in the aftermath of Rutledge's death. I'd been so consumed with my own disillusionment, my own pain, that I hadn't allowed myself to recognize how much confronting Rutledge cost him. How much it must have hurt. He lived with the emotional damage of abuse for more years than I care to count, carried the memories as deeply as the scars, and now the man who caused them is dead.

Will that free Raeth, or will Rutledge haunt him? If I could punish the people who gave my parents predatory loans and charged such exorbitant interest that it destroyed our lives, would I? Would I?

My own selfishness shames me. Seeing Raeth exact retribution hurt me in a way I still don't have words to describe and am terrified to face. But I left him alone after one of the most significant moments of his life, alone to cope with the weight of everything he suffered and everything he did because of it.

Right or wrong, good or bad, how does one begin to comprehend the scope of such a thing?

I cannot live with what he has done, with who I've become by his side. But that doesn't mean I will abandon him to this pain.

Fighting back tears, I kneel next to him. Raeth tries to block me with his arm, extending his hand palm out to ward me away. He wants to seclude himself, as he always has done. But tonight, at least, I am here. Threading my fingers through his, I pull his hand tight against my chest. He shudders as if our touch established a current that let the turmoil inside his body escape into mine.

With a sob, he catches me around the waist and buries his face in my neck, holding so tightly I can barely breathe. Our joined hands are trapped between our bodies. Hot tears soak my chemise, and all I can do is rub comforting circles on his upper back with my free hand.

"Shh," I murmur into his hair. "It's over. It's over."

I hope the words will be comforting, even if we both know it is a lie. Tears do not wash away trauma so easily. But I hold him while he weeps, every wracking sob wrenched from his soul sliding into mine like daggers.

The fire dies to a smolder. Raeth shudders and relaxes into me, and I settle between his legs to rest my head on his shoulder. Our breathing falls into sync. And when we finally climb into bed, exhausted, he wraps his arms around my waist and falls asleep with his head pillowed between my breasts and my fingers tangled in his hair.

~

WHEN WE WAKE and dress for court, a delicate web of silence hangs over us. Every movement tugs the threads, every breath, every almost-spoken word strains it until it frays around the edges. So we walk carefully and breathe softly, somehow knowing that if we do not break the silence, neither of us will be forced to confront what happened last night. And if he does not ask me whether I have reconsidered my choice, we can pretend nothing happened.

When we arrive, the tension in the air makes our fragile silence a laughably small barrier.

Members of the court stare in dazed confusion, and the way their eyes flick to Raeth and away suggests many of them hadn't wished to attend at all. Generally, the worries of the Upstairs only leak into the Undercroft insofar as they impact how closely people guard their valuables. But the events of the past months, culminating in a battle in Trafalgar Square, has left everyone shaken.

They are used to navigating crackdowns and reforms, diseases, killer fogs, and a host of other struggles. But a King who openly declares himself a faerie in an image cast onto the clouds by witches is something the Unseen Court has no experience with. The distrust in their eyes makes a shiver of dread run down my spine. I flex my hands to remind myself that the bracelets rest against my skin.

When the unease is thick enough to smother me, Raeth stands. Lamplight slides across the silver crown and pools in the bowls of the spoons. "The rumors are true. Faeries exist, and they plan to invade New London."

"But you're a faerie!" Someone shouts from the back.

"I am a refugee of the Sunset Lands," Raeth says, raising his chin. "And I have been a New Londoner longer than many of you have been alive. I have guarded you from the Constables, fed you in famine, and helped you remind the Upworlders that they cannot stomp on us without repercussions."

Some murmur in agreement, and others mutter to their neighbors. One woman gains enough courage to ask, "But where do your loyalties lie?"

"Aye!" Someone else calls. "If your people invade, how do we know you'll help us and not them?"

The crowd takes up the chorus of, "Yeah!"

"Who are my people?" Raeth shouts, the echoes of his voice silencing them into awe. He seems to have grown several inches, and the air around him warps to accommodate his presence. "Who are my people? Humans? Elves? Dwarves or Fae? No. Mine are the wretched, the forgotten, the scoundrels, and the outcasts. Mine are the abandoned, the sick, and the sore at heart." He walks down the stairs, shoulders straight, chin high, and my chest swells as tears prick my eyes. "Society says we do not fit. That there is no place for us Upstairs in the neatly planned world they built for themselves. Well, there is a place for us here!" He jams one finger at the flagstones beneath him. "And so long as we stand alongside one another, all of us, the Undercroft will stand."

Their cheer shakes the pillars, sending dust and mortar raining from the ceiling. But one dissenting voice speaks. A familiar, rugged voice. "How do we know you speak the truth?"

Tildie waddles out of the crowd, her hands folded in front of the layers of scarves and blankets that hide her squat form. "How do we know we can trust you not to manipulate and use us for your own power?"

My mouth goes dry. Tildie threatened me once to keep Raeth safe, and I suspect she would have done worse. Did Raeth plant her here for this purpose? When would he have had the time?

I cannot ask any of these questions because he turns to me, as does every eye in the room, so no one is looking at Tildie when she winks at me.

But Raeth's expression is serious, and his eyes are sincere. "No one will be forced to stay or serve in the Undercroft who does not choose to. And that includes our lady."

A soft gasp rises from the crowd and matches my indrawn breath. Raeth pulls a knife from a sheath on his hip, but it is not his silver knife. I know enough to know now that the dark metal is iron. He shows the crowd the blade as he stalks toward me. Six months ago, I would have cowered in fear. I don't know what he plans to do with the knife, but I know whatever it is will not hurt me.

"I swore once, before you all, that if I broke the terms of my pact, this knife would pierce my flesh."

Raeth stands before me, his eyes so dark I could tip forward, fall into them, and be lost forever.

*And be lost forever.*

He may have sworn an oath to the court, and he does not lie. He swore to help find my father, and I still believe he will. His vengeance on Rutledge may be justified—it is justified.

But I can still see the man's pleading eyes, Raeth's furious grimace, and the blood spreading beneath them. And I know I cannot walk this road to find my father. I cannot carry such heavy burdens on my conscience.

Raeth takes my hand, presses the hilt of the knife against my palm, and curls my fingers around it. When he drops to his knees in front of me, my mouth goes dry. And when he takes my hand to press the cold iron against his throat beneath his jaw, my hands shake.

No one breathes. I want to demand what the hell he thinks he is doing, but it is there in his eyes: he is letting me go. And letting the court watch him do it, watch him keep his word—not the letter of it, not manipulated by clever trickery or turn of phrase—but the spirit of it. If I chose to kill him now, he would allow it.

Tears sting my eyes, but I blink them back. This is not the time for tears. Heart in my throat, I let my opposite hand slide down his arm to his wrist. His pulse beats hard against my fingertips when I position the knife and press the tip into the pad of his thumb.

Blood wells, a bright red drop that slides from the side of his hand and down his wrist. I pull the coin from my pocket and stare for a moment at the embossed silver that brought me here, the head of a man with his throat cut. When I press the coin against his blood, the air goes electric, making the hairs on my forearms stand up.

A sigh escapes the court. The Undercroft now knows the King can bleed. It changes everything. And when I tug him to his feet and kiss the wound, leaving his blood on my lips, that changes everything too.

But not enough to stay.

He sheaths his knife but holds the bloody coin on his palm as I turn and leave the court.

# CHAPTER 36

*If I should like anything explained to me, it is this: why is the dearest desire of the mortal heart for certainty when certainty is the single thing we shall never have. Why is our greatest wish is immortality, only for it to be thwarted by the looming shadow of the grave.*

*It is perverse in the extreme.*

—From the diary of Willow Beauregard
Nov 12th 1902

RIPPER LEADS ME THROUGH THE TWISTS AND TURNS OF THE Undercroft with unerring confidence, the brassy click of his paws keeping time while the air warms and light contaminates the darkness.

Two Ratcatchers guard this exit from the Undercroft and bow their heads respectfully as I pass, though I no longer have the benefit of the King's protection and look nothing like a fearsome white lady. The simple grey armored dress and copper bracelets were the only things I could force myself to take from the room I shared with Raeth.

Ripper looks back at me over his brawny shoulder when I hesitate at the door of the abandoned building. Once more, I stand on a threshold in the dark with light and warmth, waiting on the other side, only this time, I am not so eager to cross it.

The peaceful shadows cover me like a blanket, promising the solace of refuge. But I cannot stay here. With a deep breath, I step into the light.

The sun batters my head and shoulders as sound assaults me from everywhere: wagon wheels, autos, barking dogs, costers shouting, pigeons and crows and–I flatten my hands over my ears to muffle the noise, but that doesn't save me from the pungent air.

Manure, exhaust, the rotten chemical odor of a nearby paper mill, and the sewage-stink of the Thames combine to make me hold my breath. But even that doesn't stop the dust-filled air from tickling the back of my throat enough to make me cough.

"You'll get used to it," one of the Ratcatchers chuckles as he closes the door.

With one hand to shade my eyes and the opposite wrist covering my nose to filter the air, I peer at the closest street sign. Harlowe Street. My heart thumps once, hard. I'm not far from home.

This time, Ripper follows me, and people stare at him in wonder as we pass, but I don't care. The only thing I have space for in my mind is whether the mechanica is still there, still ours. Do I have a home at all? Where will I go if the bank has repossessed it?

Not for the first time, the thought that I was too hasty, that I decided to leave without thinking my way through the implications of surviving alone without an income, pounds against the inside of my skull like a hammer. But I firmly ignore it. Scraping for money as I search for my father is better than becoming the sort of person I need to be to stay in the Undercroft.

A costermonger's donkey, spooked by Ripper, snorts and shies as we pass, forcing me to leap aside to avoid having my foot crushed by the wheel of his cart. The man hauls on the beast's harness, wrenching his head aside to right the cart before shouting an insult at me.

I retreat to the sidewalk, breathing hard and chastising myself for letting my attention wander in a place as casually dangerous as the streets of New London. What an ironic ending that would be after all of the dangers I have faced.

"You alright, dear?" A little old woman asks as she takes my forearm in a wrinkled hand.

The gratefulness that swells in my chest at her concern makes me want to cry, but she takes my word that I'm okay and wanders off, leaving me to gather myself and hurry on.

An auto motors by, filling the air with exhaust. Sweat rolls down my spine in a tickling rivulet, and by the time I turn onto Penny Lane, I miss the silence and relative peace of the Undercroft in a way I never expected to.

"Murders in Trafalgar Square!" A newsboy shouts at me, brandishing a paper like a weapon. "The heiress of the Wainwright Duchy arrested for treason! Read all about it!"

I slow long enough to peer at the headlines on the twine-tied stack of papers near his feet. *Grisly Deaths in Trafalgar Square; Lady Gwenevere St. James Wainwright Arrested for Murder, Conspiracy, and Treason.* The ink illustration of a brunette in cuffs is decidedly unfair. Lady St. James hadn't been a beauty by popular standards, though she was pretty enough. She certainly *hadn't* had a bulbous, warty nose, lantern jaw, and missing teeth.

But it is the headline beneath that stops me cold: *Scotland Yard in Shambles: Chief Inspector Mac Sweeney Found Dead in Office.*

A wave of dizziness hits, and the ground drops from beneath my feet. Ripper leans against my legs to steady me, and I rest my hand on his head to regain my balance.

"You alright, ma'am?" The newsboy asks.

His worried eyes roam over my face, but the gleam of opportunism in his expression is stronger. He doesn't want the responsibility of dealing with a fainting woman, but he is clever enough to know that the drama and attention would make potential customers flock around us.

I mumble something about being fine and wave him off as I stumble down the block, my head spinning. Chief Inspector Mac Sweeney was my contact at Scotland Yard. He knew I was searching for my father and that I planned to venture into the Undercroft. Could his death be tied to me and my involvement with the Covenant?

My steps slow, falter and stop.

How many people will die before I find my father? Did Mac Sweeney have a family and children who will miss him? What right do I have to search for a loved one at the expense of theirs? Why is violence at the end of every road I try to take?

Ripper tugs my skirt, pulling me out of my near trance and toward the end of the lane.

"You're right, boy," I say, shaking my head to clear my mind and trying to regain some sense of forward momentum. "I don't know anything yet, so there is no sense in torturing myself. I should just focus...on..."

The air in my lungs leaks out in a slow sigh. Beauregard's Mechanica still stands, and the sign has been freshly painted. Legs that hadn't wanted to move mere seconds ago carry me down the sidewalk at an unbecoming speed.

Everything I've known and loved, everything I've desired for months, hits me in flashes. The red brick. The windows reflecting the street behind me. The familiar creak of the sign swaying on iron chains. The door knob that fits into the palm of my hand. The little bell that chimes three times.

Dust and sunlight stream through the windows, throwing shadows on rows of shelves that are, somehow, full of new copper, brass, and steel.

Someone sanded away the blood stain and oiled the floor, overwhelming the scent of grease and old coal fires in the small furnace with wood and wax.

Something crackles beneath my foot. Mail? It had not occurred to me that everyday things like the post would continue after I left.

Dazedly, I pick up the small pile of paper and tuck it under my arm as I wade back into the place that owns every memory between seven years old and last November. My fingertips drag over the shelves, leaving clean trails in the dust. These shelves must have been stocked weeks ago, at least.

I swallow back the emotion trying to choke me as each well-known sight makes memories light up my mind like lightning flashes. Everything I sold to try and save this place, all the supplies and tools, have been returned, and more besides.

Numbly, I take the stairs with Ripper following close behind. My knees weaken with each step toward my bedroom so that when the door swings open and I see what awaits me, the ground rushes up, and I hit the floor. Somehow I remained upright, but my hip stings from the landing. Ripper buts his head against my shoulder and whines. Or is that me whining?

My arms twine around his neck, and I rest my cheek on his cool head until I feel steadier. "*Calliope's voice*, Ripper. What has he done?"

Ripper only wags his tail, leaving me to stare at my small bedroom garden that has not only been lovingly cared for but is no longer small. Plants and shelves of plants cover both walls facing the windows; their leaves turned hungrily toward the light.

I dreamed of someday creating a place like this for myself, a little refuge where I don't have to wear armor, where nothing is expected of me and I have simply to be present. And here it is, beckoning me with a reminder of another garden and the man who created it for me.

Mail slips through my fingers to land in a pile on the wood floor between my legs.

*Ms. Willow Beauregard* is scrawled across the face of a large packet in a neat script, the name marred by a bulge on one side. Hands shaking, I open the envelope. A brass key falls to the floor, and a folded bundle of paper slides out.

*Dear Madam,*

*I am pleased to inform you that the legal transfer of ownership for the commercial property at 14 Aldersgate Street, New London, has been successfully completed, and you are now the rightful owner. Enclosed, you will find the key to the premises.*

*To finalize the matter, I kindly request that you attend our office at your earliest convenience to sign the necessary documents to complete the transfer and take formal possession of the property.*

*Please do not hesitate to contact me should you require further information or wish to schedule an appointment.*

*Yours faithfully,*

*Mr. Edward H. Farnsworth, Esq.*

*Solicitor at Law*

Aldersgate? That is close to the West Side. Why do I own a building?

"I don't understand this is...this is too much. It is—" I cannot get the words out or force more air into my straining lungs. All I can do is hold Ripper and watch the square of sunlight travel across the floor and up the opposite window, turning my room gold, then orange, and finally magenta.

I sit so long that my bladder makes itself uncomfortably known.

Ripper's brass skin is cool against my palms when I take his beloved face in my hands. "I'm safe now, boy. Thank you. You can go home."

He turns in a circle once and sits decidedly down.

"Ripper, go home."

He wags his tail.

"Ripper," I point at the door, "you have done your job. Now go. Home!"

The slagging dog only lays down and rests his head on his paws with a huff.

Frustration and sorrow and regret go to war in my chest until the only way to release them is to scream, "Why is he doing this to me?"

My scream goes unanswered, the light fades from the sky, and Ripper and I lie on the floor together, watching the leaves of my plants twist in the evening breeze of the open window.

MY MORNING ROUTINE is as familiar as breathing: watering the plants, bathing, brushing my teeth, dressing my hair, fixing break-fast, checking the post, and preparing the shop for the day. I've repeated the pattern alone every morning since childhood, but this is the first time it has felt lonely. Lonely save, of course, for the Ratcatchers I've spotted lurking around the building. Apparently, I cannot entirely escape the Undercroft... or its ruler.

When I open the small pantry only to find it fully stocked, unexpected anger and frustration hit. I snatch a random jar of jam from the shelf, stomp into the small kitchen, hack a slice from the fresh loaf, and grind butter into the soft bread; bread that would not be in this pantry or be this soft unless someone bought and delivered it yesterday.

"Who asked him for this?" I grumble, shaking the butterknife at Ripper. "Who asked him to plant reminders of himself all over my life so that I cannot turn anywhere without seeing him? All this must have cost hundreds of pounds, and I cannot pay it back."

Ripper tilts his head and raises one ear, watching as I tear off a chunk with my molars, then give up and scoop a dollop of jam directly into my mouth. "It was one thing to be so extravagant while I was actively serving him," I say around a mouthful of sweet, tart strawberry jam, "but he can garner no benefit from all this? So why do it? Why leave you here with me? Did you know that if he sold you, your price could buy two or three of these buildings?"

I shove the jam back into the pantry, slam the door, and lean against it with an explosive sigh, letting my head fall back against the wood. "It doesn't matter. I cannot be the person that world requires of me. The cost is too high."

Ripper noses my hand, his muzzle clinking on the copper bracelet. The tool I created in the Undercroft, one that let me kill a woman. And the compass hanging heavy in my pocket, which also resulted in the death of a man, if by a more indirect path. How many lives am I responsible for?

When I gather all of my evidence and approach a detective, will that end in his death as well? At least the others had been trying to hurt me. I don't know if I can carry the weight of another death, of more memories of suffering.

The bell chimes three times, making Ripper and I raise our heads. Had I locked the shop last night before climbing into bed? Surely, no one was still visiting after six months of inactivity. I skip down the stairs, prepared to tell whoever wants a gadget fixed that we are closed, only to see Silk standing in the middle of the aisle, her dark hair backlit by a beam of sunlight.

The pressure on my chest lightens at the sight of her familiar silhouette. "Silk! What are you doing here?"

But when I try to take her hand in greeting, the smile freezes on my face. Bags frame her dark eyes, and lines of strain bracket her mouth. She looks bedraggled, run ragged, and a bruise darkens her cheekbone.

"When did you last sleep?" I ask, dragging her toward a chair and then turning to find something for her to drink.

She sighs and rubs dirty fingers across her forehead as if to loosen the strain, her eyes closed. For a moment, I think she will fall asleep sitting up.

"Silk," I say in exasperation, "what's wrong? Are you alright? What can I do?"

When she looks up at me, my heart plummets into my stomach like a lead weight.

"They took him," she says in a dull voice. "We tracked the Covenant last night, and they led us to an abandoned warehouse. They use lots of those, so we weren't surprised. But it was an ambush. There must have been ten of them at least, and they over-whelmed us. I—" She drops her head into her hands and shud-ders. "The only reason they didn't take me is this." She holds up the shadow cloak. "He threw it over me when I fell. But I followed them as soon as I came to." She looks up, her eyes pleading, hands clasped in the dark fabric. "I followed them. I saw where they took him, and I can get us in. I'm sure of it."

My ribcage is too small for my lungs. I cannot get enough air. And though I already know the answer, my voice comes out weak and thready when I ask, "Who did they take?"

"The King. Gwil. They killed the rest. I tried to rally the court, but the Ratcatchers have closed off the Undercroft, and they won't listen to me."

My brain spins and tumbles inside my skull as I try to piece information together, pressing the heels of my hands against my temples to force my mind—and my heart—to slow down. I need a deep breath to gather all distracting thoughts, and a long exhale to release them.

After one more slow breath, when my mind is under margin-ally better control, I say, "You followed them, and you have a way in?"

Silk nods tiredly.

"Alright," I say as I begin pacing. "We have a problem to solve, limited resources with which to solve it, and an unlikely desired outcome. Just like a bit of artifice. First, we define the problem. The Covenant already has my father, and now they have Rae—the King," I correct before remembering how particular Undercrofters are about names, "and Gwil."

I try not to picture Raeth in their hands, but the images are there anyway: his wrists bound, his body broken and bruised. I shake my head and force my mind to focus. "What is the desired outcome? The King, Gwil, and my father are free. What resources do we have to make that happen? The two of us," I gesture between us with a finger, though Silk looks spent. "My bracelets.

The cloak. The compass. And Ripper. How can we combine those things to achieve the desired outcome?"

Puzzle pieces slide in and out of place, arranging and rearranging themselves.

"Can we go to Scotland Yard and lead them to—"

"Seven gods, no," Silk exclaims, looking up. "If they do listen, which I doubt, they won't allow us to help, and they will absolutely arrest the King if they manage to save him."

That might be worth a try if I knew Raeth would live, but if a Chief Inspector isn't safe in his office, Raeth certainly wouldn't be safe in a prison, especially not bound by iron. If I only had someone to help, someone capable to rely upon... But there is no one else. Only me. I must be the capable one.

So I swallow my misgivings, square my shoulders, and raise my chin. "Let's go get them."

Ripper barks.

～

WE SPEND the next hours making plans, gathering supplies, and arguing.

"You couldn't sneak if I turned you into a cat." Silk pushes the cloak at me, but I tuck my hands behind my back.

"If I get caught or attacked, I've got this," I tap my fingers against the fabric of my dress. "Can your blouse turn aside a knife? A bullet?"

She raises a brow at my ensemble, my plain work clothes disguising the grey armored dress beneath. "You sure you trust that? At the end of the day, it's only fabric."

"It has saved my life before."

With a sigh and an eye-roll for good measure, Silk stuffs the shadow cloak into the front of the work blouse and tucks it into the top of her skirt. Both garments are worn threadbare in places and patched or darned as clothes of the working class are wont to be. Instead of looking like a charming rogue, which is always how

I've seen her, she looks like someone I might pass on the street in the morning and never glance twice at.

"Fine," she says as she pats the cloak into a more uniform lump over her belly, then jerks her chin at the dog. "But we cannot take *that* monstrosity."

"Ripper is not a monstrosity. He's a work of art. Aren't you, boy?"

Ripper, who does not realize he should be insulted, wags his tail happily. But she's right. He's far too loud to sneak anywhere. "Perhaps we can find somewhere for him to hide outside and call for him if we need him? He's capable of quite a bit of destruction if necessary."

Silk narrows her eyes at the dog. "And just how would we do that? Where can we take him and stash him that a hundred people wouldn't notice on our way?"

The dog and I look at one another for a long time. Seeming to sense my decision, Ripper whines, and shoulders my leg. "I'm afraid she's right, boy. Unless we rent a wagon of some kind and hide you inside it—"

"Someone would notice an idle wagon sitting where it wasn't wanted," Silk points out as if I don't know that.

"—we can't take you with us. Think you can stay here and guard the shop?"

"Can't you just lock him up?"

It is my turn to roll my eyes. "Do you know how heavy and powerful he is? You think my wooden door could stop him if he chose to plow through it?"

She casts an uncertain glare in Ripper's direction and shrugs. "I suppose not. You'd better hope he feels like obeying you, then. Or we'll be caught before we ever make it inside, and all the work we did to disguise your hair won't matter a bit."

I brush a curling brown lock away from my face and kneel to hold Ripper's face. "I'm going to save your master," I tell him seriously. "If I didn't have to sneak, I would take you along. But if you try to come, we will likely both be caught, and there will be no one to protect. You understand me?"

Ripper whines and drops his eyes, his tail twitching in what I interpret as a sad waggle. "You're a good boy," I tell him before kissing his cold metal nose.

When the door is closed and locked, I turn to face the street. Morning sun glances across the tops of the buildings, making the chimney smoke glow. I've done an admirable job of controlling my emotions since Silk appeared at my door, but the full weight of everything hits me as we walk away from the Mechanica.

I clasp my hands to stop them from shaking and try to breathe slowly, but my heart is doing its best to climb up my ribcage. I spent years relying on someone else to help me solve problems I didn't feel capable of solving: my father, the Guild, Scotland Yard, Raeth. And now there is no one else to rely on.

Only me.

Maybe there really was always only me. And now, it is time to find out exactly what I can do.

# CHAPTER 37

*The passing nature of pleasure and joy sometimes seem the cruelest jest, for they are as ephemeral as the sun breaking through the clouds, there for one glorious instant, and gone as quickly, leaving only the memory of warmth behind.*

*—From the diary of Willow Beauregard*
*August 19, 1901*

"NO WONDER YOU NEVER FOUND THEM," I MUTTER AS WE JOIN THE queue. "Who would have thought of looking here?

Hundreds of men and women of all races—and more than a few children—stand shoulder to shoulder outside at the gates of the mill, dull-eyed and slumped-shouldered in stained shades of brown and grey.

Those with enough spirit to chat do so quietly as we shuffle forward, no one seeming to notice the sulfurous stink that overwhelms even the constant miasma of the nearby Thames. Which means I cannot be seen noticing it either, though several other elves have cloths tied over the lower halves of their faces. I swallow back a cough and wish I would have thought of that.

"Time cards here," someone shouts from the gate, raising a handheld flag so the crowd can see. "Day workers here!" Another flag rises from the other side of the gate. "Maintain order and don't shove in. There's plenty of work for everyone today."

"And more than enough," someone nearby mutters, and someone else laughs.

Silk and I maneuver to the righthand side, edging through the shuffling bodies. The narrow opening is guarded by a man wielding a pen and a clipboard who never looks up when he demands, "Name?"

"Lewis Cooper."

"Name?"

"Maddy Churchill."

"Name?"

"Reg Harcourt."

Silk slides in front of me, her head heavy on her neck, one hand resting on her shoulder as she steps up to the gate.

"Name?"

"Lydia Turnbuckle," she says in a monotone that exaggerates her Cockney accent.

The pen scratches, the man holds out the clipboard and says, "Make your mark," and then nods Silk through.

I take her place, trying to look as casual as possible.

"Name," he says from beneath a hanging mustache.

I stutter out the first name that comes to mind. "Sylvie Bywater."

The pen scratches, and he holds out the clipboard. "Make your mark."

But as soon as I take the pen, he looks up at me through narrowed eyes. "New, eh?"

Oh, Calliope, he knows. My throat tightens up in response.

Most men don't like looking up at a woman, so I slouch as I make an X near my name. "How'd you know?"

He jerks his chin at my hands. "Those are hands for skill work, not pressing paper."

If he shouts for help or turns me in, I won't be able to make it out of this crowd fast enough to get away. My muscles tense, but if I look guilty he's more likely to find me suspicious. So I fight to maintain my composure and force myself to shrug.

He snatches the clipboard. "Don't know what you did to lose your old job, but whatever it was, don't do it here. Get me?"

I drop my eyes and nod.

He turns to the next person in the queue. "Name?"

Silk grabs my arm and jerks me into line after her as she strides toward the huge double doors of the mill muttering, "Cannot sneak to save your damn life," as we enter the cavernous mouth of the building.

Rows of monstrous Fourdrinier machines crouch like sleeping beasts along both walls of the two-story building, leaving aisles for us to creep between them. The staggered cylinders that roll pulp into paper are long and wide enough to crush any of the unwary men who crawl over them like ants with grease buckets and oil cans.

When the electricity powers on, the machines growl to life, leather belts as wide as my waist turning heavy iron wheels. Agitators at the end of the hall pump like beating hearts, sending a stream of wet pulp into the mouths of the machines. When the paper reaches the drying cylinders, puffs of humid air billow toward us, sharp with the stink of sulphur, grease, and body odor.

Luckily, huge exhaust fans circulate the sour air up and out through ventilation shafts above. In fact, the entire complex is riddled with ventilation shafts.

The grinding machines are so loud that artificers must have engraved runes for controlling sound, or we would be forced to cover our ears to protect our hearing. I lean over as I pass, trying to catch a glimpse of what runes were used on the machines, but Silk pinches my arm to keep me on track.

The stream of workers carries us down the aisle of enormous presses and into a second, much quieter room full of covered vats the size of small pools. Even exhaust fans cannot pull enough of the stink away to make this room tolerable. The chemicals in the air float into my mouth and throat, and my coughing draws laughs of derision from those wielding huge wooden paddles to agitate the pulp in the open vats.

As we travel through the complex of rooms, floors, and buildings, people peel away from the group to their areas of specialty. We keep our heads down, trying to ignore any prying eyes and avoid notice.

How Silk judges it is time to escape, I cannot tell, but in the hall between two large rooms, she pulls me aside and drags me down a narrow stairwell. We step carefully to avoid our footsteps ringing on the metal stairs, and exit into a below-ground hallway lit sparsely with industrial lights and lined with doors.

Though most of the doors are locked, one enormous bay is filled with rows of paper rolls bigger than carts, and reams of stacked paper twice my height, covered and tied with twine. Other rooms house boxes, barrels, piles of bags, rags, and other supplies either for the making of paper or equipment maintenance.

We weave between piles, the avenues like city streets, until Silk deems one corner safe enough to hide in. The large exhaust fan set about a foot into the wall is still, and only barely covers the dark tunnel behind it.

We slide into seated positions behind a stack of boxes that shield us from view, close enough to the fan for a quick escape into the dark if necessary. Silk fishes the cloak out of her blouse and holds one end invitingly toward me. "Get in. Might as well take the extra precaution since we'll be waiting a while. And it's chilly down here."

Settled shoulder to shoulder, we wait. As the hours pass, the constant vibration of working machines, stomping feet, closing doors, shouts, bells, and now and then the odd alarm, become as easy to ignore as rain on a roof.

"Why are you doing this?" Silk asks.

I startle awake to see her picking at her fingernail with the tip of her knife.

"Hmm?"

She puts the knife down and gives me an exasperated glare. "I swore an oath to the King. I know why I'm here. And I had no one else to turn to for help, save you. But why are you here? Why risk it now that you've gained your freedom?"

I consider the answer while wiping the sleep from my eyes. "If the Covenant took the King, then finding him will also likely lead me to my father."

She raises one eyebrow that says, and that's all?

"Isn't that enough?"

I cannot tell her that the thought of Raeth taken, chained, makes my stomach sick and my heart ache. That the possibility of him reliving the trauma that broke him makes me frantic with the need to tear this place apart.

"I suppose," she says finally, nodding and looking down. "People might do any crazy thing for those they love."

I swallow and look away. "How much longer?"

"A few more hours," she says. "What does your compass say?"

It lies in the concealed placket inside my vest, the one Mr. Bywater made me practice slipping my hand into. When I pull the tool out and turn the frame to the runes attuned to Raeth's magical energy, the needle swings around and wavers in a generally eastern direction.

"I never considered making it three-directional," I admit, turning the body to a ninety-degree angle. The needle immediately turns downward, quivering. "East and down. In a sub-basement, maybe?"

Silk frowns. "There's nothing for it but to search either way, I guess."

After closing the compass and stowing it away carefully, I take her hand. It is calloused, like mine only in different places, but sun-browned and capable. "Thank you, Silk. For everything."

She pats my hand but draws hers away. "Thank me when we're all safe. I don't like this place. There must be loads of hidden rooms for the Covenant to operate here if no one has ever noticed, which means they're either well hidden, well guarded, or both. I can't guarantee we'll get out once we've got in."

If I hadn't already been aware of that lovely little fact, I might have felt sick at the idea. But I've felt sick since leaving the Undercroft, and frantic since Silk appeared. Falling asleep on her shoulder was the only way my body could deal with the stress of imagining and re-imagining Raeth and my father in the bowels of this place with waxy-skinned bowler hats holding them hostage.

If they are still alive.

Mental images of what might be happening to them make the hours pass slowly. When the final bell rings, signaling the end of the workday, we do not move. When the lights flicker off, we wait. Machinery quiets. Full darkness falls. An unnatural stillness consumes place, holding within it a sense of expectation and quiet menace.

When Silk is certain the place is empty save the guards who roam the grounds in shifts, we venture out of the storage room.

I lead the way, stepping as softly as I know how, with the compass in front of me. The dark isn't complete, not like the Undercroft, and I can see enough to navigate by. Silk walks with one hand on my back, the shadow cloak making her invisible as she traces my footsteps, relying on my keener eyes to lead us through the dark.

We trail through the labyrinth of rooms, down another flight of stairs, the compass needle wavering regularly. I don't tell Silk that I haven't tested this enough to know how time and distance affect the artifice. It wouldn't change anything.

But the unease in the pit of my stomach grows with each turned corner and empty room. If Raeth never walked this way, will the compass still track him? I haven't done enough testing to know. We could be walking into the bowels of this complex with nothing to show for our efforts but empty bellies. And that is if we don't get caught.

I cannot shake the feeling that the compass isn't working like it should, but what else can we do?

The needle swings, pointing me down a long narrow hall into complete blackness. Silk pulls a small thieves' lamp from her pocket that casts a single dim beam forward into the dark, illuminating a chain hanging padlocked from the handle of a metal door. It is the only chain we have seen on a door since entering the paper mill.

My heart drops. "Can you pick locks?"

"Who do you think you're talking to," she snorts, handing me the lamp.

She pulls a rolled-up leather kit from somewhere under her skirt, unrolls it with a quick snap, and, after examining the lock, pulls two thin metal tools from their straps. One slides into the locking mechanism with relative ease, but the other must be wiggled in. Silk barely breathes, her head cocked to the side, listening for I don't know what.

But my sensitive ears pick up something else. "Silk?"

"Not now, Dove."

Careful to keep the light on the lock, I retreat a few steps and stop breathing as I listen. Footsteps. "Someone is coming."

She looks up at my whisper, her eyes wide, then bends all of her concentration on the lock. The footsteps echo down the dark hall, making the hair stand up on my neck and forearms. Whoever is coming is getting closer. Light, very faint but visible to me, lights up the wall of the T intersection at the end of this hall.

"They're close," I breathe.

If Silk unlocks the padlock, we will get through the door, but a guard will notice the missing chain and lock. Muses, I am seven colors of stupid. My heart flutters in panic as my eyes roam over the walls. There are no other doors to escape through, no side hall or stairs to climb.

When the guard turns the corner, he will see us. Only one person can fit fully beneath the shadow cloak, and I am far too tall to share it with Silk without exposing some part of me.

Perhaps she can hide, and I can let him take me as a distraction? The thought makes my stomach twist. There must be some way to—"Silk, the ventilation shaft!"

She looks up, though her hands still work the little metal tools. "What?"

Instead of trying to explain, I turn to the fan in the wall. It is set about six inches into the wall, placed a little higher than chest level. The footsteps grow louder. Heart in my throat, I push the fan until it turns to an angle that leaves a triangle beneath the blades, the support bars, and the floor of the shaft. The opening must be about two feet wide. I can fit through that.

Pushing the lantern in before me, I place my hands on the ledge and jump, catching my weight on my forearms. Silk's fingers lock into a stirrup beneath my feet and she lifts as I wriggle between the blades.

"Fergodssake, hurry," she whispers.

But my hips are caught on the fan blades, and when I try to twist, they turn with me and squeal at the mistreatment.

I freeze, the footsteps stop, and someone shouts, "Who's there?"

Silk swears, and my stomach rockets into my throat. I spin on my side, curl up like a shrimp, and drag my hips and legs through the fan. The footsteps pick up in pace. If Silk is left in the hall, she might escape notice. The cloak is magic, even if it is made for the dark. Is that a chance I am willing to take?

I spin inside the shaft, reach my hands out, and whisper, "Come on!"

Shaking her head, Silk takes my forearms, and we both pull. I am taller, but she is noticeably curvier, and the echoing footfalls are loud enough now that the guard should be turning the corner at any moment.

I set my feet against the inside of the shaft and pull, my legs, back, and arms straining. Silk's body catches on the corner, then slides into the shaft in a rush, landing half on me. She thumbs down the light on the lamp while I lay silently panting. Darkness covers us like a blanket, but that isn't safe enough. If he is a guard worth his salt, he'll shine his light into the shaft.

Pulling on Silk's wrist, I urge her silently to follow me and scoot farther down the shaft. Calliope grant there is nothing dangerous where we are heading.

"Who's down here?"

The voice is so loud it makes me freeze. Silk drags the cloak over both of us, and we lay like sardines, afraid to so much as breathe while someone rattles the chain on the locked door. From beneath the hem of the cloak, I watch light traverse the dusty wall of the duct and slide over us. It stops.

I bite my lips together, praying the disturbed dust will not make me sneeze as it tickles my nose and the back of my throat. Silk's fingers tighten around my wrist, jamming the edge of my copper bracelet painfully into the bone.

The light wavers and passes over us, and a second later, the footsteps retreat. Neither of us moves until the silence has dragged out for several minutes.

"Fucking hell, Dove. Being around you is always an adventure. Let's get out of here."

My heart refuses to calm, but I'm used to that now. The cape slides over my face as I push myself to a seated position, ready to pivot and slide toward the fan only to stop. "Do you see that?"

"See what?"

"The light. No, don't turn on the lamp. Follow me."

"Dove," she begins, then swears and follows the sound of me crawling down the duct toward a T intersection.

Light leaks in faintly from the left, in the same direction as the locked door. "Maybe we don't need to pick the lock after all."

As we crawl, the light grows, and soon, it is bright enough for Silk to see, too. Noise filters toward us, echoing and garbled through the metal ducting.

"Sounds like voices," I whisper.

She grabs my forearm, gestures to her mouth, and shakes her head before touching one ear. If we can hear them, they can hear us. Instead of crawling, we switch to scooting, which is quieter but more tiring. By the time the voices become clear, my arm and leg muscles are burning.

"Gotta stop taking them off the street," one female voice says. "They never last long enough for a decent test."

"That's only the ones we can find before the vampires get to them. Bloody greedy, they are." A male voice grunts, then complains, "Don't drop your end. This bloke is heavy."

"If we could get our hands on one that's been well fed, they might last long enough to fill the gem."

"I can't see that it matters much right now," the male voice says, getting farther away. "He won't work on it."

"Oh, he will. Eventually."

Silk and I stare at one another in the dim light as we wait for the silence to last long enough to guarantee we are alone. She nods to me at last, and I scoot to the end of the air shaft. The hall beyond is lit with only one lamp at the far end. But this opening is higher, closer to six feet from the ground.

No doorways, I mouth to Silk. If we exit here, we will have to be fast.

Her mouth thins into an unhappy line, but she nods and scoots behind me. I flip onto my stomach and slide feet first through the open triangle between the fan blades and the bottom of the ventilation shaft. This time, I turn my hips, and the fan barely moves when I slip through to land silently.

Reaching up, I guide Silk's feet through the opening, moving the fan carefully to accommodate her fuller hips. But she gets stuck halfway and starts jerking. Her body and the fan block my view, so I cannot see what is happening, even standing on my toes.

With a ripping sound and a frustrated sigh, Silk slides out into my arms, moving nearly too fast to catch. I lower her to the ground and begin to ask what is wrong, only to realize she isn't wearing the cloak.

"Bring the next one," someone calls from the end of the hall before I can ask her what happened.

She turns wide eyes on me, and we sprint on light feet in the opposite direction. When we near the corner, I slow, put my back to the wall, and lean carefully out until I can see that no one else is coming. We ease around the corner and into the first open room I can find before closing the door slowly, until only a slit of light leaks through.

Footsteps grow closer. Two or three pairs?

"Tell Grant to give them more sedative. They always get restive just before they wake up."

"Tell him yourself," comes the reply. "Last time I offered him advice, he cuffed me upside the head."

They pass between the door and the light, two dark shadows carrying a third.

"Cor, he's a strong one, inn'he? He'll last."

"We'll see."

When they're safely gone, I turn to Silk. "What happened?"

"Damned cloak stuck on a protruding nail," she says, frowning. "I couldn't get it loose and I got nervous someone would come along and see you just standing there. Didn't think it was worth the risk of waiting."

It wasn't an unlikely scenario, but losing that cloak was going to hurt. "There's nothing for it now," I say and pull out the compass. The needle swings around wildly but settles nowhere. "Something is interfering with the compass. That, or I've bollocksed it up. I think we're on our own."

After checking the hallway, we leave the room but don't quite close the door. Silk pulls a knife from her skirt and leads me down the passage. She walks on the balls of her feet like a cat, ready to spring in any direction.

The halls have an institutional feel, cold and impersonal, without the built-for-use ruggedness of the rest of the mill. I half expect to see a doctor or a nurse bustle around the corner. We turn left, then left again. At the end of the hall is another left.

"It's a bloody square," she says.

Silk slides up to a wide double door in the center of the hall that opens into the middle of the square and turns the nob experimentally. It clicks open. I prepare my bracelets, but when she eases the door open, no one is waiting to attack us. The short hall before us ends in a second-story metal catwalk circling the interior of the square. Several sets of stairs lead down to a center, roofless room built entirely of concrete.

It's like a viewing platform, I think, as I follow Silk onto the metal grating, keeping close to the wall in the shadows. We near the stairs and ease forward just enough to see into the central depressed room. My breath lodges in my throat, and dizziness hits me so hard that the only thing stopping me from collapsing is the metal rail I'm gripping like a lifeline.

In the center of the room is a work table, a toolbox as tall as I am, a small forge with exhaust piped into the wall, a barrel of oil, one of water, a chair, a rumpled cot...and my father. He is so thin that if I stare at him hard enough, I will see through him to the other side. Under the bright light of dwarven lamps, the bruises on his unnaturally pale skin are shocking.

He is here. Here, and alive.

I am moving before I can think better of it, even as Silk hisses, "Wait!"

The stairs fly under my feet, and I launch myself onto the concrete floor at a run. My father is sitting on the cot, his head in his hands. When he looks up, his expression is blank. There is no *him* behind his eyes. I slide to a stop at his feet, crouching and taking his cold, too-thin hands in mine.

"Papa?"

His brows draw together as he searches my face like I am a text in a language he cannot read.

"Papa, it's me. Willow."

His expression cracks, crumbles, and slides from his face in an avalanche. My fingers tighten around his hands as they shake. "Papa, I'm here. It's your daughter."

His pupils dilate, and there, at last, swimming up from the hazy depths of confusion in his eyes, is my father. Red flushes his neck and cheeks in a rush.

"What have you done?" He croaks. "By all nine Muses, girl, what have you done?"

His rage shocks me into leaning away from him. Tears start in my eyes. "I came to find you, Papa, I—I came to save you!"

"You said you would deliver the letter to my daughter. You swore it!"

A chill runs down my spine, turning my blood cold. He wasn't speaking to me.

Silk stands over my shoulder with her arms folded, her weight on one hip. "I kept my word. It isn't my fault she misunderstood your intentions."

# CHAPTER 38

Is the Undercroft changing me, or is it revealing something about me I've kept hidden? It's hard to tell. I find myself looking at people who would have frightened me months ago, and seeing friends instead of threats. Fate uses circumstances like a knife to prune and change the shape of whoever she chooses.

Lucinda, a lovely Welsh woman who works in the kitchen, was once the head cook in a wealthy household. But her employer couldn't keep his hands to himself. It seems fate also uses rolling pins in the absence of knives. She is now, according to the law, a murderer. And, I hope, my friend.

—From the diary of Willow Beauregard
April 1903

WHATEVER COHERENT THOUGHT HAD BEEN IN MY MIND DISAPPEARS in a wave of confusion followed by slowly dawning horror. "What letter?"

"She was never supposed to come here!" my father roars, standing up and nearly knocking me over. "I wanted to keep her away, to warn her of the danger! What have you done?"

I roll to my feet and stare as they face off like two angry cats in an alley. "Silk? What is happening?"

She sighs and rolls one shoulder in a shrug. "Archie has been difficult. Despite all the cajoling I could do, he doesn't want to finish his experiment. I did try to keep him safe, but he would rather starve himself and take daily beatings than finish the job. We needed a bit more leverage."

"What do you mean, leverage?"

"Oh, don't be dense, Dove. You're cleverer than that."

A door on the second level slams open, silhouetting the man who steps onto the catwalk. My stomach twists at the distinct shape of a bowler hat.

"Well done, Silk," he says as he reaches the bottom stair. "Though it took you long enough." Light reaches his face, and my skin goes cold. Left Hat.

"I had to be certain the King wouldn't come after her," she says.

Left Hat steps into the light, the embroidery at the lapel of his fine black suit catching the light before disappearing again. "If you'd convinced him to come along, we could have handled him here. We are prepared, after all."

"Don't underestimate him," Silk warns. "Especially not now that his construct has been repaired. I'll need to separate them and sew more discord before we take him down."

Shock and anger, unlike anything I have ever known, set my blood and my skin on fire, the change from cold to hot, making my fingertips and ears tingle. "You?" I demand, my voice trembling with rage. "It was you? You are the traitor?"

"Well," Silk shrugs, "I did try to keep you out of it. At least until Archie here decided the cost of his precious experiment was getting too high and stopped working."

"And now," Left Hat says, stepping toward me, "we have all the motivation we need to convince Mr. Beauregard to finish work on his brilliant machine."

Fury explodes in my chest in a fountain that turns my vision red, makes my muscles shake, and my hands curl into fists. I may have failed to save my father, but as soon as that disgusting creature touches me, I will activate my bracelets and cook his guts in his stomach, roast his heart inside his ribcage, and—

"Not so fast," Silk says, sliding between Left Hat and me. With an apologetic smile, she grabs my wrists, holding them away from my body. "She's hiding a rather clever weapon."

I scream in fury and jerk my wrists out of her grasp. She may be dangerous and clever, but I am faster and stronger. I will destroy her for betraying me, Raeth, and my father. For making me care about her—but Left Hat is already close enough to wrap his arms around me and trap mine against my torso.

"You let her go!" My father yells and pounds Left Hat with ineffectual fists. Only he is too weak to do any real damage. When he tries to lift a hammer and swing it at the waxy-skinned man, it drops from his fingers.

"If you don't want to see your father injured in his weakened condition," Left Hat says into my ear, "I suggest you be a good girl and allow Silk to remove whatever weapons you are carrying."

I grind my teeth in impotent rage when Silk easily unbuckles my bracelets one at a time, then holds them up to the light. "Malcolm will like to study these." She drops them into her skirt pocket. "I'll deliver them when we're done."

"Does she have anything else?" Left Hat asks.

"Not this one," Silk says, dismissing me with a flick of her fingers. "She's no threat."

"Good." Left Hat releases me, spins me around, and grabs both of my wrists. His eyes are so pale they are nearly colorless, and his skin up close is even more disturbing.

"You look like a corpse," I grind out.

He only smiles and says wistfully, "We all pay a price for the future we want." He turns to my father. "Shall I bind her here, Mr. Beauregard? Tie her to the stairs? Will it motivate you to see every cut, every bruise?" He tightens his grip until my wrist bones grind together, and burning pain radiates up my arms. I cannot stop a whimper from escaping despite locking my jaw against the noise.

"No!" My father shouts, pulling at Left Hat's arm. "No, let her go. I'll finish it. I'll finish it, I swear."

Left Hat smiles and sighs contentedly before patting my father's cheek. "Very good. Things are back on schedule, then." He pulls a pair of modern shackles from his pocket and locks them easily around my wrists. "Silk, find Miss Beauregard a comfortable room nearby, would you? And don't forget to deliver those bracelets to Malcolm."

"Certainly. As soon as you keep your end of our bargain. I don't work for free."

Left Hat stops halfway to the stairs and turns, offering her what is supposed to be an apologetic smile. "Don't tell me you truly believed we would give up our only leverage against a tool so dangerous as you? Come Silk, you know how the game is played."

She shrugs. It is a casual gesture, but the tightness around her eyes and the corners of her mouth betray her. "I expected as much."

"Then we have an understanding. You can visit her any time you like to assure yourself she is safe and happy, of course."

"Of course."

He opens his arms, palms up, as if welcoming her home. "Then we have an understanding?"

"We do," she says, dipping her chin.

I cannot tell whether he detects the fury underlying her tone, but he tilts his head to the side in a bow of acknowledgment. "Oh, and just in case," he strides back and holds out one gloved hand, beckoning with his fingers.

Silk's nostrils flare, but she doesn't argue as she digs my bracelets out of her pocket and drops them onto his palm with a clatter. He tosses them up, catches them, drops them in his pocket, and pats them once for safety. "It is always a pleasure working with you, dear girl."

Left Hat leaves by the door he entered through, and as soon as the metal clangs, I lunge at Silk with my hands curled into claws. But when I grab her blouse, my fingers will barely curl into a fist. With a sigh, she pries my fingers out of the fabric like a mother fending off the attention of an enthusiastic toddler.

"They weaken you, the cuffs," she says, brushing out the wrinkles my fingers made. "When you wear those, it doesn't matter if you're faster or stronger than me; I will win. You understand?"

With a growl of frustration, I twist my wrists against the bonds, but she grabs the linking chain and drags my wrists up so the shackles catch the light. "See the artifice? You can't fight it, so don't waste your strength. You're going to need it."

The symbols look more like the magic on my compass than any sort of artifice, but that wouldn't matter to Silk. What matters is that she is right. My body feels like a sack of wet flour. I cannot fight back. I failed.

My father sinks to his knees and wraps his arms around himself so he can sob quietly. Seeing him reduced to a shell of himself hurts more than I ever could have imagined, and my imagination has not been idle over the past months. Either anger gives me enough strength to jerk my arms away from her, or she doesn't care to hold my chain.

"You treacherous bitch," I growl. "The King isn't here, is he?"

Silk rolls her eyes. "Seven gods, you are a child." With an irritated sigh, she grabs my upper arm and hauls me toward the stairs opposite where we entered.

My father's querulous voice floats after me. "Willow?"

"I'm alright," I tell him over my shoulder. "I'm alright, Papa. I'm going to get you out of here, I swear."

Silk yanks open the door and forces me through, closing it behind us. Grief and anger are at war in my chest. I want to rage at her, but nothing comes out. She opens a room three doors from the central room on the outside wall and shoves me inside.

I right myself and glare at her. "How could you do this? I thought you served the King, the people!"

A long chain is bolted to a plate in the wall. She lifts the loose end and fastens it to the one between my wrists. "I do. But I serve myself and my family first. That's why I had to wait for you to leave the Undercroft on your own and without one of the King's damned coins in your pocket."

Once it snaps into place, the chain clatters to the floor and drags my wrists down with a snap, pulling the metal tight against the fleshy base of my thumb. That's it. I am a prisoner, along with my father. And no one is coming to save us.

When I look up, Silk is watching me, and I cannot decide whether to swear at her or to cry. All that comes out is, "I trusted you."

She sighs heavily and closes her eyes. "Only because you are a naive idiot." When she pulls me into an embrace, I snort in indignation and try to wriggle out of her grasp, but she only squeezes tighter and breathes against my ear, "You have everything you need."

When I finally fight free of her arms, she gives me a cheeky grin. "Not all friends are false friends, Dove. Sometimes, we tell the truth. Remember that."

She leaves my small room and doesn't bother to lock the door. Of course, she doesn't. My chain won't reach that far. It only reaches as far as the small cot and the chamber pot in the corner. The rest is flat, smooth, bare stone lit by a single electric bulb hanging from the ceiling. It hums with a constant whine.

My knees finally give out, and the cold floor rushes up to meet me.

I DON'T EAT the food when they slide it to me across the floor. My stomach tightens with the memory of my throat closing up and my mouth tingling as poison spread through my system. Had the poison been Silk's doing, too?

My chain doesn't reach far enough for me to lie comfortably on the cot, so I rest on my side with my arms stretched out, staring at the wall and imagining Raeth is behind me, his arm around my waist, the fire crackling on the opposite side of our room. At least he is not here, not being starved like my father.

Thinking over the path I took to get here is like walking home in the fog; I know where I am headed, but the dark shapes that should be familiar look alien, and every time I try to get my bearings, the landmarks I use to navigate life are gone.

This is what comes of trusting myself to be the competent one, to be the one who rushes in and saves the day. If I hadn't run from Raeth—and everything else about the Undercroft that scares me —I wouldn't be here. Together, we might have followed the compass and found my father, brought the Ratcatchers with us, and cleansed this place of the filth nesting here.

Instead, I am alone again, abandoned by someone else I trusted. My mind shies away from that truth, and my heart curls up to hide somewhere deep in my chest.

WHEN LEFT HAT opens my door, my muscles are stiff from lying in the same position for so long. My arms scream when he pulls me to my feet. "Time to see if we can convince your dearest father to do his job properly."

He drags me down the hall to a door on the inside corner of the square. A set of narrow stairs lead us downward into air that reeks of burnt hair and vomit. A huge window separates the room into two parts, one side for viewing and the other—my father is on the other. He cowers next to his invention, refusing to look at the machine. It is twice the size it once was, too large to fit into any travel bag, and sits atop a table with cords leading out of what used to be the charging ports.

The cords are...

"Merciful Calliope," I breathe. The links of my chains dig into my palms as my hands curl into fists. "You're using them like batteries."

He lifts my chain as if saluting me with it. "Silk said you were clever." Then he knocks on the glass.

My father turns and sees me, and his lips tighten into an unhappy frown. I lurch toward the glass, but Left Hat reacts with startling speed, backhanding me. My cheek explodes with pain that burns across my face and makes my eyeball feel as if it's about to pop. My knees give out, and I dangle by my wrists as I blink and try to overcome the dizziness.

"No!" The word is muffled through the glass, but my father's voice is unmistakable. "Don't hurt her!"

The world spins as Left Hat hauls me to my feet and secures the chain to another bolted plate. "Only making certain you know what is at stake should you lose your nerve, old boy."

My father nods vigorously, then turns to power on the machine. The chain is painfully cold, but I grip it to keep myself upright and force my eyes to focus on the other room.

The cables connecting my father's Aetheric Charger are clamped to the fingertips and earlobes of a small, pale woman. Only she isn't a woman. Not a mortal woman, anyway. She has the same charm and spellbinding beauty of Raeth and the other faerie, even in her unconscious state. Thick leather straps lock her body in place at her waist, wrists, and ankles; though she is so small, I can't imagine her breaking free.

"We do not have all day, Mr. Beauregard," Left Hat says, and though his voice is calm and pleasant, there is a threat hidden in it.

Wiping the back of his forearm across his face, my father sets the final dials and lets out a shaky breath. His fingers hover over the switch, trembling. He squeezes his eyes shut.

Power surges through the machine, and the air crackles against my skin as it fills with the suffocating bite of ozone.

The woman screams.

Her body arches, straining against the leather so hard that the muscles on her face look as if they will tear through her skin. Tendons stand stark on her hands, and blood vessels begin bursting in her cheeks, leaving splotchy bruises.

"Stop." The plea leaks out of me unconsciously, and I grab Left Hat's arm, but the screaming fades, and my father backs away from the machine, tears streaming down his pale face.

He raises his hands and shakes his head. "I can't. I can't. I can't." The words flow out of him in an unceasing mutter, like water through a broken sieve.

"Finish the test, Mr. Beauregard," Left Hat growls.

"I can't, I can't, I can't, I can't—"

With an animal snarl, Left Hat grabs the back of my neck and slams me face-first into the glass. Breath rushes out of me as the chain wrenches my arms to the side. Pain blooms in my left cheekbone where it smashes into the glass.

"Finish the test!"

My father's grief-stricken eyes lock on my face, and his chin wobbles. I try to shake my head, but Left Hat tightens his grip, and my vision condenses to a tunnel.

"Don't do it!" I shout with my remaining breath.

The world spins as Left Hat wrenches me away from the window and sinks his fist into my stomach. My dress absorbs the blow, sending heat spreading to my back to disperse the impact so nothing ruptures, but enough force hits my diaphragm that the muscle spasms. All the strength bleeds out of me, and I land on my hip, arms stretched above me, gasping for air that won't come.

But Left Hat isn't done. He lifts me off the floor by the front of my shirt as easily as if I were a child and cocks back a fist. "Finish. The. Test."

My father's eyes are red-rimmed, and tears streak his face. His gaze flits between me, the machine, and the groaning woman strapped to the chair. With a moan, he curls in on himself, his shoulders hunching up to his ears, and he turns away to huddle against the wall, sobbing.

Left Hat bears his teeth in a furious grimace. I don't feel the punch land.

# CHAPTER 39

*Raeth is a faerie. I've seen and I believe it, yet I still do not understand how it can be true. It would have been easier to believe him a vampire or some other monster long since chased from civilization by technology.*

*Mortals are safer now than we were before things like guns and electric lights—at least, we think we are —but what if all turning on the lights has done is chase monsters further into the shadows where they are harder to spot? If faeries exist, other things may also lurk in the dark. How does one reconcile themselves to such a world?*

*—From the diary of Willow Beauregard*
*June 1903*

"HE FAILED AGAIN. HE IS TOO BROKEN TO CONTINUE. NOT EVEN A threat to his daughter forces him to comply."

"They will not be happy."

"I know that, Malcolm. You think I am unaware?"

"If the charger is not ready, the invasion will fail." Someone coughs. "King Obyrron's minions are already here. They can show up unannounced at any time. Do you want to be the one to explain why they cannot usher his armies into New London?"

"Why do you persist in threatening me with things I already know?"

The haze of unconsciousness lifts slowly, enough that words—which were nothing more than blurry sounds moments before—become clear. I hurt too much to move. I can barely breathe, thanks to a shoulder digging into my stomach. But I remain as still and limp as possible.

The other voice—Malcolm?—lowers into an angry hiss. "Because nothing else gets through your thick skull, and I do not want to die!"

"No one will die," Left Hat says. I recognize his voice as it buzzes against my limp body.

"Is that so?" Malcolm sneers. "Perhaps you should explain that to all the dead Covenant members whose bodies still litter Trafalgar Square."

"They were expendable."

"Were they? As I am? As you are? You think vampire blood flows so freely that we can simply get more from anywhere?" Malcolm coughs, and it is a racking, wet sound.

Left Hat's voice softens, almost concerned. "How long has it been?"

"Two days. Already, I feel as if I can barely see or hear. And it will take at least another week to manufacture more serum."

"You take too much, Malcolm."

"If you would simply convince our guest to finish his invention, we wouldn't have this problem. So do your fucking job, Bernard! And get rid of her before she wakes up."

"She's not waking up any time soon," Left Hat/Bernard says. "I made sure of it."

Cool air brushes my face as we move, the motion making my head swim. Darkness creeps back in and drags me under.

IN MY DREAMS, I watch my father turn away from me over and over; I am a child, standing in the rain before an open door that leaks light and warmth into the darkness, but it closes; I am an adolescent, showing my father the crooked butterfly I made from the discarded bits of scrap, but he pats me on the head and tells me to practice my runes before dropping the sculpture onto the recycle pile.

I am an adult with an early acceptance letter to the Artisan's Guild in my trembling fingers as my father tells me that what the shop really needs is another Artificer.

My father turns away. Away. Away.

I am bruised and bleeding, begging him not to hurt the faerie woman anymore. So he lets the Bowler Hat hurt me instead. I asked him to do it. It was the right thing to do. So why is my chest threatening to crack open?

My ribcage splits with a creaking sound, spilling my beating heart onto the cold floor. No. It isn't my chest. That sound is the door opening. They're coming back to hurt me.

Panicked, I roll to my feet, but the chain pulls tight, and I slide off the cot instead, hitting the floor with a pained oof. The door closes, leaving a bowl of soup barely steaming on the floor next to a thick slice of bread.

I am not too afraid or dulled by grief and surprise to ignore the food this time. If they poison me, at least I will die quickly. The lukewarm soup burns the inside of my cheek. When I run my tongue across the mangled flesh, I feel the impact of Left Hat's fist and the grinding of my teeth against my cheek.

Or was his name Bernard? Had I heard that, or was I dreaming?

I have to soak the bread in the broth to soften it enough to eat, and by the time I slurp the last of the cold soup, my stomach still hurts, but it isn't quite so hollow. My mind, however, is full enough to spill out of my ears.

Sitting with my back against the cot, I put my elbows on my knees and rest my pounding head in my hands, trying to ignore the deep ache in my ribs and the swelling on my cheek. They will heal soon enough, so long as I stay alive. And if I am to live and get my father out of here like I promised, I have to think.

Deep breath in, slow breath out, repeat. Repeat. Repeat. Until everything fades away but what I can conjure in my mind.

The Covenant of the Silver Dawn hired my father for his Aetheric Charger so they could use it to facilitate the invasion of New London. The Faerie invasion, I can only assume, given the connection to Lord Rutledge and his goals.

But when my father discovered what they planned to do with it, and that they wanted to use faeries to power it, he refused to keep working. So, they resorted to torture. And, now, to using me as manipulation.

Which they were only able to do because Silk lured me in, a lamb to slaughter, and I followed her like Bo Peep's damned sheep. Anger swells in my chest, making my thoughts clearer, sharpening every memory of the last twenty-four hours until they cut.

She tricked me into coming here, turned me over, shackled me to the wall, and stole my bracelets. So why didn't she take my compass? When Left Hat asked whether I carried any other weapons, she knew I had it. My fingertips brush across the hidden pocket. Mr. Bywater concealed it so carefully that only someone who knew where it was there would think to look.

The compass is there, nestled safely against my skin. And so is something else. Blood singing in excitement, I turn my back to the door and fish around for the opening to the placket concealed against my ribs. Smooth metal warmed by the heat of my body greets my fingertips; not the flat cylinder of my compass...my copper bracelets.

I saw Silk take them and give them to Left Hat. But I know my own work, and these are my bracelets.

My mind flies backward across memories, picking and sorting them just as I would with the pieces of disassembled artifice, matching one side, one hint to another, until it makes a complete picture. The bracelets she took from me may not be the same ones she pulled from her pocket when Left Hat demanded them. And when she hugged me and said, you have everything you need, was this what she meant?

I slide the bracelets on, forcing them beneath the layers of clothing just above the iron shackles. They're too tight on my forearms, but I will live with the discomfort. Pushing myself to my feet, I pace and swing my arms, letting the chain rattle as the energy of my movement charges the bracelets with static electricity.

Silk had wanted something from Left Hat, a payment. He'd denied her, and she had been angry about it. In fact, she'd said she expected it. Which meant she must have planned for this scenario. When we snuck in, did she know about the ventilation shafts? Did she plan to leave the shadow cloak inside one?

My heart races as I realize I have a way out. I cannot pick locks, but I can certainly crawl through tunnels as long as the fans are inactive. That thought chills my blood. I very much doubt I will be able to haul my father through the ducts and then into the paper mill without being spotted. And as soon as they realize he is gone, they will start hunting us.

Heels of my hands pressed hard against my temples, I grit my teeth and force myself to focus. There must be an answer. I wrack my brain until my eyeballs hurt, playing scenario after scenario in my mind.

The door handle clicks. I freeze and clutch the chain against my chest.

Right Hat enters. It has been half of a year since I saw his face and it is still etched in my mind. All Bowler Hats look sick, with grey waxy skin stretched tightly over their bones, but Right Hat looks sicker than most. His hollow eyes are red-rimmed and sit on dark purple cushions. Veins of the same color are visible beneath his skin, crawling under his eye sockets and across his sharp cheekbones.

"I see the calculation in your eyes, girl. Rest assured, this is a fight you cannot win. Behave yourself, or I will be forced to hurt you."

I believe him. His tone holds none of the casual politeness of Left Hat and all of the menace. Still, when he slides his key into the bolt to unlock my chain, the temptation to jerk the metal out of his hand and swing it at him like a club nearly overcomes me.

It is a short walk from my room to the laboratory door, down the flight of stairs, and back into the room with the window. My father is curled against the wall, his arms wrapped around himself. Another faerie is strapped into the chair, this time a young boy with horns curling from his brown hair and a smattering of freckles across his sharp cheekbones.

Left Hat is waiting for us. And this time, he has a knife.

"What happened to the woman," I ask faintly, remembering the conversation Silk and I overheard while hiding in the ventilation shaft.

Right Hat gives me a blank stare. "She outlived her usefulness."

"Don't be so surly, Malcolm," Left Hat says as he fastens my chain to the wall.

"So...you're going to kill this boy? He's only a child!"

Malcolm grabs a fistful of my hair and wrenches my head around to stare into my face. "Do you know how many children mortals have killed all because you gave them the title of monster?" His breath smells like the inside of a sepulcher. "Do you?" He shakes me, making my head swim, and my fingers curl into his jacket to try and steady myself.

The temptation to activate my bracelets is so strong I have to bite the inside of my cheek until the copper taste of blood fills my mouth. I will have one chance to use this weapon. One. I cannot waste it.

Left Hat wrenches Malcolm's hand away. "If you cannot control your temper, you can leave."

"No," Malcolm snarls as he fixes the lay of his jacket. "No, I want to see you fix this."

After a polite nod from Left Hat, Malcolm backs to the other side of the small viewing area and folds his arms expectantly.

"You have one last chance, Mr. Beauregard," Left Hat says loudly enough for my father to hear through the glass. He takes my chain and hoists my wrists above my head, pinning me against the wall.

My squeak of protest means nothing to him. And, apparently, less to my father, who only curls further in on himself and shakes as he weeps. Left Hat lifts the knife, turning it so the lamplight slides across the blade.

"You can either finish the machine or watch your daughter bleed. If you refuse, we have no further use for you. Or her. The choice is yours, Mr. Beauregard."

Oh, *bloody slagging hell.* My skin tightens, retreating from the blade as fear crawls over every inch of me with needle-sharp claws. Almost worse than the fear is the knowledge that if he tries to cut me anywhere but my face or hands, the dress will stop the blade. And then he will realize everything I am hiding: my armored dress, the compass, my bracelets.

Any hope I may have had for escape will be gone.

My father presses his palms over his ears and sobs but never looks up. He knows what will happen but will not—or cannot—force himself to move. The knife lowers, caressing my cheek. When the point pricks under the edge of my jaw, I suck in a breath of shocked pain and jerk my chin up, trying to ease the pressure.

Warmth trickles down my neck and into the collar of both blouses, filling the room with the salt smell of blood.

"It has begun, Mr. Beauregard." Left Hat turns the knife so my father can see red streaks across the silvery blade. "Only you can stop it."

But he won't. He can't. My breath comes in panicked gasps as my eyes flit from the unconscious faerie boy to my father and his damned machine, the invention he has sunk so much of our lives into.

The knife descends again, and I suck in a breath as the tip hovers over my stomach.

"I can do it!" I shriek. "I can do it. I can make it work."

The knife stops as Left Hat regards me through narrowed, colorless eyes.

"She's lying," Malcolm spits. "Lying to save her own life."

Left Hat turns my face toward his with the edge of the blade. "Would you lie to me, Miss Beauregard?"

"No," I pant, trying not to move so much as a hair. "No. I know that invention; I've helped my father with it for most of my life. I can make it work. I know I can."

Malcolm is tense as a loaded spring, and he unleashes his unspent energy on me. "Lies! We can't afford to start over if she destroys it. Enthrall the bitch and make her prove it."

"That is a waste of serum," Left Hat says, but he never takes his eyes off my face.

"Then cut her throat and be rid of them both. We'll find another artificer. Unless you want to explain to the King's minions why we failed."

Left Hat's jaw works, but he finally shakes his head and sheathes his knife. He unbuttons his jacket, pulls his arm out, rolls up his sleeve, and takes a small leather case from his pocket. Inside is a vial of red liquid and a syringe. With a practiced motion, he draws a discreet amount of liquid into the syringe and slides the tip of the needle into the vein inside his elbow.

Malcolm watches with hard, hungry eyes, his lips twitching.

Left Hat's muscles clench so hard I can hear his joints pinging, and when he looks tight enough to snap, he relaxes with a long, satisfied sigh. His head falls back, and his groan is so sensual I would have blushed if I wasn't so slagging scared.

With quick, careful motions, Left Hat replaces his equipment, rolls down his sleeve to cover the line of injection scars, and replaces his jacket. You'd never know he just injected himself with a strange serum except that when he looks into my eyes, his glow with a hypnotic yellow light.

It's like looking at a full moon for so long you can fall upward into it, weightless. I float away into those eyes, severing all connection to control of my body, to the pain in my face, wrists, and muscles. Relief rushes in and overwhelms every thought, smothering my sense of self.

"You will not lie to me, Miss Beauregard," Left Hat says, his voice thrumming through my veins like champagne, floating to my head, making me dizzy.

I want to say no, that I would never dream of lying to him, but my muscles refuse to move.

"You will tell me the entire truth without reservation," he continues. "Won't you?"

Now that he has asked me a question, my body springs to life. "Yes," I say, relieved to obey.

"Good girl. Can you make the Aetheric Charger function properly without catastrophic failure?"

Thank the Muses, another question I can answer. "Yes, I can."

"Will you do so?"

"Yes, I will."

"How will you do it?"

A dozen sketches and schematics, hundreds of hours of tinkering with my father, of brainstorming and revising, come hurtling back through my mind. "I need to examine it first," I say slowly, "to see what he has changed. But I know I can do it."

"How do you know it?"

His voice penetrates my chest and wraps tendrils of compulsion around my heart. Even if I wanted to hide the truth, which I don't, I could not stop myself from speaking it. "I am a better artificer than he is. And I have used artifice to hurt people before. He hasn't."

Left Hat leans away from me with a gasp. The yellow light fades from his eyes, and he catches himself on the wall, his head hanging while he pants. With a sickening rush, I fall back into my body, into a sea of throbbing pain and confusion that leaves me crumpled in a dizzy heap with my palms pressed to the cold stone floor.

"Does that," Left Hat pants, "satisfy you, Malcolm?"

Malcolm jerks me to my feet and scowls, his pale eyes boring into me with physical force. My stomach rolls and turns over. If I vomit, I hope I do it right down the front of him.

"She may not be lying, but that doesn't mean she's capable. Just remember one thing, girl. We don't have to hurt you to hurt you. What Bernard did to your mind? Imagine he told you to use this," he pulls a knife from somewhere beneath his jacket and points the tip at my cowering father, "on him."

The thought makes me retch because I would have done it. I would have watched myself press the blade into his skin without even the desire to stop.

"What did he do to me?" I choke.

"I gave you a taste of the future," Left Hat says. His voice is weak, and sweat gleams on his forehead. He isn't much better off than I am. But deep conviction colors his words. "I've shown you what the world will look like when monsters are no longer forced hide in the shadows. When science and technology take the best nature can give us and improves upon it for those who are worthy. You can either help us build that future or be crushed by it."

"If she does what she claims she can," Malcolm says, shaking me.

"I can," I promise.

But when he releases my chain, my legs buckle. Whatever Left Hat did left my limbs so hollow I can barely move.

"She's no use to us now, in any case," he says. "Put her back. We will give her the chance to prove herself tomorrow. But be warned, Miss Beauregard. You will get one chance before the pain starts."

⁓

WHEN MALCOLM LEAVES me in my room, I lean against the wall, slide to the floor, wrap my arms around my knees, and breathe. I need a few moments to reflect on everything I've learned.

And what I've done.

My body is still wretchedly weak from whatever control the serum gave Left Hat over my mind. It is no wonder they resorted to other means, such as torturing me, to motivate my father. If they'd used that serum on him, he would have been useless for artifice. In all honesty, he wasn't much better than useless now.

So, getting us out of here will rest entirely on me and the tools I have at my disposal. At least my experience in the Undercroft has strengthened my ability to improvise. I'm going to need it to pull off the idea that has been building in my mind since volunteering to finish the Charger.

It is a mad plan, one that will probably get both my father and me killed. But if what the Hats say is true, not only is the Covenant inviting a faerie invasion, but they are doing it for the benefit of monsters who kill and feed on mortals. If I cannot save my father and myself, then the least I can do is prevent such a future from coming to pass.

Determination settles on and over me, shielding me from the fear that has been gnawing at my guts since Silk appeared at my door. I swing my arms up as far as the chain will allow, then swing them back down, creating energy for my bracelets to store.

There isn't time to be afraid when work needs doing. And for my plan to succeed, I will need a *lot* of stored energy.

# CHAPTER 40

I took a rare day off and walked to Hyde Park today. The beauty of this world simply cannot be overstated. Sometimes, I think a life spent merely appreciating it would be a life well spent. It is no wonder the Muses chose art, music, and poetry as forms of worship.

Then again, as I walked home, I saw the squalor of the parts of New London that get ignored for lack of funding, the exhausted faces of factory workers, the hungry eyes of orphaned children, and it is incomprehensible that such sublime beauty can exist alongside such cruelty and neglect.

—From the diary of Willow Beauregard
June 15, 1902

THE BRACELETS ARE ONLY A FEW DEGREES SHY OF BURNING MY ARMS. I spent hours thinking and moving, moving and thinking, letting my restless energy sink into the runes and heat the copper. I should sleep to give myself at least a chance of being effective tomorrow, but all I can do is lay on the cot, stare at the buzzing lightbulb, and piece together information—because if I move much more, the bracelets will burn me, and the last thing I need is for Left Hat to investigate why I stink of roasted meat.

So, I lay quietly on the cot with my fingers wrapped around the chain and try to accept that the world I thought I knew does not exist. Faeries are real, they are trying to invade mortal lands, and the Covenant of the Silver Dawn plans to use my father's invention to help them. That, and some sort of serum made of vampire blood that doesn't only grant them the healing powers of a vampire but also the ability to enthrall someone, at least for a short time.

And, because he stands in the way, they've been trying to assassinate Raeth.

At least he is safe and able to protect his folk. I close my eyes and imagine him lounging on the chaise by the hearth, a glass of whisky in one hand, firelight tangling in his hair and reflecting in his dark eyes.

Seeing him murder Lord Rutledge had scared me deeply. I did not think I could live side-by-side with such violence. It was at odds with everything I thought I wanted for my life, for the person I wanted to be. But I am planning something just as bad, planning to kill people not in the heat of battle, but cold-bloodedly. Perhaps afterward, I will have the space for guilt or grief.

For now, the fear that spreads over and inside of me, that sits deep and cold and heavy in my gut, leaves no room for other emotions. Until then, I close my eyes and think of Raeth, Tildie, and Gwil, safe in the Undercroft. Ethel, safe with her parents. If I am successful, perhaps I can keep them all safe a little longer.

~

AFTER DRAGGING me from my small room and down the stairs into the lab, Left Hat seizes the back of my neck and forces my face inches from my father's invention. "You will ensure this machine drains the magic from faeries and funnels it into this object." He jerks my head in front of a garnet the size of my fist. It sits on the opposite end of the table, glowing like a fresh drop of blood. "Can you do it?"

Swallowing the fear and grief knotting my throat, I nod.

"Willow, no," my father uncoils from his self-protective stance and takes my arm, his eyes imploring. "Don't do this thing. They will use it to—"

A sharp slap from Left Hat leaves my father clutching his cheek and stumbling away.

"None of them would be here if you had done your job, elf," Left Hat says, his voice conversational despite the violence. "Remember that."

He gives both of us a warning glance that needs no words. When the door closes behind him, he does not lock it. Where would we go, after all? A moment later, Left Hat enters the viewing chamber, safe behind artifice-reinforced glass. Should the machine malfunction, he and Malcolm will be safe. Probably. My father and I? Bits of us will likely be spattered on that window.

But worrying about malfunctioning artifice will not make my hands steadier. I take a deep breath to pull in all my worries, exhale to release them, and rub my sweating palms together. I need calm nerves for my plan to work, calm nerves, and a clear mind.

Crouching and pretending to examine the invention so it hides my face from view, I whisper low enough for my father's sensitive, elvish ears to hear me. "I'm going to get us out of here, but I need you to help me."

He rests one hand on my shoulder, but his voice isn't comforting. "You can't. I've tried."

"Well, I'm trying now. And my plan will work."

His hand falls away, and he swallows audibly. "They'll kill us."

"Maybe. But not before I stop them from helping the faeries invade." Louder now, "Come on, tell me about these changes you've made."

Haltingly, at first, my father points out the adjustments that have altered the invention, allowing it to pull and store magic instead of electricity. "It's just another sort of energy," he says, his voice growing stronger the longer he speaks.

I listen with one ear while pulling a coil of thick copper wire from a box of material. The copper is smaller than I'd like, but I think I can make it work. Runic inscriptions will come first, added while the wire is straight. It's much harder to inscribe curved surfaces, and probably impossible with my hands bound. Bending the copper wire into coils without altering the runes is danger-ously tricky, but it's my only option. So, I must inscribe the instruc-tions into the metal with a slight degree of stretch. Then, when I bend the copper, the lines will meet properly.

My father talks, and I etch runes with deliberate care. Now that they've got a job to do, my hands stop shaking, and my worry fades. I sink into the routine of engraving, letting my inner voice walk me through the process; the coils themselves will do most of the work, but I need them to amplify energy as well, without blowing myself up.

Papa leans over me to see what I've done, and his hand tightens on my arm. "Willow, that is—"

An over-the-shoulder glare is enough to silence him before he says something dangerous. He swallows again. I cut my eyes toward the window where the Bowler Hats are watching. My father may be terrified and weak, but he isn't stupid. He gives me a wobbly smile of approval for their sake, and I begin on the second coil.

My stomach growls loudly, but I ignore it. I cannot spare atten-tion for the raw soreness in my wrists, the ache in my ribs, or any of the other pressing bodily needs making themselves known. Every ounce of my attention and skill is required to work faster than I ever have.

My father turns dials and makes small, meaningless adjustments to appear as if he is helping. "How will you test them?"

"I can't," I murmur, turning the coil to examine the runes. "So pray to the Muses I got this right."

If he wasn't already so pale, the sick expression that tightens his features would have turned him green. He knows the danger as well as I do. If I haven't chosen the right runes, or if I have warped a line too far in turning the coils, anything...anything could happen. This is why artifice takes so long, why it must be tested on paper, tested on blanks, tested, and tested again before a final stamp and maker's mark can be added.

I am jumping fifty steps ahead and risking both our lives to do it.

"I'll pray to the Smith instead," my father chokes. "Hopefully, Dwarven gods listen to elves, too."

If they do not, we are in trouble. But it is the only chance we have.

He lets me finish the coils in peace, adding a comforting pat to my back or shoulder here and there. But my mind is so focused on the last twist of the copper wire that I barely notice. If I can get these on my wrists before the Hats stop me, and activate my bracelets—which are now so full of energy my skin stings with the heat of it—I can get us out of here.

A distant scream rips my concentration to shreds, and I startle with a gasp. My father's head whips toward the sound, and we stand frozen as a second scream joins the first before it dies. The room shudders as something slams into a nearby wall, making mortar dust shower from the ceiling.

Left Hat and Malcolm exchange a surprised glance before bolting out of the observation room. We flinch at a smattering of staccato gunfire, and Papa grabs my shoulders as if he can protect me from whatever is happening Upstairs.

Shouting. More gunfire. Crashing and screaming. But we are alone, and this is my chance. I pinch my fingers together to slide the coils up over my wrists. Once I get them on, they will amplify the power of my bracelets and—they catch on the iron. The coil won't fit.

Oh bloody damned hell, I did not account properly for the size of the manacles. The coils are millimeters too small, fucking millimeters!

Why didn't I measure twice? I place the coils on the table and stand staring at my failure with stinging cheeks, burning wrists, and a sick, sinking feeling in my guts. This would have worked. I know it. I have to think of a way around it, but I cannot bend the coils any more than I already have or risk destroying the artifice.

An explosion rocks the lab, sending Papa and me to our knees and making the garnet slide off the table and clatter to rest against the wall. Dust thickens the air until it's hard to breathe.

"Willow, come on!" Papa grabs my arm and pulls while covering his nose with his opposite elbow. "We can't stay here! If this is our chance, we've got to take it."

The screaming comes back in full force, high-pitched yowls of pain so bestial no human could have made them.

Papa continues dragging at me, his panicked face is more moving than his arguments. His eyes apologize and beg all at once, and I cannot force myself to tell him no.

Numbly, I let him pull me up the stairs. I do still have the bracelets. They were not made for fighting, but they are better than nothing. Papa eases the door open, and the noise and smell hit us like a physical force.

I swallow convulsively at the sharp copper and salt smell of blood. When we step into the corridor, the carnage makes my stomach crawl up my throat. It looks as if someone flung buckets of red paint at the walls, spattering the pale surfaces before it pooled on the floor. Red footprints of different shapes and sizes smear through the puddles and lead in confusing directions.

Here and there lay torn bits of clothing, motionless bodies, and limbs.

My stomach heaves, and I clap my hands over my mouth.

Papa makes a retching sound but drags me onward anyway. We

tiptoe around and over the viscera, holding our breath. The racket increases, and someone roars from the hall behind us, the sound so guttural it electrifies my muscles until they scream run!

We stumble around the corner to the sight of more death. The halls are all the same, replicas in a perfect square, but this one I recognize because of the exhaust shaft, only this time the fan is working, filling the air with a low thrum.

The exit is near.

Now, I am dragging Papa. Freedom is so close I can ignore the horrid smells and sounds. A figure flies through the air at the end of the hall and hits the wall with bone-shattering force. They fall in a limp heap, nothing more than a tangle of limbs. Running footsteps and gunfire follow.

"We've got to get out of here," I breathe, but it's too late.

Several figures retreat into our hall in lockstep, their backs to us as they fend off whatever is chasing them. We turn to run, but Malcolm stalks toward us with a snarl on his face, and Silk strides beside him. When she sees me, her expression hardens, and she draws her pistol, but not before she winces.

Whatever guilt she might feel doesn't stop her from yelling, "I will kill her!"

Papa and I back up, but there is nowhere to go. Malcolm surges forward and grabs Papa by the throat. His face turns red, and I scream.

But Silk yanks me sideways and wraps her arm around my throat, the barrel of the pistol cold against my temple. Fury ignites in my chest, and I grab her wrist to activate my bracelets.

"Don't be stupid, Dove," she growls in my ear, shaking me. "I'll shoot you before you can burn me, and then we'll both die."

Which leaves no one to protect Papa.

Without waiting for an answer, she turns us to face the oncoming Covenant.

They back toward us, pistols and knives raised as a dark figure prowls around the corner. My heart stops. My head spins. I cannot breathe or think, only watch as Raeth, fully unmasked in his fae form, discards a dismembered arm as casually as the bone of a gnawed drumstick.

He is smiling, his sharpened canines on grisly display. Blood drips from the inch-long claws at the tips of his fingers to patter on the floor. As he closes with the defenders, the holes in his shirt prove how many times he has been shot, cut, and stabbed.

"I will kill her," Silk repeats and presses the barrel hard enough to bend my neck.

Raeth stops and holds his arms in a placating gesture to the side, but the smile has not left his face. His eyes are entirely black and trained on me. They roam over my body, locking on the blood staining the neck of my blouse, the bruise I am certain is on my cheek, my raw, blood-smeared wrists beneath the iron chains.

He growls, and six pistols fire in response.

My scream is drowned by the deafening thunder.

Sulfurous gun smoke fogs the air between us, hiding everything but the dark smears of the Covenant. No one moves. The only sound is the hardworking exhaust fan that labors to clear the air.

When the smoke fades, Raeth hasn't moved. Only now, he is angrier.

"So much for handling him," Silk says, with amused irritation. "I warned you not to underestimate the King."

Malcolm ignores her and tells Raeth, "If you take another step, they die."

"Be still and don't provoke him," Silk whispers in my ear when my fingers tighten on her arm. "Malcolm doesn't have Bernard's restraint. He will kill your father."

"Release them," Raeth says, his voice rich and warm and cajoling. It washes over the hall like a shot of whisky, making everyone sway a little. "Release them, or I will kill you all."

Pistols lower or waver at the powerful compulsion in his voice, but Malcolm appears untouched. He pulls a knife from his belt, spins my father, and jams the tip under his jaw. Papa's body tightens like a stretched rubber band as blood rushes down his neck.

"Stop!" I scream, jerking against Silk's arm. She neatly kicks the back of my knees, and they buckle. Mighty Calliope, I want to spin and attack her. I would be strong enough without these damned manacles. But she's right. Malcolm would kill my father.

Five more Covenant members enter the hall behind Raeth with Left Hat at their center. "Thank you for joining us," he says. "Unfortunately, we weren't prepared for visitors, but I've changed that. These are iron bullets, Your Majesty. Unless you'd like to be ripped to shreds, I suggest you come quietly."

Raeth is a walking army, but he cannot fight iron. He might withstand a few iron wounds, but not this many. I've got to help. If I activate my bracelets, I may be able to take Silk and Malcolm down and distract them long enough for Raeth to attack or flee.

"Release the woman, and you have my word that I will not kill another Covenant member," he says.

Left Hat sighs. "We need the woman, unfortunately. And you are not in a position to negotiate."

"You may have overwhelming force, but I guarantee that you, at least, will die before they muzzle me," Raeth swears, and the threat is all the more chilling for the flat, soft tone of his voice.

"You don't need Willow, please," my father chokes, though speaking makes the blade push farther into the delicate skin beneath his jaw.

Raeth takes in the scene in an instant, and his eyes narrow. "Is this your father? The one you sold yourself to me to find?"

Papa's eyes cut toward me, wide with shock and pain.

"Oh yes," Raeth says as if he is enjoying the dismay on my father's face. "She bartered herself to me for my help finding you. She was a sweet little morsel to corrupt. I should thank you for walking out and leaving her alone."

Despite everything, blood rushes to my cheeks in a hot flush of shame.

"It wasn't fair, really," Raeth continues. "She didn't have a chance. I suppose I owe you for allowing me to take her inno-cence. I'll make you a deal: release the woman, and I will freely surrender."

His intention hits me like a hammer in the chest. I know what he is doing and why. Oh, merciful Calliope, no.

"My father cannot finish the tests," I blurt to Malcolm, grip-ping Silk's forearm as hard as the manacles allow. "You've broken him, he cannot—"

"I will do it," Papa growls, his eyes fixed on Raeth. His voice, his bearing, is more confident than I have seen it since I first found him. "If he will trade himself for Willow, I will finish the Aetheric Charger. I will do it today."

Raeth's plan is now flowing like a river, dragging everyone else along in the current. I can feel it pull me under, forcing me to watch the chain of events unfold without being able to stop them.

He and Papa will use themselves as a shield for me, no matter what I have to say on the matter.

Malcolm and Left Hat exchange a charged glance as more Covenant come running through the open exit, weapons drawn.

"I think we will keep the woman for security," Left Hat says, taking a step toward Raeth, "and take you, too."

"Is he the one who did that to you?" Raeth asks me, ignoring the enemies closing in around him.

I lock my jaw, refusing to answer, but he sees the truth in my eyes. So fast the motion is impossible to track, Raeth spins and lunges, his claws flashing. The black bowler hat topples as Left Hat's head falls from his body.

Gunfire erupts, and Silk drags us to the floor.

Malcolm shouts, "Hold your fire!"

Raeth drops the limp body that used to be Left Hat, the corpse now riddled with bullets from being used as a shield.

"Fuck," Malcolm growls as he watches the head of his compa-triot roll to a stop against the wall. Left Hat will not heal from that.

"I will finish it," Papa insists, his voice high-pitched. "I will finish it, I swear! Release my daughter. If he will be the subject, I will finish it and fully charge the jewel. You'll have all of the power you need to break the spell."

Damn these men, they are conspiring against me! How can they expect me to give myself up and let them suffer when they are the only two people on earth who have ever cared for me even a little?

"Listen to him, or more will die before you stop me," Raeth warns. "Escort her out, and I will allow you to bind me with iron. Ignore this offer, and I will kill as many as I can before I die." He points at Malcolm with one clawed finger. Left Hat's blood drips from the tip. "Beginning with you."

"No," I croak as Silk drags me to my feet. I cannot let Raeth do this, cannot let him turn himself over to torture and death, not for me. I know the deep, festering wounds his captivity left on his body, on his spirit.

"You owe me nothing," I say, trying to make my voice as cruel as possible, though it shakes. "You were no more than a useful tool to me. I used you."

He ignores me and stares pointedly at Malcolm, who finally wavers under his black gaze and snarls, "Fine. Get her out of here."

Covenant members part as Silk drags me toward the door.

Raeth watches Malcolm, refusing to look at me. Muses, no. I cannot let him do this.

Tears spring to my eyes as I lunge toward him, fighting for every step against Silk's hold, the toes of my boots dragging and slipping in the blood. I have to make him stop. Sharp words rip out of my chest and cut their way up my throat. "I never wanted you. I never cared in the least. You were only a means to an end."

He won't look at me.

"You must believe me. I only got close to you because I wanted to turn you over to Scotland Yard! Why won't you listen? I planned to betray you and the Court. I lied! You were right; I lied the whole time!"

He's not going to change his mind. The bastard is going to let them take him and shove me out into the dark, where I can do nothing.

"No! Don't do this! I hate you! Do you hear me? I hate you!"

Silk pulls me, kicking and struggling through the open door that separates the Covenant from the Paper Mill.

Raeth meets my gaze, at last, a single, dark-eyed glance that exposes his soul so clearly it makes makes the world disappear.

One corner of his mouth twitches in what should have been a smile before he looks away. "I know."

A Bowler Hat leaps forward and locks a thick iron collar around his neck. He deflates, landing on his hands and knees, chest heaving. The Covenant swarms him from every side.

"No!"

Silk shoves me. I trip over my feet and land hard on my hip, barely able to catch myself with my bound wrists.

"Either call the dog and get out of those stupid chains," she hisses, "or run and don't look back."

The door closes with a resounding bang, leaving me alone in the dark.

# CHAPTER 41

Papa was trying to teach me about escape runes today, the ones that let energy out of the system if it stores too much power. I couldn't form mine right, and I was so angry. I threw my pencil across the room, and I said I didn't want to do this anymore. We'd already been at it for hours. I was so tired.

He was frustrated that I didn't understand this as easily as the other runes. He yelled at me that I needed a skill if I wanted to keep myself off the street, and I'd better apply myself instead of throwing fits.

Then he left. When he came back, he went to his room. I've been practicing since then. I think I got it perfect now.

—From the diary of Willow Bowbriar
May 18, 1869

~

I THROW MYSELF AT THE DOOR AND POUND ON THE METAL, BUT I cannot budge it, especially not weakened by the magic of the manacles that bind my wrists. And *nine muses,* they sting from the heat of the bracelets and the skin rubbed raw by the metal. A sob of helpless frustration bubbles up from my chest, and I sink to the floor in a puddle.

Even through the door, the sound of the Covenant dragging Raeth to the lab is clear. They will strap him to the chair where my father's damned machine will suck the magic, and the life, from his body. The Aetheric Charger will help the faeries invade, and the Unseen Court will topple without Raeth, destroyed by the power struggles of those eager to replace him. Will his successor be as competent as concerned for the well-being of the people?

Or will they keep all the power and profit for themself, like the politicians and wealthy business owners, leaving those who need the Divvy to starve and die on the street?

Raeth has many weaknesses, but failing to care for his people is not one of them. They need him, and he doesn't deserve to face torture and death again, especially not for me. I will not leave this place knowing he saved me by sacrificing himself.

But my damned hands are bound, and my bracelets are burning, and if I don't release some of the energy, I'll scream. I need a safe place to transfer the energy, or the electricity will take the path of least resistance and jump into the iron, which will hurt terribly if it doesn't kill me.

A series of pipes and wires are bolted to the wall, carrying electricity and water through the paper mill and into the complex used by the Covenant. Industrial buildings still rely on electricity as a cheaper option than sun-powered artifice, and electric bulbs have a particular weakness.

Wrapping both hands around the pipe and gritting my teeth, I activate the bracelets. Static electricity crackles like pins and needles over my skin. But once it finds the pipe, the energy rushes into the metal, becoming a flowing current.

Now that Raeth is no longer fighting the Covenant, the hall is quiet, so I clearly hear the lightbulbs overload with added energy, emitting a high-pitched hum before popping in sprays of glass. As soon as the metal stops burning me, I disengage the bracelets and cry in relief. I hadn't realized how hard it had been to ignore the pain.

An alarm sounds from somewhere in the paper mill, and my heart sinks. If they find me here, they'll either drag me out for trespassing or, if they're in active league with the Covenant, do something worse.

The fan behind me jumps back to life, creaking, then picking up speed. Had the burst of electricity stopped it, too? I discharge a bit more, listening as the circuits overheat, stutter, and the fan slows, only picking up again when I stop interfering

I stare at the fan for several seconds, watching the blades open and close the triangle of space beneath. That is the shaft Silk left the shadow cloak in. Bits of information hit me like I'm standing exposed in a hail storm, each a painful ping that, when taken together, hurt so much it makes me flinch.

Call the dog and get out of those stupid chains.

I dig my fingers into the hidden pocket to fish out my compass and find, tucked alongside it, a key. The urge to laugh makes me clench my teeth in a furious smile as I jam the key into the lock and let the manacles fall at my feet. If we make it out of this alive, I am going to kiss that woman and then hold her down and shake her until her teeth rattle. Maybe something worse.

I don't know what game she is playing or whose side she is on. All I can think about is getting my hands on that cloak and calling for Ripper. Though how I'm meant to do that, I do not know. Raeth said my blood bonded him to me, but how will he come if he cannot hear me? And if, by some miracle he does sense me, he won't make it through the Mill without being noticed.

But maybe that doesn't matter. If no one can stop him, he can bulldoze through the walls as far as I care. So long as Raeth and my father are free.

First, though, I need to get out of sight. Another short burst of electricity stops the fan, and I throw myself into the shaft between the blades. The stink of overheated metal reaches me as I squeeze through the opening, but the engine has already begun to whine.

I reach as far forward as I can and drag myself into the shaft, turned half sideways, but a blade slams into my calf and grinds with a cranking noise as the motor struggles. My leg is trapped between the blade and the two brackets on either side of the fan's center. Sitting up, I brace my arms for leverage and haul myself backward, scraping the skin off my shin and losing my shoe. My toes barely avoid the next swipe of the blade as the fan whirs back to life.

That was close. I may as well leave the other shoe and my stockings here. The last thing I need is to slip on the smooth stone floor while running for my life.

Balancing speed with silence, I scoot back into the dark and try to call Ripper with my mind. I picture him—bulky brass body and bead-black eyes, his mouth open in an imitation of a doggy grin, and think, come to me, boy. I need you.

For good measure, I relive my walk through the city with Silk, the paper mill, imagining the locked metal door, and the lab, myself pushing those thoughts into the atmosphere so Ripper can hear them. That will have to be enough.

As I pull myself along in the dark, my fingers slide across the silky black fabric of the shadow cloak. It slips soundlessly across the metal floor of the duct without so much as snagging on anything. Shaking my head at the layers of Silk's lies, I feel along the edge of the cloak until the closure ties slide between my fingers. It fastens around my neck as if it wants to be there.

A bellow of pain shakes the air, making my arms tighten with gooseflesh.

*Raeth.*

With the cloak tucked between my legs to stop it from flap-ping, I pull myself faster toward the faint light and whirring fan. There must be a lantern somewhere in the hall because I can see just enough to make out the black blur of the fan blades ahead. Another quick burst of electricity stalls the blades long enough that I can slide through, this time fast enough not to get caught.

My bare feet hit the floor soundlessly, and I pause to shake out my hands. The surges of electricity are starting to make them tingle.

With the cloak pulled tight around me and the hood low over my eyes, I creep forward. My burst of electricity knocked out all the electric light bulbs, giving me enough shadow to disappear into. If I can move slowly enough, I can sneak through the halls without being seen. But the thought of my father causing Raeth the sort of pain he inflicted on the other faeries makes it almost impossible to fight the urge to run.

Back pressed to the wall, I lean around the corner far enough to see down the hall. A burly man shoves my father into the lab, growling something about preparing the machine, and then follows him in, closing the door behind them.

Two other guards stand outside another door, one with a pistol and the other holding a dagger. Raeth must be inside.

Fear tightens my throat as I imagine taking a bullet, but the dress beneath my outer garments is supposed to be as good as a suit of armor, so, jaw clenched, I turn the corner and ghost into the hall, riding the darkness along the wall. The cloak is as good as its name, making me nothing more than a shadow as I edge closer to the Covenant members.

A boom so loud it hurts my eardrums makes me cringe as shockwaves shudder through the building.

"What the bloody hell was that?" The gun-wielding guard demands.

"I don't really want to find out," says the other, looking right past me to the turn in the corridor.

I freeze and hold my breath.

"If you want enough serum to change, you'd better find out."

"After all the shit that's happened tonight, I'm not sure I still want in."

The gun-wielding guard turns his pistol on the other and snarls, "Watch your mouth and do your fuckin' job."

The knife-wielding guard swears and takes off down the hall at a trot. Right toward me. I flatten myself against the wall and turn my face away, looking down so no part of my skin is exposed. The cloak warms, like sinking into a bath, and the guard passes within a foot of me. When I see his feet turn the corner, skipping around a puddle of blood, I release a quiet sigh.

Time to take advantage of whatever the booming is.

I ease up the hall, nearing the guard's pistol hand, jaw aching from how hard I've clenched my teeth. The lantern is nearby, casting steady yellow light in a circle near the door. He'll see me moving before long. I've got to be fast.

My muscles burn in protest as I force them into a burst of speed, bolting the last few feet into the light. He hears me, turns, swears, and raises the pistol. But I am already too close. Grabbing his wrist with one hand as I dart forward, I push his gun hand upward and activate the bracelet by jamming my wrist against his.

Electricity flows out in a rush. His muscles lock up, and he gasps, trying to flinch away from the sudden pain, but I've already pressed my other hand flat against the left side of his chest to complete the circuit.

He stiffens, his body rigid as a board, mouth open but unable to gasp as the electricity freezes his diaphragm and flows through his heart. When I release him, he goes limp, and I fumble for his gun, but my hands are numb and clumsy.

He doesn't have the waxy skin of the Covenant members I've fought in the past, and he doesn't recover from injury like they do. While I fight my hands into submission, clumsily grasping his pistol, he merely lays there, gasping and wide-eyed as his last breath rattles in his chest.

Another man is dead by my hand. I will not vomit. I will not.

I have to watch my shaking fingers grasp the doorknob to

ensure I've got it, but it turns silently despite my clumsiness. The room is small and bare, a mirror image of the one they held me in, only this one has an iron cage in the center. Raeth lays inside it, shirtless and bruised on the bare stone floor, the iron collar glowing dully in the light leaking in through the open door.

Grief and helpless anger close my heart in a fist and squeeze. I never should have come to him asking for help. If I'd only trusted myself to find my father, this never would have happened. But I can make it right. I have to make it right.

Closing the door behind me, I throw myself to my knees in front of the chained padlock and fish the key Silk gave me out of my pocket. "Raeth?"

The only light in the room is whatever slips beneath the closed door, but it is enough to let me see his horror-stricken face as he raises his head. "No. Dove, what are you doing?"

"Getting you out of here," I mutter, trying to fit the key into the lock. Damn, my traitorous fingers!

"You have to leave before they come back."

The bit slides into the lock but doesn't turn. Panic laces my blood with frantic energy as I wiggle the key and shake the door. Maybe it's just rusty or old? Silk did this with little metal tools. I should be able to do it with an actual key. I wiggle the metal again, shoving it against the locking mechanism. It has to open. It has to!

A cold hand settles over mine. "You can't fix it this time, Dove."

Tears blur my vision, turning his pale face into a watery smudge in the dark. "Yes, I can. I won't leave you here. I can save you."

Raeth grunts as he uses the bars to pull himself toward me. The iron has drained him of his natural strength, leaving him as weak as any mortal, as it stops his innate healing. It has also stolen the powerful aura that makes his presence feel like a physical force in the air around him. But his gaze holds me effortlessly, and the tenderness in his eyes stops the breath in my lungs. He must be in so much pain, yet he folds both hands over mine and says in that sun-warmed honey voice, "You've already saved me in every way that matters."

A sob of denial claws up my throat, but he cups my cheek with one hand and slides his thumb over my lips. "Listen. They are going to kill me, and neither of us can stop it. But *you* can escape. Leave this place, go to the Undercroft, and protect the people. They are the only hope the city will have when the King invades. Order Gwil to reach out to Lady St. James's housekeeper. She will know what to do to get the lady's help."

"Lady St. James? She's in prison for treason."

"Not for long, not if I know the woman like I think I do. She will help you protect the people. Now go before they come back."

My palm slides over his, and I turn my face to press my cheek against his palm. "No."

"If they kill us both, the people will have no one to protect them. They trust you. You can do this. Willow, please." His voice drops to a choked whisper. "Don't make me watch them hurt you."

Footsteps echo in the hall, growing louder. Another *boom* makes us flinch, this one loud enough to be in the next room.

"Hide in the shadows," Raeth hisses, sliding away from me and back to the center of the cage.

Tears stream down my cheeks as I push myself into the corner and wrap my arms around my knees beneath the cloak.

Raeth's whisper is soft in the dark, barely audible above the shouting in the hall. "Willow?"

"Yes?"

After an instant of hesitation, he speaks a word, one similar to his name but in an accent I've never heard. The sound vibrates, hanging in the air like the reverberation of a struck bell. A shiver of awareness rolls over me at the sound of it.

"That is my true name," he admits, hesitant. "Will you speak it, just once? I want to hear it from your lips before they take me."

His *name*. I thought my heart could not hurt worse than it did seeing him caged like an animal. I was wrong. The memories of faerietales from my book return to break my heart one word at a time, reminding me of the secret power of a Faerie's name.

I once told Raeth to tell me something that would put him in my power; he'd given me part of his story. Now he is giving me his name, the single truth that lay at the very heart of what he is.

Choking back a sob, my heart slamming against my ribcage, I speak his true name, breathing it into the air as a prayer so soft only he will hear it. He sighs like a man who has finally found what he spent a lifetime searching for, and closes his eyes.

"He's dead!" Someone shouts from the hall. The door swings open and bangs against the wall, outlining the silhouette of a man. He searches the dark room, his eyes passing over me to land on Raeth. "He's still in his cage! It wasn't him. Search the halls!"

I curl into myself, hands clasped over my mouth, chest burning with the need to cry. Two Covenant members enter behind the first man to unlock the cage and drag Raeth to unsteady feet. He doesn't fight back. He gave his word, after all. They don't bother closing the door as they haul him out by both arms.

"Secure him," the first man says, "then join the rest. Find out what that fucking noise is and stop it. We need to finish this before there are any other interruptions."

As if to illustrate the speaker's point, another boom sounds, and the vibration rumbles through the floor and up my legs. A door opens and closes. Running feet retreat down the hall. I fight to calm my breathing, but my mind and body don't respond to my commands. I am locked in place, pinned by the weight of all that is happening, and the spiderweb of possible futures that hinges, unaccountably, on me.

Logic says I should do what Raeth asked of me. Aren't the lives of the people of this city worth his sacrifice? If Raeth dies and there is no one to wear the mantle of Cutthroat King, the Unseen Court will dissolve in internal strife as the Lords of the Undercroft vie with one another for power. They need a leader strong enough to hold them together, especially in the face of a faerie invasion.

I try to imagine myself in that role without Raeth by my side... and fail.

He may be a monster. He may be able to kill a dozen men, rob a dozen homes, and disappear into a cloak of shadows. He may be a villain. But he is *my* villain. If the Unseen Court falls apart, they will do it without me.

I shake out my hands, working a little warmth back into my fingertips, and stand. With some surprise, I remember I've taken a gun. My hands are still clumsy, and I don't know if firing a pistol is the same as firing my father's shotgun, but muses help me; I am willing to try.

Jaw set, I pull the cloak tightly about me and stride into the hall. The Covenant guards have already left to investigate, and the door to the lab is unguarded. This is it. I can use some of my previous plan, and I will have to extemporize, but I can do it.

I will fix this.

With whatever courage I can scrounge together pulled about me more tightly than my cloak, I open the door. The burly Covenant member who pushed my father into the lab barrels into me at a run. We stumble backward over the outstretched leg of his fallen comrade and hit the ground with enough force to drive the breath from my lungs.

He grunts in surprise but recovers quickly and punches me in the ribs as we fall. Heat spreads across my chest from the impact. We hit the ground, and the weight of his body drives the air from my lungs as my head bounces off the floor and the gun skitters away from my limp fingers. White flashes across my vision.

Muses grant me strength, I cannot fail now! I gasp and flail, trying to keep him away from me long enough to bring the world back into focus. My diaphragm engages, and I manage to gasp and clear my vision.

The burly man looms above me, face drawn into tight lines of fury, eyes flat and murderous. When he draws his fist back to punch me again, lamplight glints off the dark iron of a knife blade. He didn't punch me at all. He tried to kill me.

The knife plunges once more, this time at my stomach, but the dress turns the blade aside, absorbing the impact even though the pressure of his strike makes me curl up to protect myself.

Animal fear steals my I need to get a hold of him and activate my bracelets, but he bats my flailing hands away.

Metallic thudding echoes down the hall in a rolling staccato, and something big and bright cannons through the air above me, crashing into the man with a fleshy thump. I roll onto my side, gasping, to see Ripper tearing the man to literal pieces. My call worked. I'm not alone.

But I don't have time for surprise, elation at Ripper's presence, or disgust at the carnage. More Covenant members are sure to follow this one, and soon. Panting, I struggle to my hands and knees and retrieve the pistol while trying not to notice what Ripper is doing to the man.

"Guard the door, boy!" I shout and throw myself into the dark stairway, closing the door behind me.

The lab is crowded. My father is hunched over the Charger, working furiously, sweat already darkening the back of his shirt. Malcolm and other Covenant members watch from the opposite room, peering through the glass as Raeth bellows in agony, his body arching off the chair where the leather straps fail to hold him down.

For an instant, everything slows, and every detail becomes sharp as shattered glass; the garnet is glowing with energy, casting red light over the charger, my father, Silk, and Raeth. The Cutthroat King is bleeding where the cables attached to the charger pinch through his skin; his scars are on display, his lips are purple, great dark smudges frame his eyes already, and every vein, every tendon and ligament strains against his bruised skin.

The iron collar fastened around his neck rattles as he flings his head back and forth, trying to escape the pain. Sweat plasters his dark hair to his forehead, and lines of strain bracket his mouth. His head swivels in my direction, nostrils flared, and for a moment, realization and horror make him freeze with wide eyes.

He mouths the word "No" before another scream is torn from his lips.

# CHAPTER 42

*If making beautiful things glorifies the Muses, and making useful things glorifies the Smith, do I practice two religions? Does the dwarven forge god hear the prayers of elves? If he does, I hope he will answer mine and help the Muses bring Papa home.*

*—From the diary of Willow Beauregard*
*October 25, 1902*

SOMETHING SNAPS INSIDE ME. FEAR MAKES ME GO COLD, BUT THE fury expanding in my chest replaces it, melts the ice, and turns into an inferno so hot it forces me, for a moment, out of my body. I watch as I curl my barely functional fingers into the back of my father's shirt and yank him away from the machine.

He trips over my feet and lands on his arse, but I have no attention to spare for him. Silk stands in the dark corner behind Raeth, arms crossed. I raise the pistol at her and order, "Pick the lock."

She grins at me and pulls the small leather tool kit from her pocket.

I dismiss her and turn my attention to Raeth. We lock eyes. The weight of what is happening to him, what he allowed himself to be subjected to, lands on me like falling stones. His eyes are opaque with pain suffered on my behalf.

And now I must ask him to endure more. "Do you trust me?"

He swallows and licks his lips but never takes his gaze from mine. "Always."

That one word is enough to break my heart. In a low enough voice not to be overheard, I speak his true name, allowing the syllables to roll off my lips like the pronouncement of doom. "You will not move from that chair until I give you leave."

Energy crackles in the air, making every hair on my body rise. Raeth's eyes widen in shock, but he nods, chest heaving, and bears down as I begin changing the settings on the machine. I've barely thought this through, but I know it will work. It must.

"Willow, no!" My father yells.

Ripper roars, gunfire explodes from Upstairs, and I look through the window at Malcolm. His expression is slack with shock. Silk pries the collar off Raeth at last; I flip the final switch to reverse the flow of energy and bare my teeth at the waxy-skinned bastard with a feral smile.

If we die here, I am going to take this damned machine with me.

The garnet glows with the whirring, pulsing magic stolen from Raeth and every other faerie my father has killed with his machine. When the flow is reversed, the power rushes from the garnet and into the Aetheric Charger, making it incandescent with power before the magical energy rushes back through the cables toward Raeth.

Malcolm leaps at the glass and pounds both fists on it hard enough to make the reinforced material wobble in its case. "No!"

When Raeth screams this time, unholy pleasure is mixed with

the pain. He arches off the chair as magic floods back into him. Buckles pop, leather straps tear, and color floods his skin.

"Hang on!" I yell again, grab the machine, activate my bracelets, and force extra electricity into it.

Raeth's head falls back, his arms flung to his sides, glowing with the power I am forcing into his body. Everything they took from him, and more, returns in a torrent that must be so painful I can hardly comprehend it.

But he will need the power to escape this place. I release the Charger and Raeth at the same time with a short, "Now!"

Raeth lunges out of the chair, his muscles taut with power, his chest heaving, and rips the cables from his body with a snarl. The metal teeth of the clamps leave small, bloody wounds that heal instantly.

"No!" Malcolm pounds on the glass again. His furious eyes shift from Raeth to me. With a grimace, he rips a bloodstained leather case from his pocket and removes a pre-filled syringe he must have taken from Left Hat's body. That serum will make him a walking weapon.

Turning to my father, I shake out my hands to force sensation back into them and recharge the energy I used. "Look at me. Do not look Malcolm in the face, no matter what. You hear me?"

He nods jerkily.

"Put the copper artifice on my wrists."

He stares at me, then at the coils I created earlier, which lie discarded on the ground. Understanding dawns in his eyes. "Willow, you can't! You'll damage your hands!"

I want to snarl at him that I know the danger. I am not stupid enough to sacrifice my hands—the only thing that makes me valuable— for no reason, but all that comes out is, "Do it now!"

Covenant members are already flowing out of the viewing room and into the hallway, where Ripper is the only thing standing between them and us. "We don't have time!"

He takes my discarded coils from the work table and forces

them over my tingling hands onto my wrists. "You're a good artificer," he says, squeezing my forearms. "They'll work."

But he doesn't believe it, and his forced hope isn't comforting. If the coils work, we may live, but there is a good chance they will also make me useless, both to him and to Raeth. Still, any chance is better than dying here as test subjects for the Covenant or tools for the invasion.

Raeth brushes past my father, jerks me into his arms, and kisses me hard enough that my teeth cut the inside of my lips. His skin is warm beneath my cold hands, and his fingers thread through my hair to keep me close.

"Seven gods, you are a glorious force of destruction," he says against my lips and smiles wolfishly.

I grin back, the fury that took me over warring with my fear and the joy of seeing him as he should be: powerful and in control. "Let's get out of here."

"Wait," Silk says, holding up an open hand, her brown eyes huge and desperate. "My niece! Please. She's here, but I can't get her out on my own. If she dies, everything I've done will have been in vain."

Everything falls into place: Silk's behavior, her careful manipulation, her betrayal. She planned it all to free her niece, who must be the 'leverage' Left Hat spoke of.

Part of me, the gentler part, wants to forgive her immediately. After all, what terrible things have I done in the name of saving my father? But the other part, the furious part, wants to leap across the intervening space and punch her in the face.

Raeth must see my warring emotions because he says gently, "She came to me, and led me to you," even as Ripper roars in challenge and something hits the wall upstairs with stunning force. "She's under my protection. At least for now."

"She *betrayed* you."

"I know."

The man I met six months ago would have killed her without a second thought, and here he is, offering her mercy while our lives are in danger. That should fill my heart, but all I can feel right now is grim determination to get us out of here alive.

Gritting my teeth, I nod, toss her the pistol I stole, raise my coil-enclosed fists, and tell Raeth, "Keep me between you and iron."

He glances at the coils, and his eyes widen as he realizes the implications of my makeshift tools."No. I can handle this. Stay behind me."

"We need every advantage we can get. If you go down, none of us will walk out of here."

"Willow," he begins, but then sees something in my eyes, something that convinces him I will not be moved. Perhaps he sees my determination to get him out of here even if I must betray his trust by using his true name to compel him.

Could I do that? If it meant saving his life? Muses forgive me, I think I could. I might do anything if it meant saving his life.

The muscle in his jaw flexes and locks, but he nods once. "Tell me when they run out."

Before I can respond, the door bursts open. Someone got past Ripper.

I throw myself in front of Raeth and smash the coils together. The bracelets activate, sending energy flooding the copper. The runic sentences light up as electricity swirls through them, and a magnetic field springs to life as the muscles in my hands tighten and lock, forcing my fingers to curl painfully.

The report of gunfire rolls through the little room like thunder, making my ears ring. But the sudden magnetic field deflects the iron bullets just enough that they smash into the glass over Raeth's shoulder. It worked. Merciful Calliope, it worked.

Raeth leaps over me in an arc, landing on the stairs and slamming into whoever shot at us. His fist shoots out and through the chest of the man with the gun. I disengage the bracelets, and the muscles in my hands unlock enough to flex my fingers, though it hurts terribly.

But pain will not stop me from ripping the cords and cables

out of my father's machine. I don't know how they intend the invention to help the fae invade New London, but they certainly won't be able to use it when I'm through.

Papa watches in horror as I destroy a lifetime of work. Then, with a cry, he picks up the Aetheric Charger and smashes it on the floor with whatever strength he has left, kicking the damaged bits until they lay in pieces at our feet. Tears stream down his face.

"Dove!" Raeth shouts.

I drag my father from the warped machine and up the stairs with Silk behind us, brandishing both pistols. We burst into the corridor to see Ripper barrel down the hall with a leg in his mouth and a Covenant member clinging to his back. Bodies and body parts litter the hall. And Malcolm is there, ready.

He throws himself at Raeth, his eyes glowing yellow, iron knives in both hands as he flies through the air like a leaping cat. My stomach drops in terror. I know what happens when their eyes glow like that.

Raeth throws a hand up, catching Malcolm by the throat. The man's feet dangle in the air.

"Vampiric magic does not work on Aes Sidhe. Didn't you know?"

Fear blossoms in Malcolm's eyes before he slashes at Raeth's arm. But Raeth tightens his grip, leans back, and kicks Malcolm in the stomach. He flies backward ten feet, leaving his throat in Raeth's bloody fist.

Silk slides out from behind Raeth and fires at the incoming Covenant, her mouth set in a thin line of determination. Luckily, Malcolm is the only member with the waxy skin and yellow eyes of someone taking the serum. The rest are mere humans.

Ripper slides to a stop near me, his mouth a gory mess of blood, torn clothing, and strings of flesh. He wags his tail. It is so ridiculous and awful that I cannot stop myself from laughing. "Good boy. Go get 'em!"

His feet slide on the wet stone as he turns and flings himself at the Covenant alongside Silk. I pull my father behind me and turn to see Malcolm stand. The open wound in his throat is already closing. Holy Muses.

Raeth stills, but not because of Malcolm. Behind him, a woman and a beast round the corner. She looks human but moves like a predator, with smooth grace and lithe muscles bunching and shifting, so compelling I have to force myself to look away. Only a faerie is capable of commanding attention like that.

At her side stalks something like a panther, greenish stippled fur covering a compact body with long back legs, a stub tail, broad shoulders, and a wide, boxy head. It must be more than two feet high at the shoulder.

"What is it?" I ask, my voice a bare whisper.

"Mistcat," Raeth snarls.

Silk screams my name, and without thinking, I raise my hands, slamming them together to activate the bracelets. Electricity buzzes into the copper but also pours over and through my hands, cramping the muscles so tightly that I gasp at the pain.

Two bullets buzz inches past Raeth's right shoulder, bent by my magnetic field, and smash into the wall, sending rock chips flying. One slices across my ear as I spin toward the danger, leaving a trail of burning pain so minor compared to my hands that I barely notice it.

Silk spins outside an attack and uses the force of her spin to smash the butt of her pistol into the head of a snarling woman. Her opponent crumples, leaving two Covenant members the space to fire at Raeth. I hold the magnetic field, my arms raised to cover Raeth's torso. The earlier pins and needles of pain in my hands are now knives, stabbing deeply as my bracelets expend the last of the stored electricity.

I won't be able to renew the energy in my bracelets fast enough to raise another shield, and I am no fighter. Even with elven speed and strength, I could not fight two people.

The energy fizzles, then fades. The magnetic field falls. A Covenant fighter slams Silk into the wall, snarling as he holds her by the lapels and shouts "Traitor!" in her face. I can't protect her. I have nothing left with which to fight.

My father crouches against the wall behind me, his hands over his head, all but unnoticed as the Covenant closes in from one side and the faerie woman stalks us from the other. The mistcat lets out a rumbling growl and leaps, claws extended.

Ripper flies through the air with a roar and smashes into the leaping beast. They slam against the wall feet beyond Raeth and hit the ground, rolling and snapping. Behind them comes the fae woman. She darts through the melee, knives in hand, slashing, spinning, and thrusting with such speed that her movements are barely more than a blur.

Raeth dodges, using his claws to attack instead of blades. His attention is focused on the battle, so he does not see the other Covenant member raise his pistol. My bracelets are empty, and my hands are cramped and useless. So I throw my body between Raeth and the barrel.

Gunfire explodes. An impact, like being kicked in the stomach by a mule, sends me stumbling backward to trip over the fallen bodies of dead Covenant.

"No!"

"Willow!"

The shouts blur together as I fall. From the corner of my eye, I see Silk jam a knife into the ribs of her opponent, kick the man off her blade, and launch herself at the woman who shot me.

Then I hit the ground on my back and the world goes hazy.

# CHAPTER 43

PAPA'S WORRIED FACE FLOATS OVER MINE, AND HE SAYS SOMETHING I cannot hear over the ringing in my ears. For a moment, it becomes a rubber band, stretched until it is taught, still and vibrating with stored motion.

I can still breathe, so the magic symbols must have absorbed the force of the bullet. But as the impact is converted to heat, it wraps around my chest and back, making sweat break out on my brow. I can feel every drop form on my skin, every individual muscle in my hands cramp, every heartbeat drum against my breastbone.

But I am still alive.

The rubber band breaks, the ringing dies, sound rushes back, and everything snaps to normal speed.

"Get up!" Papa shouts, yanking my arm.

I wobble to my feet with Papa's hands steadying me. Ripper stalks back and forth between us and the prowling Mistcat. When the beast lunges at us, Ripper hurls himself in front of it with a hollow metal rumble.

Beyond them, Raeth and the faerie woman fight, swirling and twisting in a complex dance only one of them will walk away from. But Papa shakes my arm until I turn.

Malcolm. He must have circled the hall from the opposite side to come at us from behind, far from Raeth and Ripper. His iron knives won't affect me like they do Raeth, but they are still sharp and large enough to kill. And my jacket is already so hot with stored energy that I do not know how much more it can hold.

Silk stands shoulder to shoulder with me, holding her pistols by the barrels and panting hard. As dangerous as she is, Silk, at her best, is no match for Malcolm. And when he turns his yellow eyes on her, she stiffens as if she's been shocked. Then, her body relaxes, and her face empties of all traces of thought or personality.

Oh no.

A sneer warps his face. "Subdue them. Kill them if they will not submit."

Silk turns, her eyes blank. She stalks toward me, pistols held loosely, not even blinking. An hour ago, it would have been easy to let my bracelets lock up her muscles, but there isn't enough energy left to do more than give her the shock one might get after walking on a carpet in stocking feet.

My natural speed and strength *might* be a match for her deadly skillset were I rested and had the use of my hands, but we are far beyond that slim possibility.

My only chance is to wait for Malcolm's serum to run out. As I back away, she closes the distance with athletic strides, arms held out and balanced for action. She'll kill me and not realize what she did until Malcolm's power over her mind eases. But how long will that take? Not long enough to save my life.

Throat tight with fear, I yell, "Ripper!"

The dog abandons his fight and gallops toward me. I drop to my knees, finger pointed at Malcolm. Ripper pounds down the hall with the mistcat behind him, his metal claws digging furrows in the stone floor as he gathers himself and leaps, hitting a stunned Malcolm in the chest and bearing him to the ground.

Silk wobbles and blinks in confusion, then goes down under the Mistcat with a surprised scream. She has no armor, and that beast's claws are over an inch long. I scramble to my feet and throw myself at its back. My hands are useless, so I wrap my arms around its neck and plant my feet, using the full force of my legs and back to haul it off of her.

It turns on me with a furious yowl and sinks its teeth into my arm. Heat blossoms in my sleeve as I fall backward, trying to turn and trap the beast beneath me.

Someone screams.

Metal screeches as it warps.

Papa calls my name.

But I ignore it all and force my body down and down, pinning the mistcat as it tightens its jaws and rakes its back claws along my belly. My dress blossoms with heat as it tries to absorb and distribute the force, ratcheting the temperature higher. Higher. It's too much to bear. It radiates like an oven, like the steam off a boiling pot.

A scream of fear and pain rips up my throat.

I slam the bracelets together, praying to the Muses that I've moved enough to store a bit of energy. The buttons depress. I shove my cramped hands against the beast's chest, and a jolt of electricity buzzes into its body. I've only managed to generate enough electricity to lock its muscles for an instant, but that is long enough for me to back away.

I cannot see through the tears blurring my eyes, and I cannot tear myself out of my clothes, not with fingers too cramped to move and too numb to feel the small buttons. Little whimpering fills the air as I back away, fumbling uselessly with the buttons as my dress cooks me alive. Smoke rises from the hem of the skirt and stings my nostrils.

Hands are on me, tearing. I scream, flailing my arms, swinging my bracelets like weapons, as I cry.

"I've got you, Dove, be still."

*Raeth.*

Someone catches me as my legs give out. A ripping sound. Cool air hits my scalded skin, making a wave of gooseflesh prickle across my body. The relief makes me sob. Raeth thumbs the tears from my eyes and holds my face steady until I can see again. His dark eyes regard me from a foot away. His brows are drawn together, forehead creased in worry. Blood spatters his cheek.

"Are you alright?" I manage to ask, though my voice is thick with tears.

He shakes his head and brushes my hair back from my face. "Only you would worry about someone else's wellbeing after you've been scalded. Seven gods, Dove. Are you alright? Can you stand?"

Everything hurts; my skin stings, my ribs are bruised, and the cramping extends from my fingertips to my forearms. Raeth is currently the only thing holding me up.

But my legs are mostly functional. "I think so."

He kisses my forehead, perhaps the only place on my body that doesn't hurt.

"Good," Silk says. "Then we've got to get Daisy and get out of here. More Covenant are on the way, and if she was here, other faeries won't be far behind."

Was? I glance down the hall to look for the faerie woman, but Raeth brushes my cheek with his fingertips, bringing my eyes back to him. "Don't."

Silk takes off at a jog. Her knees are still unsteady from being enthralled, but she plows determinedly onward.

Raeth reaches out as if he wants to lift me into his arms but hesitates. My corset and chemise are scorched around the edges, the skin beneath red and angry everywhere but my feet, head, and hands.

"I can walk," I assure him. It's the only thing I can do.

His mouth thins into an unhappy line, but he nods before picking up the tatters of my torn dress and hurling it hard against the wall. The force overloads the fabric, which bursts into flames and lands on Malcolm's body. His suit catches fire. Tongues of flame lick across his torso and spread to those nearby.

Raeth turns my face back to his, forcing our eyes to meet and blocking the grisly sight. "Stay close to me, Dove. I'll carry you if you need me to."

DEATH IS EVERYWHERE. The hall stinks of blood and voided bowels. The broken bodies should be sickening, but numbness steals over me, thankfully separating me from the rest of the world. I can tell the air is cold because I shiver uncontrollably, but I note that fact with the same detachment as noticing the sky is cloudy or a dress is blue.

When we stop, I stare at the plain door before us and try to remember how we got here, but cannot recall what passages we took.

Silk retrieves her lock-picking tools, but Raeth waves her aside, leans back, and kicks the door below the handle. The frame warps, disengaging the lock, and Silk rushes in. A moment later, she emerges with a little girl wrapped around her torso. The girl's small legs are clamped around her waist, red head pressed into the curve where her neck and shoulder meet.

"This way," Silk says, and we are moving again.

Shouting echoes toward us from somewhere. Ripper barks. We hurry through a room similar to the one they kept me in, and leave through another door, down a series of stairs, and into a narrow hall lit only by a torch Silk carries. We run until my leg muscles burn, stumbling to a halt only when a heavy metal door blocks our path.

Silk takes the handle, but the door doesn't move. She sets her shoulder against it and pushes. Then slams the side of her body into the metal, careful of the small, shivering child she carries.

"No," she growls, desperation in her voice for the first time. "They've locked it. The bastards have locked it. Shit!"

She kicks the metal door in frustration once, twice. It doesn't move. Raeth tells her to step aside, but she sobs and kicks the door again. "There's no point, majesty. It's three inches thick and locks from the other side. Even you cannot break through this fucking thing."

The four of us stand there, staring at the heavy door, listening to the echoes of feet, shouting, and the distant whine of an alarm bell. Reinforcements have arrived, as she said they would. And smoke is beginning to flavor the air.

I fight to force my numb mind back into action, to think of a solution, but holding any thought is like trying to stop water from slipping through my fingers. I don't know how to get us through the door. All I know is that we are trapped on this side of it, and the Covenant is coming.

Raeth tucks me against his side, barely touching my skin, and kisses my hair. Papa looks at me with haunted eyes, his face drawn in lines of hopelessness. After everything, we are doomed to simply stand here and wait as the Covenant comes for us. I'd like to cry, but I don't think I can.

"Compel me to break it down," Raeth says.

"What?"

He lifts my chin. "I can't do it on my own. The pain will force me to stop. But if you use my name, I won't be able to help myself."

He wants me to order him to destroy his body, so we have a chance to escape.

I'm barely able to force the word through the tightness in my throat. "No."

"If you don't," he says softly, "everyone will die. I cannot let you die, Willow."

Ripper barks.

The dog is battered from fighting, his metal shoulder warped from breaking into the stronghold, and one eye socket is so dented his eye looks sideways. Scratches from mistcat claws make long furrows down his back, luckily missing the runic sentences.

But his mouth is open in a doggy grin, and his tail wags when he turns to face the door.

"Ripper, no," I breathe.

But Raeth crouches and lays his palm on the dog's brass head.

The two regard each other for a few heartbeats as the alarm sounds in the distance. Finally, Raeth motions us back and away from the door to give the dog room.

Ripper backs up several paces, sets his shoulders, and charges. His metal claws scrape deep gouges into the stone as he builds up speed. Hundreds of pounds of metal and artifice crash into the door with a mighty *crack*. He bounces off it but leaves a dent as large as my head in the bottom half near the handle.

The sound of distant footsteps grows louder.

Ripper's shoulder is bent at the wrong angle. But he backs up again, lowers his head, and leaps into a run.

*Boom!*

His head is twisted to the side as he resets himself, metal neck warped beyond repair. But he prepares to charge again.

*Boom!*

The impact tears the joint of his right front paw, and the limb dangles uselessly. The glug-gug of his heart pump struggles to force hydraulic fluid through his damaged joints. But the dog sets his remaining feet and rushes the door.

*Boom!*

The door bows outward from the frame, bent almost enough for us to squeeze through. Ripper no longer resembles a dog so much as a dented piece of scrap. Hydraulic fluid leaks from his bent joints, leaving a shining trail of dark liquid on the floor behind him.

But his tale wags as he hobbles backward, the warped panels scraping against one another. Ripper sets himself and forces his twisted limbs to bear his weight as he squares his broken shoulders. With a last growl, Ripper launches himself forward, dragging every bit of speed from his broken body to batter the door one last time. Torchlight gleams off his brass hide as he passes, making the once elegant artifice shine for an instant before he's gone.

*Boom!*

The metal door bows inward, tearing a twisted hole on the outside edge large enough for us to squeeze through. What is left of Ripper's body lies wedged between the metal and the frame, nothing more than a wreck of destroyed brass.

His tale wags weakly once. It doesn't wag again.

Heart aching and trembling with exhaustion, I hobble forward and try to wrench his body free of the door, but my fingers won't bend enough to take hold of him. Every time I think I've got a grip, my hands slide free. I thought I was beyond crying. I was wrong.

Papa sidles up next to me. Silk joins him. And Raeth leans in to grasp what is left of Ripper's shoulders. Together, we drag his remains from the wreckage of the door.

"We can't leave him," I hear myself say.

"No. We can't." Raeth solemnly distributes Ripper's pieces between the three of us, and we cradle them as the treasures they are.

Raeth leans down to lift me into his arms, but hesitates. "This will hurt, Dove."

"Everything hurts." My scalded skin is no more than a drop of water in an ocean of pain, vast and pitiless. He lifts me into his arms and carries what is left of both Ripper and me through the hole as smoke and the echoes of footsteps chase us into the dark.

# CHAPTER 44

Some years after my father adopted me, I went looking for the home I shared with my parents. I'd dreamed of the place one night, and the need to see it again grew in my chest until I thought I would burst if I couldn't satisfy it. When I stood before the building at last, comparing my memories with the reality of the place, I learned something: eyes that look backward always wear rose-colored glasses.

My memories were tinted with love and laughter, it's true, but also made brighter, sharper, and more vivid by the desperate hope for comfort I could only find in an idealized past. The reality of the water-stained stone and broken glass did not compare favorably. Either that or I was no longer the sort of person who could see the promise of what had been.

Watching the mechanica emerge from the dark, I feel as if I am standing on that street again, staring at the home that was stolen from me. The familiar brick facade doesn't resemble the haven from my memories; just a storefront in a moderately impoverished part of town. But my father rushes toward the doors as if the light of heaven shines through the dark windows.

Silk rubs Daisy's back, her expression tired but content under the bruises and spatters of blood. "We're going home, too," she says quietly.

Raeth's response isn't cold, but it isn't kind, either. "Don't come back."

She grins at him over Daisy's matted red hair. "Oh, you'll never see me again, majesty. Count on it." But when she places the bits of Ripper she's been carrying on my lap, her grin falters and dies. "I wish I didn't have to say the same for you. I won't apologize. Daisy needs me, and I would have done worse to get her out of there. But I'm glad you're damned clever, and I didn't have to." She nods, turns, and strides into the dark. Before I lose sight of her, she turns, still walking backward, and shouts, "Make the future you want for yourself, Dove. To hell with everyone else."

Raeth and I watch until the dark swallows her. Without asking, he carries me inside, kicking the door closed behind us. Papa is leaning over the counter, his head resting on his forearm, the opposite arm bent over the back of his neck as if protecting his head. His slender form shakes with quiet sobs.

I should go to him, comfort him. After everything he has suffered, he needs to know he's safe. But Raeth doesn't put me down, and I can't bring myself to ask him to. He passes my father and carries me up the stairs, finding my bedroom in the dark as if he has been there hundreds of times.

The bed sinks as he places me on the mattress and sets Ripper's remains beside me. Then he wraps me carefully in a blanket, lights my small dwarven stove, and pours the water from my basin into the kettle.

"Where are your salves?" He asks. "And don't tell me you don't keep any; I know better."

Numbly, I gesture to a shelf above my chest of drawers. He inspects them, finds what he is looking for, and returns to the little stove. It takes a while for even a dwarven stove to heat enough to boil water, but once the kettle is steaming, he pours the water back into the basin, adds a few drops of oil, and the scent of lavender fills my room.

He kneels before me, steam rising from the basin.

"They'll come for us," I say as he slides the copper coils off my wrists, followed by the bracelets. The pieces of Ripper, he stacks gently by the window.

"Yes. But not tonight. Or in the foreseeable future."

"Why not?"

"Because now that I know where they are," he says as he washes my face with the warm, rough cloth, "I am going to fire-bomb the whole fucking place."

I shiver and close my eyes. The washcloth slides over my skin in an echo of another time Raeth washed me, but now the lavender soothes my burned skin, and no trace of desire thickens the air. When he finishes, the water in the bowl is pink, and his jaw is set.

Raeth remains on his knees, moonlight from my window hugging his bare torso like a lover. I'm glad he doesn't use his glamour to hide his scars. Glad he is safe and strong and capable of protecting the Undercroft. I instinctively raise a hand, wanting to push his hair back from his forehead, but freeze when I see my hand. It is cramped into a twisted claw, and I cannot force the muscles to move or relax.

A spear of icy grief pierces my chest. Everything that brought me joy and made me useful came from my hands.

And they may never recover.

"I will not ask you to come with me," Raeth says, resting his hands on the outside of my thighs. "I have already cost you more than you can bear. More than I can stand."

He searches my face for something, his eyes finally straying to my mouth. Is he looking for permission? When my gaze mirrors his, that is permission enough.

Raeth holds my face gingerly and closes his eyes as he leans toward me, brows pinched together as if he is in pain. But his lips are soft, brushing lightly over mine as if he thinks too much pressure will shatter me. He is probably right.

There is no demand in the caress, only a tender question, one asked with trembling lips and a furrowed brow.

One I cannot answer.

If I go back with him, I will be a liability. Will my hands will ever recover? If they do, how much use they will be to those I care for? I cannot be the White Lady or help his people with useful artifice without the use of my hands. I will be a burden. How long before he resents me for it?

Worse, how long before I grow so calloused by the violence and lies of the Unseen Court that I no longer recognize myself? Before I, like Ripper, am nothing more than the leftover pieces of someone who used to be valuable?

I close my eyes and lean into the kiss, letting myself revel in the taste of him, drawing as much of his warmth into myself as I can, like an autumn bloom clinging to the last rays of the sun.

Because this kiss is the first breath of winter, painful and beautiful as frost, and just as fragile. And, when it is over, all that is left is the impression of what was, empty as a footprint in the snow.

I open my eyes, and Raeth is gone.

A silver coin sits on the coverlet next to me, glowing coldly in the moonlight.

"STRANGE, ISN'T IT?" My father says as his strong fingers dig into the cramped muscle at the base of my thumb, working the salve into my skin. "Someone taking care of you for once? I think it does us both some good, honestly."

His voice is overly bright, as if optimism will convince my muscles to relax and my fingers to regain sensation. As if his bright demeanor will subdue his grief.

My skin is red from the friction of the massage, and I suppress a wince as he tackles a knot of sore muscle. "You don't have to do this."

He ignores me, as he has twice a day for the past three days. "I don't think it will be long before you're ready to do a few simple repairs."

I snort, and he shakes my hand good-naturedly. "You are making progress. That's something to be grateful for."

"I held a spoon this morning. That won't be very helpful when you reopen the mechanica."

"It's more than you could do two days ago."

"It's not enough," I say, pulling my hand from his grip and pinching it between my knees.

Irritation enters his voice, and he crouches beside my chair to look me in the eye. "Enough for what, Willow? Enough for *what*?"

When I don't answer, he stands and stalks to his office.

SUNLIGHT WARMS my face and torso as I sit cross-legged on the floor before my window. A breeze blows my curtains in a ghostly dance and ruffles the leaves of my plants. They rub against one another in a dry whisper that is more like music than any song could ever be.

Enough sensation has returned to my hands that I can feel the chill of the brass as my fingers trace the lines of what used to be Ripper's head. He and my plants are my only company, as Papa has given up trying to cheer me.

I had tried to wash a bowl after breakfast, but it slipped through my fingers and shattered. When he bent to pick up the pieces, I'd pushed him away. "I've got it."

"Why won't you let me help you?"

"I told you, I can do it."

"It's okay to accept help while you heal," he'd said, and I could hear the fraying edges of his temper despite how hard he tried to control his voice.

"I don't want your help!"

He threw up his hands. "I don't know what else you expect of me."

"Nothing!" I shouted at him, perhaps for the first time in my life. "I expect nothing of you but what you have always done."

"What is that supposed to mean," he demanded, his face pale.

"Let me handle it on my own. I'll deal with the unpleasant side of things, so you don't have to."

He swallowed, and his fists clenched and unclenched. "I see. I see what this is about."

I stared at him as if he were losing his mind. It wasn't his fault my temper was ragged after days of pain and inactivity, but I couldn't seem to help myself. "Do you? That would certainly be a novel experience."

"You're angry at me for...because I couldn't protect you."

The memory of him turning away to cower while Left Hat beat me made me shudder and wrap my arms around myself. I looked down so I wouldn't have to see his grief-stricken face.

"You told me to," he whispered.

I hadn't wanted him to hurt the fae woman any more than he did. It was the right thing to do. And yet... Raeth wouldn't have let them beat me, no matter what it cost him.

I had fled up the stairs, unable to look at my father, knowing it was unfair to blame him and not able to stop myself.

With a sigh, I look down at the dented and warped remains of my friend, who sacrificed himself to save us. The late afternoon sun warms the metal and makes it glow.

"DAMMIT, Willow, if you don't give yourself time to heal, you'll keep injuring yourself, and you won't be useful to anyone!"

I glare at my father as he snatches my hand and presses a rag to the puncture on my left forefinger. But he is as angry as I am, and he rips the awl out of my opposite hand and hurls it across the room.

The half-engraved piece of brass follows, my clumsy runes clattering to the floor nowhere near the scrap pile.

"What if I don't heal?" I demand, jerking my hand away and pressing the cloth against my wound. "What if I remain useless? Will you find another apprentice? Will you get rid of me?"

His mouth drops open, as shocked as if I'd slapped him. But he controls himself and wipes the back of his hand across his lips. "Great Calliope, daughter. Is that what you think of me? That I will turn you out the moment you stop being useful?"

The very thought of it, and the sound of my greatest fear rolling from his tongue, makes my throat close with grief. "What else—" I choke and press my hands to my stomach to stop myself from saying, *what else am I good for?* Because even in my mind, the phrase makes my blood cold. "Why else would you keep me?"

Tears spring to his eyes, and he pulls me against him and wraps his arms around me like he did when I was a child, petting my hair as the sobs that have been trapped in my chest for days finally fight their way free.

When my tears fade, he brushes the hair out of my eyes and says, "I keep you in my life because you are you, Willow. That is all you ever have to be. And the fact that you ever thought otherwise is my failure. Oh, muses, I am sorry. I'm sorry for everything."

As my hands slowly regain strength and dexterity, and I begin easing carefully back into the familiar chores I've handled most of my life, my father also slips back into his old habits. Sometimes, I see his office light on far into the night as he drafts new inventions. I often take him a plate when he forgets to eat.

Sometimes, I hear him crying downstairs at night, but when I knock on his door, he pretends he does not hear me. He loves me, and he is sorry, but his life has always been in his mind. And my life has always been in service to his.

I stalk through the mechanica like a caged animal, looking not so much for something to do as for someone to be. I tidy what I can, arrange new stock, and when none of it fills the hole in my chest, retreat to my room and the plants that have always brought me peace.

My fingers trace the shape of leaves, stems, and petals, letting their quiet beauty seep into my soul. And I picture another garden, a miracle in the dark, growing where plants should not exist.

"Why do you love them so?" the flower vendor in the Thieves' Market asked me once.

What was my answer? "They don't require you to be any sort of person. They never ask anything of you. They simply exist..."

Not long afterward, Raeth had given me my garden and said, "Usefulness isn't the only measure of value. Nor even the most important one." And earlier, before he knew me. "I don't want your skills. I want you."

My hand slips clumsily into my pocket and my fingers curl around the silver inside, warm from my body heat.

"Willow?"

I turn and jerk my hand guiltily from my pocket, forcing myself not to blush. Papa stands at my door with his hands folded in front of him. He is still too thin, but his color is better, and his eyes are less dull. "Hmm?"

"The past few days," he says, walking hesitantly into my room, "I have been thinking. Remembering, really. And thinking about what you said."

"Papa, don't—"

He holds up a hand. "I never planned to be a parent. I think you know that. I never thought myself suited for it. An old bachelor," he laughs uncomfortably and sits on my bed, "that's what I thought I would be."

"A famous inventor, old bachelor," I amend.

He smiles shamefacedly and shrugs. "I suppose, yes. But then you showed up on my door and looked up at me with those soulful eyes, so full of hope and pain, and..." he raises one hand helplessly, "I was lost. You didn't show some great skill or cleverness while standing there in the rain. I didn't open my home to you because I thought you would grow to be the most talented artificer I'd ever know. I did it because I thought you needed me."

The bed creaks as I sit beside him and place one hand over his. "I did. I still do."

"No," he says with a sad smile. "No, I was the one who needed you. And somehow, you knew that. You became everything I needed, and I was so proud that you were like me that I never saw the truth."

I swallow past the tightness in my throat. "What truth?"

"That you became everything I needed, when what you needed was to be like *you*. To chase your dreams and do things your way."

Warmth spreads through me like the sun coming up. I can only nod and look down at our joined hands as he places his other hand atop mine.

"Can you forgive me? Not only for not seeing you, but for all of it?"

I don't try to control my expression or my voice. If my chin trembles and my voice wavers, that's okay. Our eyes meet, and his are earnest and sad, couched with more lines than before he left. He looks older and more tired, and seeing the age on his face hurts in an obscure way.

What else can I say but, "Of course I can, Papa."

He smiles and lets his forehead rest against mine with a soul-deep sigh. "Thank you. I was terribly afraid you wouldn't. I don't think I could have lived with myself. You cannot imagine the torture it has been, watching you suffer and knowing I caused it, at least in part." He leans back far enough to see my eyes and pats my hand. "I'm glad we've got that hammered out, and we can put it behind us. I've been dying to tell you my plans for the shop. You're going to love them. And now that the mortgage is paid, we will have much more money to work with. We can do amazing things."

I smile at him, but my chest tightens, and my stomach curls up on itself. "That's wonderful, Papa."

"I knew you'd think so. You're healing well, better than I

expected. I think you'll be back at the bench in no time. Once you balance the books, I'm sure you'll find enough extra money to afford a few spare sheets of brass or copper for your little art projects between repairs. We can clear a bit of shelf space so you can sell them and put some spending money in your pocket. How does that sound?"

My future unfurls like the petals of a flower, and inside, I can see everything we planned for, everything we worked at for years. Instead of hope and expectation, a great hollowness spreads inside me. Will such a future be possible when the faeries invade, if they do, or when the Covenant regroups?

And, maybe more importantly, is it the future I want? One where the next year and the year after are the same as the last year and the last five before that, where I will always, on some level, be merely an extension of his dreams? In that future, even if he wants to, my father will never truly see me enough to let me go. And I will never be strong enough to step away from him.

I shoot to my feet, still holding my father's hand, but barely able to stand still as energy floods my veins. I cannot tell if it is the need to run or fight, but if I don't move soon, I will fly apart.

"Papa, you know I love you."

His eyes widen. "I know it. What's this about?"

I take his face in my hands and memorize every feature. Beneath the aging skin and the lines of care is the face of the younger man who took me in out of the cold, and loved me in the best way he knew how.

I press a kiss to his forehead. "Thank you. For this life, for giving me what you could. Thank you."

When I leave, he doesn't try to stop me.

# CHAPTER 45

Unlike the last time I entered the Thieves' Market, the air is warm. Unlike last time, other pedestrians cross the square with hurried gaits, passing beneath the street lamps like moths, their worn brown and grey coats fluttering behind them. And, unlike last time, I cross the square in front of the church with determination instead of fear.

The silver coin is warm in my hand, and I hold it like a talisman as I skip up the few steps to the door of the church and stop. This may be the last time I look at a threshold, knowing my life will change forever when I pass through it. I entered this church six months ago, believing I had no other options. Now I know what waits for me.

At least, I know what I hope waits for me. And, if I am wrong, I will find something new to hope for. Chin high, I grip the wrought iron door handle and push, not because someone is relying on me and not because obligation drives me, but because I choose to.

"Unwise decision, miss," a deep voice says from the shadows to my right.

One of the Ratcatchers who guard the entrance to the Undercroft, no doubt. Coin prepared, I pull my hood off and let my hair spill down my back as I turn toward him. Even in the dim light, the locks are bright enough that I cannot be mistaken for anyone else.

"Hell," a feminine voice hisses. "It's the white lady."

If they react violently, I have no bracelets to protect me. Though they rest in my pocket, I haven't worn them since Raeth pulled them from my wrists. The only thing that may keep me safe is their belief that I have the King's goodwill.

"You got a coin, white lady?" The deep voice asks as a man steps forward. The lamp light leaking through the open door and broken windows reveals a heavy frame and the black mourning band pinned around his upper arm.

He hooks his thumbs into his belt and gives me a thoroughly suspicious once-over. But when I open my fingers to reveal the King's Coin, he raises a brow. "You certain you want to do this?"

"Yes."

Voices break the silence, light leaks into the velvet darkness, and the scent of roast mutton, stew, yeasty bread, yeastier beer, and sweating bodies overwhelms the faint mineral and mildew stink of the tunnels. It must be Court night. My heart rate picks up, but not with the same fear that drove me six months ago. This time, it's hope, which is probably why it hurts more.

Arguing echoes toward us, angry voices that make my blood cold.

"You know how this works," the big man says, gesturing at the great hall with his chin as we near the arched door.

"I do."

"Be about it, then. And good luck."

He leaves me there, confident either that I won't cause trouble or that the other Ratcatchers will handle it if I do. I'm unsure about either of those things, but I pull my hood up before passing through the arch.

"—we expect you to protect us when you're one of them?"

A woman stands in the center of the aisle, her feet spread and braced, pointing a finger at Raeth. I ease through the crowd along the back wall, catching glimpses of his black-clad figure. He isn't sitting on the throne or lounging as usual, but standing.

"What threat have I failed to protect you from?" He asks in a surprisingly calm tone.

Someone else shouts, "That wasn't against your own people!" Which is followed by a chorus of *Yeah!*

Tension makes the air thick, and all around me are faces creased in lines of worry. Raeth raises both hands, palm out, and the murmuring dies to a hush of shifting feet and wringing hands.

"I have protected you from the constables, from starvation and the cold, from those posh cunts in fancy carriages who would exploit you for their own gain. What makes you think I will not fight the faeries, too, for your sake?"

"How?" The small, delicate voice comes from a little girl, no more than twelve, holding her red hat against her chest with both hands. "How, if they've got magic like the stories say?"

Raeth doesn't patronize her by crouching or talking softly. He points up and out to the surface. "Have you seen the marks on the stone near the entrances to the Undercroft?"

"Those old runes?"

"Not runes," he says, lowering his voice so the crowd leans forward to listen. "Those are wards. Magic symbols that won't let any faeries pass unless they carry my coin, given to them freely and sealed to me. The tunnels are thick with them."

Murmurs of surprise accompany exchanged glances.

"Does that mean there's other fae here besides you?" A man demands.

This time, the exchanged glances are suspicious, and the people shift as if trying to put more room between themselves and the people next to them. The mood in the room is tenuous, shifting unpredictably between hope and fear. I thought Raeth addressed this, but the fear of invasion runs deep, and the Undercrofters are naturally suspicious.

Raeth raises his chin and his voice is a challenge. "I will never turn away refugees fleeing oppression, dwarf, human, elf, or fae.

496

And if the faerie King does invade, you will need every member of the Unseen Court on your side, mortal and fae alike."

Something clicks in my chest, like a gear fitting neatly in place. Though it makes my throat dry with fear, I slip my hands into my pockets and slide my bracelets on. I still have not recovered my fine motor skills, but my hands are healed enough for this.

When I press my wrists against my thighs and depress the rune-inscribed button, static electricity crackles over my skin, clothing, and hair. The hood drops, and tendrils of white-blonde hair rise as if on a phantom breeze while little blue sparks of static sizzle across my skirt. Without the copper coils to amplify the electricity, it only makes my skin tingle and the hairs on my arms rise. But the visual effect is entirely more arresting.

The crowd gasps and retreats, leaving a circle around me a dozen feet across.

"The White Lady," they whisper.

The weight of a hundred gazes falls on me, follows me as I walk down the center aisle. A red trail of hastily cleaned blood mars the stone in my path. Someone died tonight. I step over the blood, never looking down, while the Unseen Court parts before me, opening a lane directly to the dais where Raeth, The Cutthroat King, stands.

They shift and whisper as he watches me approach, his expression as cold as if he's never seen me. But his fingers tighten on the silver crown held negligently in one hand. "I am afraid, Madame, that the time for supplicants is past."

His voice makes a chill run down my spine. I raise my chin and let the electricity fade. "I am not here to beg for help."

The King raises a brow, interested. "Then why have you forsaken the safety of the Upstairs and braved these dangerous halls?"

Fear arrives at last. It tightens in my guts and makes my heart beat as if it's trying to escape my chest. "Because the Unseen Court and its King are in danger. So, I've come to propose an alliance."

"What do you offer that benefits the Unseen Court?"

That bastard. Those words in his gently mocking voice are daggers well-placed, and he knows it. He's always known it. But I am not the same woman I was when I entered the Undercroft, and I will not be cowed, not now. So I answer, in as confident a voice as possible, "Myself."

Silence blankets the room, and Raeth stands slowly. He prowls down the stairs, as dangerous as I have ever seen him, black eyes fixed on me. The crowd backs away, pressing against the far wall.

Raeth eyes me, weighing and judging. His Adam's apple bobs. "A prize of incalculable value, no doubt. And what would you demand of the King in return for such a generous offer?"

I can smell him: cinnamon and tobacco, a hint of red wine from the glass discarded near the throne. His nostrils flare as he passes within a foot of me, and I know he can smell me, too. His senses are more acute than mine, so he may be able to feel the heat of my body in the air between us.

"Don't be afraid now, Dove," he murmurs for my ears alone. "Not when the stakes are so high."

My heart is beating so hard I can hear the blood pounding in my ears. But he's right; I cannot turn back now. This is a chance I must take.

"In return for my oath," I respond, loud enough for the crowd to hear me, "I require an equal promise of the Cutthroat King."

A crooked smile tugs at the left corner of his mouth. "Under what terms, lady?"

"What terms will you offer?"

Now, his smile is wolfish. "I will neither give nor accept less than complete surrender."

"And I will neither give nor accept less than complete equality."

I cannot drag my eyes from Raeth's face, but I can hear the shocked gasps of the crowd. The air is electric with anticipation. Will the King grant his power to another? This is the sticking point, the hinge on which everything turns, and my guts twist like snakes in my stomach as he circles.

When he finally stops before me, his gaze is direct and intent, and his voice is soft as he removes the crown. "Agreed."

My heart leaps, and the crowd also responds, leaning forward, their eyes locked on us. I am pushing him, I know. Not only asking him to be vulnerable with me, but to make himself vulnerable—to give up some of his power—in the eyes of his court. To trust me, and *them*, to stand with him. But if I am going to stay, I must ask for one more concession.

"And," I begin, raising my voice so the Court can hear me clearly, "I require more than simply protection for the Unseen Court."

He raises one brow as he tilts his head. "Oh?"

"So long as we restrict ourselves to existing within an oppressive system, it will always create new victims."

His eyes narrow. "What are you suggesting, lady?"

"That we destroy the system and replace it with something new."

Silence. I can only wait. If he turns me down here, I must turn and leave the Undercroft, no matter how much it hurts. Survival alone cannot be enough. If we are unwilling to fight for a world where people are not used and abandoned, then maybe we don't deserve it. And I am done with living a life others choose for me.

"There will be casualties, lady. More far-reaching than you can imagine. Systems of such entrenched power do not fall cleanly. The people will suffer, even if we succeed."

His voice is low and serious, his eyes earnest... because he must have considered this before. He has weighed the cost and prioritized the safety of the people over their freedom. But he made the decision alone, just as he decided to protect himself by cutting love out of his life.

Taking his hand, heart in my throat, I turn to the crowd. "What does the court say? Is this a battle you are willing to fight?"

There are no exchanged glances this time. No murmurings or suspicious glares. As one, they advance, encircling us. Gwil steps out of the crowd and looks between the King and me, his massive jaw flexed and a look in his eyes I have never seen before.

At last, he says, "I am willing," and kneels.

Emotion forms a lump in my throat.

One person follows, knuckles on the ground, head bowed.

Another, and another kneels, until the Unseen Court is on its knees and the air is filling with the murmurs of "I am willing."

Raeth's voice sounds choked when he says, "It appears the Court accepts your proposal."

Merciful Calliope, I cannot breathe. How I manage to turn and look at Raeth, I do not know, but I force myself to ask, "Do you accept mine?"

"For how long?"

His pupils are huge and dark, and his pulse hammers wildly at the base of his throat. When he traces the lines of my face with his fingertips, I cannot stop myself from shivering and leaning into the touch.

"For how long?" I repeat, afraid to hear the answer but desperate for him to be the one to say it.

His thumb caresses my bottom lip, and when he meets my eyes, the honesty in his spears my heart to my ribcage. "Till the stars die."

"Till the stars die," I breathe. "Do you swear it?"

"I swear it," he says, and the air around us lights up with the power of a faerie promise given openly. We are bound as surely as if connected by runes or cables.

Tears spring to my eyes. "And I swear it."

Raeth is kissing me, his mouth warm and demanding, his fingers in my hair, his chest pressed hard to mine, our hearts beating against one another. My ears are ringing—or is that the Court cheering?

He takes my hand and turns us to face them. "Does anyone question my lady's right to preside over the Unseen Court at my side?"

Silence. We turn, ascending the steps side by side, and Gwil raises a fist. "The Cutthroat King and the White Lady!"

"The King and the Lady!" The crowd screams.

## THE END

*To read more about Willow, Raeth, and Lady Gwen St. James, start with Vanished, Book One of The Gwen St. James Affair*

*For a free ebook, join the Newsletter on Towerroompublishing.com*

# EPILOGUE

## Raeth

"We have not been able to track them, Majesty," Gwil says around a mouthful of whatever pastry Tildie fished from her cloak of blankets and scarves. "Will the Lady have her compasses ready soon?"

"Shortly," I allow and swirl the red wine in my glass to give myself a moment to think. "Tildie, you said the hobs found no bodies in the ashes of the paper mill?"

Tildie shakes her head and adjusts the scarves that cleverly hide her form. She prefers not to use a glamour when she doesn't have to, and the shapeless blanket hides her stubby legs and long arms as well as any glamour might.

"We was thorough," she says, shaking her head. "What's worse, there weren't no trace of the machine, either. Not even the twisted bits you mentioned."

The last gulp of wine slides cold down my throat. "They've retreated to regroup, then. When the compasses are finished, we will distribute them to the Ratcatchers. I want detailed reports. If I am to impose upon Lady St. James and her crew during her trial, I will need a compelling reason."

"Giving her some trace of the bastard what shot her ought to be proof enough," Tildie snorts.

"The lady need have no fear of the man who shot her," I remind them.

Gwil turns green at the reminder of what Lady St. James's paramour did to the Covenant member who dared to hurt her. We found only pieces of him. "That bugger scares me."

"Only a fool wouldn't fear him," I agree and stand. "It will be enough. Lady St. James knows much of what is happening, but not all of it. And we will need her help in the coming months. Gwil, prepare the Ratcatchers. Tildie, reach out to the hedge witches."

They both bow before leaving me alone in the great hall. The Covenant of the Silver Dawn has been broken but not derailed. Their plans reached farther than the Aetheric Charger, farther than simply recruiting the faeries to help position monsters in the place of power they lost with the advent of technology. And if we are to survive, I must discover what it is.

I have spent days searching and planning, building our defenses, and making arrangements for long-term food storage. The undercity itself will help us with clean water, thanks to the genius of the coalition that built the original city of London thousands of years ago. But it won't save us, not without help.

The threads of fate twist and curl on one another, stretching into the future toward a hundred unacceptable outcomes. If I don't account for all of them, I'll fail. And my people cannot afford failure. I know what King Obyrron will do when he invades and how he will subjugate and control mortals.

The threat he presents to my people, but most importantly to *her*, makes the darkness in my soul wake up and unfurl its claws. The darkness has been quieter lately, easier to restrain. But the thought of Obyrron harming Willow makes it surge to the surface and claw at my self-control.

I taste the copper bite of blood on my tongue, the only thing that will satiate the raw, violent need to protect her by whatever means necessary. My cheek stings for a moment before the cut heals, but it is enough to stop me from turning and sprinting to our room. Enough to stop me from dropping my glamour and dragging my claws through flesh. For now.

Out of long force of habit, I do not use my natural speed in the Undercroft, But it is late, and my need to see Willow, to hold her and breathe in the rosemary scent of her skin, is so overwhelming that I cannot wait another moment.

In seconds, I am at our door. Music leaks through the wood and stone, a tinny waltz on strings. A smile curves my lips. We danced to this waltz in her garden. Silently, I turn the knob, magicking the latches so they slide open with soundless ease. Just one benefit of having lived in this hole for so long.

It wouldn't have mattered if I'd bowled down the door screaming. Willow would not have heard me. When she is invested in a task, nothing else exists.

The picture before me is one that fills my chest with such contentment that the pressure of it crushes my heart and forces the darkness into submission. Peace steals over and through me, unusual and intoxicating. The sensation is so addictive it's no surprise I could not resist her, even when I tried.

She bends over her workstation, chatting with the piece of bronze she hammers. Fire and lamplight guilds her moonlight hair, which is pinned atop her head, leaving her pale elegant neck on display, little curls hugging the curve of her ear.

I know how that spot tastes, how it feels on my tongue and between my teeth.

The leather apron, baggy trousers, and blouse she wears shouldn't be attractive. Willow, in her ice queen gown is so regal and elegant that she would bring even the faerie court to its knees. But this version of her is my favorite.

I want to fly across the room, pull her into my arms, bury my face in her glorious hair, and feel her heartbeat against my skin.

But I hold myself back and watch instead. Denying myself will make the moment I finally touch her all the more satisfying.

"Nearly there," she tells the metal as she turns and examines it. "You'll fit perfectly, won't you?"

Her habit of speaking to inanimate objects makes my ribcage squeeze my lungs. I'd found the habit interesting, even amusing at first. Then I realized why she did it, why she made friends of chairs and tapestries and plants; because inanimate objects could never abandon or judge her. Now, when I hear her talk to a bit of metal or question a plant as she prunes and waters it, I can only wonder at how she managed to stay so kind, so fucking *good*, despite the way life has treated her.

She blows a hair out of her face, another adorable habit, and holds the curved metal up to the light. "Will you look at that, boy? I think it may be a better fit than your last piece! Don't tell your master, though. I doubt he would appreciate it."

"Appreciate that you are a far better craftsman than I am?" I say, finally allowing myself to cross the room toward her, drawn like a magnet to iron.

Willow jumps and turns, her cheeks flushed with surprise, extraordinary pale green eyes wide. If she knew that exact expression is the only reason I sneak up on her, she would never make it again. Except, of course, when I enter her. Then her eyes flare wide, and her lips part in a gasp, her cheeks flush just as they are now.

She rolls her eyes at me. "I am no such thing. Of course," a speculative look crosses her face, "you could always prove me wrong and help me finish."

She holds out the hammer, knowing I will not touch it but hoping anyway. The mere idea of engraving a bit of artifice makes my stomach heave as remembered pain sears a dozen cuts along my back and torso.

*His* voice echoes in my mind. *"You seem to like the kiss of the iron, boy."*

The memory makes my muscles tense, and the glamour that

makes me appear more human falters. My claws bite the inside of my palms. But Willow's eyes are soft and searching, as if she can see beneath the anger to the softer parts of me. She believes I am a better man than I know myself to be, and that trust makes it easy to force my darkness back and settle it like a growling hound.

"I would rather appreciate your work," I say instead.

It isn't a lie. Willow is the most naturally gifted artisan I have ever seen, save perhaps a certain dwarven artificer who works with Lady St. James. But that isn't the whole truth, either. Not lying while telling not-quite truths is a specialty of mine.

And she knows it.

"Fine," she waves the hammer at me in dismissal, "but someday you will create again. I know it."

I shrug. It isn't that I don't feel the pull of the metal or the hunger to feel it come to life in my hands. But my body remembers the danger too well. "Time will tell, I suppose. Show me the new piece?"

She grins like a little girl, proud of her first drawing. I will never tire of the joy that lights up her features when she shows off whatever she is working on, and nothing has given her greater joy than this project.

Willow bends and fits the new piece against Ripper's side. "Just look at this! I've curved his ribcage here to give his chest more room for a bigger hydraulic pump. I think I can build a backup into his system so that if his main pump takes damage, he can function until I repair it."

The twisted remains of my artifice dog sit on the floor, each bit laid out with precision so she can painstakingly repair those that can be repaired, and forge new pieces for those that must be replaced. When I'd carried the brass carcass to her, she'd cried and thrown her arms around my neck.

"That's clever," I agree. "Perhaps I can find more robust tubing as well. That should make him less likely to leak fluid if he is damaged."

She smiles at me. "Perfect! Then we'll make his insides as armored as his outsides."

Her pleasure hurts me in ways I cannot fathom. "Even if you repair every piece," I warn, "he may not—" but the confidence in her eyes stops me.

"He will. I know it."

I've learned not to argue with that confidence. But I hate to see her disappointment. If she fails, the pain of it will cut me, too. I've spent so long carefully keeping emotions at bay that experiencing them so strongly with her is like warming a frozen limb by the fire. It hurts, though it is proof I'm still alive. A fact I doubted for too many years to count.

"I believe you, then. Will you still have time to make more art for the shop?"

She stares down at the pieces of Ripper waiting to be brought back to life. "I'd like to finish him first. He's earned our time and attention, don't you think?"

"I do."

"Besides, there are still a few pieces that haven't sold. I'll head Upstairs tomorrow. I think the flower lamp has a buyer."

"And here you thought you could not sell your art. It turns out you were mistaken."

"Don't rub it in," she says, though she smiles, and a pleased flush colors her cheeks.

"Take Gwil with you when you go. With Lady St. James's trial so close, the streets aren't safe. And the Ratcatchers are reporting Bowler Hat sightings again."

Her face falls. I hate to destroy that smile, but I can't let her risk the Upstairs with so much uncertainty troubling the city.

"I will," she promises. "Though he won't like it much."

"Gwil is capable of a few hours of discomfort. Can you leave Ripper for a bit? I've more news of the Covenant."

Her expression turns serious. She replaces each tool with surgical precision, peels off her apron, and joins me by the fire. Of course, she hesitates long enough to water a plant on her way.

But when she sits, her attention is entirely focused on me. I'd noticed that about her immediately. When Willow gives someone her attention, she gives it entirely. Her eyes are clear glass that invites me to look inside while she probes the darkest parts of me.

For someone as guarded as I must be, it is both an invasion and an irresistible lure. She is promise of light and warmth; things barely out of reach for one who makes his home in the dark. If she is a flame, then I am the foolish moth, but damn me if burning isn't worth it.

"Tell me," she says.

"The Covenant was broken, but not destroyed." I explain everything we've learned about their movement and what we suspect. "I think I should take this to Lady St. James."

Her pale brows rise. "How will you reach her? With her trial so close, she must be surrounded by guards."

"That doesn't mean much to me," I say, leaning back on my chair. "They won't stop me from reaching her."

"I always forget about your glamour. Alright, but what good will that do us?"

"She has resources I do not."

Willow grins. "That must have been hard to admit."

"You have no idea of the pain I am in."

"I'm proud of you."

"As you should be."

Her pleased grin is addictive, but she is quick to return to business. "I'm nearly finished with the compasses. Gwil has promised to bring me a new stamp for the needles. The last one broke."

"Good. Then we can send the Ratcatchers out. There is one more thing."

"What?" She frowns at my tone and braces herself.

I hesitate only a moment. This will worry her, but if I trust her the way I've sworn to, the way my soul so desperately yearns to, then I cannot try to protect her from the truth. "They found no trace of your father's invention in the rubble of the paper mill."

Willow catches her breath. She is smart enough to know what

that means. "You don't think they can replicate it without him, do you?"

"I cannot say," I shrug, "but if they did not keep detailed notes, they are fools. Tildie tells me they found syringes in the ashes, so they did not think the evidence of their vampire blood serum was more important than the invention."

"That makes sense." She frowns and rubs the tips of her fingers against her forehead. "No one who found a syringe could guess they are alchemizing vampire blood, even if they analyzed whatever fluid happened to be left inside; whatever wasn't damaged by the heat, anyway. But a talented artificer certainly could discover the use of the Charger with enough time to study it. And since we've hidden Papa, they'd have to find someone else."

"Which, of course, means we are not done with the Covenant."

She rubs her forearms against a shiver. "You're certain no one will find him?"

"Of course." I resist the urge to pull her into my arms for comfort. This protective instinct, the desire to safeguard someone else from harm not because her existence serves me or because I do not wish to see her suffer as I suffered but because she *deserves* it, still catches me off guard.

Part of me wants to squash the feeling, to stamp it out until it is no more than a smear on my heart. I cannot afford such vulnerability and maintain my place and my power. If my power slips, so does my safety and my ability to protect the people.

But another part, the strongest part, revels in the knowledge that she trusts me enough to show me her weakness, though I do not deserve it. In a way that still does not make sense to me, I *want* to deserve it.

"Good," she says, her expression hardening. "Because I am not done with them, either."

That makes me smile. An honest smile, which is still feels strange on my face but good. I stand and pull her into my arms, exactly where I long to have her. "Have I told you how much I enjoy your ferocity?"

She tightens her grip on me, nails digging into my back through my shirt with a sweet pain that makes my nerve endings sing. "Once or twice."

Her heart speeds and the heat of her body seeps into me through our clothing. My fingers slide through her hair to dislodge pins. They hit the carpet with dull *pops* as the silky, glorious mass tumbles down her back, cool against my forearms.

I let my glamour slip a little, enough to watch her eyes soften and grow dreamy under my influence before I claim her mouth. My sweet Dove melts into me with a whimper, a sound that makes the blood gather between my legs in a dizzying rush as her breasts press hard against my chest. I never thought such a gentle creature would enjoy the violence I crave, but she does, and the knowledge makes me hard in a rush.

When she bites my lip, a growl rumbles in my chest, and I drag her up my body by her thighs, letting her lock her legs around my hips before sitting her on the closest flat surface.

Seven gods, she is sweet. Watching her pale fingers unbutton my fly makes my blood turn to fire in my veins. How can I want to possess her so thoroughly, to own her, body and soul, to leave my touch stamped on her very bones—and yet desire to cherish and protect her, even from myself, all at once?

"These," I say as I fight with her britches, "are a far greater inconvenience than your skirts."

She slides my trousers over my hips, leaving nothing between her hands and my flesh. "Good things are worth fighting for, majesty."

She squeaks when I yank her off the table and tear her britches down the middle. "My work trousers!"

"I'll buy you new ones," I snarl, sinking my fingers into the silky muscles of her hips, "ones that aren't so hard to remove."

Her skin makes a slapping sound as I drop her onto the table again, but she doesn't notice. In fact, my gentle Dove has grown to enjoy the ragged edges of my desire. All of her attention is on my fingers, where they dig into her thighs as I slide them toward her center. The green in her eyes is all but gone, swallowed by dilated pupils and heavy lids, her pale lashes like hoarfrost on the branches of a frozen tree.

She is already slick with desire, the scent of her salty and sweet in the air between us, her mouth hot and hungry, and bloody fucking hell; I want to savor and ravish her at once. If she knew how the little sounds she makes drive me to the edge of my self-control—

Willow lifts her legs, wraps them around my hips, and pulls me toward her, trapping my hand between us. With a sultry grin, she leans back on her hands, leaving herself fully open to me in every way.

But it is the trust in her eyes that destroys and unmakes me. Her trust unravels every fiber of what I am. Wanting to be worthy of her weaves the broken parts of me into something new, something I don't quite recognize but hunger for with each breath, each heartbeat.

"God's breath, Dove," I breathe, pulling her hips toward me. She watches our bodies touch, watches me slip inside. Her eyes widen, her mouth falls open, and her lashes flutter as she gasps. My entire body clenches so tightly my muscles might snap my bones.

The heat and pressure of her body seep into me, and there in her eyes is the welcome my soul has ached half a century for.

She braces herself with one hand on the back of my neck and kisses me wildly, her mouth sweet and tart as wild strawberries.

When she says against my lips, "Harder," all thought, all restraint, evaporates.

Willow welcomes me with her body, arching into every thrust. She welcomes me with her heart, opening for me and blunting my sharp edges without removing them. She welcomes me with her mind, forcing honesty from my soul in a way I never wanted or expected. She knows my darkness, has seen and touched it with both hands and doesn't shy away from me. Instead, she becomes the light.

And she does all of it with the generous spirit that made me love her in the first place.

We bite and bruise one another in our passion, leave marks of possession and hunger on each other's skin, and deeper than that; marks that do not disappear with time but are felt years, decades later, if they fade at all.

Her inner muscles tighten impossibly around me, pulling as I drive into her, losing myself inside her one thrust at a time.

A fine sheen of sweat makes her skin luminous in the lamp-light, and her brows draw together as her climax forces her body to tense. My thumb circles the slick knot of her pleasure as my own reaches a peak, the pressure building between my legs and spiraling outward in waves. Her eyes roll as her head falls back, her nails drawing blood in a sweet rush.

When she cries my name, my true name, the combination of pain and the pleasure of being known, *truly known,* forces me over the edge with her.

SOMETIME LATER, when she lies pressed to my side in our bed, her hair fanned across my chest and arm, she says, "Will we survive what's coming? I cannot imagine an army of beings as fierce as you descending on the city without destroying it."

I turn my head to stare at the tapestry. Years ago, more years than I care to count, I found the thing in the home of a wealthy merchant I'd been contracted to remove from an unfavorable busi-ness negotiation. My first instinct had been to destroy the damned thing. It was, after all, a painful reminder of my country and the warring King and Queen who chased me from my home.

But it was too beautiful to destroy, even if it did not nearly touch the glory of the true Titania and Obyrron. And it was a reminder of a different kind. That beauty is deceiving, a facade that can hide a cruel heart. But then I met Willow and discovered that the beauty of a kind heart cannot be hidden. That the beauty of a kind heart transforms everything around it.

"I don't know," I admit before kissing her head. "But we will fight for the future together. I swear it."

And with Willow by my side, the future does not seem so dark, no matter what else it might hold.

# DICTIONARY AND
# PRONUNCIATION GUIDE

## DICTIONARY

If you read this guide before reading the book, please be aware that some definitions or pronunciations have the potential to spoil characters or plot points.

- **White Lady:** A type of ghost or spirit often associated with tragic love, betrayal, or death. White Ladies are common in various cultural traditions, especially in Germanic, Slavic, and Celtic folklore. They are typically described as ethereal, pale, and dressed in white, which symbolizes purity, mourning, or death.
- **Rune:** Symbols with specific magical or functional properties inspired by the ancient writing systems of Germanic and Norse peoples.
- **Hob:** A type of household spirit or goblin from British and Northern European folklore. Often considered a helpful but mischievous creature, hobs are akin to brownies, kobolds, or house elves in mythology.

- **Construct**: A mechanically or artificially created entity or being, often blending advanced technology with Victorian aesthetics and an air of the fantastical.
- **Guestright:** A sacred tradition found in many mythological, historical, and cultural narratives, symbolizing the inviolable bond between a host and their guest. It reflects the values of hospitality, trust, and mutual respect. This custom often carried profound moral, social, and sometimes even supernatural consequences for its observance or violation.
- **Thieves' Cant:** A specialized, secretive language or code traditionally associated with rogues, thieves, and criminal networks in folklore and literature. Designed to allow clandestine communication that can be understood by those in the know while remaining unintelligible to outsiders.
- **Divvy:** A regular distribution of resources or wealth among the members of the Unseen Court.
- **Ratcatchers:** Enforcers of The Cutthroat King
- **Aes Sidhe:** Figures from Irish mythology, representing a race of supernatural beings associated with the Otherworld, nature, and the ancient Celtic pantheon. Their name translates to "People of the Mounds" (*Aes* meaning "people" and *Sidhe* referring to fairy mounds or hills).

## PRONUNCIATION GUIDE

- **Aes Sidhe:** Pronunciation varies by region but generally "Eyes Shee" or "Ees Shee"
- **Raeth:** RAYth
- **Calliope:** Ka-LIE-oh-pee
- **Bowbriar:** BOW-bryar

- **Aetheric:** EE-thair-ick
- **Artifice:** Art-if-iss
- **Carinachea:** Care-in-AY-sha
- **Rune:** Roon

# TIMELINE
# GSJA

All novels in the Gwen St. James Affair world

**SPRING 1899**
BLOOD AND SILVER

standalone featuring
Alix and Cyrus

**FALL 1900**
VANISHED

**SPRING 1902**
MOONSTRUCK

**WINTER 1902**
SPELLBOUND

**1902-1903**
THE CUTTHROAT KING

standalone featuring
Willow and The Cutthroat King

**SUMMER 1903**
BEDEVILED

**SUMMER 1903**
FORSAKEN

**1905**
THE MOONSTONE MIRROR

**1906** DISPUTED

www.towerroompublishing.com